William Dougal Christie

A Life of Anthony Ashley Cooper

first Earl of Shaftesbury, 1621-1683 - Vol. 1

William Dougal Christie

A Life of Anthony Ashley Cooper
first Earl of Shaftesbury, 1621-1683 - Vol. 1

ISBN/EAN: 9783337094713

Printed in Europe, USA, Canada, Australia, Japan

Cover: Foto ©Raphael Reischuk / pixelio.de

More available books at **www.hansebooks.com**

A LIFE

OF

ANTHONY ASHLEY COOPER,

FIRST EARL OF SHAFTESBURY.

1621—1683.

BY

W. D. CHRISTIE, M.A.,

FORMERLY HER MAJESTY'S MINISTER TO THE ARGENTINE CONFEDERATION
AND TO BRAZIL.

.

TWO VOLUMES.

VOL. I.

London and New York:

MACMILLAN AND CO.

1871.

A LIFE

OF

ANTHONY ASHLEY COOPER,

FIRST EARL OF SHAFTESBURY.

VOL. I.

TO THE

Seventh Earl of Shaftesbury, K.G.

THIS LIFE OF HIS

CELEBRATED AND MUCH MALIGNED ANCESTOR

Is Inscribed,

IN ACKNOWLEDGMENT OF

AID KINDLY GIVEN FOR THE WORK,

AND AS A

MARK OF PERSONAL RESPECT.

a 2

PREFACE.

I PUBLISHED, some twelve years ago, a volume of papers illustrating Shaftesbury's Life to the Restoration, then intending to make a second similar volume with the papers which I had collected for the remaining and more important portion of his life. Several causes delayed the prosecution of the second volume; and I ultimately judged it better to relinquish it, and to prepare from the materials which I had acquired a connected biography of Shaftesbury. The first volume of this work contains, either incorporated into the narrative or inserted in the Appendices, all the important materials of the volume of 1859.[1] The remainder of this work, after Chapter VIII. of the first volume, is entirely new.

The original materials for this Life of Shaftesbury have been chiefly derived from the following sources:—
1. The papers preserved at St. Giles's, to which the present Lord Shaftesbury has given me access. 2. The Locke papers in possession of the Earl of Lovelace.

---

[1] "Memoirs, Letters, and Speeches of A. A. Cooper, first Earl of Shaftesbury, Lord Chancellor, with other Papers illustrating his Life. Edited by W. D. Christie." London, 1859.

3. The papers of Mr. Thynne, afterwards Viscount
Weymouth, nephew of Shaftesbury's first wife and of
Sir William and Henry Coventry, and cousin of Lord
Halifax, which are at the Marquis of Bath's seat at
Longleat. 4. The Archives of the French Foreign
Office. 5. The Domestic Papers of Charles the Second's
Reign, in our State Paper Office.

I have also found much material, hitherto unworked
for the study of Shaftesbury's character and career, in
the large collection of Diaries, Correspondence, and
Biographies of Shaftesbury's time published in the
present century. Truth is gleaned, and new light .
obtained, from casual notices in such works as the
Diaries of Pepys and Evelyn, the Rawdon Papers,
and the Diary and Correspondence of Henry Sidney,
afterwards Earl of Romney.

The reader will see by my references in notes what
great aid I have derived from the valuable work of M.
Mignet, founded on the documents in the Archives of
the Foreign Office in Paris, on the negotiations relative
to the succession to the Spanish throne in the reign
of Louis XIV., beginning with the Pyrenean treaty and
Louis's marriage with Maria Theresa of Spain and ending with the treaty of Nimeguen and the marriage of
Charles II. of Spain with Marie Louise, niece of Louis
XIV.[1] In this work M. Mignet has minutely traced the

[1] " Négociations relatives à la Succession d'Espagne sous Louis XIV. ;
ou Correspondances, Mémoires, et Actes diplomatiques concernant les
Prétentions et l'Avènement de la Maison de Bourbon au Trône d'Espagne,
accompagnés d'un Texte historique, et précédés d'une Introduction. Par
M. Mignet, Membre de l'Institut, &c." 4 tomes 4to. Paris, 1835.

negotiations and intrigues between England and France
from the beginning of the reign of Charles the Second
to the Peace of Nimeguen of 1678, and has given to the
world a large important addition to the valuable materials for the history of England in Charles the Second's
reign, which were published in the last century by Sir
.John Dalrymple.[1] It is surprising that this important work of M. Mignet has been so little noticed and
known in England. Its great size, and its being part
of a very voluminous series of government publications of original documents on the history of France,
have probably stood in the way of general circulation.
But there are few histories which equal this bulky
work in attractiveness, for the documents are arranged
with exquisite skill and connected by a commentary
displaying all the graces of M. Mignet's charming
style.

I may mention that I have myself carefully examined
in the French Foreign Office the despatches of the
French Ambassadors in England for the years 1659
to 1665, 1669, 1672 to 1674, and 1679 to 1681.

When engaged in examining them, in the year
1850, seeing the immense bulk of the correspondence,
and finding it impossible to attempt to go carefully
through the whole, I suggested to Lord Palmerston,
then at the head of the Foreign Office, that it might

---

[1] "Memoirs of Great Britain and Ireland, from the Dissolution of the
last Parliament of Charles II. until the sea-battle of La Hogue." 3 vols.
4to. 1771, 1773, 1788.

be worthy of the consideration of our Government to
incur a moderate expense for making complete copies,
if the French Government would permit it, which
might be rendered accessible in England to historical
inquirers, or even published to the world. Lord Palmerston received the suggestion with his invariable
kindness, and acted with characteristic promptitude.
I was immediately authorized to incur a reasonable
expense on the public account, for the copies of the
despatches from England of the reign of Charles the
Second; and Lord Normanby, then our Ambassador in
Paris, was instructed to apply for the permission of
the French Government. The permission was refused.
A distinction was made between allowing individuals
to make extracts by special permission and under the
supervision of the Director of the Office of Archives,
and allowing the publication of the whole series. I
hope that this decision may yet be reconsidered. These·
despatches now belong to history. They are, alas! the
best sources for the history of English government
during a period of humiliating memories, when the
English Sovereign, some English Ministers, and many
English legislators were the mendicant retainers of the
French King, and when the chief business of the
French Ambassador in London was the base one of
bribing members of Parliament to worry the King,
and bribing the King to resist the Parliament. Large
extracts from these despatches have been published by
Sir John Dalrymple, M. Mignet, and others; and more

are published in this work. No reserve can now lessen the shame for both nations of the known flagrant corruption by Louis. the Fourteenth of our King and public men.

Some writers having cast discredit on Dalrymple's valuable work, and doubted the truth of Barillon's statements about money given to members of Parliament,[1] I wish to say that I have always found Dalrymple's extracts correct and fair, that I believe him to be an honest, as he is unquestionably an able, writer, and that I can see no good ground for disbelieving Barillon's accounts of his disbursements, which not only leave untouched but place in a strong light the honour of Shaftesbury and Russell, while they prejudicially affect the reputation of Algernon Sidney.

The want of a Life of the First Earl of Shaftesbury has been often mentioned by historical writers.

Shaftesbury has been indeed unfortunate in his fame. He lived in times of violent party fury; and calumny, which fiercely assailed him living, pursued him in his grave, and still darkens his name. He lived in times when the public had little or no authentic information about the proceedings of members of the Government or of Parliament, when errors in judging public men were more easy than now, and when venal pam-

---

[1] See the Introduction to the "Letters [of Lady ˈRussell," &c., 8vo. 1801, and Lord John Russell's "Life of William Lord Russell," chap. x.

phleteers, poets, and playwriters drove a profitable
trade in libels on public men. The power of Dryden's
poetry eclipsed all the efforts of the inferior versifiers
who battled for Shaftesbury and the Whigs: and the
undying verse of the brilliant, but not conscientious,
author of "Absalom and Achitophel" and "The Medal"
has been a powerful cause of Shaftesbury's condemnation by posterity. Another of several causes has been
the willing credulity of Hume, a prejudiced friend of the
Stuarts, whose attractively written History long swayed
the public mind. The falsehoods of detraction have
produced counter falsehoods of excuse and eulogy, and
the result has been a great agglomeration of errors. It
will be seen from the first piece in the Appendices of
this volume that Shaftesbury formed in old age the
design of placing his own story before posterity, and
vindicating his fame from the calumnies of contemporary faction. He has left but a small fragment, which
terminates at the moment of his entrance into public
life, before attaining the age of twenty-one.[1] There is,

---

[1] Mr. Martyn says that a work, of which the fragment in Appendix I.
of this first volume was only the beginning, was entrusted by Shaftesbury, when he fled to Holland, to the care of Locke, who, after
Shaftesbury's death and Algernon Sidney's execution, burnt it from
fear of the Court. (Life, i. pp. 3, 10.) He gives no authority for these
statements, and I am not aware of any. There is no reference to this
story in any Life of Locke, nor in any of his published correspondence,
nor in his letters existing at St. Giles's (among which, besides many to
the grandson, the author of the "Characteristics," are some written
shortly after Shaftesbury's death to his widow and his son), nor in any
of the Shaftesbury papers, nor in the Locke papers which I have
examined at the Earl of Lovelace's. Nor is there much reason to believe
that Shaftesbury had regularly composed this work beyond where the
fragment abruptly terminates. It is possible that the two short
passages referring to events in 1640 (see pp. 35-6 of this volume),

I think, no sufficient authority for the story of his Memoirs having been burnt by Locke. But there is no doubt that Shaftesbury's distinguished grandson, the author of the "Characteristics," cherished the hope that his illustrious friend and tutor, the intimate friend of Shaftesbury in his later life, would write a biography of his departed patron. There can be no doubt that Locke's powers of analysis, knowledge of human nature, and zeal for truth, applied to the portrayal of Shaftesbury's character, which he had had great opportunities of studying, and to the history of his life and times of which he had personal knowledge, would have produced a most excellent work. Boswell records a *dictum* of Dr. Johnson: "They only who live with a man can write his Life with any genuine exactness and discrimination, and few people who have lived with a man know what to remark about him." Locke would have known what to remark. When Locke died, leaving only a small collection of crude materials, just enough to show that he had meditated a biography, there came for a moment a new gleam of hope to the grandson, piously attached to Shaftesbury's memory, that the work which Locke had failed to execute might be

and the fragment of a narrative composed by Shaftesbury of events shortly before the Restoration, printed in Chapter VII., may have been intended for a continuation of the Autobiography ; but I am inclined to believe that the short narrative of events between Richard Cromwell's fall and the Restoration was composed about the time of the Restoration. The paper headed "The Present State of the Kingdom at the Opening of the Parliament, March 1679," printed in the second volume, in Chapter XVI., may have been a part of Shaftesbury's Autobiography, but it is quite as likely to be a distinct memorandum.

undertaken by his distinguished nephew and executor, the future Lord Chancellor King. But here
again came disappointment.

The fourth Earl of Shaftesbury, the son of the author
of the "Characteristics," who was born in 1711 and
succeeded to the title in infancy in 1713, was very
anxious, on reaching manhood, for a biography of his
great ancestor and an effective vindication of his fame;
and, shortly after he became of age, he placed all
the materials in his possession at the disposal for
this purpose of Mr. Benjamin Martyn, who had
been recommended to him as competent for the
task. Mr. Martyn was the author of a successful tra-
gedy, called "Timoleon," now forgotten, and a friend
of Dr. Birch, the well-known literary and historical in-
quirer of the last century. He appears to have begun
the work in the year 1734, and he was employed
upon it for some years. The fourth Earl and other
members of the family took an active interest in it;
and there are many judicious notes by the fourth
Earl preserved among Lord Shaftesbury's papers. Mr.
Martyn's work, when completed, did not satisfy his
patron. It is evident that Martyn had no knowledge
of history, and no capacity for writing such a work. In
the year 1766 the work was consigned by the fourth
Earl to Dr. Sharpe, Master of the Temple, for improve-
ment. The fourth Earl of Shaftesbury died in 1771;
his son then placed the manuscript in the hands of Dr.
Kippis, the editor of the *Biographia Britannica*. Dr.

Kippis appears to have made many suggestions. The work was then printed. No cobbling could make a good book of a bad one; and the fifth Earl was justly dissatisfied with the performance, when in print. It is stated that the whole impression was destroyed with the exception of two copies. One copy exists at St. Giles's; another, having found its way into the hands of Mr. Bentley, the publisher, was edited in 1836 by Mr. George Wingrove Cooke, the author of the "History of Party."[1] Mr. Cooke erred greatly in his estimate of the value of the work which he edited, and in his own notes and additions to the narrative increased the stock of errors about Shaftesbury.

One serious mistake made by Mr. Wingrove Cooke is in ascribing to Shaftesbury the authorship of a Letter on Toleration, which is among the papers at St. Giles's, and which he considers "an early sketch, from which Locke's Essay upon the same subject was afterwards filled up." Locke is undoubtedly the author of the manuscript at St. Giles's.

I stated, perhaps too strongly, in the notes to the volume which I published in 1859, an opinion of the improbability of Locke's being the author of the small fragment of a biography, which has been printed in Locke's works with the title "Memoirs relating to the

---

[1] " The Life of the First Earl of Shaftesbury, from original documens in the possession of the family, by Mr. B. Martyn and Dr. Kippis, now first published. Edited by G. Wingrove Cooke, Esq., author of 'Memoirs of Lord Bolingbroke,' " 2 vols., 1836. Dr. Kippis's connexion with the work does not justify his being named as joint author.

Life of Anthony Earl of Shaftesbury." [1] There are some flagrant inaccuracies in that fragment for the period of the Civil War. The manuscript of the fragment, which is at St. Giles's, is in Locke's handwriting. Practically it is for the most part a series of statements relative to Shaftesbury's early life, of which Locke himself knew nothing, and which he probably jotted down from Stringer's information, as so much raw material to be afterwards worked upon; and Stringer, though a perfectly respectable man, is inaccurate, confused, and injudicious. It contains a few statements of opinions of Shaftesbury, which Locke learnt directly from his conversations. In all else, I remain of opinion that Locke is not to be held responsible for the Memoir, found in his own handwriting, beyond his having written out for future study and use information given him by another or others.

I have not been able to find among Lord Shaftesbury's papers the rest, and doubtless the larger portion, of the Memoir of Shaftesbury by Stringer, of which a fragment for the years 1672 and 1673 is printed at the end of the second volume. It is clear that Martyn saw a longer Memoir, and took much from it for both the earlier and later parts of Shaftesbury's life. It would have been satisfactory to see the remainder of Stringer's Memoir, as no reliance can be placed on Martyn's judgment, and it may have been sometimes inaccurately represented by Martyn, or it may have

---

[1] Locke's Works, vol. ix., p. 266, 3d edition, 1812.

contained information which he has omitted to extract.
But, on the other hand, it is clear that Stringer's accuracy is not to be relied on, and that many of Martyn's
errors are derived from Stringer. Of Shaftesbury's
early life Stringer would have known nothing of his
own knowledge. In the years 1672 and 1673, for
which Stringer's Memoir is before us, he was in close
connexion with Shaftesbury, being one of his Secretaries
when he held the office of Lord Chancellor. He had
been previously Shaftesbury's solicitor, and continued
to be so after Shaftesbury's removal from the Chancellorship, and he remained a confidential friend till
Shaftesbury's death. But Stringer's Memoir, even for
this period, though containing much useful information
and fundamentally true, as it is throughout honest, has
many mistakes of exaggeration and imperfect judgment,
which show that he is far from being an altogether safe
guide. Stringer's Memoir was written about seventeen
years after Shaftesbury's death, and twenty-seven years
after Shaftesbury ceased to be Lord Chancellor. It
was written when he was an old man, and his death,
which was in 1702, may have stopped an unfinished
work. He undertook to write the Memoir in consequence of the disparaging treatment of Shaftesbury in
Sir William Temple's Memoirs, published in 1691.
Lapse of time, failure of memory, and warm zeal for
the good name of his departed patron, whom he loved,
would have all combined to impair the value of a work
written by a man who in his best days had no literary

power, and of whom his widow ingenuously says that writing was not poor Mr. Stringer's talent.[1]

I have occasionally referred to a manuscript at St. Giles's, which is a vindication of Shaftesbury from the aspersions of Bishop Burnet in the "History of his Own Time," first published in 1724, and which was written by a Mr. Wyche, who had been an amanuensis in Shaftesbury's service. The manuscript bears the title, "A Vindication of the Character and Actions of the Right Hon. Anthony late Earl of Shaftesbury, late Lord High Chancellor of England, from the Detractions and Misrepresentations of the late Right Reverend Gilbert Bishop of Sarum, by Philoecus." This Vindication is more a dissertation than a biography: it is long, and unskilfully written: I have found it occasionally useful, but I have not thought it worth printing.

Lord Campbell's Life of Shaftesbury in his "Lives of the Chancellors" is freely criticised in this work. Those who have followed the criticisms on other Lives by Lord Campbell will not expect that his Life of Shaftesbury should be one of great accuracy. It is perhaps one of the most inaccurate. In the volume which I published in 1859, when Lord Campbell was alive and Lord Chancellor, I inserted a minute dissection of the first chapter of his Life of Shaftesbury, which covered the period from his birth to the Restoration. It is a satisfaction to me to know that I criticised Lord

---

[1] Letter of Mrs. Hill, Stringer's widow, to Lady Elizabeth Harris, Appendix VIII. of vol. ii.

Campbell, when he was alive, as freely as I do now after his death. I am more anxious now to offer to his memory the respect which I expressed for him when he was living; and I therefore proceed to repeat the substance of observations which I made in the Preface to my volume of 1859. I repeat, then, that it is not easy, with every desire to avoid offensiveness, to make a long and minute criticism in an agreeable manner. I hope I shall not be thought to over-estimate the talents required for writing an accurate Life, or for exposing the inaccuracies of another. A great author, in a biographical work which, in spite of much injustice, and notwithstanding great subsequent additions of knowledge, has achieved lasting fame, and is always read with enjoyment, has modestly gauged the requirements for literary biography; and legal or political biography is not dissimilar. "To adjust the minute events of literary history," said Dr. Johnson in his "Lives of the Poets,"[1] "is tedious and troublesome; it requires indeed no great force of understanding, but often depends upon inquiries which there is no opportunity of making, or is to be fetched from books and pamphlets not always at hand." There can be no doubt that, if Lord Campbell had taken the necessary time, and put out all the powers of his acute and vigorous mind, to write a careful biography of Shaftesbury or any one of the Chancellors, he might have left little employment for critics. As it is, he does not

---

[1] In the Life of Dryden.

depend on his Lives for lasting reputation. It will, however, always be no mean embellishment of the solid fame which he has secured, that, in the evening of a life of great professional labours and successes, he found amusement and relaxation from high duties in pursuits of literature, and in composing a long series of biographies which, if often inaccurate, are always lively and agreeable, and, if often unjust, are always unjust in ignorance and without determination of injustice. I should be sorry to be unfair towards one who, in my early life, honoured me with his friendship; and whose strong intellect, kindly nature, public services, and great career have my respect and admiration.

I wish specially to mention my obligations for assistance and advice often kindly given by an old and warm-hearted friend, Mr. John Forster, the author of "The Statesmen of the Commonwealth," the "Life of Sir John Eliot," the "Life of Goldsmith," and many other works.

W. D. C,

32, DORSET SQUARE, LONDON,
April, 1871.

CONTENTS.

CHAPTER VI.

1658—1659.

CHAPTER VII.

1659—1660.

CHAPTER VIII.

1660.

CHAPTER IX.

1661—1664.

CHAPTER X.

1664—1667.

APPENDICES.

ILLUSTRATION.

INDEX.

negotiations, peace of Nimeguen, 265—276; French bribes and subsidies, 267, 268 (and see Dutch war, Louis XIV.).
Fuller, Dr., Bishop of Lincoln, letter from him to S., ii. 193.

G.

"Gantelope" (gauntlet), running the, a punishment for deserters, i. 81.
Gardening, apple trees planted by S. at Wimborne St. Giles, ii. 49; remarks by S. on planting timber trees, on the sycamore, and wall fruit, 50; Locke's observations on vines, olives, &c., written at the request of S., 49; Evelyn's remarks on the sycamore, 50; letter from S. to Locke, 61; S. commissions Locke to buy orange and other trees, vines, and seeds for him, 220, 221.
Gardening in the seventeenth century, i. App. I. xviii.
Gentry of the West of England in the seventeenth century, i. 25.
Godfrey, Sir Edmund Bury, murder of, ii. 296, 409.
Godolphin, Sidney, made Privy Councillor, ii. 352; with Sunderland and Laurence Hyde, chief ministers, nicknamed "the Chits," 353.
Goldsmiths' Hall, fines for recovering sequestered estates received at, i. 70.
Government interference in Parliamentary elections (see Parliament).
Grafton, Duke of, son of Charles II. by Duchess of Cleveland, married to daughter of Arlington, ii. App. II. xiii.
"Granadoes" used by S. in the storming of Abbotsbury, i. 62; proposed to be used to murder S., ii. 350.
Grey, Lord, his calumnies against S., ii. 400; joins S., Monmouth, and Russell, to raise an insurrection, 445; his account of participation of S. in intended rising, 447, 448.
Grimstone, Sir H., letter to S. on the state of the records, ii. App. IV. lv; notice of him by Burnet, lvi.
Guerden, Dr., first tutor of S., i. 12, App. I. vi.
Guinea stock, speculations of S. in, ii. 226.
Guizot, M., his notices of S., i. 186, 190; on the offer of the throne to Monk, i. 217.

H.

Habeas Corpus Act carried by S., its provisions explained, ii. 333, 334; said to have been carried by a trick, 335.
Hale, Sir Matthew, a member of the Law-Reform Commission (1652), i. 87.
Halifax, Lord, his relationship to S., i. 22, 121; made Privy Councillor, ii. 84; his mission to France during the Dutch war, Colbert's account of him, 85; his

ignorance of the design to establish Popery, 86; presents petition of S. for release from the Tower, 257; his proceedings as Privy Councillor, 328; promotes design for introducing the Prince of Orange, 341; opposes bill for exclusion of Duke of York, 375, 376; address for his removal, 381; speeches in Committee of Privy Council, advising arrest of S., App. VII. cxviii.
Hallam, his opinions of S., ii. 472.
Hampden, his attempted arrest by Charles I., i. 55.
Hampton Court Palace offered to, but refused by, Cromwell, i. 103.
Hanley bowling green, Dorsetshire, i. 25.
Harwich, flight of S. from London, his stay at, ii. 451.
Haselrig, Sir Arthur, his description of the ejection of the "Rump" Parliament, i. 93; refuses to sit as one of "Cromwell's Peers," 133; his influence as a member of the Rump, 173, 188; his intrigues with Monk described by S., 212; excepted from the "Pardon and Indemnity Bill," his life spared on an address from Parliament, supported by S., 241, 243.
Hastings, Mr., account of him by S., i. App. I. xv.
Hawking, practised by S., i. 14.
Hawles, Sir John, condemns Chief Justice Pemberton's charge on the trial of S., ii. 425.
Hebden, the Russian resident, his notices of S., i. 274.
Henrietta Maria, Queen of Charles I., her letter to S. as to payment of her pension, i. 317.
Hertford, Marquis of, commands the Royal army, i. 43.
Hewson, Colonel, one of "Cromwell's Peers," attacked in a speech by S., i. 161.
Highmore, Rev. John, chaplain to S., his letter to S. on the "Meal-tub" Plot, ii. 351.
Hill, Mrs. (widow of Stringer), letter from, on Burnet's misrepresentations of S., ii. App. VIII. cxxiii.
Holland (see Dutch war).
Holles, Denzil (afterwards Lord Holles), his relationship to S., i. 11; his litigation with S., 39; his opposition to Cromwell, advice to him by S., 78; co-operates with S. in the House of Lords, ii. 200; presents petition of S. for release from the Tower, 257; letter from him to S., their early litigation and late friendship, 365.
Hooke House, Dorsetshire, proposed by S. to be garrisoned, i. 69.
Horses belonging to S., his instructions when in the Tower for their sale, ii. 418.
Howard of Escrick, Lord, committed to the Tower, ii. 411.
"Humble petition and advice" to Cromwell to assume the title of King, i. 130;

A LIFE

OF

ANTHONY ASHLEY COOPER,

FIRST EARL OF SHAFTESBURY.

LIFE OF SHAFTESBURY.

CHAPTER I.

1621—1639.

ERRATUM.

Vol. I. page 19, line 22, *for* "wish" *read* "wit."

and sisters-in-law, Lady Savile, mother of Lord Halifax, and Lady Pakington—Sketch of his youth.

ANTHONY ASHLEY COOPER, the future Earl of Shaftesbury, was born on July 22, 1621, the nineteenth year of the reign of James the First. He has himself been careful to note that he was born "early in the morn," and that he was "the eldest child then living of his father and mother."[1] His father was John Cooper, created in the next year a baronet, of Rockborne in Hampshire.[2] His mother was Anne, the only child of Sir Anthony Ashley, knight, who was also in

[1] Autobiographical Sketch of 1646 prefixed to Diary, Appendix II.
[2] Rockborne is close to the borders of Wiltshire and Dorsetshire, and within a few miles of Wimborne St. Giles.

LIFE OF SHAFTESBURY.

CHAPTER I.

1621—1639.

Birth and parentage — Baronetcies of father and maternal grandfather—The Coopers and Ashleys—Sir Anthony Ashley—Death
of mother and of father—Sir A. A. Cooper a King's ward—
Losses of property by Court of Wards—Litigation with Sir Francis
Ashley and Denzil Holles—Sir A. A. Cooper's wealth—His
guardians—Goes to Exeter College, Oxford, when sixteen—His
life at Oxford—Entered at Lincoln's Inn—Marries at eighteen
daughter of Lord Keeper Coventry—Predictions of a German
astrologer—His brothers-in-law, Henry and Sir William Coventry,
and sisters-in-law, Lady Savile, mother of Lord Halifax, and Lady
Pakington—Sketch of his youth.

ANTHONY ASHLEY COOPER, the future Earl of Shaftesbury, was born on July 22, 1621, the nineteenth year
of the reign of James the First. He has himself been
careful to note that he was born " early in the
morn," and that he was " the eldest child then living
of his father and mother."[1] His father was John
Cooper, created in the next year a baronet, of Rockborne in Hampshire.[2] His mother was Anne, the only
child of Sir Anthony Ashley, knight, who was also in

---

[1] Autobiographical Sketch of 1646 prefixed to Diary, Appendix II.
[2] Rockborne is close to the borders of Wiltshire and Dorsetshire,
and within a few miles of Wimborne St. Giles.

the next year made a baronet, of Wimborne St. Giles in Dorsetshire. He was born in his grandfather's house at Wimborne St. Giles, near Cranborne; "he was nursed," he has written himself, "at Cranborne by one Persee, a tanner's wife."[1]

The date of Sir Anthony Ashley's baronetcy is July 3, 1622, and that of Sir John Cooper's the day after. The order of baronets had been created by James the First ten years before, and in the present year he completed the number, two hundred, of which it was originally provided that the order should consist, and which, it had also been stipulated, was never to be exceeded. Every baronet then paid one thousand and ninety-five pounds for the honour. No one was admitted to it who was not possessed of a thousand pounds a year, clear of encumbrances, and who could not prove descent from a grandfather on the father's side who had borne arms.[2]

" My parents on both sides of a noble stock, being of the first rank of gentry in those countries where they lived,"—is Shaftesbury's own account of his ancestry.[3] The Coopers appear to have been persons of consideration in the West of England, for at least two generations before Sir John Cooper, the father.[4] Henry the Eighth granted the manor of Paulet in Somersetshire, taken from the Gaunt's Hospital in Bristol, to Richard Cooper of Rockborne, Sir John Cooper's grand-

---

[1] Autobiographical Sketch.
[2] By the rules of the order every baronet was also a knight; so Shaftesbury, in the Fragment of Autobiography, describes his father as " knight and baronet." (Appendix I.)
[3] Fragment of Autobiography, Appendix I.
[4] Collins's Peerage (Brydges), iii. 545.

father.[1] Sir John Cooper's father was member of Parliament for Whitchurch, in Hampshire, in 1586. and received the honour of knighthood from Queen Elizabeth. Sir John Cooper himself sat in the House of Commons for Poole, in the first and third parliaments of Charles the First, 1625 and 1628.[2]

Shaftesbury's lineage on the mother's side was more ancient and distinguished. The Ashleys, a younger branch of an ancient Wiltshire family,[3] had been planted at Wimborne St. Giles since the reign of Henry the Sixth; and their ancestors, traced through heirs female, had been lords of that manor from before the reign of Edward the First.[4] Sir Anthony Ashley inherited the property late in life, on the death of his cousin, Sir Henry Ashley, without issue.[5] He had been bred to public employment, and had probably already enriched himself in the service of the State. He had been for many years one of the Clerks of the Privy Council. In 1589 he went as Royal Commissioner in Norris and Drake's expedition against Portugal, and in 1596 he was Commissioner for embarking the troops and Secretary to the Council of War in the expedition of Lords Effingham and Essex against Cadiz.[6] Essex knighted him with many others after the capture of Cadiz. On his return home he was charged with

---

[1] Collinson's Hist. of Somersetshire, iii. 100.
[2] Willis's Not. Parl. ii. 411. He was John Pym's colleague.
[3] Coker's Survey of Dorsetshire, p. 14.
[4] See the Ashley pedigree in Hutchins's Hist. of Dorsetshire, iii. 174.
[5] Burke's Extinct Baronetcies, Ashley of Wimborne St. Giles.
[6] Camden, Ann. Elizabeth (Hearne), p. 720. Strype's Annals of Reform. iv. 400. Some of Shaftesbury's biographers have made the mistake of calling Sir A. Ashley Secretary at War to Queen Elizabeth. There was no such office in those days.

peculation, was imprisoned, and was for some time in disgrace. When, late in life, he became the proprietor of Wimborne St. Giles, he was a liberal benefactor of the parish. He rebuilt the parish church, and built and endowed almshouses for the relief of eleven old persons.[2] He is said to have introduced the cultivation of cabbages from Holland.[3]

Shaftesbury appears to have derived from his mother's side the "pigmy body" of Dryden's satire. He describes Sir Anthony Ashley as "of a large mind in all his actions, his person of the lowest," and he says that "his daughter was of the same stature;" while of Sir John Cooper, his father, he says that he was "very lovely and graceful both in face and person, of a moderate stature, neither too high nor too low."[4]

Old Sir Anthony Ashley felt the liveliest interest in the grandchild born to inherit the ancient possessions of his house. He caused him to be christened, in deviation from custom, with the double name of Anthony Ashley; "for notwithstanding," says Shaftesbury, "my grandfather had articled with my father and his guardians that he should change his name to Ashley,

---

[1] Archæologia, xxii. 172 ; Birch's Mem. of Q. Eliz. ii. 49, 95, 144, 171. Several letters preserved in the Cotton and Lansdowne MSS. in the British Museum show that Sir A. Ashley's official life was not free from suspicion on other occasions.

[2] Hutchins's Hist. of Dorsetshire, iii. 193.

[3] Evelyn's "Acetaria, a Discourse of Sallets:" " 'Tis scarce a hundred years since we first had cabbages out of Holland, Sir Anthony Ashley of Wiberg St. Giles in Dorsetshire being, as I am told, the first who planted them in England."—The "Acetaria" was published in 1699. Ben Jonson in his "Volpone," first acted in 1605, describes a busy newsmonger as receiving weekly intelligence "out of the Low Countries in cabbages."

[4] Fragment of Autobiography, Appendix I.

yet, to make all sure in the eldest, he resolved to alter his name so that it should not be parted with."[1] In the same year, 1621, in which Anthony Ashley Cooper was born, the old grandfather, then in his seventieth year, married a second wife, a very young lady, by name Philippa Sheldon, related to the great favourite, the Duke of Buckingham. But this second marriage seems to have made no ill-will; a daughter born to Sir John and Lady Cooper two years later was christened Philippa after Lady Cooper's stepmother. Sir Anthony Ashley lived long enough to choose his grandson's first tutor, whom he chose because he was a Puritan, and he died, at the age of seventy-six, on January 13, 1628.[2] Anthony Ashley Cooper was then in his seventh year.

Six months after his grandfather's death Anthony Ashley Cooper's mother died of small-pox. Her death was on the twentieth of July, 1628. She left two children besides Anthony,—a daughter Philippa, two years

[1] Fragment of Autobiography.—Two Christian names were then uncommon. Sir Simonds D'Ewes, having occasion to name Sir A A. Cooper in 1641, in his Journal of the Long Parliament, explains, "He named Anthony Ashley in his baptism" (Harl. MSS. in British Museum, 162, p. 213 a). Cromwell is said to have called him Marcus Tullius Cicero, the little man with three names. (Martyn's Life of Shaftesbury, i. 168.) Camden mentions that there was a provision in Sir John Cooper's marriage settlement, that, if he or any of his heirs should obtain a peerage, the title was to be Ashley (Britannia, Gibson's ed. i. 63); and this is confirmed by a note of the fourth Earl of Shaftesbury preserved in the family papers, stating on the authority of Mr. Stringer, that Sir A. A. Cooper was ignorant of such a stipulation when he chose the title of Baron Ashley after the Restoration, and was much rejoiced, on his afterwards becoming acquainted with the settlement, that he had unwittingly complied with this provision.

[2] Sir A. Ashley's young widow married Carew Raleigh, the son of Sir Walter, and survived her second husband, who died in 1667. Sir A. Ashley's first wife, Shaftesbury's grandmother, was Jane, daughter of Philip Okeover, Esq., of Okeover in Staffordshire.

younger than Anthony, and a son George, two years younger than Philippa.[1]

Sir John Cooper afterwards made a second marriage with Lady Morrison, widow of Sir Charles Morrison, knight, of Cashiobury in Hertfordshire, and one of the daughters and co-heiresses of the great City mercer, Sir Baptist Hicks, created by Charles the First Viscount Campden.[2] He died within three years after his first wife's death, March 23, 1631. He had no children by his second wife. She had had one daughter by Sir Charles Morrison, who lived to inherit Cashiobury, and who passed it to the family to which it still belongs : for she became the wife of the gallant, ill-fated Lord Capel, the victim of one of the Commonwealth High Courts of Justice, and was the mother of the not less ill-fated Earl of Essex, a political associate of Shaftesbury in the reign of Charles the Second, whose mysterious death in the Tower on the morning of Lord Russell's trial is one of the melancholy incidents of the Rye House Plot. Cashiobury being the jointure house of his second wife, Sir John Cooper lived there frequently with his family after his second marriage, and Cashiobury was thus the home of Lord Shaftesbury during a portion of his boyish years.

Sir Anthony Ashley Cooper had lost both his parents before he completed his tenth year. He inherited, with other property, very extensive estates in the four counties

---

[1] Philippa Cooper married Sir Adam Brown, baronet, of Betchworth Castle in Surrey, and died at a very advanced age in 1701. (Aubrey's Surrey, ii 307.) George Cooper married, in 1647, one of the daughters and co-heiresses of Alderman Oldfield, of London.

[2] Banks's Dormant and Extinct Peerages, iii. 140.

of Hampshire, Wiltshire, Dorsetshire, and Somersetshire.[1] But Sir John Cooper had encumbered this inheritance by gambling and extravagance, and the young baronet's fortune was now further injured by the gross injustice of a relative, by maladministration of the Court of Wards, and by great litigation.

Inheriting estates held by tenure of knight-service of the Crown, Sir Anthony Ashley Cooper became a King's ward; and all his property so held was, during his minority, under the control of the Court of Wards. Sir John Cooper had left considerable debts, and now, by corrupt means and by the active instrumentality of Sir Francis Ashley, a brother of old Sir Anthony, an order for sale was obtained from the Court of Wards, by which the young baronet's interests were greatly injured. Sir Francis Ashley was the King's serjeant, and as such had great influence with the Attorney of the Court of Wards. Thus he obtained a decree of sale in which his own friends were named commissioners to the exclusion of the trustees appointed by Sir John Cooper,[2] and properties were sold, much below their

[1] See the report of the Inquisition held at Rockborne under the Court of Wards after Sir J. Cooper's death, in Collins's Peerage (Brydges), iii. 546. The only property there mentioned, out of the four western counties, is "in the county of Middlesex, a messuage in Holborn, called the Black Bull, and divers tenements in Muschamps." It appears from the Diary, that Ely Rents, Holborn, formed part of Sir John Cooper's estate (Append. II., November 29, 1647). Sir A. A. Cooper inherited other property, which did not come under the Court of Wards. In the Diary are mentioned a plantation in Barbadoes and an estate in Derbyshire (March 23, 1646; September 11, 1649).

[2] Sir Francis Ashley does not appear to have been one of the commissioners himself, though Shaftesbury, in the Fragment of Autobiography, says that he was. Many papers relating to these proceedings are preserved in the records of the Court of Wards in the Chapter House, where I have seen a list of the commissioners, which does not contain Sir F. Ashley's name.

value, to Sir Francis Ashley and some of the commissioners themselves. The trustees, however, refused to convey the lands to these purchasers, and applied to the Court of Wards for time to sell to greater advantage, and for permission for Sir Anthony Ashley Cooper to buy, he having property not in wardship from which he could do so. This was refused, unless the purchaser should consent. One, the purchaser of Pawlett, consented;[1] but Sir Francis Ashley and Mr. Tregonwell, a Dorsetshire neighbour, who had contracted for Rockborne, were obdurate. The trustees were then ordered by the Court to convey the estates to those purchasers who insisted; they refused, and were put in prison and not released till they had executed the conveyances.[2] " Thus," says Shaftesbury, in his Autobiography, " was my estate torn and rent from me before my face by the injustice and oppression of that Court, near relations, and neighbours, who, I may truly say, have been twenty thousand pound damage to me."

Shaftesbury proceeds to relate how he ultimately

---

[1] Pawlett was bought for Sir A. A. Cooper for 2,500*l*. (Diary, Jan. 21, 1648.) His property of Ely Rents, Holborn, was bought for him for 1,800*l*. (Ibid. Nov. 29, 1647.)

[2] The account in the text is taken from the Fragment of Autobiography. But who were " the trustees " imprisoned is doubtful. The three trustees appointed by Sir John Cooper's will were Sir Daniel Norton, Mr. Edward Tooker (his brother-in-law), and Mr. Hannam of Wimborne; the last declined to act. It appears by a note among the papers at St. Giles's, that Robert Wallop and Francis Trenchard were committed to the Fleet, June 16, 1634, for refusing to assign Damerham and Loders to Sir F. Ashley. It is therefore probable that sales had been actually made by the trustees of Sir John Cooper's will to friends in trust for Sir Anthony; and that Wallop and Trenchard, the friends to whom Damerham and Loders were so sold in trust, were the trustees imprisoned. Wallop was in this way trustee for Ely Rents. (Diary, November 29, 1648.)

recovered Rockborne, and behaved generously to his ungenerous neighbour's descendant :—

" Yet Mr. Tregonwell had not good success in his hard dealing, for he was so greedy of a good bargain that he looked not into his title, and this manor proved entailed on my father's marriage with my mother, my father having left this out of the fine he passed on all his other lands when he conveyed them for the discharge of his debts, not intending to sell the place of his father's bones, especially when his other land would more than serve to pay all. This blot was soon hit, when I came to manage my own matters ; and Mr. Tregonwell's grandchild and myself came to an agreement, I suffering him to enjoy his own and his lady's life in the manor, in which I designed to bury all animosity or ill-will as well as lawsuits betwixt the families."

With Sir Francis Ashley there was further litigation. The trustees, after the forced conveyance, preferred a bill against him to enforce execution of a trust to which the property was subject, and which he tried to evade. Sir Francis, knowing that the trustees derived the means of litigation from an estate of Sir Anthony's which was not in wardship, then made an endeavour to bring this property within the control of the Court of Wards. The property thus exempt from wardship had come to the young baronet from his grandfather, probably under his mother's marriage settlement, and the deed had been drawn by the famous Noy, who was at this moment Attorney-General. Shaftesbury, describing these proceedings when he was an old man, speaks of this last

endeavour of Sir Francis Ashley as a wicked design for
the total ruin of his fortune. His trustees made him
go himself to Noy to endeavour to prevail on him to
be his counsel. The influence of the Attorney-General
in the Court of Wards would probably be all-availing;
but he might, on the other hand, be unwilling to appear
against the Crown.

" Mr. Noy was then the King's Attorney, who being
a very intimate friend of my grandfather's had drawn
that settlement; my friends advised that I was in great
danger if he would not undertake my cause, and yet
it being against the King, it was neither proper nor
probable he would meddle in it for me; but weighing
the temper of the man, the kindness he had for my
grandfather, and his honour so concerned if a deed
of that consequence should fail of his drawing, they
advised that I must be my own solicitor, and carry
the deed myself alone to him, which, being but thirteen
years old, I undertook, and performed with that pertness that he told me he would defend my cause
though he lost his place. I was at the Court, and he
made good his word to the full without taking one
penny fees." [1]

Sir Francis Ashley appeared for himself.

" My Lord Cottington was then Master of the Wards,
who, sitting with his hat over his eyes, and having
heard Sir Francis make a long and elegant speech for
the overthrowing of my deed, said openly, ' Sir Francis,
you have spoke like a good uncle.' Mr. Attorney Noy
argued for me, and my uncle rising up to reply (I
being then present in Court), before he could speak two

[1] Fragment of Autobiography.

words, he was taken with a sudden convulsion fit, his mouth drawn to his ear, was carried out of the Court, and never spoke more." [1]

This was in 1634, and in 1641 there was still litigation about Sir Francis Ashley's purchases between Sir Anthony Ashley Cooper and the heir of Sir Francis, the celebrated Denzil Holles, who had married Sir Francis Ashley's only child. [2]

The exactions and corruptions of the Court of Wards were soon to have an end.   The Civil War broke it up, and its functions then ceased, never to be revived, for one of the first acts of the legislature after the Restoration was the abolition of the Court of Wards and the military tenures connected with it; and Sir Anthony Ashley Cooper was then able to avenge the losses of his youth by giving a helping hand for the abolition. [3]

There is no reliable account of the extent of Shaftesbury's fortune, but with all the losses of his youth he undoubtedly remained a wealthy man.   The rental which he inherited is stated to have been eight thousand

[1] Sir Richard Baker notes Sir F. Ashley's death as, "by the will of God," November 20, 1635. (Chronicle, p. 417, ed. 1684.) Noy, who was made Attorney-General in January 1634, died August 9, 1635. (Howel's Letters, i. 241; Notes and Queries, 1st Ser. i. 211.) There must therefore be a mistake in Baker's date of Sir F. Ashley's death. Sir F. Ashley was a conspicuous defender of the arbitrary system of Charles the First, and was committed to custody by the House of Lords in 1628, on account of the violence with which he argued at the bar of that House for the Crown, against the Petition of Right.

[2] It appears by a note preserved among the family papers that Sir F. Ashley had promised to reconvey Damerham and Loders, two of the manors he had become possessed of, to Sir A. A. Cooper, when he became of full age, and that there was a suit against Holles to compel execution of this promise. On February 13, 1637, the Court declared the promise voluntary and not binding, and pronounced Holles's demurrer good in bar of Sir A. A. Cooper's suit.

[3] "Sir A. A. Cooper spoke against the Court of Wards and for the Excise." (Parl. Hist. iv. 148, November 21, 1660.)

a year,[1] which would be equivalent to more than twenty thousand at present. He estimates his losses by the Court of Wards at twenty thousand pounds, which at the then rate of eight per cent. interest would be a loss of 1,600*l.* a year. He may have made some addition to his property by his three marriages with daughters of peers,—of Lord Coventry, the Earl of Exeter, and Lord Spencer of Wormleighton. He was, through life, careful of his fortune and eager to improve his income by trade and speculation. On the other hand it is to be said, both to the honour of his character and as a sign of his wealth, that there is no trace of his having made any unworthy gains in the confiscations of the Commonwealth, or of his having received or sought any of the various grants so profusely given by Charles the Second among his ministers and courtiers.

After his father's death Sir Anthony Ashley Cooper, with his brother and sister, lived with one of the trustees of his father's appointment, Sir Daniel Norton, at Southwick, near Portsmouth. His first tutor, the Puritan whom Sir Anthony Ashley had chosen, now left him. This tutor, by name Guerden, became afterwards a physician, and, Shaftesbury says, had great practice in London. Shaftesbury was an acute discerner of character; and if the following account of his first tutor gives the recollections of a boy of ten, his powers of discernment must have been developed early : "This man was moderately learned, a great lover of money, and had neither piety proportionable to the great profession he made, nor judgment and parts to support the

[1] Rawleigh Redivivus, p. 6 ; Martyn's Life, i. 36.

good opinion he had of himself; but he served well
enough for what he was designed for, being formal, and
not vicious."[1] In Sir Daniel Norton's house he had
for tutor a Mr. Fletcher, of whom all that Shaftesbury
tells us is, that he was "a very excellent teacher of
grammar."

He now went often to London, in term-time, with Sir
Daniel Norton, who was obliged frequently to go there
on his ward's business. "He very often took me with
him," says Shaftesbury, "as thinking my presence,
though very young, might work some compassion on
the Court, or those that should have been my friends."
Sir Daniel Norton died in 1635, and the three young
Coopers then went to live with another trustee, Mr.
Tooker, who had married a sister of Sir John Cooper,
and who lived at Salisbury, and at Madington, eight
miles from Salisbury. Lady Norton had wished that
they should continue with her, looking to the young
baronet as a good match for one of her daughters, and
Shaftesbury owns that his young heart was a little
touched. "Truly, if the condition of my litigious
fortune had not necessitated me to other thoughts for
support and protection, the sweetness of the disposition
of that young lady had made me look no further for a
wife." He chose to go and live with his uncle Tooker,
and his brother and sister accompanied him :—

"My uncle Tooker and Sir Walter Erle both also
pretended to take care of me; Sir Walter Erle's son,
Mr. Thomas Erle, being of the same age with me, and
there being the nearest friendship betwixt us was

[1] Fragment of Autobiography.

imaginable in our years, which increased as we grew
older, and never to expire but in both our deaths. But
my being so very young was assisted with the troubles
I had already undergone in my own affairs, having now
for several years been inured to the complaints of
miseries from near relations and oppressions from men
in power, being forced to learn the world faster than my
book, and in that I was no ill proficient : yet I had for
my diversion both hounds and hawks of my own. I
chose my uncle Tooker, my surviving trustee, for my
guardian, he being most versed in my affairs, my nearest
relation, and had the reputation of a worthy man, as
indeed he proved. He was a very honest, industrious
man, an hospitable, prudent person, much valued and
esteemed, dead and alive, by all that knew him." [1]

Having had for about a year before going to the
University a third tutor, of whom no more is known
than that he was a Master of Arts, of Oriel College,
Oxford,[2] Sir Anthony Ashley Cooper was sent to Oxford
in 1637, at the age of sixteen.[3] He was entered as a
gentleman-commoner at Exeter College,—the college
chiefly resorted to from the western counties of England,
which was then flourishing under the mastership of
Dr. Prideaux, afterwards Bishop of Worcester. Shaftesbury says in his Fragment of Autobiography, that he
was "under the immediate tuition of Dr. Prideaux," and
in the short sketch of his early life, written in 1646, he
calls Dr. Prideaux his tutor, and mentions that Mr.

---

[1] Fragment of Autobiography.
[2] Autobiographical Sketch prefixed to Diary.
[3] His name had been entered, according to Anthony Wood, in Lent
Term, 1636. (Ath. Oxon. ed. Bliss, iv. 7.)

Hussey, "since minister of Hinton Martin,"[1] was his servitor. He stayed at Oxford not much longer than a year, and during this time he was entered as a student at Lincoln's Inn, and he probably went up to London from Oxford to keep law terms.[2]

It is likely that Sir Anthony Ashley Cooper gave little attention at Oxford to the studies of the University, but it cannot be doubted that his brilliant abilities and strong will, afterwards so conspicuous on the world's stage, were otherwise exhibited. The cares of life had come early upon him and disturbed in boyhood the regularity of his education; he had "learnt the world," in his own expressive words, "faster than his book;" but the manly business of his boyhood had doubtless helped to quicken the development of his understanding and mould that character, compounded of grave failings and many excellent dispositions, which has made for him so chequered a fame. Shaftesbury's speeches and writings give ample evidence of early culture.

His talents and genial character, aided by a liberal allowance and his social position, made him a leader among his college contemporaries. The following account of himself at college is not over-modest, but it has all the air of truthfulness:—

"I kept both horses and servants in Oxford, and was allowed what expense or recreation I desired, which liberty I never much abused; but it gave me the oppor-

---

[1] In Dorsetshire; and Shaftesbury, who was lord of the manor, had doubtless given his old servitor the living.

[2] Some of Shaftesbury's biographers have incorrectly made him member of Gray's Inn. His name is one of the last entered in the Lincoln's Inn register, in 13 Car. I., 1637-8. Lord Falkland's name is within four or five before it.

tunity of obliging by entertainments the better sort, and supporting divers of the activest of the lower rank with giving them leave to eat, when in distress, upon my expense, it being no small honour among those sort of men that my name in the buttery-book willingly bore twice the expense of any in the University. This expense, my quality, proficiency in learning, and natural affability easily not only obtained the good-will of the wiser and elder sort, but made me the leader even of all the rough young men of that college, and did then maintain in the schools coursing against Christchurch, the largest and most numerous college in the University."[1]

Shaftesbury's account of "coursing" at Oxford, and of his own achievements in resisting the "tucking" of freshmen and a designed alteration of the "size" of college beer, is a most curious contribution to the knowledge of Oxford University life in the seventeenth century.

" This coursing was in older times, I believe, intended for a fair trial of learning and skill in logic, metaphysics, and school divinity, but for some ages that had been the least part of it, the dispute quickly ending in affronts, confusion, and very often blows, when they went most gravely to work. They forbore striking, but making a great noise with their feet, they hissed, and shoved with their shoulders, and the stronger in that disorderly order drove the other out before them; and, if the schools were above stairs, with all violence hurrying the contrary party down, the proctors were forced either to give way to their violence or suffer in the throng. Nay, the Vice-Chancellor, though it seldom has begun when he was

---

[1] Fragment of Autobiography.

present, yet being begun, he has sometimes unfortunately been so near as to be called in, and has been overcome in their fury once up, in these adventures. I was often one of the disputants, and gave the sign and order for their beginning; but being not strong of body, was always guarded from violence by two or three of the sturdiest youths, as their chief, and one who always relieved them when in prison, and procured their release; and very often was forced to pay the neighbouring farmers, when they of our party that wanted money were taken in the fact, for more geese, turkeys, and poultry than either they had stole or he had lost : it being very fair dealing if he made the scholar, when taken, pay no more than he had lost since his last reimbursement.

" Two things I had also a principal hand in when I was at the college. The one, I caused that ill custom of tucking freshmen to be left off: the other, when the senior fellows designed to alter the beer of the college, which was stronger than other colleges, I hindered their design. This had put all the younger sort into a mutiny ; they resorting to me, I advised all those were intended by their friends to get their livelihood by their studies, to rest quiet and not appear, and that myself and all the others that were elder brothers or unconcerned in their angers, should go in a body and strike our names out of the buttery-book, which was accordingly done, and had the effect that the senior fellows, seeing their pupils going that yielded them most profit, presently struck sail and articled with us never to alter the size of our beer, which remains so to this day.

" The first was a harder work, it having been a foolish custom of great antiquity, that one of the seniors in the evening called the freshmen (which are such as came since that time twelvemonth) to the fire, and made them hold out their chin, and they with the nail of their right thumb, left long for that purpose, grate off all the skin from the lip to the chin, and then cause them to drink a beer-glass of water and salt. The time approaching when I should be thus used, I considered that it had happened in that year, more and lustier young gentlemen had come to the college than had done in several years before, so that the freshmen were a very strong body. Upon this I consulted my two cousin-germans, the Tookers, my aunt's sons, both freshmen, both stout and very strong, and several others, and at last the whole party were cheerfully engaged to stand stoutly to defence of their chins. We all appeared at the fires in the hall, and my Lord of Pembroke's son calling me first, as we knew by custom it would begin with me, I, according to agreement, gave the signal, striking him a box on the ear, and immediately the freshmen fell on, and we easily cleared the buttery and the hall; but bachelors and young masters coming in to assist the seniors, we were compelled to retreat to a ground chamber in the quadrangle. They pressing at the door, some of the stoutest and strongest of our freshmen, giant-like boys, opened the doors, let in as many as they pleased, and shut the door by main strength against the rest; those let in they fell upon, and had beaten very severely, but that my authority with them stopped them, some of them being considerable enough to make terms for us, which they did; for Dr. Prideaux being called out to suppress the mutiny, the old Doctor, always favourable to youth offending out of courage, wishing with the fears of those we had within, gave us articles of pardon for what had passed, and an utter abolition in that college of that foolish custom."[1]

---

[1] Fragment of Autobiography. Anthony Wood describes this practice of "tucking," as existing in Merton College when he entered in 1647.

Sir Anthony Ashley Cooper left Oxford before the usual time, and too soon to take a degree ; and on the twenty-fifth of February, 1639, when yet only eighteen, he was married to Margaret, a daughter of Lord Coventry, the Lord Keeper. His uncle and guardian, Tooker, had suggested this marriage, thinking that he had need of powerful friends. Sir Anthony, writing in 1646, when this lady was alive, describes her as " a woman of excellent beauty and incomparable in gifts of nature and virtue." She died suddenly in 1649 ; and on the occasion of her death, Cooper wrote, in what is generally the most meagre and prosaic of diaries, this touching and exquisite piece of praise :—

" She was a lovely, beautiful, fair woman, a religious, devout Christian, of admirable wit and wisdom, beyond any I ever knew, yet the most sweet, affectionate, and observant wife in the world. Chaste, without a suspicion of the most envious, to the highest assurance of her husband ; of a most noble and bountiful mind, yet very provident in the least things ; exceeding all in anything she undertook, housewifery, preserving, works with the needle, cookery, so that her wish and judgment were expressed in all things ; free from any pride or froward- ness, she was in discourse and counsel far beyond any woman."

A German astrologer, Dr. Olivian, was one of Shaftes- bury's friends and companions in boyhood. He had been in old Sir Anthony Ashley's house when the young heir was born there ; he cast his nativity, and predicted for the infant a great career. He imbued the boy with a faith in astrology, which, according to Burnet,

Shaftesbury retained in manhood.[1]   Relying on his art, he had now endeavoured to persuade the young baronet to marry the sister of a Dorsetshire neighbour, Mr. Rogers.   Shaftesbury thus tells the story :—

"This match Dr. Olivian, my great friend, earnestly pressed me to, not only as it was every way suitable and fit for me, but, as he positively affirmed, he saw by his art there would be feuds and great danger to me if it was not a match, and, if it were, he could assure me she would prove a vast fortune; professing he had no concern in it above mine; and I did truly believe so, but I told him I could not see a possibility of her being so great a fortune, or having considerable addition to her present portion, since her father had divers sons and sons married.   He replied he was sure of the thing, but could not tell me how it should be; and this lady, after marrying my Lord Maynard, by the death of her brothers and strange unequal humour of her father, came to be a very great fortune indeed."

Thus one part of the prediction was verified; the feuds and troubles predicted also arrived.   Mr. Rogers became a rival for the hand of Margaret Coventry, and Sir Anthony never forgave the offence.   "For Mr. Rogers, hearing where my address was, did, by the favour of my Lord Cottington, then a suitor to the elder sister, earnestly press to be admitted a servant to my mistress, but neither she nor her friends would admit it; but yet

[1] "He had the dotage of astrology in him," says Burnet, "to a high degree; he told me that a Dutch doctor had from the stars foretold him the whole series of his life." (Own Time, i. 96.)   Another story is told in "Rawleigh Redivivus," p. 7, of a prediction by the German doctor that Sir Anthony would have a narrow escape from drowning on a certain day, and the prediction is said to have been verified.

the offer and attempt was so open and avowed that it began a never reconciled feud betwixt us, he having offered me the highest injury, and merely out of malice." [1]

Sir Anthony Ashley Cooper's marriage with a daughter of Lord Coventry connected him with three persons who bear important parts in the politics of the reign of Charles the Second. Henry Coventry, one of his wife's brothers, was Secretary of State during seven years of that reign; he had before been employed in diplomacy, and was joint plenipotentiary with Holles for the treaties of Breda. He was a man of probity, genial character, good judgment, and superior though not splendid abilities. Sir William Coventry, another brother, was a man of greater mental mark; he was Secretary of the Lord High Admiral and the chief administrator of the Admiralty in the first seven years of Charles the Second's reign, was one of Charles's chief advisers at the time of Clarendon's fall, which he much helped to bring about, and was at that time, according to Burnet, expected to become chief minister; [2] but he suddenly

---

[1] Fragment of Autobiography.

[2] Burnet's Own Time, i. 265, and Lord Dartmouth's and Speaker Onslow's Notes. Sir W. Coventry has been erroneously supposed to be the author of the "Character of a Trimmer," which was written by his more celebrated nephew, Lord Halifax. Coventry distinctly denies the authorship in an interesting letter to his nephew, Thomas Thynne, afterwards Lord Weymouth, preserved at Longleat. He follows up the denial of the authorship of the tract by avowing himself to be a Trimmer. "I have not been ashamed to own myself to be indeed a Trimmer, not according as the Observator paints them, but (as I think the name was intended to signify) one who would sit upright, and not overturn the boat by swaying too much on either side." Sir W. Coventry died in 1686, and left by his will 2,000l. to the French refugees, and 3,000l. to redeem slaves in Barbary. (Lady Russell's Letters, i. 193; Savile Correspondence, published by the Camden Society, pp. 293-5.) Marvel, in a satirical poem of 1667, introduces

lost the fickle King's favour, and was afterwards for
many years one of the most able and respected members
of the House of Commons. A sister of Sir Anthony
Ashley Cooper's wife married Sir William Savile, baronet,
of Thornhill in Yorkshire and Rufford in Nottinghamshire; and of this marriage was born the witty, accomplished, and eloquent Lord Halifax, who came to be a
chief minister towards the end of the reign of Charles
the Second, and was successively one of Shaftesbury's
friends and coadjutors, and one of his keenest adversaries in the last troubled years of Shaftesbury's life.
Talent was largely given to the children of Lord
Keeper Coventry; another of his daughters, who
married Sir John Pakington, a distinguished Cavalier
baronet, is believed with good reason to have been
the author, or one of the authors, of the " Whole Duty
of Man." [1]

An orphan at the age of nine; at war, while a boy,
with the rapacity and injustice of relatives; forced, as
he says of himself, to learn the world faster than his
book, and called early by business to the thoughts and
cares of manhood ; having inherited in childhood a title
which was then a considerable distinction, and growing
up to be the possessor of a large estate; with no father's

Sir William and Henry Coventry as the chosen leaders of the supporters
of Government in the House of Commons during Charles the Second's
first Dutch war :—

> " All the two Coventries their generals chose,
> For one had much, the other nought to lose.
> Not better choice all accidents could hit,
> While hector Harry steers by Will the wit."

[1] See Ballard's Learned Ladies, p. 320.

authority to control, or mother's love to render gentle
guidance, Sir Anthony Ashley Cooper grew up to
manhood under circumstances which may serve to
account for something harsh and jarring in the course
and character of the Earl of Shaftesbury.

CHAPTER II.

1639—1644.

Lives, after marriage, with his father-in-law—Hanley bowling-green in Dorsetshire—Sir A. A. Cooper's neighbours—Lord Digby—Visit to Worcestershire with Mr. Coventry—Elected member for Tewkesbury, at age of eighteen, for the Short Parliament of April 1640—Termination of Fragment of Autobiography—The Parliament quickly dissolved—Lord Coventry's death in January 1640—Letter of John Coventry, February 1640—Lord Savile's forged letter—Petition of twelve peers to the King for a parliament—Returned in a double return for Downton to Long Parliament—Petitions—Holles said to have prevented his being seated—Came forward for the King in Dorsetshire in spring of 1643—Dispute about his being made Governor of Weymouth and Portland—Ultimately appointed—Letter from the King to Marquis of Hertford—Appointed King's Sheriff of Dorsetshire—In February 1644 goes over to the Parliament—His statement of his motives made before the Committee of both Kingdoms.

SIR ANTHONY ASHLEY COOPER, being still a minor and not yet in possession of his property, lived, after his marriage, with his father-in-law the Lord Keeper, at Durham House in the Strand, and at Canonbury or Canbury House in Islington.[1]

He frequently visited Wimborne St. Giles, and improved his acquaintance with his Dorsetshire neighbours. Bowls was then a favourite game of the English gentry, and the county bowling-green a place of gathering. Sir Anthony frequented a bowling-green at Hanley,

[1] The Lord Keeper rented these two houses : Durham House from the Earl of Pembroke, and Canonbury or, as it was called, Canbury House from the Earl of Northampton.

not far from Wimborne St. Giles, which was the weekly
resort of the leading gentlemen of the eastern part of
Dorsetshire. Here he used to meet his enemy, Mr.
Rogers.

"The eastern part of Dorsetshire had a bowling-green
at Hanley, where gentlemen went constantly once a
week, though neither the green nor accommodation
was inviting; yet it was well placed to continue the
correspondence of the gentry of those parts. Here I
omitted no opportunity, and it was often given, to show
Mr. Rogers, where his coach and six horses did not a
little contribute to their envy. His garb, his discourse
all spoke him one that thought himself above them;
which, when observed to them, they easily agreed to.
My family alliances and fortune, being not prejudiced
either by nature or education, gave me the juster
grounds to take exceptions; besides my affable, easy
temper, now with care improved, rendered the stiffness
of his demeanour more visible." [1]

Shaftesbury has sketched in his Autobiography the
characters of most of the leading gentry of Dorsetshire and Somersetshire at the time of his marriage.
The longest and most finished of these sketches,—that of
Mr. Hastings of Woodlands,—is generally known, having
a place in the collection of the "British Essayists." [2]
It is a graphic description, written with great humour,
pungency, and vigour. Most of the persons whom he

----

[1] Fragment of Autobiography, Appendix I.
[2] It is in the "Connoisseur," No. 81, August 14, 1755. It was first
printed in Dr. Leonard Howard's "Collection of Letters and State
Papers," published in 1753. Horace Walpole, in his "Royal and
Noble Authors," made a mistake, which has been generally copied, in
saying that it first appeared in Peck's "Desiderata Curiosa," where it
is not to be found.

has sketched are unknown to fame. But one young man who appears on this list of Dorsetshire gentry,— Lord Digby, afterwards the second Earl of Bristol,—was in four years from this time Secretary of State to Charles the First, and had a long political career, in which great abilities and great advantages were always prejudiced by vanity and indiscretion. " The Earl of Bristol was relieved from all business, and lived privately to himself; but his son, the Lord Digby, a very handsome young man, of great courage and learning, and of a quick wit, began to show himself, he being highly admired by all ; and only gave himself disadvantage with a pedantic stiffness and affectation he had contracted."

Shaftesbury's account of himself at the beginning of manhood, of his high animal spirits which pain could not conquer, of his playfulness in society, and of his wit and address which won for him at the age of eighteen a seat in the House of Commons, would suffer by any abridgment :—

" My wife continuing at her father's house, my Lord Keeper's eldest son, Mr. Thomas Coventry, an honest, fair, direct man, carried me with him to see his house in Worcestershire, where we stayed some time ; and I grew in great respect in those parts for a pleasant, easy humour, but especially in the town of Tewkesbury by an accident. They having invited their neighbour, my Lord Keeper's son, to a hunting in the chace near them and a dinner at their town after, all the neighbour gentry were called in to grace the matter, who failed not to appear and pay a respect not only to the town, but so powerful a neighbour. At the hunting I was taken with one of my usual fits, which for divers years had hardly missed me one day, which lasted for an hour, betwixt eleven and one, sometimes beginning earlier and sometimes later betwixt those times. It was a violent pain of my left side, that I was often forced to lie down wherever I was; at last it forced a working in my stomach, and I put up some spoonfuls of clear water and I was well, if I may call that so, when I was never without a dull aching pain of that side. Yet this never abated the cheerfulness of my temper; but, when in the greatest fits, I hated pitying and loved merry company, and, as they told me, was myself very pleasant when the drops fell from my face for pain; but then, my servant near me always desired they would not take notice of it, but continue their diversions, which was more acceptable to me; and I had always the women and young people about me at those times, who thought me acceptable to them, and peradventure the more admired me because they saw the visible symptoms of my pain, which caused in all others so contrary an effect. At this hunting the Bailiffs[1] and chief of the town, being no hard riders, were easily led by their civility to keep me company, and being informed of my humour, we were very pleasant together, and they thought themselves obliged with my respect, as liking their company and being free with them. On the other hand, I was ready to make them any return of their kindness, which quickly offered itself, for part of our discourse had been of an old knight in the field, a crafty perverse rich man in power, as being of the Queen's Privy Council, a bitter enemy of the town and Puritans, as rather inclined the Popish way. This man's character and all his story I had learnt of them. At dinner the Bailiffs sat at the

---

[1] The chief officers of Tewkesbury were two Bailiffs, annually elected by the burgesses, twenty-four in number, from their own body.

table's end ; Sir Harry Spiller and myself, opposite to
one another, sat near them, but one betwixt. Sir Harry
began the dinner with all the affronts and dislikes he
could put on the Bailiffs or their entertainment, which
enraged and discountenanced them and the rest of the
town that stood behind us ; and the more, it being in
the face of the best gentlemen of the country, and when
they resolved to appear in their best colours. When the
first course was near spent, and he continued his rough
raillery, I thought it my duty, eating their bread, to
defend their cause the best I could, which I did with so
good success, not sparing the bitterest retorts I could
make him, which his way in the world afforded matter.
for, that I had a perfect victory over him. This gained
the townsmen's hearts, and their wives' to boot ; I was
made free of the town, and the next parliament, though
absent, without a penny charge, was chosen Burgess by
an unanimous vote.

"During this time of my youthful days and pleasant
humour, I had one accommodation which was very
agreeable, a servant that waited on me in my chamber,
one Pyne, a younger brother of a good family, every way
of my shape and limbs and height, only our faces and
the colour and manner of our hair was not alike ; mine
was then a flaxen inclined to brown, soft, and turning at
the ends ; his was dark brown, thick, bushy, hard, curled
all over. My stockings, shoes, clothes, were all exactly
fit for him ; my hat, though my head was long and big
and his round and little, yet he wore his hair so long
and so thick that it served him reasonably well, that
being the only part of my clothes that he could not buy
and fit me by his own trial. His great felicity was to
wear my clothes the next day after I had left them off,
so very often appearing in the same suit of clothes I had
worn the day before. He had a strong mechanic genius ;

he quickly learnt to trim me, and all the art of any
tradesman I used, but especially he was an excellent
sempster; he sewed and cut out any linen for men or
women, equal if not beyond any of the trade, and he
never went without patterns of the newest fashions;
and, as soon as I alighted at any place, I was hardly in
the parlour before my man had got to the nursery or
laundry, and, though he was never there before, his confidence gave him entrance, and his science in that art
they had most use of gave him welcome, and his readiness to teach and impart his skill, and to put them and
their ladies into the newest fashions, gave him an intimacy especially with the most forward and prating
wenches ; those he expected his best return from, which
was, besides the usual traffic and commerce of kisses
(the constant trade betwixt young men and women), the
intelligence of all the intrigues of the family, which he
with all haste conveyed to me, and I managed to the
most mirth and jollity I could. My skill in palmistry
and telling fortunes, which for my diversion I professed,
was much assisted by this intelligence, and gave me
choice of opportunities which some would have made
worse use of than I did."

"Thus," adds Shaftesbury, "I have set down my
youthful time. What follows is a time of business
which overtook me early, and the rest of my life is not
without great mixtures of the public concern, and must
be much intermingled with the history of the times."

And here, unfortunately, where the public interest of
Shaftesbury's life begins, ends the Fragment of the
Autobiography, in which he has related with so much
spirit and humour the story of his youthful years, and

which he began in old age to compose, in order to vindicate his fame for posterity from many calumnies of malice and faction.

In the short autobiographical sketch of 1646, Sir Anthony Ashley Cooper says of the election for Tewkesbury: "In March, 1640 he was by a general and free election of the town of Tewkesbury chosen their first burgess for the parliament, in which short parliament he served them faithfully." There was no contest, and by "first burgess" must be meant that he was named first in the return of two members. The election for Tewkesbury was with the magistrates and all inhabitants paying scot and lot, and the number of electors was probably about four hundred. Sir Anthony had not yet completed his nineteenth year; but it was not uncommon then, and for long after, for minors to sit in parliament, though their doing so was contrary to law.[1]

This parliament, which met on the thirteenth of April, 1640, was Charles the First's fourth parliament; and eleven years had passed since he had dissolved his third parliament in anger. The long interval had been marked by many arbitrary acts, by great discontents, by events memorable in English history; by Sir John Eliot's death in prison, the imposition of ship-money and Hampden's resistance, a multitude of arbitrary procla-

---

[1] At one time in James I.'s reign, there were counted forty members under age, some of them being only sixteen. The poet Waller sat in the House of Commons when only sixteen. Monk's son is said to have been only fourteen when he took part in a debate on Lord Clarendon's impeachment, November 16, 1667; but that he was so young is doubtful. The practice of minors sitting was put a stop to after the Revolution by a clause of the Triennial Act, which makes void the election of a person under twenty-one. See Hatsell's "Precedents," ii. 9.

mations, many cruel punishments in the Star Chamber and Court of High Commission, a large introduction under Archbishop Laud's government of Romish practices into the Church, and lastly an endeavour to force a liturgy on the people of Scotland, which raised a rebellion in that kingdom. The formidable appearance in arms of the Scotch Covenanters obliged Charles at last to call a parliament. The Privy Council had unanimously advised it; yet the King would not adopt their advice, until every member of the Council had promised to support him in extraordinary ways of raising money, if the parliament proved untoward.[1] Charles was very soon convinced of the untowardness of this parliament. He endeavoured to obtain an immediate supply, promising to allow the parliament to continue to sit for the discussion of grievances. The House of Commons, however, insisted that grievances should first be discussed. The parliament was dissolved in three weeks.

There is no sign of Sir Anthony Ashley Cooper in the Journals, or in the accounts which we have of the debates, of this short-lived parliament, and no information whatever about his proceedings. It has been generally assumed that he now voted blindly for the King. But it has also been generally assumed that, on the first breaking out of the Civil War, he was an

[1] Clarendon State Papers, ii. 81. Secretary Windebank to Sir A. Hopton, December 13, 1639 : "But before his Majesty would declare his resolution for this way, he was pleased to put another question to the Board, whether, if the parliament should prove as untoward as some have lately been, the Lords would not then assist him in such extraordinary ways in this extremity as should be thought fit, which being put to the vote, the Lords did all unanimously and cheerfully promise that in such case they would assist him with their lives and fortunes in such extraordinary way as should be advised and found."

adherent of the King; whereas he himself states that, as late as September 1642, after the King had set up his standard at Nottingham, he had "not as yet adhered against the Parliament." It was natural to infer that the young son-in-law of the Lord Keeper Coventry would vote on the King's side; and most of his own relatives were on that side also. But Cooper, as a young man, was very likely to think and act for himself. It is to be inferred from his account of his election for Tewkesbury that the feeling of the electors, with whom he had ingratiated himself by banter of Sir Harry Spiller, was Puritan.[1]

Lord Coventry, Cooper's father-in-law, and the Lord Keeper, had died about three months before the meeting of this parliament,—before Cooper was elected for Tewkesbury, and before the completion of a year after Cooper's marriage with his daughter. He died on the fourteenth of January, 1640, "to the King's great detriment," says Clarendon, "rather than to his own."[2] His young son-in-law, who was beginning life as his own master with wealth, inherited station, great talents, and eager temperament, probably lost by his death a wise and useful counsellor. Sir Anthony continued to live with his mother-in-law at Durham House and Canonbury, till, at the end of a twelvemonth after Lord Coventry's death, she gave up the two houses; and then he went to live

---

[1] Mr. Martyn says that Cooper was very diligent in his attendance in this parliament, and "every day wrote an account of their proceedings." (Life, i. 47.) No authority is given for this statement, and I have found no trace among Lord Shaftesbury's papers of such a journal. Mr. Martyn does not say that he had seen such a journal: had he seen one, he would doubtless have given extracts.

[2] History of the Rebellion, ii. 64.

and keep house with his brother-in-law, the second Lord Coventry, at Dorchester House in Covent Garden.[1]

A letter to Cooper from another brother-in-law, John Coventry, the eldest son of the Lord Keeper by his second wife, who was Lady Cooper's mother, is the only vestige among the papers at St. Giles's of Cooper's private correspondence in early life. This letter was written in the short interval between the Lord Keeper's death and Cooper's election for Tewkesbury. John Coventry is mentioned by Shaftesbury in his Autobiography as one of the leading men of Somersetshire at this time.[2] The following letter shows him a candidate for the county for the parliament called for April. It is superscribed, " To my truly honoured brother Sir Anthony Ashley Cooper, Baronet, Durham House, present these."

" DEAR BROTHER,—I hope you all came safe home on Tuesday night, as I did in the morning, for my horses began to find their legs again. We are here canvassing very hard. Mr. Smyth and Mr. Alexander Popham are pitched upon by the Robins; Sir Ralph Hopton and I as yet stand single ; what we shall do I know not Here is great exceptions taken, as I am told, at me for reporting that Mr. Alexander Popham was a banquerout, and that the Robins had made choice of Robin-hood as

[1] Autobiographical Sketch prefixed to Diary.
[2] He was father of Sir John Coventry, who obtained notoriety, in Charles the Second's reign, by a speech in the House of Commons reflecting on the King's amours, and by the savage assault made on him in consequence by a band of courtiers and ruffians instigated by Monmouth, which greatly inflamed the House of Commons, and led to the passing of an Act " to prevent malicious maiming and wounding," which was familiarly known as the Coventry Act (22 & 23 Car. II. c. i.).

an outlaw and incapable of being chosen. This is said
to be dispersed here by a letter of Sir Francis Doding-
ton's from London. I remember at Durham House
being asked (I think by yourself) whom the Robins
would make. I answered, I thought Robin-hood, naming
Mr. Kirton or Mr. Stroud, and Mr. Aish the clothier.
'Tis true, I said, that some of them had a mind to Mr.
A. Popham, but I knew he had refused to stand, and
that some men did doubt whether he was eligible in
respect of his brother's debts, for which I had heard he
stood outlawed. But sure I think you have not heard
me press anything with sharpness and barbarism against
him, as is pretended. This was at the table, and if I
mistake not, Mr. Ingram was present. I know Sir
Francis hath acquaintance with him ; possibly he might
tell him somewhat. Be pleased, I pray you, to speak
with Mr. Ingram and know whether he told him anything, or anything more than I admit, and let me hear
from you by the return of the post what he saith, and
what your remembrance is. If he divulged not this,
you have a dangerous pack of servants. Let none see
this letter or know the contents but Mr. Ingram. Thus
in haste, with my service to my sister and my lord and
the rest of your good company, I remain,

" Your faithful brother and servant,

" J. COVENTRYE.

" ORCHARD, *February* 29, 1639.[1]

" Keep this letter safe till I see you."

The parliament which met on the thirteenth of April,
1640, having been abruptly dissolved on the fifth of May,
Charles the First proceeded again to try his extraordinary
ways of raising money. But these were soon found

---

[1] February 1639, is old style for 1640.

unavailing. The Scotch army crossed the Tweed and
routed the King's forces. As a last hope of avoiding
a parliament, Charles summoned all the peers of the
realm to meet him at York. But before the day fixed
for their assembling, he found himself constrained to
call a parliament, and he announced to them, when
they met, his resolution. The parliament which had
been hastily dissolved in the spring is known as the
Short Parliament; that which met in less than six
months after, on the third of November, 1640, was the
celebrated Long Parliament.

Two short notes by Shaftesbury, on occurrences
between the dissolution of May and the meeting of the
next parliament, which may have been intended for the
continuation of his Autobiography, may here be inserted.[1]
The first refers to the letter sent by Lord Savile to the
Scotch Commissioners, urging an invasion of England,
with a number of forged signatures of leading noblemen
added to his own, which led the Scotch army to enter
England in August.

[1] These two passages occur in Locke's "Commonplace Book," under
date December 1680, and are printed in Lord King's "Life of Locke,"
vol. i. p. 222. The letters A. E. S. being appended to one of the
passages in Locke's manuscript, Lord King conjectured that these
initials meant Anthony Earl of Shaftesbury; and the conjecture has
been confirmed by two references in Martyn's "Life of Shaftesbury"
(i. pp. 115, 119) to a manuscript of Shaftesbury's as authority for the
same statements. I have not found the passages thus referred to
among the papers at St. Giles's. Martyn may have seen them, and
they may have been since lost, or he may have only learnt about them
from references by Stringer. Reference is made to one of these
passages in a note of the fourth Earl's, which is preserved. The
passages may have been fragments to form part of the introductory
historical sketch in the Autobiography which terminates so abruptly
at the Reformation, or they may have been detached notes written in
1680, for Locke's and Stringer's information. Locke sets them down
in his "Commonplace Book" as notes for Rushworth's "Collections."

" This second coming in of the Scots was occasioned and principally encouraged by a letter which the Lord Saville, afterwards Earl of Sussex, writ with his own hand, and forged the names of a dozen or fourteen of the chiefest of the English nobility, together with his own, which he sent into Scotland by the hands of Mr. H. Darley, who remained there as agent from the said English lords until he had brought the Scots in. At the meeting of the grand Council, when the English and Scots lords came together, the letter caused great dispute amongst them, till at last my Lord Saville, being reconciled to the Court, confessed to the King the whole matter." [1]

The second note is on the presentation of the petition to the King for a parliament, signed by twelve peers,[2] and contains startling statements, which are, however, confirmed by Bishop Burnet's narrative.

" This petition was presented to the King at York, by the hands of the Lord Mandeville[3] and the Lord Edward Howard.[4]   The King immediately called a Cabinet

---

[1] A note of the fourth Earl of Shaftesbury, among the papers at St. Giles's, points out the importance of Shaftesbury's testimony to the story of Lord Savile's forgery.   Dr. Lingard expressed a doubt as to the truth of the story ; but it is too well attested to admit of reasonable doubt.   Mr. Sanford has since published a long circumstantial account of the transaction, from a MS. in the British Museum, Add. MSS. 15,567.   See Sanford's " Studies and Illustrations of the Great Rebellion," p. 171, and Hallam (Const. Hist. ii. 125, note).

[2] Mr. Hallam has given an incorrect list of the twelve peers who signed this famous petition : the names of Lords Paget, Wharton, and Savile appear in his list, instead of the Earls of Rutland and Exeter, and Lord Howard of Escrick.   Compare Hallam, ii. 127, note, with the list in Lords' Journals, iv. 188.

[3] Lord Mandeville, eldest son of the Earl of Manchester, had been called by writ to the House of Lords, with the title of Baron Kimbolton, by which name he is best known to us.

[4] Edward, younger son of the Earl of Suffolk, created Baron Howard of Escrick in 1628.   His son, the third baron, obtained an unenviable fame in Charles the Second's reign by his evidence against Russell and Sidney.

Council, wherein it was concluded to cut off both the
lords' heads the next day; when the Council was up,
and the King gone, Duke Hamilton and the Earl of
Strafford, general of the army, remaining behind, when
Duke Hamilton, asking the Earl of Strafford whether
the army would stand to them, the Earl of Strafford
answered he feared not, and protested he did not think
of that before then. Hamilton replied, if we are not
sure of the army, it may be our heads instead of theirs;
whereupon they both agreed to go to the King and alter
the counsel, which accordingly they did."[1]

Sir Anthony Ashley Cooper was not again elected
for Tewkesbury. He was a candidate for Downton in
Wiltshire, a borough in which he had property, and
which was near his seat at Wimborne St. Giles; and
he was one of two candidates returned on a double
return. Neither he nor his rival could sit until it
was decided which had the right. Cooper says, in
his Autobiographical Sketch written in 1646, that the
Committee of Privileges decided in his favour, but
that no report had been made to the House. "For
this happy parliament," he writes,—being in 1646, when
he wrote, a strong Parliamentarian,—"he was chosen

---

[1] Bishop Burnet tells the same of Lord Wharton and Lord Howard
of Escrick, presenting other petitions. "The Lord Wharton and the
Lord Howard of Escrick undertook to deliver some of these, which they
did, and were clapt up upon it. A council of war was held; and it
was resolved on, as the Lord Wharton told me, to shoot them at the
head of the army, as movers of sedition. This was chiefly pressed by
the Earl of Strafford. Duke Hamilton spoke nothing till the council
rose; and then he asked Strafford, if he was sure of the army, who
seemed surprised at the question: but he upon inquiry understood
that very probably a general mutiny, if not a total revolt, would have
followed, if any such execution had been attempted." (Own Time,
i. 29.) Lord Wharton was not one of the petitioners. Burnet's
variances, which are probably mistakes, may enhance his substantial
confirmation of Shaftesbury's story.

a burgess for Downton in Wiltshire, in the place of
Mr. William Herbert, second son to the Earl of Pembroke, who was chosen knight also of a county in
Wales ; Mr. Gorge, eldest son to the Lord Gorge, was
also returned; but at the Committee for Privileges, it
was clearly decided for Sir Anthony, yet no report
made of it." This is probably quite correct. It
appears by the Journals that the question had been
referred to the Committee of Privileges, and a day
fixed for the hearing, in February 1641 ; but the
Journals then contain no further notice of the matter.
Thus the question remained in abeyance and the seat
vacant, and Cooper was kept out of the House.[1] The
case is not singular.   Sir John Bramston gives an
account of a similar proceeding with his own petition
for Bodmin, which, he says, was decided in his favour
in Committee, but that the chairman, Serjeant Maynard, would never report.[2] Obstruction may have been
given to Cooper, as Sir John Bramston thinks that it
was given in his case, from political motives. But
Denzil Holles, who was a leader in the party opposed
to the King, is said to have exerted himself, for private
reasons, to prevent Cooper from obtaining his seat.
The authorities for this statement are not unexceptionable ;[3] but there is a fact which suggests that

---

[1] Downton returned two members ; the return of one, Sir Edward
Griffin, was undisputed.   Sir E. Griffin adhered to the King, and, his
seat having been declared vacant, a new writ was issued in September
1645, and Mr. Thistlewaite was then elected in his place.
[2] Sir J. Bramston's Autobiography, published by the Camden Society,
p. 160.
[3] Locke's Memoir in Works, ix. 271.   Martyn's Life, i. 143.   The
identical statement in these two places was doubtless derived from
Stringer, and is introduced in order to prove Sir A. A. Cooper's magna-

Holles had an interest in excluding Cooper from the House, and which, if Holles has been calumniated, will account for the imputation. Holles was at this time prosecuting a suit in the Court of Wards against Cooper, arising out of his father-in-law Sir Francis Ashley's proceedings after the death of Cooper's father; and there is an entry in the Commons' Journals on February 10, 1641, a few days before the reference of the question of the election to the Committee of Privileges, recording a permission given to Holles to proceed with the suit. Sir Simonds D'Ewes in his Diary gives a fuller explanation of the resolution: "It was agreed in the House that Mr. Hollis, a member of this House, having a suit against Sir Anthony Ashley Cooper (he named Anthony Ashley in his baptism), being an elected member of this House, but the election being in controversy, and he not yet admitted to sit as a member, was allowed to proceed in the suit, being in the Court of Wards, and demand publication of witnesses."[1]

In 1645, after Cooper had joined the side of the Parliament and fought for it, he made an endeavour to get seated on the same petition for Downton, but still unsuccessfully. There is an entry in the Commons' Journals, September 1, 1645, that Sir Walter Erle was ordered to report on Sir Anthony Ashley

nimity in not revenging himself on Holles, when called before the House of Commons, a few years after, as is alleged, to give evidence about transactions of Holles at Oxford. But this story of his being called as a witness against Holles is clearly a romance. See note at p. 41.

[1] Harl. MSS. in British Museum, 162, p. 213 a.

Cooper's election, but again no report was made. At last, on the eve of the Restoration, in the last days of the Rump of this parliament, which Cooper had then prominently helped to resuscitate, he obtained a decision in his favour, and was declared to have been duly elected for Downton in 1640.[1]

Sir Anthony Ashley Cooper was therefore excluded from taking part in the great parliamentary contests of the beginning of the Long Parliament, which ushered in the Civil War. He was of age on the twenty-second of July, 1642. He had then not yet proclaimed himself a partisan. But swords had been then already drawn in the great quarrel of King and Parliament. On the twenty-fifth of August, the King set up his standard at Nottingham; and Cooper, who was at the time visiting in Nottinghamshire, at his brother-in-law Sir William Savile's at Rufford, was present at this ceremony, but only as a spectator. "He was with the King," he says of himself, "at Nottingham and Derby, but only as a spectator, having not as yet adhered against the Parliament."[2]

In the spring of 1643, after the failure of the negotiations at Oxford, Cooper came forward in Dorsetshire on the King's side.[3] He says of himself that at this

---

[1] January 7, 1660.

[2] Autobiographical Sketch prefixed to Diary.

[3] The following account of Sir A. A. Cooper's proceedings, while he supported the King's party, is derived from his own statements in the Autobiographical Sketch, written in 1646, and from Clarendon's "History of the Rebellion;" it is in complete contrast with the absurd, extravagant statements, to which some have given credence, contained in Mr. Martyn's Life, and in the fragment of a Memoir printed among Locke's works. The accounts given by Mr. Martyn, and in the Locke Memoir, are as follow. Sir A. A. Cooper, being a young man of twenty-two, is represented to have proposed to the King, in an inter-

time he "was by the gentlemen of the county desired to attend the King with their desires and the state of view at Oxford, to undertake the general pacification of the kingdom, if the King would authorize him to treat with the parliamentary garrisons and promise a new and free parliament. The King is said to have observed, "You are a young man, and talk great things;" but to have given Sir A. A. Cooper the authority he desired. All Cooper's plans are represented to have been spoilt by Prince Maurice, and on Cooper's complaining to the King it is said that "the King shook his head with some concern, but said little." It is further stated that, after this first grand project was broken by Prince Maurice, Cooper started another, which was that the counties should all arm and endeavour to suppress both the contending armies, that Cooper brought most of the sober and well-intentioned gentlemen of both sides throughout England into this plan, and that this was the origin of the "clubmen;" that Cooper was now so strictly watched by the Court, which had become jealous of him, that he could not maintain the necessary correspondence with distant counties ; that at this time the King wrote a very complimentary letter begging him to come to Oxford, but that his friends dissuaded him from going, telling him that danger lurked in the King's civility ; that Goring, who commanded a force in those parts, had orders to seize Cooper; that he invited himself one day to dine with Sir Anthony, who upon this took fright and fled to the Parliament's quarters. Most of this is downright falsehood ; it is in itself sufficiently improbable that Sir A. A. Cooper, when so young, should have been encouraged in such grand undertakings, and the story abounds in anachronisms. The clubmen, whom Cooper is said to have brought forward, did not appear on the stage before the spring of 1645, more than a year after Cooper had left the King's cause. Mr. Godwin has pointed out this anachronism (Hist. of Commonwealth, i. 439, note). Goring had no command in the west at the time when Cooper left the King's cause in February 1644; he had a command there in the following autumn. It will be observed that Shaftesbury in his Autobiographical Sketch makes no allusion whatever to the clubmen, which is not consistent with his having been the originator of so important a movement. There appear to be in the whole of this elaborate story, two, and only two, facts, on which this superstructure of confused error has been raised : 1st, that Cooper attended the King at Oxford in 1643, with a deputation from his county ; and 2d, that he received a flattering letter from the King shortly before his defection. It is not unlikely that Cooper, in supporting the King's cause, assumed a somewhat independent tone, and that his own exaggerated accounts in later life led a hearer, who had no personal knowledge of the events of this time, to misrepresentation. Another gross historical error occurs in a story told for the glorification of Cooper in the Locke Memoir, and likewise told by Mr. Martyn, of his being called by the Parliament as a witness against his old private adversary, Holles. Holles being accused in the House of Commons of having transacted separately with the King when he was sent with other commissioners to Oxford to treat of peace, it is stated that Cooper was called as a witness by Holles's accusers, as he was with the King at Oxford at the time, and that Cooper refused

the county." Clarendon says that the King resolved
at this time to send the Marquis of Hertford with
an army into the western counties, "the rather because
there were many of the prime gentlemen of Wiltshire,
Dorsetshire, and Somersetshire, who confidently undertook, if the Marquis went through these counties with
such a strength as they supposed the King would spare
to him, they would in a very short time raise so considerable a power as to oppose any force the Parliament
should be able to send;" and later, after the surrender
of Bristol, Clarendon gives as one of the reasons why
the King determined to divide his western army, and
detach a portion under Prince Maurice and the Earl
of Carnarvon to Dorsetshire, "some correspondence
with the chief gentlemen of Dorsetshire, who were
ready to join with any considerable party for the
King, and had some probable hopes that the small
garrisons upon the coast would not make a tedious
resistance." Dorsetshire was entirely in the hands of
the Parliament, who held all the ports, and Clarendon

to give any answer and persisted in his refusal, though threatened to
be sent to the Tower. Now the separate conversation with the King,
which was made a charge against Holles, took place in November 1644,
nine months after Cooper had quitted the King's party. In the Memoir
in Locke's works, it is mentioned that Holles's separate transaction
with the King was on the occasion of the treating at Uxbridge, which
was even later, in the beginning of 1645; but this is only one error
more. The account in this Memoir and that of Mr. Martyn evidently
proceed from the same source; and that source is doubtless Mr.
Stringer. Locke probably took these stories from Stringer, and wrote
them down, without examination at the time, in a rough draft of a
biography designed for subsequent correction. It is not impossible
that Shaftesbury, in old age, may in conversation with his friends have
given a somewhat false colour to the story of his early life; and there
is a remarkable passage in Burnet, accusing him both of boasting and
of disingenuousness in speaking of his relations with Cromwell. (Own
Time, i. 96.)

speaks of Dorchester as "the most malignant town in England."[1]

The Marquis of Hertford, as commander-in-chief of the western army, had commissioned Cooper, with Sir Gerard Napier, Sir John Hele, and Sir William Ogle, to treat with Weymouth and Dorchester for their surrender; and Cooper had raised at his own expense a regiment of foot and a troop of horse, and received from Hertford commissions as colonel of the regiment and captain of the troop.[2] Hertford had given him also a commission appointing him governor of Weymouth and the island of Portland, when they should be taken for the King. In August, Dorchester, Weymouth, and Portland all surrendered to the Earl of Carnarvon, immediately on his arrival with his army from Bristol. Very shortly afterwards, the Marquis of Hertford ceased to be commander-in-chief, the King desiring to give the chief command to Prince Maurice, who accordingly succeeded him. Cooper, hearing that Prince Maurice was not disposed to respect the commission which Hertford had given him to be governor of Weymouth and Portland, and that he wished to appoint some one else, went off immediately to Hertford, who was at Bristol, to press his claim. He had indeed already acted on Hertford's commission by nominating a commander for Portland. Hertford, who had lately, before his removal from his command, had a similar question with Prince Rupert about the governorship of Bristol, took up Cooper's case warmly. Weymouth and Portland had, in truth, been

[1] History of Rebellion, vii. 94, 154, 155.
[2] Autobiographical Sketch prefixed to Diary.

surrendered before he had actually ceased to be commander-in-chief, and he made it a question of his own
honour with the King that the commission which he
had given to Cooper should be confirmed. Clarendon,
who was at Bristol, being then the King's Chancellor of
the Exchequer, has given a detailed account of this
incident, and describes Cooper as "a young gentleman
of that country, of a fair and plentiful fortune, and one
who, in the opinion of most men, was like to advance the
place by being governor of it, and to raise men for the
defence of it without lessening the army, and had, in
expectation of it, made some provision of officers and
soldiers, when it should be time to call them together."
Hertford spoke with Hyde on the subject, and Cooper
himself applied to him for his intercession : "And Sir
Anthony came likewise to him [Clarendon], who was of
his acquaintance, and desired his assistance, that, after
so much charge he had been put to in the expectation
of it, and to prepare for it, he might not be exposed to
the mirth and contempt of the country." Hyde wrote
to the King, who was before Gloucester, then besieged
by the royal forces, and he also "wrote to the Lord
Falkland, to take Sir John Colepepper with him, if he
found any aversion in the King, that they might together
discourse and prevail with him." The King refused.
Hertford was so much hurt that he talked of retiring to
his own house to live privately and quietly, seeing that
he had no more credit with the King. Hyde then went
to the King ; and, according to his own account, written
long after, when his feelings towards Shaftesbury were
soured, "at last, with very great difficulty, he [Hyde]

did so far prevail with his Majesty, that he gave a commission to Sir Anthony Ashley Cooper to be Governor
of Weymouth, which he was the more easily persuaded
to, out of some prejudice he had to the person who he
understood was designed to that government." [1]

Such is the detailed account given by Clarendon of
this incident, of which he had excellent opportunities of
knowledge. Cooper himself makes no allusion to the
difficulty and dispute, simply saying that, after Hertford's removal, he " had a continuation of all his commands under the King's own hand." Clarendon has
omitted to mention that the King wrote to Hertford,
signifying his consent to the appointment of Cooper and
of the person whom he had named to command under
him at Portland, but at the same time urging him to
endeavour to persuade Cooper and his nominee to
resign after a short interval, and then, on their resigna-
tions, to confer with Prince Maurice about the selection
of successors of greater experience and military knowledge. The following is the King's letter to Hertford,
which completes the story :—

" CHARLES R.

" Right trusty and right entirely beloved cousin and
councillor, we greet you well. Upon the hearing of some
difference about the command of our town of Weymouth
and our castle of Portland, signified to us by our Chancellor of the Exchequer, we have written to our nephew
Prince Maurice, that our pleasure is that Sir Anthony
Ashley Cooper and the person appointed by him remain
in those commands according to the tenor of your com-

---

[1] History of Rebellion, vii. 199.

mission granted to him; which though out of respect to
you and your grant we have thought fit to do, and that
nothing like an affront may fall upon the gentlemen
entrusted by you, yet being informed of the youth of
the one and the want in both of experience in martial
affairs, and of the importance of those places and how
likely they are, being ports, to be attempted by the Parliament forces by sea, in which case, for want of an able
and experienced commander, they may run great hazard
to be lost, to the great prejudice of our affairs, we
earnestly recommend it to you to prevail with them
willingly to resign their commands after they have held
them so long as that they may not appear to be put
from them, nor your commission to have been disregarded
by us. And we recommend to you so to advise with our
nephew about the persons to succeed them therein that
both these places for the security thereof may be in the
hands of more able soldiers, and that (if such persons
be there to be found) these soldiers may likewise be
persons of some fortune and interest in those parts for
the better satisfaction of the gentry of that country.
And so not doubting of your ready compliance herein,
we bid you heartily farewell. Given at our camp before
Gloucester, the 10th day of August, 1643.

" To our right trusty and right entirely beloved cousin
and councillor, William Marquis of Hertford." [1]

After this, Cooper was made sheriff of Dorsetshire for
the King, and he says that he was appointed president
of the King's council of war in the county.[2]

But in a few months a great change took place. In
the beginning of January 1644, Cooper resigned the

---

[1] From a copy among Lord Shaftesbury's papers at St. Giles's.
[2] Autobiographical Sketch prefixed to Diary.

government of Weymouth and all his commissions under the King, and a few weeks after he went over to the Parliament. He presented himself in the Parliament's quarters at Hurst Castle, on the Hampshire coast, on the twenty-fourth of February, and thence proceeded to London, where his wife joined him, after a year's separation. She had remained in Shropshire with her sister, Lady Thynne, while Cooper had been doing military service for the King in Dorsetshire.[1]

While Cooper represents his resignation of his commissions as voluntary, and his change as purely the result of conviction, Clarendon has stated that he was removed from the government of Weymouth, and that he abandoned the King's cause from pique;[2] and this explanation of Cooper's change has been generally accepted without inquiry. There is no doubt that Cooper was not ostensibly removed, and so far Clarendon's statement is unquestionably inaccurate. Clarendon's accuracy in details can never be relied on, and when he wrote his History, in exile, thirty years

---

[1] Autobiographical Sketch prefixed to Diary.

[2] Hist. of Rebellion, viii 60. Colonel Ashburnham succeeded Cooper as governor of Weymouth, and Clarendon says that Cooper was removed to make way for him. He goes on to say that Cooper "was thereby so much disobliged that he quitted the King's party and gave himself up, body and soul, to the service of the Parliament, with an implacable animosity against the royal interest." It is stated in "Rawleigh Redivivus" that Cooper was affronted by Ashburnham's being sent into Dorsetshire with a commission as governor of the county which overrode his own authority as sheriff; but this little biography is a catchpenny publication of no authority, and the object of the writer was to prove Shaftesbury an injured man. Bishop Burnet ascribes Cooper's desertion of the King's cause to an incident which would have occurred, and which is related in the Locke memoir as occurring, before he became governor of Weymouth, viz. Prince Maurice's breaking an engagement which he had made with one of the Dorsetshire towns, on its surrendering to him for the King. (Own Time, i. 96.)

after these incidents, he was angry with Shaftesbury. It is even probable that Cooper's own account of his conduct is entirely correct, and that he had no cause for resentment. Certainly, if Cooper had been pressed to resign the government of Weymouth in compliance with the King's wish as it had been conveyed to the Marquis of Hertford, his resignation might have been a virtual removal. But there is no trace of evidence of any endeavour made by Hertford or any one else to persuade Cooper to resign, and it is quite likely that the King's suggestion of his resignation, made at the time by way of compromise between Hertford's and Prince Maurice's pretensions, was not afterwards thought of. It is beyond dispute that Cooper was appointed sheriff of Dorsetshire for the King after the decision of the question about the government of Weymouth. And there is no reason to doubt Cooper's own statements, written in 1646, that he was courted and treated with honour by the King to the last days of his remaining on the King's side, and that he had a promise of a peerage and received a complimentary letter from the King only a few days before he went over to the Parliament.

"He now plainly seeing the King's aim destructive to religion and the state, and though he had an assurance of the barony of Ashley Castle,[1] which had formerly belonged to that family, and that but two days before he received a letter from the King's own hand of large promises and thanks for his service, yet in February he delivered up all his commissions to Ashburnham, and

---

[1] In Wiltshire, whence the Ashleys of Wimborne St. Giles came. See Coker's "Survey of Dorsetshire," p. 14.

privately came away to the Parliament, leaving all his estate in the King's quarters, 500*l.* a year full-stocked, two houses well furnished, to the mercy of the enemy, resolving to cast himself on God and to follow the dictates of a good conscience. Yet he never in the least betrayed the King's service, but while he was with him was always faithful."

On his arrival in London, Cooper appeared, on the sixth of March, 1644, before the standing Committee of the two Houses, now called Committee of both Kingdoms, and made a statement explanatory of his coming over to the Parliament, of which notes have been preserved. As these notes come from the Committee, and not from Cooper, they may be relied on as a report of what he said of himself; and this is Cooper's account, publicly given, of his actions and motives, when he was exposed to easy detection of any inaccurate or disingenuous statement. There would have been enough distrust among those to whom he went, and enough anger among those whom he left, to ensure his being exposed, if he had acted from resentment at a marked affront.

" Sir Anthony Ashley Cooper, bart., saith that he was Sheriff of Dorcester this year, and late Governor of Weymouth, but he hath delivered up his commissions of Governor and Colonel the first week of January 1643.[1]

" He came into the Parliament quarters at Hurst Castle, in Hampshire, upon the 24th of February.

" He brought in a certificate under my general's hand, certifying his coming into the Parliament quarters before the 1st day of March.

1 January 1644, according to the present mode of reckoning.

" He saith he came there being fully satisfied that there was no intention of that side for the promoting or preserving of the Protestant religion and the liberties of the kingdom, and that he left 600*l.* per annum well stocked there; and is fully satisfied of the justness of the Parliament proceedings: 800*l.* near Oxford, under their power: 2,000*l.* per annum in the King's quarters in Wiltshire and Dorsetshire and Somersetshire.[1]

" He saith he had not made known his intentions to any.

" That those that should come in before the 1st of March, the Parliament would give them their lives and liberties, but for their estates that was wholly to be disposed of to the use of the public; only if they took the Covenant and behaved themselves likely to deserve well of the Parliament, they should be allowed forty or fifty pound per annum. Mr. Kirby's letters certified so much.

" He saith above a month before he heard of the Parliament declarations he delivered up his commissions and was resolved to return to the Parliament; being fully satisfied of the injustice of that cause, and of the justice of the Parliament, he was resolved to come into them without looking to any conditions whatsoever.

" He saith he hath seen the Covenant, and desires to take the Covenant when this Committee shall tender it unto him.

" A better testimonial of his purposes of coming in, and intentions to leave them, and that he is very cordial for the Parliament, being able to do you good service, and discovery of their designs and of their strength, and

---

[1] From the Royalist Composition Papers in the State Paper Office, First Series, 16,561. It is evident that these are very rough notes made at the time Some part of the notes is in cypher; the rest very badly written.

wherein they might prepare against your enemy both upon Poole and Wareham, by Mr. Hildeley, one of the Committee there."

This document renders it impossible to believe that Cooper was superseded or slighted. He probably acted, according to his nature, impetuously. But there is much reason to think that he acted conscientiously. The time of his change was a time when any man doubting or wavering would be strongly moved to decide himself. The King had summoned his friends of both Houses to assemble as a parliament at Oxford in January 1644; the Parliament had lately concluded the "Solemn League and Covenant" with Scotland. Other persons of importance left the King's party at this very time, alleging disgust at the treaty made by Ormond for the King with the Irish rebels, and the favour shown to Roman Catholics. Among these were the Earl of Westmorland and Sir Edward Dering, who gave their reasons in language very similar to that of Cooper, that "there was no intention of that side for the promoting or preserving of the Protestant religion and the liberties of the kingdom."[1] Sir Gerard Napier, Sir Anthony Ashley Cooper's neighbour and friend, went over with him to the Parliament. A royalist gentleman writes from Oxford, in March 1644: "Sir Anthony Ashley Cooper and Sir Gerard Napier are both run away to the Parliament from their brethren the

---

[1] Ludlow, i. 106 ; Whitelocke, pp. 81, 82. Holland is by mistake named instead of Westmorland by Mr. Hallam (Constitutional History, ii. 233, note). Lord Inchiquin was another convert at this time on account of Ormond's treaty of cessation with the Irish rebels.

Commons here."[1] This is a royalist who writes, and, writing when Cooper's desertion was fresh, he imputes no bad motive. It is right also to remember that in the beginning of 1644, when Cooper left the King's party, the King's friends were hopeful, and the King's fortunes by no means low. The result of the campaign of 1643 had been on the whole favourable to the King's arms. In Dorsetshire and the western counties especially, where the Parliament had had a decided ascendency in the spring of 1643, the ascendency of the King was as decided at the close of the campaign.[2] A year earlier or a year later, Cooper might have been described as going over to the more powerful party. Another proof of disinterestedness is furnished by the fact that, leaving the King's side when he did, he left much of his property at the King's mercy; for most of his posses-

---

[1] Carte's Life of Ormond, iii. 254. Mr. Arthur Trevor to Ormond, March 9, 1644. Mr. Trevor's words do not necessarily mean that Cooper went from Oxford : Charles's parliament was then sitting there, and Cooper, if he had remained among the royalists, would have been probably recognised there without difficulty as member for Downton. It is said in "Rawleigh Redivivus" (p. 17) that he went from Dorsetshire, taking his brother's house, which would be near Salisbury, on the way.

[2] Clarendon writes of the condition of the west in the spring of 1643 : "Dorsetshire and Devonshire were entirely possessed by the enemy, and all the ports upon the western coasts were garrisoned by them. The Cornish army [for the King] was greater in reputation than numbers." (Hist. of Rebellion, vi. 151.) Contrast this with his account of the state of things in October. "He [the King] was now master of the whole west ; Cornwall was his own without a rival ; Plymouth was the only place in all Devonshire unreduced, and those forces shut within their own walls ; the large rich county of Somerset, with Bristol, the second city of the kingdom, entirely his ; in Dorsetshire, the enemy had only two little fisher-towns, Poole and Lyme ; all the rest was declared for the King. And in every of these counties he had plenty of harbours and ports to supply him with ammunition, and the country with trade. In Wiltshire the enemy had not the least footing, and rather a town or two in Hampshire than any possession of the county." (vii. 298.)

sions lay in the western counties, where the King then was uppermost.

Mr. Martyn, and Lord Campbell who has followed him, have given an exaggerated impression of the warmth- of Cooper's reception by the Parliament, and the importance attached to his joining them. They state that the Parliament specially appointed a Committee to receive and examine him,[1] and Lord Campbell says, that "the Parliament was contented to receive him on his own terms." He was examined, like any one else, by the standing Committee of both Kingdoms; and it will be seen in the next chapter that it was not until after five months, and after some military service, that he was permitted to compound for his estates by a fine of five hundred pounds; that, eighteen months later, when he had performed much military service, he could not gain admission into the House of Commons, although a Committee had previously decided that he was duly elected in 1640; and that he was not entirely cleared of delinquency until the beginning of 1652, eight years later. The importance likely to attach to him as a Parliamentary convert is also a material point for consideration in the question of Cooper's motives.

[1] Martyn's Life, i. 141.

CHAPTER III.

1644—1653.

SIR ANTHONY ASHLEY COOPER was far advanced in his twenty-third year when, after some ten months' service on the King's side, he went over to that of the Parliament. Here, as in other parts of Dryden's sketch of his history in "The Medal," the satirist's animosity has outrun accuracy :—

> " A martial hero first with early care,
> Blown, like a pigmy, by the winds to war ;
> A beardless chief, a rebel ere a man,
> So young his hatred to his prince began."

It may be convenient here to take a short retrospect, and briefly define the present position of affairs between the King and the Parliament. The body now exercising power and directing war at Westminster, was very different from the parliament which had assembled there in November 1640. This parliament had, in May 1641, legally framed an act to prevent dissolution without its own consent. The Bishops were excluded from the House of Lords by another act, legally passed in February 1642. In the same month, an ordinance for regulating the militia, agreed to by both Houses, was presented to the King, which nominated a lord lieutenant for every county, to obey the orders of the two Houses, and to be irremoveable by the King for two years. To this ordinance, transferring for two years the government of the military force of the nation from the King to the two Houses of Parliament, Charles refused his assent. The King's rash attempt to arrest Hampden, Pym, Holles, Haslerig, and Strode in the House of Commons, had hurried Parliament to this militia ordinance; and on the King's refusal, the two Houses took the matter into their own hands, passed the ordinance without the King's consent, and resolved to place the kingdom in a posture of defence. Here, then, was one definite issue between the King and the two Houses,— which should have the control of the military force of the nation? Other demands were made by the Parliament before the Civil War actually began. In the meantime, the King had established himself at York, and the Lord Keeper Littleton had joined him there, carrying with him the Great Seal from Westminster. At

York, in June, nineteen propositions were presented to
the King from the two Houses, containing, among
others, the following demands:—That the appointments
of all privy councillors and officers of state should be
subject to approval by the two Houses; that the
education and marriages of the King's children should
be under the control of Parliament; that Roman Catholic
peers should be excluded from the House of Lords; that
the government and liturgy of the Church should be
reformed as the two Houses might determine; that the
militia and all fortified places should be confided to
persons approved by the two Houses; and that no
peers hereafter to be made should sit in parliament
without the consent of both Houses. To these propositions the King's assent could not have been expected.
Military preparations had already been made on both
sides, and civil war was inevitable. It began in August.
Now, the House of Commons sitting at Westminster
was reduced by the secession of nearly a hundred
members who adhered to the King, and of the House of
Lords about forty, only a third of the whole number,
remained at Westminster.[1] In 1642 and 1643, fortune
favoured the King's arms. The Parliament now, in
1643, urged the Scotch to come to their aid, declaring
their eagerness to reform the Church of England on
Presbyterian principles, and their fear of the King's
bringing against them an army of papists and foreigners.
The articles of cessation made by Ormond in Ireland
with the Roman Catholic rebels, and the bringing over

---

[1] Hallam, Const. Hist. ii. 203, note; Sanford's Studies and Illustrations of the Great Rebellion, p. 498.

of Irish troops to reinforce the King's armies, added fuel to the flames, and angered many of the King's friends. The famous treaty known as " The Solemn League and Covenant " was concluded between the English and Scotch Parliaments : the Covenant, which was to be a test of fidelity to the parliamentary cause, bound its subscribers to endeavour to preserve the Scotch Church as it was, and bring those of England and Ireland into conformity with it in government, doctrine, and practice ; to labour for the extirpation of popery and prelacy; and to preserve the rights and privileges of the parliaments, and the liberties of the kingdoms, and the King's person and authority in aid of the true religion and liberties of the nation. A Scotch army of twenty-one thousand men now crossed the border, in January 1644. The Scotch Commissioners at Westminster were joined with a Committee of both Houses for direction of affairs; and to this joint Committee was given the name of the Committee of both Kingdoms. The King had summoned all his adherents of both Houses to assemble as a parliament at Oxford, on the twenty-second of January, 1644. There was a call of the two Houses on the same day at Westminster; thirty-five peers acknowledged this call, and two hundred and eighty members of the House of Commons are said to have attended at Westminster, about a hundred more being absent on parliamentary service.[1]

---

[1] This statement is in Whitelocke's Memorials, p. 80. Mr. Hallam thinks that there is a mistake in the statement, and that the number of adherents of the Parliament was not so great. Mr. Sanford, who has examined this portion of English history very laboriously, supports Whitelocke's statement. (Studies and Illustrations, p. 498.) The two

In the middle of May 1644, two parliamentary armies left London, under the Earl of Essex and Waller, with ulterior destination for the West, but to be guided by the movements of the King, who was at Oxford. Abingdon and Reading quickly falling into their hands, the King, with a small body of attendants, leaving his army, suddenly quitted Oxford, where he found himself in imminent danger of being besieged. He was followed by Waller into Worcestershire, managed with great skill and energy to elude Waller's pursuit, and within three weeks after his escape from Oxford he was again there at the head of his army, relieved of the presence of Essex's forces, which had gone into Dorsetshire, and thinking himself strong enough to cope with Waller's, which would probably return in pursuit of him. The King shortly after marched out of Oxford to meet Waller. The two armies met, at the end of June, at Cropredy Bridge, where the advantage of the fight was with the King.

In the meantime, Essex had entered Dorsetshire with his army ; he quickly retook Weymouth for the Parliament, the King's governor, Colonel Ashburnham, who had succeeded Cooper, abandoning it immediately on Essex's approach, and retiring into Portland Castle ; and he then marched to Lyme, which Prince Maurice, who had been long besieging it, quitted as soon as he heard of the taking of Weymouth, " with some loss of reputation," says Clarendon, " for having lain so long with such

hundred and twenty-eight members of the House of Commons, whose signatures to the League and Covenant in September 1643 are printed in a tract in vol. iv. of the Somers Tracts, are clearly not all the parliamentary adherents.

a strength before so vile and untenable place without reducing it." The defence had been conducted by the indomitable Blake, who next maintained an equally surprising defence against the royalist besiegers of Taunton. Prince Maurice, on abandoning the siege of Lyme, put a garrison of five hundred men into Wareham, and went off to Exeter with the main body of his forces. Essex followed him, and Prince Maurice retired into Cornwall. The King, no longer troubled by Waller, marched into the West after Essex, and ultimately discomfited Essex's army in Cornwall.

Sir Anthony Ashley Cooper, in July, was permitted by the Parliament to go down into Dorsetshire for military service. He says himself: " After Weymouth was taken in [1] by the Lord General Essex, the Committee for Dorset going into the country, desired Sir Anthony's company with them, which he did." [2]

On the third of August he received a commission to command a brigade of horse and foot, with the title of Field Marshal General.[3] Cooper's first military service was in the taking of Wareham. Together with Colonels Sydenham and Jephson, he proceeded to besiege that town with twelve hundred horse and foot; and they were afterwards joined by Lieutenant-General Middleton, with a thousand horse. They began to storm the out-

---

[1] " Taken in ;" the usual phrase of the time when speaking of taking a town : it occurs also in Clarendon.

> " You durst not think of taking in a heart
> As soon as you set down before it."
>   SUCKLING, *Brennoralt.*

[2] Autobiographical Sketch. There is an entry in the Commons' Journals, July 10, 1644, of permission given to Sir A. A. Cooper to go into Dorsetshire.

[3] A copy of the commission is among the papers at St. Giles's.

works on the tenth of August, when the garrison immediately capitulated, three hundred undertaking to serve the Parliament against the rebels in Ireland.[1] The governor of Wareham for the King was Colonel O'Brien, a brother of Lord Inchiquin, who had lately left the King's service for the Parliament in disgust at Ormond's cessation with the Irish rebels; and it is supposed that O'Brien had not been hearty to defend Wareham.

Cooper says that he attended, by order of the Dorsetshire Committee and Council of war, at the bar of the House of Commons, to relate the taking of Wareham, but there is no entry to this effect in the Journals. His statement, however, is doubtless correct. Four days after the taking of Wareham, he was added by a vote of both Houses to the Committee for governing the army in Dorsetshire; and on the same day, his case was referred to the Committee for Sequestrations sitting at Goldsmiths' Hall, to consider on what terms his estates should be restored to him.[2] The Committee made a report in a few days, recommending that he should be permitted to compound by a payment of five hundred pounds, and the House immediately adopted

[1] Autobiographical Sketch of 1646; Rushworth's Collections, pt. 3, vol. ii. p. 697; Vicars's Parl. Chron. iv. 5; Whitelocke's Memorials, p. 98; Comm. Journ. Aug. 14, 1644. These different accounts vary in details, and it is difficult to reconcile them entirely. From the accounts in Rushworth and Vicars, it would appear that Colonel Sydenham and Sir A. A. Cooper bore the chief part in this action. The Commons' Journals record, August 14, that letters of thanks were sent by the Parliament to Middleton and Jephson. Cooper was probably thanked in person, as he attended at the bar of the House of Commons to relate what had been done.

[2] Comm. Journ. August 14. Lord Campbell erroneously places the taking of Wareham after these votes of August 14, which were the reward of his service.

the report.[1] The five hundred pounds were never paid, and it appears from a note preserved in the family papers, that the fine was discharged by Cromwell, thirteen years later, in 1657.

On October 25, Cooper was appointed Commander-in-chief of the Parliament's forces in Dorsetshire,[2] and he took the field with ten regiments of horse and foot, fifteen hundred men in all, to encounter Sir Lewis Dives of Sherborne Castle, who was about the same time appointed the King's commander-in-chief in Dorsetshire.[3]

In the meantime the King had followed Essex into Cornwall, and there completely defeated him. The King then returned to Exeter, and in the beginning of October passed into Dorsetshire, and stayed a few days at Sherborne.[4] The Parliament, on receiving the news of Essex's disaster, had successively despatched two armies under Waller and Manchester, to check the King, who now hurried on from Sherborne to attack Waller near Andover. Here he gained an advantage over Waller: at Newbury, where he fought Waller's forces joined with Manchester's, and contended against an army double of his own, he neither conquered nor was defeated; and he then carried off his army to Oxford, arriving there himself on the twenty-third of November.[5]

---

[1] Comm. Journ. Aug. 22.
[2] Autobiographical Sketch. The original commission is at St. Giles's.
[3] "Sir A. A. Cooper, with fifteen hundred horse and foot from several garrisons, took the field to encounter Sir Lewis Dives." (White-locke's Memorials, p. 109, October 1644.) See also Vicars's Parl. Chron. iv. 62.
[4] Clarendon, Hist. of Rebellion, viii. 148.   [5] Ibid. viii. 164.

In the beginning of November, Cooper took by storm
a Cavalier garrison at Abbotsbury, the house of Sir
John Strangways. A minute and graphic account of
this action is in existence, written by Cooper himself.
The following draft of his report to the Committee for
the Parliament for Dorsetshire, in his own handwriting,
is among the papers in Lord Shaftesbury's possession.

"Honourable,—Yesterday we advanced with your
brigade to Abbotsbury as a place of great concern, and
which by the whole council of war was held feasible.
We came thither just at night, and sent them a summons
by a trumpeter, to which they returned a slighting
answer and hung out their bloody flag. Immediately
we drew out a party of musketeers, with which Major
Baintun in person stormed the church, into which they
had put thirteen men, because it flanked the house.
This after a hot bickering we carried, and took all the
men prisoners. After this we sent them a second
summons under our hands that they might have fair
quarter if they would accept it, otherwise they must
expect none if they forced us to a storm. But they
were so gallant that they would admit of no treaty, so
that we prepared ourselves for to force it, and accordingly fell on. The business was extreme hot for above
six hours ; we were forced to burn down an outgate
to a court before we could get to the house, and then
our men rushed in through the fire and got into the hall
porch, where with furse fagots they set fire on it, and
plied the windows so hard with small shot that the
enemy durst not appear in the low rooms : in the meantime one of our guns played on the other side of the
house, and the gunners with fire balls and granadoes
with scaling ladders endeavoured to fire the second

story, but, that not taking effect, our soldiers were forced to wrench open the windows with iron bars, and, pouring in fagots of furse fired, set the whole house in a flaming fire, so that it was not possible to be quenched, and then they cried for quarter; but we having bet [1] divers men before it, and considering how many garrisons of the same nature we were to deal with, I gave command there should be none given, but they should be kept into the house, that they and their garrison might fall together, which the soldiers with a great deal of alacrity would have performed, but that Colonel and Major Sidenham, riding to the other side of the house, gave them quarter; upon which our men fell into the house to plunder and could not be by any of their commanders drawn out, though they were told the enemy's magazine was near the fire and, if they stayed, would prove their ruin, which accordingly fell out, for the powder taking fire blew up all that were in the house, and blew four score that were in the court a yard from the ground, but hurt only two of them. Mr. Darby was of the number, but not hurt. We had hurt and killed by the enemy not fifteen, but I fear four times that number will not satisfy for the last mischance. Captain Heathcock and Mr. Cooper (who did extreme bravely) were both slain by the blow of the powder. Captain Gorge, a very gallant young gentleman, is hurt in the head with a freestone from the church tower and shot through the ankle, but we hope will live. Lieutenant Kennett to Major Peutt, who behaved himself very well, was blown up with the powder and slain; and Lieutenant Hill, who went a volunteer and was sent in to get out the soldiers, was blown up with the rest, yet since we have taken him strongly [2] out of the rubbish

---

[1] So in the manuscript, apparently; the meaning must be "lost."
[2] So in the manuscript.

and hope to preserve him. The house is burnt down to the ground, and could not be saved. We have prisoners Colonel James Strangways, Major Coles, and three captains, besides a hundred foot soldiers and thirty horse, all Strangways his whole regiment. Sir William Waller's officers all of them have behaved themselves extreme gallantly, and more than could be expected in their readiness and observance for your commands; we cannot say to whom you owe the most thanks, only Lieutenant-Colonel Oxford we are extremely obliged to for his nobleness in joining in this expedition, though without command, only on our entreaty. Captain Starr and Captain Woodward behaved themselves extremely well. Our men are so worn out with duty and this mischance that we are necessitated to retire to Dorchester to refresh them. If you have anything in particular to command us, we shall most readily obey you. To-morrow we have a council of war of all the officers, and then we shall conclude of what may be of most advantage to your service, and by God's blessing will faithfully prosecute it. Colonel Sidenham has yet afforded us no ammunition; all his men are supplied from us hitherto besides. He makes not up his regiment either of horse or foot; he has withdrawn one more company this day. We have given him orders that all the prisoners that are officers should be sent to you. We humbly desire you will be pleased to consent to no exchange for any of them until Haynes be exchanged.

"A. A. COOPER."

Another account of the storming of Abbotsbury has been preserved in Vicars's Parliamentary Chronicle, written by an officer who was under Cooper in the engagement, and who speaks with the highest admiration of Cooper's gallantry. "About the eighth of this instant November," says Vicars, "we received credible information out of the West by a letter from a commander of note and quality, of the storming and taking of a strong garrison of the enemy's, which was Sir John Strangwaies his house in Dorsetshire, and had been a very ill neighbour to our renowned garrison of Lime, which service was most bravely performed by that valiant and loyal patriot, Sir Anthony Ashley Cooper, Commander-in-chief for the Parliament in that county." The letter is as follows; it confirms Cooper's account in all material particulars ; the name of the officer who wrote it I have not discovered :—

"SIR,—We marched from Dorchester to Abbotsbury, where Colonel James Strangewayes and all his regiment were in garrison; they held both the house and the church which joined to the house : it was night before we summoned it, and they in a scorn refused the summons of Sir Anthony Ashley Cooper, a very active and noble gentleman, and Commander-in-chief, whereupon he sent his Major-General with a considerable party against the church, who presently assaulting it took it and all the men in it prisoners, without the loss of one man of our own. After this we summoned them in writing, the second time, to yield on fair quarter or else to expect no mercy, if they forced us to storm them. To this also they disdained to return an answer; upon which denial we fell on, and after as hot a storm as ever I heard of, for six hours together, it pleased God at last to give us the place. When by no other means we could get it, we found a way by desperately flinging in fired turf-fagots into the windows. And the fight then grew so hot that our said Commander-in-chief (who to his perpetual renown behaved most gallantly in this service) was forced to bring up his men within pistol-shot of the house, and could hardly then get them to stay and stand the brunt, yet in all this time (God be praised) we had but three men killed and some few wounded. Now when as by the foresaid hot assault half of the house was on a light fire,[1] and not to be quenched, then at length Colonel James Strangways called out for quarter, which our Commander-in-chief was resolved no man in the house should have, in regard they had so desperately and disdainfully scorned his summons, and also in regard that the Cavaliers' custom was observed to be to keep such paltry houses and pilfering garrisons against any of our armies, that they might thereby be sure to do us mischief, and (by reason of our observed clemency) to have their lives at last granted to them : but some of our commanders upon one side of the house, contrary to the mind of our said Commander-in-chief, and against the opinion of all the officers, in his absence had given them quarter, which being granted them, we instantly rushed into the house, which being on a light fire and their magazine in it (I believe rather accidentally than, as some reported, purposely and treacherously), to set on fire four or five barrels of gunpowder, and blew up between thirty and forty of our men ; yet, the Lord be blessed, myself and the rest were even miraculously preserved.

" We took prisoners Colonel James Strangewayes, Sir John Strangewayes his son, governour of this garrison, his Major and three Captains: and not three of his whole regiment but were either killed or taken, and the house was wholly burnt down to the ground, and we thereby freed of a pestilent and pernicious neighbour.

[1] " A light fire," an old expression for " a bright fire."

Colonel Bruen and Mr. Crompton behaved themselves very worthily in this action, and Captain Starre incomparably bravely.

"Yours,

"C. A."[1]

Soon after the taking of Abbotsbury, Cooper marched to Sturminster, and the royalists evacuated the castle on his approach: thence he marched to Shaftesbury, and forced the royalist garrison of that town to quit.[2] The following instructions to Cooper from the Committee for Dorsetshire, without other date than " Poole, eight at night, 1644," were probably written in November, between the taking of Abbotsbury and the expedition to Shaftesbury :—

" NOBLE SIR,—We have received your letter and have considered the particulars.   In that which concerns the altering your quarters, we hold it most fit to be resolved on by the council of war upon the place, according as you have intelligence of the motions of the enemy. Only we shall intimate that, before Shaston[3] be resolved on, it may be considered how safe a retreat may be made, if a body of the enemy's horse advances to Blandford. . . . . We are very sensible of the necessity of supplying the soldiers with some money, and have sent you twenty pound, whereof we are fain to borrow ten.   If we had more, you may be assured those should not want that deserve so well and are so modest in their demands.   You are now in a convenient quarter to raise money on malignants, therefore we desire you to make

---

[1] Vicars's Parl. Chron. iv. 67.   This work is so scarce that I may be excused for extracting the whole of a letter so closely connected with Shaftesbury's history.

[2] Autobiographical Sketch of 1646.   [3] Shaftesbury.

use of the opportunity to the best advantage, and you
shall be confident of our approbation. We have nothing
else at present but that we are,

" Your very loving Friends,

THO. ERLE,	ELIAS BOND,
RI. BRODRIPP,	THO. HENLEY,
RI. BURIE,	RI. ROW.

"Poole, eight at night, 1644."[1]

These instructions show great straits for money. The
following memoranda were probably written about the
same time by Cooper for the Governor of Poole :[2]—

" 1. That if they cannot immediately send us a supply
of horse, that orders be forthwith sent for the with-
drawing the Sussex foot, and that the rest be disposed
into their several garrisons. The keeping them together
in a body does devour that provision should be sent into
the garrisons and destroys the county, besides these few
horse we have (being not above a hundred) are wholly
taken up with providing for them.

" 2. That if a considerable party of horse, sufficient to
relieve Taunton, cannot be sent us presently, we desire
that some few may be spared, with which added to
those we have already we shall be able to victual our
garrisons and subsist in the county. However, we
shall be better able to subsist without than with the
Sussex foot.

" 3. Under a thousand horse it will be now difficult to
relieve Taunton, the enemy having received the addition

---

[1] From Lord Shaftesbury's papers at St. Giles's.
[2] They are among the family papers at St. Giles's, in Shaftesbury's
handwriting, without any date, and with the heading, "Memo-
randums for the Governor of Poole." They must have been written in
November 1644.

of a hundred horse lately from the King's army. under
Colonel Cooke, so that with those horse that lie near
Salisbury they are able to march fifteen hundred horse
and dragoons.

" 4. The enemy being resolved to fortify round the
skirts of Somerset, as Sherborn, Sturten Candell, Shafton,
to make it a safe quarter for his retreat and to drive all
the parts of the counties of Dorset and Wilts unto their
quarters, being resolved both their horse and foot shall,
if they be forced to retire, live on the skirts of these
two counties,—quære, whether it will not be necessary
for us to garrison Hooke House,[1] and, if we cannot force
them from Shafton or Sherborn, to garrison in some
other strong houses near those places by which their
incursions may be restrained.

" 5. The enemy being possessed of Ivychurch and
Langford Houses, from which they make perpetual
inroads into the eastern part of our country, and bring
the northern part of Wiltshire into contribution to them,
—quære, whether we should not garrison Falston House,[2]
by which we are sure to cut them off from troubling
this county, besides we shall gain the contribution of a
considerable part of Wiltshire.

" 6. Quære, whether it be not absolutely necessary to
pluck down the town of Wareham, it being impossible
for us to victual; if Sir W. Waller ever draw away his
foot, the town is left naked and exposed to the pleasure
of the enemy, who will certainly possess it unless it can

---

[1] Hooke House, near Beaminster, the property of the Marquis of
Winchester, the celebrated defender of his house in Hampshire, Basing.
Hooke House was burnt down in 1647. (Hutchins's Hist. of Dorset,
i. 494.)

[2] Ludlow mentions Falston House as garrisoned for the Parliament
in 1645, with one of his relatives, Major William Ludlow, as governor.
(Memoirs, i. pp. 148, 158.) Falston, Ivychurch, and Langford Houses
were all near Salisbury. Langford belonged to Lord Gorges; it is
now called Longford, and belongs to the Earl of Radnor.

be made no town. And there can be no argument against the demolishing it, being extremely mean-built, and the inhabitants almost all dreadful malignants, besides the keeping it will certainly starve more honest men than the destroying it will undo knaves.

"7. A few foot in Lulworth with a troop of horse will keep Corfe far better than Wareham. And the lesser number of foot we keep, the more horse and dragoons we shall be able to maintain, with which the business of this county must be done.

"8. If they are unwilling to destroy the town of Wareham, it may be left for a horse quarter; and they have direction, when they are forced to quit it, to set it on fire.

"9. That the horse of the county be all reduced into a regiment, and there may be two troops allowed the governors of Poole and Weymouth, Weymouth troop to be commanded by Major Sydenham, otherwise it will be impossible to keep them together or in any command.

"10. That the Committee name whom they will have to be colonel of their horse, and that they will assign how many troops he will allow in the regiment and whose troops these shall be, and that they will send to my Lord General for a commission for the colonel.

"11. That there be twenty musketeers in every troop and a full troop of dragoons at least in the regiment."

A letter to Sir Anthony from London, November 5, 1644, from Mr. John Collins, who appears to have had the charge of his private affairs, mentions that no step is being taken at Goldsmiths' Hall for the recovery of his composition-fine of five hundred pounds, and speaks of law-business still pending in the Court of Wards :—

" Upon my late speech with Mr. Allen,[1] I find no other but that your business at their Hall rests in peace. In the Court of Wards business nothing stirs as yet. In the matter of indictment of your tenants the City solicitor is someway calling upon it, but I have used some means lately to allay him, and, if that hold not, I must get the Court moved for a further postponement until the next term."

The following letter to Cooper from Colonel Butler, who commanded at Wareham, and was directing the siege of Corfe, again shows the great want of money with the Parliament's forces in Dorsetshire.

" SIR,—I have written in a former letter the three foot of Colonel Raynesborough's are immediately to be drawn off for Abingdon ; the men are loth to leave the siege if they may have money and provision. To-morrow they expect pay, for they buy all by the penny. I beseech you do what may be done to send money with all speed, for it is a business of great concernment, and I likewise beseech you to do what you may for Mrs. Squib. We have sent to Poole and Weymouth for men and ammunition. I pray you do your utmost to second our desires, and in sending to London, but especially send money, and now be doing for your country and for God's cause. A little now will be worth a great deal hereafter. I pray send money, money ; and that will take Corfe Castle, which is in no strong condition.

" Sir, I am,
" Your faithful servant,
" Warham, Dec. 18, 1644.   ROBT. BUTLER.

" To my honoured friend Sir Anthony Ashley Cooper, at Wimborne, these present."

[1] Doubtless Alderman Allen, an active Parliamentarian.

In December, Sir Anthony Ashley Cooper received
orders from the Parliament to proceed with all his
Dorsetshire forces to the relief of Taunton, where Blake,
who had before so gallantly defended Lyme, was maintaining another equally gallant defence against the
royalists under great disadvantages. Cooper, who had
the chief command, was joined in this expedition by a
force under Major-General Holborn, and Edmund
Ludlow also joined with two hundred horse from Wiltshire.[1] The besiegers immediately retired on the arrival
of this relieving force. Cooper wrote to the Earl of
Essex from Taunton, announcing the easy success of
the expedition:—

"MAY IT PLEASE YOUR EXCELLENCY,—The last night
we brought all our carriages safe to Taunton with our
horse. We find the castle in no great want of victual,
only of powder and salt. The town began to be in great
distress, and it almost a miracle to us that they should
adventure to keep the town, their works being for the
most part but pales and hedges, and no line about the
town. The enemy endeavoured twice to force it, but
were repulsed; and since they have only kept them in
by a quartering round about the town at a mile or two
distance. Notwithstanding, the townsmen made daily
sallies and got in store of victuals, without which it had
been impossible for them to maintain such numbers of
unnecessary people. The enemy on Friday last have

---

[1] Autobiog. Sketch. Ludlow, i. 135 ; Vicars's Parl. Chron. iv. 77. It
would appear from the accounts in Ludlow and Vicars, that Holborn
had the chief command, but Cooper distinctly states in his thoroughly
reliable Autobiographical Sketch of 1646, that he had a commission
from Essex to command in chief. Holborn made various marauding
excursions against garrisoned houses about Taunton. See the passage
in Vicars referred to.

quitted their garrisons in Wellington, Wyrwail,[1] and Cokam Houses; the two last they have burnt, and as I saw him they have quitted Chidock House, whether it be out of fear or to make a body able to encounter with us, we cannot yet understand; but Sir Lewis Dives his running up with his horse to the Bridgewater forces argues the latter; however, we are in a very good condition, if they receive no assistance from the King's army, which we most fear; this country being of so great import to the enemy that it will be worth their engaging their whole army, which may prove a successful design to them, if we have not a considerable strength ready on all motions of the enemy to advance to our assistance. I shall only humbly offer this to your Excellency's consideration, to whose commands I shall always render myself faithful and obedient, as becometh your Excellency's most devoted, most humble servant,

"ANTHONY ASHLEY COOPER."[2]

This letter was read in the House of Commons on December 24, and was copied by Sir Simonds D'Ewes

[1] So in the manuscript; Wyrwail may be Worthele near Plymouth. Cokam House is Colcombe near Colyton in Devonshire, and belonged to Sir John Pole. Chidock or Chideock House belonged to Mr. Arundel, a Roman Catholic. Wellington House was burnt down by the royalists in the next year.

[2] This letter is in Sir S. D'Ewes's Diary, preserved in the British Museum, Harl. MSS. 166, p. 1696. It was first printed by the author in the "Memoirs, Letters and Speeches, &c. of Earl of Shaftesbury," 1659. There is an entry in the Commons' Journals, December 24, 1644: "A letter from Orchard from Sir Anthony Ashley Cooper directed to my Lord General, concerning the relief of Taunton, was this day read. Ordered, that it be referred and earnestly recommended from this House to the Committee of both Kingdoms, to send a new, speedy, and considerable supply of forces into the West." It is also stated in Whitelocke's Memorials, Dec. 23, 1644, p. 121: "Letters from Sir A. A. Cooper informed of the relief of Taunton town and castle, held out to admiration by Colonel Blake, notwithstanding his great want of ammunition and provisions, and that the works there were inconsiderable."

into his Diary. The letter was not entered in the
Journals. It is a striking and amusing specimen of the
way in which Shaftesbury's character has been prejudiced
by biographers, that Lord Campbell,—who had never
seen the letter, and knew no more than was to be learnt
from the simple notices in the Journals of the House
of Commons and in Whitelocke's Memorials, that Sir
Anthony Ashley Cooper had written a letter concerning
the relief of Taunton,—has said, imaginatively, that "he
wrote a flaming account of the exploit to the Parliament, taking greater credit to himself than Cromwell in
his despatch announcing his victory at Dunbar." A
more modest and plain statement than that of Cooper's
letter on this occasion can hardly be conceived. The
House of Commons resolved, after the reading of
Cooper's letter to Essex, that the Committee of both
Kingdoms should be urged to send speedily a strong
reinforcement to Taunton; and Waller and Oliver
Cromwell were ordered into the West in the end of
February for the relief of Taunton.

Thus ended the year 1644, a year of great military
activity for Cooper. The next year was passed more
tranquilly. The following is his own account in his
Autobiographical Sketch, written in January 1646, of
his proceedings during 1645 :—

"In May he received divers commissions from the
Committee of the West, the chief of which was to
command in chief the forces they designed to beleaguer
Corfe Castle, which forces he was to receive from
Colonel Weldon, who then commanded in the West;
but when Sir Anthony came into the country, he found

Weldon blocked up by Goring, so that being not supplied with men, he was forced to return. In June he went with his lady to Tunbridge, where he for six weeks drank the waters. In September his lady went to Oxted, in Surrey, to her aunt Capel's,[1] where her mother also was, and they both sojourned there. In October he went down into the country, and sat with the Committee constantly, most commonly as chairman. In December he was employed by the Committee, with Colonel Bingham, to the General, who lay then at Autree,[2] in Devon, to obtain an assistance of force towards the besieging Corfe Castle, which they obtained.[3] In the end of this month he returned to Oxted in Surrey."

This is the concluding passage of the Autobiographical Sketch prefixed to the Diary, which begins on January 1, 1646. Cooper's military service had come to an end. It was, doubtless, terminated by that new-modelling of the army in 1645 which was attended by the Self-denying Ordinance, and which substituted Fairfax for Essex as Commander-in-chief, gave Cromwell great advancement, and removed most of the Presbyterian leaders from commands in the army, replacing them by Independents. As Cooper had not been admitted a member of the House of Commons on his petition, the Self-denying Ordinance probably did not apply to him;

[1] Lady Capel, sister of Lord Keeper Coventry's second wife: she was wife of Sir Henry Capel, knight, of Hadham, Herts, and had been previously married to Sir Thomas Hoskins of Oxted.

[2] Ottery St. Mary; the General was Fairfax, who had now succeeded Essex.

[3] Corfe Castle surrendered after a long siege, in April of next year, to Colonel Bingham. Mr. Martyn and Lord Campbell erroneously state that Sir A. A. Cooper took Corfe in 1644.

but he had connected himself with the Presbyterians on his coming over to the Parliament, and he was precisely one of the class of officers whom the promoters of the "New Model" of the army did not desire to include in the new arrangements. It is certain that he had no quarrel with the Parliament, or with its officers in the West. This is sufficiently proved by his own account of his proceedings during the year 1645, which has been quoted, and by his subsequent unintermitted attention to various local duties in the service of the Parliament.[1]

In the autumn of 1645, after he had ceased to serve as an officer of the army, Sir Anthony made an attempt to obtain admission as a member of the parliament through his original petition for Downton. An entry in the Journals informs us that, on September 1, Sir Walter Erle was ordered by the House to report on a future day concerning Sir Anthony Ashley Cooper's election. But there is no subsequent entry of a report. Cooper was not admitted.[2] The explanation of his failure is, doubtless, to be found in the ordinance, which had been passed in the previous year, that no peer or commoner who had been in the King's quarters should be admitted again to sit in either House. Whitelocke records, on September 18 of this year,

---

[1] Lord Campbell, whose biography was written on the plan of imagining a bad motive for every action, says : "He was suddenly satiated with military glory, and after this brilliant campaign never again appeared in the field : whether he retired from some affront, or mere caprice, is not certainly known."

[2] The other seat for Downton, held by Sir Edward Griffin, who adhered to the King, was at this time declared vacant, and a new writ was issued, September 1645.

that " Sir A. A. Cooper professed his great affection to
the Parliament, and his enmity to the King's party
from whom he had revolted, and was now in great
favour and trust with the Parliament." This probably
refers to some declaration of political faith made in
support of his endeavour to gain admission to sit for
Downton.

The seven or eight years which followed were passed
in comparative tranquillity, and were chiefly occupied
with the business of private life and performance of
local duties. Excluded from Parliament, Cooper accepted all the events and changes which these years
witnessed, and submitted to the mutilated and reduced
Parliament as the existing authority, and acted under
its orders. It is much to be regretted that his Diary,
which extends from the beginning of 1646 to the
middle of 1650, is little more than a meagre chronicle
of visits, journeys, domestic incidents, and pecuniary
transactions, and does not contain one single comment
on any of the great political events which are crowded
into this period: for these years witnessed the entire
defeat of the royal cause and the disruption of the
victorious parliamentary party, the humiliation of the
Presbyterians by the Independents and of the Parliament by the army, the consolidation of Oliver Cromwell's power, the trial and execution of the King, and
the establishment of a Commonwealth, without King
or House of Lords, under the supremacy of the small
remnant to which military violence had reduced the
House of Commons, and which history has. branded
with the nickname of the Rump.

Though Cooper conformed always to the authority
of the actual sovereign power, it is certain that his pre-
dilections and chief personal relations were with the
members of the Presbyterian party. At the time of the
Restoration he was regarded one of this party. A story
is told, which may have some truth in it, of his having
endeavoured at the beginning of the contest between
the Presbyterian majority in the House of Commons
and the army, which ended in the forced exclusion of
the Presbyterian members, to moderate the zeal of
Holles against Cromwell. The incident referred to in
the following story, which is related by Locke, was in
the spring of 1647; it is told by him, however, with
that tone of evident exaggeration of Cooper's importance which characterises the whole of Locke's fragment of a memoir. The King was now vanquished, and
a prisoner in the care of the Scotch Commissioners and
army. The House of Commons wished to reduce their
army, and to despatch a portion for service in Ireland.
The army, assembled near Saffron Walden, clamoured
for payment of arrears, and an imperious petition was
presented from the army by three emissaries at the bar
of the House. The House passed a resolution in disapproval of the petition. Another was set on foot in
the army, when a motion was made in the House of
Commons by Holles to declare the petition seditious,
and its promoters traitors; and there was private talk
of calling Cromwell to account. Cromwell left the
House while the discussion was proceeding, and went
straight to the army. Locke's story is as follows:—

" It happened one morning that Sir A. A. Cooper,

calling on Mr. Holles on his way to the House, as he often did, he found him in a great heat against Cromwell, who had then the command of the army, and a great interest in it. The provocation may be read at large in the pamphlets of that time, for which Mr. Holles was resolved, he said, to bring him to punishment. Sir A. A. Cooper dissuaded him all he could from any such attempt, showing him the danger of it, and told him it would be sufficient to remove him out of the way by sending him with a command into Ireland. This Cromwell, as things stood, would be glad to accept; but this would not satisfy Mr. Holles. When he came to the House the matter was brought into debate, and it was moved that Cromwell and those guilty with him should be punished. Cromwell, who was in the House, no sooner heard this, but he stole out, took horse, and rode immediately to the army, which, as I remember, was at Triplow Heath; there he acquainted them what the Presbyterian party was a doing in the House, and made such use of it to them that they, who were before in the power of the Parliament, now united together under Cromwell, who immediately led them away to London, giving out menaces against Holles and his party as they march, who with Stapleton and some others were fain to fly; and thereby the Independent party becoming the stronger, they, as they called it, purged the House, and turned out all the Presbyterian party. Cromwell, some time after, meeting Sir A. A. Cooper, told him, I am beholden to you for your kindness to me; for you, I hear, were for letting me go without punishment, but your friend, God be thanked, was not wise enough to take your advice." [1]

[1] Locke's Works, ix. 278. See for an account of what passed in the House, April 30, 1647, Ludlow, i. 190, and Holles's Memoirs, p. 89.

This story, as told, contains several historical inaccuracies, such as occur in other parts of Locke's
memoir.[1] Fairfax was at the time General-in-chief, not
Cromwell; and no motion appears to have been made
in the House against Cromwell. There is apparent
confusion between the proceedings against Holles,
Stapleton, and other Presbyterian members in 1647 and
the violent general "purge" by the army in December
1648. But it is quite probable that Cooper tried to
temper Holles's zeal, and that Cromwell afterwards
spoke of the matter to Cooper.

Cooper was high sheriff of Wiltshire for the Parliament during the year 1647, and leave was given him
to reside out of the county during the year of his
shrievalty.[2]

Some passages of his Diary extending from January
1, 1646, to July 10, 1650, are here selected, which have
interest in connexion with his life and character, or
with the habits of the time.

On February 5, 1646, Cooper records a surgical operation :—" I had a nerve and vein cut by Gell and
two more, for which I was forced to keep my chamber
twelve days." On February 12, "I had another nerve
and vein cut."

On April 1, 1646, he mentions that two Dorsetshire
boys of his neighbourhood, fifteen years old each,
bound themselves to him for seven years for his plantation in Barbadoes, to receive 5*l.* each at the end of
the time.

---

[1] See note, pp. 40–42.
[2] Comm. Journ. Dec. 1, 1646, Jan. 6, 1647; and see further on, p. 82.

The Dorsetshire quarter sessions were held on the seventh and eighth of April, "this time kept at Dorchester, and not at Sherborne, for security." The magistrates did bloody work : "Nine hanged; only three burnt in the hand," is Cooper's summary of their deeds.

A few days after, the Dorsetshire Committee, of which Cooper was one, "sat in the Shire Hall, at Dorchester, by the ordinance for punishing pressed soldiers that ran away on the 15th of January last, when three were condemned to die, two to run the gantelope,[1] two to be tied neck and heels and one to stand with a rope about his neck."

On July 27, there is an entry of a domestic incident : "My wife miscarried of a boy ; she had gone twenty weeks. Her brother John[2] in jest threw her against a bedstaff, which hurt her so that it caused this."

In August he attended the assizes at Salisbury and Dorchester, being, he says, in the commission of oyer and terminer for the whole circuit. The judges were Mr. Justice Rolle and Serjeant Godbolt. On August 10, the assizes began at Salisbury, and Cooper took the oaths as a justice of the peace for Wiltshire.

"August 11 : Sir John Danvers came and sat with us. Seven condemned to die; four for horse-stealing, two for robbery, one for killing his wife, he broke her neck with his hands; it was proved that, he touching her body the day after, her nose bled fresh ; four burnt in

---

[1] Old spelling of *gauntlet* or *gantlet*. The word is said to be of Dutch origin ; *gant*, all, and *lopen*, to run.
[2] John Coventry, the eldest of the Lord Keeper's sons by his second wife; see p. 33.

the hand, one for felony, three for manslaughter; the same sign followed one of them of the corpse bleeding.

"August 12.—I and the Sheriff of Wilts begged the life of one Prichett, one of those seven condemned, because he had been a Parliament soldier. I waited on the judges to Dorchester."

At Dorchester the assizes terminated on the fourteenth :—

"Five condemned to die, two women for murdering their children, one of them a married woman; one for murder, one for robbery, one for horse-stealing : three burnt in the hand, one for manslaughter, two for felony. Chibbett condemned for horse-stealing. The Justices begged his reprieve, he having been a faithful soldier to the State."

A few days after, on the seventeenth, he went Bryanston bowling-green, where he "bowled all day."

On October 1 he mentions :—"I went to Shaftesbury to the council of war for Massey's brigade, and got them removed out of Dorset." The Parliament had ordered that this brigade should be disbanded.[1]

In December, he enters :—

"I was by both Houses of Parliament made High Sheriff of the county of Wilts. I was by ordinance of Parliament made one of the committee for Dorset and Wilts, for Sir Thomas Fairfax his army's contribution."

In March of next year, 1647, he attended the judges as sheriff, at the Wiltshire assizes :—

"March 13 : The judges came into Salisbury, Justice

---

[1] Ludlow's Memoirs, i. 181.

Roles[1] and Serjeant Godbolt. They went hence the 17th
day. I had sixty men in liveries, and kept an ordinary
for all gentlemen at Lawes his,[2] four shillings and two
shillings for blew men. I paid for all. There were
sixteen condemned to die, whereof fourteen suffered.
George Philips condemned for stealing a horse; I got
his reprieve, and another for the like offence was reprieved by the judge. Three more were burnt in the
hand, then condemned."

On March 29, he and his wife had another disappointment—" My wife miscarried of a child she was
eleven weeks gone with."

During this month of March, Cooper adds, "I raised
the country twice, and beat out the soldiers designed
for Ireland who quartered on the county without order,
and committed many robberies." These were very likely
soldiers of the disbanded Massey's brigade, of whom
Ludlow says that many gave trouble in Wiltshire, and
ultimately enlisted themselves to serve against the rebels
in Ireland, the Parliament having sent instructions and
officers for that purpose.[3]

In June he took his wife to Bath, where she stayed
five weeks. "June 15 : We came to Bath, where my
wife made use of the Cross bath, for to strengthen her
against miscarriage."

The August Wiltshire assizes began at Salisbury on
the fourteenth and ended on the eighteenth. The
judges this time were Godbolt, now a Judge of the

[1] Mr. Justice Rolle, afterwards made Chief Justice of the King's
Bench, in 1648. He was one of the two judges seized in their beds at
Salisbury, in Penruddocke's royalist rising in 1655, and had then a
narrow escape of his life.
[2] Lawes's.   [3] Ludlow's Memoirs, i. 181.

Common Pleas,[1] and Serjeant Wild, afterwards Chief
Baron. "Four condemned to die: one for a robbery,
two for horse-stealing, one for murder. Luke, that was
for the robbery, I got his reprieve." Cooper adds, "I
kept my ordinary at the Angel, four shillings for the
gentlemen, two for their men, and a cellar."

On November 12, there is a curious entry of a speculation :—"The little ship called the 'Rose,' wherein
I have a quarter part, which went to Guinea, came to
town this term (blessed be God!). She has been out
about a year, and we shall but make our money."

On the twenty-ninth :—"My wife was delivered at
seven o'clock in the evening of a dead maid child; she
was within a fortnight of her time."

For the first half of the year 1648, Cooper had
attacks of ague. On February 14 he enters in his
Diary, "I fell sick of a tertian ague, whereof I had but
five fits, through the mercy of the Lord." This ague
prevented his sitting with the judges at the assizes in
March. He had ceased to be Sheriff of Wiltshire,
having received his writ of discharge on February 11
from his uncle Tooker, who succeeded him. Again, on
April 29, there is an entry: "I fell sick of a tertian
ague, whereof I had but two fits, through the mercy of
the Lord."

In July he was made a commissioner of the ordinance
of Parliament for a rate for Ireland for Dorsetshire, and
also, by ordinance of Parliament, was made one of the
commissioners for the militia in Dorsetshire.

---

[1] He had been made a Judge, April 30, 1647: he died in the next
year. (Foss's Judges, vi. 318.)

The ordinance for the trial of Charles the First was passed by the House of Commons on the sixth of January, 1649. The trial began on the twentieth; on the twenty-seventh sentence was passed, and on the thirtieth the King was executed. Even this great event elicits no mention in Cooper's Diary. He was travelling at the time, and he merely notes his movements. On the twenty-ninth, the day before the execution, he left his house at Wimborne St. Giles to go to London, and on the thirtieth he travelled from Andover to Bagshot. The entries in the Diary are these:—" January 29 : I. began my journey to London, and went to Andover. —30 : I went to Bagshot.—31 : I came to London, and lodged at Mr. Guidott's, in Lincoln's Inn Fields." This is all.

In the next month he records : " I was made by the States a justice of peace of quorum for the counties of Wilts and Dorset, and of oyer and terminer for the western circuit."

In July 1649, a heavy domestic calamity befell him, the sudden death of his wife :—

" July 10 : My wife, just as she was sitting down to supper, fell suddenly into an apoplectical convulsion fit. She recovered that fit after some time, and spoke and kissed me, and complained only in the head, but fell again in a quarter of an hour, and then never came to speak again, but continued in fits and slumbers until next day. At noon she died; she was with child the fourth time, and within six weeks of her time."

She had had no child born alive. They had been married nine years and a half. Cooper's glowing and

touching eulogium of his wife, which here follows in
the Diary, has been already quoted.[1]

In little more than nine months Cooper was again
married. One of the last entries in his Diary records
his marriage, on April 25, 1650, with the Lady Frances
Cecil, sister of the Earl of Exeter, a royalist nobleman.

A few days before this marriage, on April 19, Cooper
entered in his Diary : "I laid the first stone of my house
at St. Giles's."[2]

After the execution of Charles the First, Cooper continued obedient to the existing supreme authority, acted
as a magistrate, took the engagement to be faithful to
the new Commonwealth without King or House of
Lords, and acted as a commissioner to administer the
engagement in Dorsetshire. He mentions in the Diary
that he was sworn as a magistrate for the counties of
Wilts and Dorset, and acted for the first time since the
King's death, on August 16, 1649,—about a month after
the loss of his first wife. He subscribed the engagement, with a number of his brother magistrates, at
Salisbury quarter sessions, on January 17, 1650. On
January 29 he sat at Blandford, on a commission from
the Council of State, to give the engagement. On the
thirty-first he started for London, where he arrived on
the second of February, and he there received a new
commission to himself and others for giving the engagement in Dorsetshire.

The Diary ends abruptly on July 10, 1650. In the

---

[1] See p. 19.
[2] The right wing of the present house was built in 1651. (Hutchins's
Hist. of Dorset, iii. 186.)

following year Cooper's wife bore him a son, who was christened Cecil, and who died in childhood. On the sixteenth of January, 1652, was born another son, Anthony Ashley, who lived to inherit his father's possessions and titles, and transmitted them to a son of his own, the distinguished author of the "Characteristics."

From the termination of the Diary in July 1650 to the beginning of 1652, there is no information as to Sir A. A. Cooper's proceedings. But it is certain that he remained constant in allegiance to the Rump Parliament. On the seventeenth of January, 1652, he was named by this Parliament one of a Commission for the reform of the laws. A Committee of the Parliament had been named for the same purpose some time before, but the slowness of its proceedings caused great dissatisfaction. It was now resolved to appoint a Commission of twenty-one members, none of whom should be members of the Parliament, to assist the Committee. Sir Anthony Ashley Cooper was the last-named of the twenty-one Commissioners. The first-named, and probably the leading member of the Commission, was Matthew Hale, the future celebrated Chief Justice. These were associated with a motley group, in which were a few lawyers, three officers of the army, Desborough, Tomlinson, and Packer, and the notorious preacher, Hugh Peters, who, after the Restoration, was one of the victims selected to expiate the execution of Charles the First, and was tried and sentenced to death by a body of judges of whom one was Cooper.

This Commission, guided chiefly by Hale, drew up a

digest of the laws, and prepared various excellent drafts of measures, some of which, designed to simplify and cheapen legal proceedings and facilitate conveyances, Cooper afterwards procured to be passed by the Barebone's Parliament. The celebrated Marriage Act of the Barebone's Parliament, prescribing the celebration of marriages before magistrates, was one of the measures prepared by this Commission.[1]

On the seventeenth of March, 1653, it is entered in the Journals :—"Resolved by the Parliament that Sir Anthony Ashley Cooper, baronet, be, and is hereby,

[1] See the collection of Acts prepared by this Commission in Somers' Tracts, vol. vi. They were printed by order of the Barebone's Parliament, immediately after its assembling. Several of these measures had been reported to the Rump, but none appear to have been passed by that parliament. It appears from two entries in the Journals (January 20, 21, 1653) that the Commission prepared a digest of the laws, of which the Parliament ordered three hundred copies to be printed. Various measures were referred by the House to this Commission for their advice, among others a bill for a general register of lands (Journ. Feb. 2, 1653). This bill had not come back from the Commission when the Rump was dissolved, April 20, 1653. The registry bill appears to have been strongly pressed on the Rump by petitions from without (Journ. July 22, 1652), and the long time spent in discussing it by the law reform Commission caused great complaints. Ludlow complains of the lawyers spending three months on the word "incumbrance" in this bill (i. 430), and see Cromwell's speech to the Barebone's parliament (Carlyle, ii. 198). Whitelocke, who was a member of the Committee of the Rump which this Commission was appointed to assist, complains of the impracticability of Hugh Peters in this Commission. "I was often advised with by some of this committee, and none of them was more active in this business than Mr. Hugh Peters the minister, who understood little of the law, but was very opinionative and would frequently mention some of the proceedings of the law in Holland wherein he was altogether mistaken." (Memorials, p. 521.) Peters says of himself, "I rather was there to pray than to mend laws, but I might as well have been spared." Hale, writing on the amendment of the laws after the Restoration, speaks of the impracticability of the law reformers of the Commonwealth, and admits the unwillingness of the lawyers to aid them, saying that they feared to increase the difficulties of a general settlement of property if the King should be restored, and feared also to increase the difficulties of a restoration. (Hargreave's Law Tracts, p. 274.)

pardoned of all delinquency, and be, and is hereby, made capable of all other privileges as any other of the people of this nation are." Now, therefore, very shortly before Cromwell's ejection of the Rump of the Long Parliament, Cooper was at last admitted to all privileges, and made capable of sitting in Parliament. There is not the slightest reason for supposing, as some biographers have imagined, that Cooper had recently given offence to the Parliament, or that he had ever acted against it since he quitted the King's party.[1]

[1] Mr. Martyn, to explain this entry in the Journals, has invented that the Parliament, after the battle of Worcester, had some suspicions of Cooper and arrested him as a delinquent, and afterwards pardoned him in order to secure his friendship as against Cromwell (Life, i. 163). Lord Campbell has improved on Mr. Martyn's statement. "In the beginning of 1652, he became a member of the famous Commission for the reform of the law; but he soon found this very dull work, and being shut out from all civil and military distinction, he became highly discontented, and muttered so loud against the reigning authorities that he was actually taken up as a delinquent; but nothing could be proved against him except some intemperate speeches, and it was resolved by the House, 'that Sir A. A. Cooper be pardoned of all delinquency.'" The dislike of the Law-reform Commission, in which Cooper took great interest, the discontent, the loud mutterings, the arrest, and the proved intemperate speeches, are all imagination.

CHAPTER IV.

1653—1656.

Cromwell's ejection of the Rump—Reasons for the act—Temporary Council of State—A Convention summoned—Meets, July 4, 1653—Sir A. A. Cooper a member—Proceedings of Barebone's Parliament—Parties in that assembly—Questions of Church and Law Reform—Cromwell allied with the moderate party—The Parliament resigns its powers to Cromwell, December 12, 1653—Cooper had acted with the moderate party and Cromwell, and had promoted the resignation—Idle rumour that Cromwell meant to make Cooper Lord Chancellor—Cromwell refuses to be King, and is made Protector—Cooper said to have pressed him to be King—Cooper one of the new Council of State—The Instrument of Government—Milton serves under the Council—Cooper elected to the new parliament for Wiltshire, Poole, and Tewkesbury—Sits for Wiltshire—Ludlow's account of the Wiltshire election—Parliament meets, September 3, 1654—Cromwell's difficulties with the Parliament—He dissolves it—Cooper ceases to attend the Privy Council—His estrangement from Cromwell—Ludlow's mistakes about this estrangement—Death of Cooper's second wife in 1654—Story of Cooper wishing to marry Cromwell's daughter Mary—He marries, in 1656, a daughter of Lord Spencer of Wormleighton—Her character—She survives Shaftesbury.

FOUR years of the government of the Rump Parliament had prostrated the forces of the enemies of the Commonwealth in the three countries, and had also divided that body within itself, and made it obnoxious, for various reasons, to large portions of the republican party. These four years had likewise consolidated the power of the army, and established the ascendency and fixed the ambition of Cromwell, its victorious general. Those who interpret a great career by a single motive,

and do not allow the possibility either of generous
desires to the objects of their antipathy or of human
weaknesses to their idols, will ascribe Cromwell's suppression of the Rump, according as they may be his
admirers or his depreciators, to pure patriotism or un-
scrupulous ambition. It is more probable that ambition
and a persuasion of public advantage combined to move
Cromwell to this act. The force of circumstances and
his own superiority of character had made him master
of the destinies of the country, and he would have been
more than human if he had been unwilling to grasp
supreme power when it was within easy reach. The
Rump had committed many errors, which Cromwell
probably exaggerated, and, as is inevitable even for
the wisest holders of power, had made many enemies,
whom Cromwell probably encouraged and deluded. But
a numerous executive is especially unsuited to a time
when the ravages of revolutions are to be repaired, and
the discord of civil wars to be laid to rest, and a nation
placed again in the way of tranquil progress after
storms ; and Cromwell might not unreasonably or unjustly persuade himself that his own clear head and
strong hand could better provide for the interests of
the Commonwealth than a distracted and damaged
assembly, in which some able and upright men were
swamped by pedants, adventurers, and fanatics.[1]

[1] There is no information as to the exact number of members of the
Rump Parliament, *i. e.* the remnant of the Long Parliament recognised
as members after the execution of Charles I. It was probably about
180. The largest number ever recorded as voting is 122, at the election
of the Council of State, November 24, 1652. The ordinary attendance
of members was about fifty. Ludlow counted 160 who had sat in the
House since 1648 as alive in April 1659. (Mem. ii. 645).

The immediate cause of Cromwell's violent dissolution of the Rump was a dispute as to when their power
should terminate, and how their successors should be
appointed. A bill for regulating the election of future
Parliaments had long been before them, and the slowness with which they proceeded in it had occasioned
many reproaches. With great difficulty they had been
prevailed on, in November 1651, to fix a day for the
termination of their own power; and the day fixed was
three years distant, the third of November, 1654. The
bill for the election of future Parliaments provided a
much more popular scheme of representation than that of
the ancient constitution; it was the same as that which
Cromwell afterwards adopted in the mixed constitution
known by the name of the "Instrument of Government," though now he was vehemently opposed to it,
arguing that for the election of a sovereign assembly it
was a dangerous experiment in the distracted condition
of the country. Cromwell urged that the Presbyterians
could not be kept out of an assembly popularly elected.
This party had fought with the heir of the late King
against the Rump; they had been vanquished in the
field, and Prince Charles was an exile. "Let them
not," said Cromwell, "peril the republic, and revive
prostrate pretensions by a popular election which must
introduce many Presbyterians into power." He called
upon the Rump to name an early day for the termination of their own power, and to nominate a sovereign
body of moderate number as their immediate successors.
Both these demands were refused. The Rump were
now as impatient to pass their bill as before they had

been dilatory; and at last, on the twentieth of April, 1653, as they were hurrying the bill through its last stage, in spite of an understanding with Cromwell that on that day no progress should be made with it, Cromwell brought a handful of soldiers into the House and violently broke up the assembly.[1]

[1] See Cromwell's account of his reasons for taking this step in his speech at the opening of the Barebone's Parliament, which may be read in the "Parliamentary History," or in Mr. Carlyle's work. I find it difficult to reconcile Cromwell's objections to the popular character of the scheme of representation proposed in the bill with another charge which he distinctly makes against the Rump, that they designed by this bill to continue their own power. I cannot suppose, with Mr. Carlyle, that the bill contained a clause providing that every member of the Rump should be a member of the new parliament without election. (Cromwell's Letters and Speeches, ii. 177.) Perhaps Cromwell meant to say that the bill either would lead to a virtual reproduction of the Rump, or must let in a number of Presbyterians: excluding clauses sufficiently stringent to keep out Presbyterians might have produced the former result. Or perhaps Cromwell, whose object was to justify himself and abuse the Rump, did not consider very nicely all that he said against them. The election of the Parliament of 1654, under the same plan of representation, verified Cromwell's expectations as to the Presbyterian party. There are two well-known graphic descriptions of Cromwell's ejection of the Rump, Ludlow's (ii. 455) and the Earl of Leicester's (Blencowe's Sydney Papers, p. 139); but though their descriptions are graphic, neither was an eye-witness. Whitelocke, who was present, gives a very tame account of the scene. Two interesting notices of this event, which will be new to most readers, by members who were ejected, occur in the debates in Burton's Parliamentary Diary. Sir Arthur Haselrig: "We were labouring here in the House on the act to put an end to that parliament, and to call another. I desired the passing of it with all my soul. The question was putting for it, when our General stood up and called in his lieutenant with two files of musqueteers, with their hats on their heads, and their guns loaden with bullets. Our General told us we should sit no longer to cheat the people. The Speaker, a stout man, was not willing to go. He was so noble that he frowned, and said he would not out of the chair, till he was plucked out; which was quickly done, without much compliment, by two soldiers, and the mace taken." (iii. 98.) Mr. Reynolds, who is evidently badly reported says: "I never desired any earthly thing with more earnestness, to see that parliament fairly dissolved, and another provided to build up. The question being put to dissolve—with a very loud Yea. This done, persons came to the door. One came in, and sweetly and kindly took your predecessor by the hand, and led him out of the chair. I say sweetly and gently. This was never known abroad, how near the

The Rump sat no more, and the sovereign power of the Commonwealth was now in the hands of Cromwell, the commander-in-chief of an obedient army of eighty thousand men.

In a few days Cromwell appointed a Council of State to transact the ordinary duties of executive government. It consisted of thirteen members, including himself. He continued to exercise the sovereign power with the advice of his Council of officers,[1] and he proceeded, in accordance with the recommendation which he had made to the Rump, to arrange for the nomination of a temporary sovereign assembly.

parliament that conquered others was to conquering themselves." (iii. 209.) It appears, from these two statements of persons present, that the question, that the bill do pass, was actually put. M. Guizot has published an interesting letter of M. de Bordeaux, the French Minister in London, giving an account of this dissolution. (Hist. de Cromwell, vol. i. App. No. 23.) M. de Bordeaux' account of Harrison's taking the Speaker from the chair curiously agrees with Reynolds's : "Le dit major (Harrison), le chapeau à la main avec tout respect, s'en alla à la chaire du Speaker, et lui baisant la main le prit par la sienne et la conduisit hors du parlement comme un gentilhomme ferait une demoiselle." M. de Bordeaux also puts into Cromwell's mouth a short speech accusing the Parliament of tyranny and corruption, and declaring his resolve to place the government in the hands of a few respectable men, "entre les mains de peu de gens, mais gens de bien."

[1] The continued exercise of the sovereign power by Cromwell and the Council of officers after the establishment of the Council of State puzzled contemporaries (Blencowe's Sydney Papers, p. 142), and has puzzled Mr. Godwin, who describes the Council of officers and the Council of State as two co-ordinate powers. (Hist. of Commonwealth, iii. 528.) I think there is no doubt that Cromwell appointed the Council of State for ordinary purposes of administration, retaining in his own hands the sovereign power, which he continued to exercise with the advice of the Council of officers. The Council of State consisted of Cromwell, General Lambert (his son-in-law), General Harrison, General Desborough (Cromwell's brother-in-law), Colonels Stapeley, Sydenham, Philip Jones, Tomlinson, and Bennet, Sir Gilbert Pickering, Walter Strickland, John Carew, and Samuel Moyer. It exemplifies the inaccuracies of contemporary writers, that Lord Leicester calls the Council of State a council of ten (Blencowe's Sydney Papers, p. 141); and Heath names Fairfax and Deane as members of it. (Chronicle, p. 343.)

Six weeks were spent in deliberating on the composition of this body. At last, early in June, summonses were issued to a hundred and forty-two persons, of whom a hundred and twenty-four were nominated for the counties of England, six for Wales, six for Ireland, and six for Scotland.[1]

Sir Anthony Ashley Cooper was nominated, with nine other members, for Wiltshire. He accepted this nomination, and was one of the leading members of this assembly, and a zealous supporter of Cromwell's views.

This is the body known by the name of the Barebone's Parliament, so nicknamed from one of its members, a notorious fanatic, who bore the singular name of Praisegod Barebone or Barbone. A large proportion of its members were religious enthusiasts, Anabaptists, Fifth Monarchy men, and followers of other sects into which the Independents were subdivided, and tradesmen and men of small means and humble position. Cromwell, having determined to call together such a body, was compelled to consult those on whom his power depended, and who had supported him in his measures against the Rump. The ministers of the

[1] Hobbes mentions one hundred and forty-two as the number of summonses issued (Behemoth, Part iv.) Cromwell in his address to the assembly on its meeting says that they were "above a hundred and forty." A member of the assembly to whom we owe the fullest account of its proceedings, says that two, and two only, refused their nominations. (Somers Tracts, vi. 269.) One of those who refused was probably Fairfax. See Godwin, iii. 524. The list of the members printed in the Somers Tracts (vi. 246) contains only 139 names. Mr. Hallam incorrectly states 120 as the number of the assembly (Constit. Hist. ii. 329); this is the number said to have attended on the first day. Dr. Lingard incorrectly makes the number of members for England 139, and the total 156. (Hist. of England, xi. 4.)

Independent congregations throughout the country were chiefly advised with as to the persons to be nominated.[1] On the other hand, Cromwell's means of choice among the gentry were necessarily limited. It may be inferred from what followed that, if he had been free to pursue his own inclinations, he would have appointed fewer fanatics and tradesmen, and more country gentlemen and lawyers. As it was, it excited astonishment that he should have succeeded in obtaining the services of so many gentlemen of birth and fortune as did take their places in this assembly.[2] Among these were Lord Eure, who sat a solitary peer in this assembly, Lord Lisle, the eldest son of the Earl of Leicester, Sir Charles Wolseley, Sir Gilbert Pickering, Cooper himself, Edward Montagu and Charles Howard, who were afterwards Earls of Sandwich and Carlisle. Other names occur in the list of members, which are at this day leading names in the counties which their bearers were called to represent. Very few officers of the army were nominated; and Cromwell abstained from nominating himself or any of his principal officers. One of the first proceedings of this body, after it was constituted, was to add Cromwell, Generals Lambert, Harrison, and Desborough, and Colonel Tomlinson, to their number; and Cooper was appointed to go at the head of a deputation to Cromwell, "to desire him to afford his

[1] Thurloe's State Papers, i. 395 ; Somers Tracts, vi. 269.
[2] Compare Whitelocke, who expresses such astonishment (Memorials, p. 559) with Clarendon, who admits, reluctantly, that "there were amongst them some few of the quality and degree of gentlemen, and who had estates, and such a proportion of credit and reputation as could consist with the guilt they had contracted." (Hist. of Rebellion, xiv. 15.)

presence and assistance in the House as a member thereof." [1]

This assembly met on the fourth of July, 1653. Cromwell addressed them on their first coming together in a long speech, full of religious phraseology, in which he justified his dissolution of the Rump, laid before them the great task which they were called to perform of settling the Commonwealth on firm foundations, and urged them to proceed in a spirit of forbearance and conciliation towards the numerous Presbyterian portion of the nation. At the conclusion of his speech, Cromwell delivered to the assembly a written instrument, by which he formally devolved on them the sovereign power, to hold it for a period of sixteen months, until the third of November, 1654. Three months before that day they were to nominate a body of equal number as their successors, who again were to sit for a twelve-month, and to make permanent provision for the future government of the Commonwealth.

The first business of the assembly was prayer. The commencement of their proceedings is thus described by one of themselves: "The fourth of July, 1653, those thus assembled and empowered did adjourn themselves from Whitehall to the Parliament-house, to meet the next morning at eight of the clock, and then to begin

---

[1] Comm. Journ. July 5, 1653. Cromwell was invited to sit as member of the Council of State. A difficulty seems to have been started as to whether members could be added to those named in the original instrument, without a new instrument; and they probably thought to get over the difficulty in this way. See Blencowe's Sydney Papers, p. 149. After the addition of these members, all the members of the Council of State which Cromwell had appointed were members of the assembly.

with seeking God by prayer; which accordingly they
did, and the service was performed by the members
amongst themselves, eight or ten speaking in prayer to
God, and some briefly from the Word, much of the presence of Christ and of His Spirit appearing that day, to
the great gladding of the hearts of many; some affirming
they never enjoyed so much of the Spirit and presence
of Christ in any of the meetings and exercises of religion
in all their lives as they did that day. In the evening
of that day, Mr. Francis Rouse was called to the chair,
and chosen Speaker; and then the House was adjourned
to the next day, when the House appointed to pray
again three or four days after, which accordingly was
done by the members, principally by such as had not
done service before, when also the Lord General was
present, and it was a very comfortable day."[1] No words
can describe more vividly the prevailing character of
this assembly. Cooper, Howard, Montagu, and others
who had joined this assembly as politicians, must have
been far from feeling comfortable in witnessing these
proceedings.[2]

[1] Somers Tracts, vi. 270. Compare Thurloe, i. 338, and Blencowe's
Sydney Papers, p. 148.
[2] There is no evidence, and it is not at all probable, that Cooper,
any more than Montagu or Howard, led in these prayers: they were all
members of a moderate party in this assembly, which steadily opposed
the fanatics, and ultimately broke it up.   Dryden's fierce lines in
"The Medal" are satirical exaggeration, and, so far as concerns the
charge against Cooper of selling himself to Cromwell, downright misrepresentation :

> "Bartering his venal wit for sums of gold,
> He cast himself into the saint-like mould :
> Groaned, sighed, and prayed while godliness was gain,
> The loudest bagpipe of the squeaking train."

Lord Campbell, improving on tradition, and without any evidence,
says that Cooper "pretended to have received the new light, after

The assembly adopted the name of the Parliament of the Commonwealth of England. They enlarged the council which Cromwell had appointed to the number of thirty, and among the additional members now appointed was Sir Anthony Ashley Cooper.

It soon became apparent that from this assembly a healing of divisions was not to be expected; and if Cromwell had bestowed on it the sovereign power in the hope that it might become the instrument of his own elevation, any such hope must soon have been abandoned. Two parties, very nearly equal in numbers, appeared in the assembly. One party acted with Cromwell, and endeavoured to temper the violent counsels of the other, more especially in the questions of tithes, presentations to livings, the maintenance of a clergy in connexion with the Government, and the reform of the laws and of the Court of Chancery. The violent party of root and branch reformers wished to abolish tithes and rights of presentation, and to leave the clergy entirely to the choice and control, as well as to the contributions, of their congregations. Cromwell's party were ready to give up tithes, but wished to retain them until some less irritating mode of payment of clergy were provided; they urged that rights of presentation were property, and desired to preserve them, subject to the check of a body of commissioners empowered to eject unworthy clergymen, and having a veto on nominations. As regards the law, the violent party were for

the fashion of the Independents," and that, "on the meeting of the House, he joined zealously in 'seeking the Lord,' along with the great body of fanatics of which it was composed."

constructing a complete code of new laws on principles
from which all the lawyers recoiled as fanatical : Cromwell's party opposed this proposal, and thought it sufficient to reform the laws according to the recommendation
of the Commission appointed by the Rump, over which
Hale had presided, and of which Cooper had been a
member. Almost immediately after the meeting of the
assembly, a committee for the reform of the law was
appointed, of which Cooper, being the first named, was
probably chairman; they applied themselves to consider
the various projects of measures which the Commission
had prepared; and Cooper from time to time introduced
bills to the House, some of which were passed. A vote
for the abolition of the Court of Chancery was passed
without a division, but disputes afterwards arose between
the two parties as to the provision to be made for the
future administration of equity and the decision of pending suits ; and the violent party, getting impatient, were
prevented only by the casting vote of the Speaker from
carrying a motion for the immediate abolition of the
Court of Chancery, without any provision being made
for these purposes.[1] On other occasions the violent
party succeeded in obtaining small majorities. It was
clear that Cromwell was not strong enough in the
assembly to master its fanatical elements, and keep it
in the ways of prudence and conciliation. The Presbyterian clergy who had been planted through the country
while their party was predominant in the Long Parlia-

---

[1] " It wanted not much but that all the caterpillars of the land had
been all banished the town, as formerly the poor cavaliers were, one
voice only reserving them for a time, which will not be long."
(Letter in Thurloe's State Papers, i. 577.)

ment, the Universities, and the Inns of Court, were all struck with terror at the designs of the violent party. Some of their proceedings gave offence to the army.[1] Cromwell made up his mind to put an end to this Parliament.

In the first days of its sitting, a committee had been appointed to consider the question of tithes. The appointment of this committee, carried by a majority of seven, had been a victory gained by the moderate party, who had thereby parried a motion for the abolition of tithes. It was afterwards referred to this committee on tithes to propose a plan for rejecting unworthy clergymen. The moderate party prevailed in the committee, and on the third of December they presented a report, recommending the continuance of tithes, and the appointment of commissioners, to be divided into circuits, and joined with four or five residents in each county, for the ejection of ungodly ministers and induction of godly successors. The violent party opposed the adoption of this report ; a debate arose on the first paragraph, which lasted for five days, and which ended by a vote, carried by a majority of two, against agreeing with it.

This vote determined the existence of the assembly. It was passed on Saturday, the tenth of December. During the next day Cromwell arranged his plans. On the morning of Monday his friends mustered early, and one of them, Colonel Sydenham,[2] moved that " the sitting of this Parliament any longer as now constituted will not be for the good of the Commonwealth, and that

[1] Thurloe, i. 368; Somers Tracts, vi. 274.
[2] The same who had acted with Cooper in his first military service for the Parliament, the taking of Wareham, in 1644, and afterwards at the storming of Abbotsbury. See pp. 59, 63..

therefore it was requisite to deliver up unto the Lord General Cromwell the powers which they received from him." This motion was seconded by Sir Charles Wolseley. After some debate, the Speaker, who was one of Cromwell's partisans, rose without putting the question, and, followed by about forty members, and preceded by the serjeant bearing the mace, proceeded to Cromwell at Whitehall. A resignation of the powers of the assembly was then written out, signed by the members present, and given to Cromwell. He accepted the resignation with professions of astonishment and sorrow. About seven-and-twenty members had remained in the House, and were consulting what they should do, when two officers entered and requested them to withdraw. They refused, and the officers brought in soldiers, forced them out, and locked the doors. The paper of resignation lay at Whitehall, to be signed by any other members who might choose to add their signatures; and ultimately it had eighty signatures, which enabled Cromwell to say that the sovereign power had been returned into his hands by a majority of this Parliament.

Cooper's name is not mentioned in the accounts which we have of the termination of the Barebone's Parliament; but there is no doubt that he acted with those who brought about the resignation of its powers. He had been constantly a teller for the moderate party in divisions in this Parliament. He was appointed one of Cromwell's Council of State immediately after the termination of the Barebone's Parliament.[1]

---

[1] Mr. Martyn, in a series of extraordinary misstatements, represents Cooper as systematically opposing Cromwell in the Barebone's Parliament, and describes Colonel Sydenham's motion for the resignation of its powers as a step hostile to Cromwell. (i. 164.)

Two incidents recorded in the Journals show how
much Sir Anthony Ashley Cooper was devoted for the
present to Cromwell and his policy. He reported from
the Council of State to the Parliament on the case of
the republican agitator, John Lilburne, who had been
banished by the Rump on pain of death if he returned
to England; who, after Cromwell broke up the Rump,
had returned and had been arrested by order of Cromwell's Council, and sent to trial; who had been tried
and acquitted by a jury amid threatening demonstrations
in his favour of large masses of the lower orders, and
whom the Council, through the medium of Cooper, now
recommended the House to retain in custody, notwithstanding his acquittal, for the peace of the nation.[1] On
another occasion, he was deputed by the House to convey
to Cromwell an offer to place Hampton Court at his
disposal, in exchange for New Hall in Essex, which he
then occupied, and he reported to the House Cromwell's
grateful refusal.[2]

There was an idle rumour during the few days which
intervened before the new government was settled, that
Cromwell had appointed Cooper Lord Chancellor; but
there is no reason to believe that Cromwell had thought
of such an appointment.[3]

---

[1] Comm. Journ. Aug. 27, 1653.
[2] Ibid. Sept. 20, 26; Thurloe, i. 477.
[3] It is said in an intercepted letter from Thomas Crocker to Francis
Edward, printed in Thurloe's State Papers (i. 645): "I hear the councillors are all named last night, the officers chosen, and several
honours to be conferred: amongst others, Lambert, who is now, as I
conceive, general of the three nations, to be made a duke; my Lord
Say to be chamberlain of the household; which is yet in doubt, whether
he will accept or refuse; my Lord Chief Justice St. John to be lord
treasurer; Sir Anthony Ashley Cooper, chancellor; both which have

At a council of officers assembled by Cromwell on the
day on which the Barebone's Parliament was broken up,
an elaborate scheme of a constitution was resolved upon,
which placed the government of the Commonwealth in
a single person, styled Protector, assisted by a Council
of State, and a Parliament popularly elected, according
to a reformed scheme of representation, similar to that
which had been projected by the Rump. The elaborate-
ness of this scheme shows that it must have been
already for some time under consideration ; and Cromwell may have designed to submit it to the Barebone's
Parliament, before he gave up hopes of managing that
assembly. Lambert, who proposed the scheme to the
Council of officers, said that it had been two months in
preparation. There were those who had proposed that
Cromwell should now be made King. Indeed the scheme
was originally drawn up, with the title of King for the
chief magistrate. Cromwell refused this title,[1] and it

accepted." This is the only allusion which exists to a design of
appointing Cooper chancellor, and it is easy to see that these are idle
stories.   Yet Lord Campbell has built upon this valueless statement a
singular superstructure of error. He first represents Cromwell as
having offered the great seal to Cooper *before* the calling of the Barebone's Parliament : "After the expulsion of the Long Parliament he
intrigued with Cromwell, who was anxious to secure him, and held out
to him the prospect of being appointed Lord Keeper of the Great
Seal." Then Lord Campbell supposes that, in the Barebone's Parliament, Cooper's "views on the Great Seal were considerably dashed by
the bill for 'the immediate and total abolition of the Court of Chancery,'"
and thinks that his opposition to this bill may have led to the statement
that he opposed Cromwell in the Barebone's Parliament, whereas it is
known that Cromwell also disapproved of that bill. Lastly, Lord
Campbell thinks that the ultimate estrangement between Cooper and
Cromwell probably arose "from the *promise* about the Great Seal not
being fulfilled."

[1] A speech of Cromwell in 1657 to a large number of officers who
then opposed his taking the title of King, which was printed for the
first time by the editor of Burton's Diary from a MS. in the British
Museum, is the authority for this statement. "He [Cromwell] said

was settled that the "single person" of the new constitution should be styled Protector, and hold his power
for life.   Cromwell was to be the first Protector, and
his successors were to be elected by the Council   The
constitution now promulgated by Cromwell and the
Council of officers is known by the name of "The
Instrument of Government."

Bishop Burnet has said of Cooper that he was one
of those who most pressed Cromwell to accept the
kingship.   An attempt has been made by Mr. Martyn
to discredit this statement, but there is no improbability in the statement, which doubtless refers to this
period, when Cooper was a zealous and leading supporter
of Cromwell.[1]

There was only an interval of four days between the
end of the Barebone's Parliament and the installation
of the new Constitution and of Cromwell as Protector.

that the time was when they boggled not at the word king, for the
instrument by which the government now stands was presented to his
Highness with the title King in it, as some then present could witness,
pointing at a principal officer then in his eye, and he refused to accept
of the title." (Burton, i. 382.) Lambert is probably the officer here
referred to.   Ludlow says, "Some were said to have moved that the
title might be king." (ii. 477.)

[1] Hist. of Own Time, i. 97.   The whole passage is as follows : "He
[Shaftesbury] pretended that Cromwell offered to make him king. He
was indeed of great use to him in withstanding the enthusiasts of that
time.   He was one of those who pressed him most to accept of the kingship, because, as he said afterwards, he was sure it would ruin him."
There is no doubt that Cooper aided Cromwell against the enthusiasts,
and nothing is more probable than that he was one of those who urged
Cromwell to take the title of King.   But that Cromwell should have
offered to make Cooper king is not quite so likely; and if Cooper afterwards gave the reason which Burnet imputes to him for his advice to
Cromwell, he was guilty of a ridiculous untruth.   Shaftesbury may
have boasted in his later years, and may have endeavoured dis-
ingenuously to excuse some of his earlier actions ; but, on the other
hand, Shaftesbury may have bantered Burnet, and certainly Burnet is
spiteful to Shaftesbury.

Cooper was one of fifteen members of the Council of State named in the Instrument of Government. A salary of a thousand pounds a year was assigned to each councillor, but Cooper, who did not remain a member of the Council much longer than a year, never received any salary.[1]

It is desirable to give an account of the leading provisions of this constitution at the birth of which Cooper assisted.

It has been already said that the Protector was appointed for life, and that, after Cromwell, future Protectors were to be elected by the Council. There was no restriction on their choice, except that none of the late King's children, line, or family, could be elected. The Council was to consist of not more than twenty-one nor less than thirteen members. Fifteen were named in the Instrument of Government, and Cromwell and a majority of the Council were empowered to fill up the number twenty-one before the meeting of the first parliament. After that time a scheme of election, jointly by the Council, the Parliament, and the Protector, was provided. A member of Council could only be removed by the judgment of a tribunal jointly appointed by the Council and the Parliament.

---

[1] This is accidentally proved by a paper printed in Thurloe's State Papers (iii. 581), giving an account of payments to members of the Council from its first appointment to the end of 1655. In the debates on the Indemnity Bill in the Convention Parliament after the Restoration, Cooper is reported to have said, in opposing a proposal that all officers of the Protectorate should refund their salaries, "He might freely speak, because he never received any salary." (Parl. Hist. iv. 73.) Some letters published by M. Guizot (Hist. de Cromwell, vol. ii. Appendix, No. 3) mention Cooper as taking a prominent part, as member of the Privy Council, in Cromwell's reception of the French ambassador, April 1654.

In the constitution of the Parliament there was a great and a wise change from the mode of election of the old English House of Commons. It was to consist of 460 members; 400 for England and Wales, 30 for Scotland, and 30 for Ireland. In the distribution of the numbers for England, there was a great increase in the number of county members, many small boroughs were disfranchised, and members were given for the first time to several large towns. Few towns returned more than one member, and the number of members for each county and for the boroughs included in it was made as nearly proportional as possible to the contribution of the county towards the public expenditure. It was left to the Protector and Council to settle the distribution of the sixty members for Scotland and Ireland. The qualification for an elector was the possession of two hundred pounds of real or personal property. The elected were to be twenty-one years of age, and "such, and no other than such, as are persons of known integrity, fearing God, and of good conversation." Those who had taken part against the Parliament since the first of January, 1641, unless they had afterwards given "signal testimony of their affections thereunto," were to be incapable of electing or of being elected to the first four parliaments ; Roman Catholics, and those who had been in the Irish rebellion, were disqualified for ever. For the first three parliaments the members elected were to have a certificate of approbation from the Council, without which they were not to be allowed to sit; and there was to be a clause in every indenture of return prohibiting the members from altering the government as settled in a single person and in a parliament by the present Instrument of Government.

The first parliament was to meet on the third of September, 1654, about eight months after the promulgation of the Constitution. A parliament was to be called once in three years, and was not to be adjourned, prorogued, or dissolved without its own consent, for five months after its meeting.

Where the command of the forces of the commonwealth was to be placed, and whether any, and what, checks were to be placed on the Parliament in legislation,—the two great questions which had been battled with the late King, and which had brought him to the block,—were difficult problems to be solved by the framers of this constitution, who desired to restrain the power of the Parliament, and yet to avoid all appearance of a monarchical element. It was provided that the disposal of the militia was to be vested in the Protector and the Parliament jointly, and, when Parliament was not sitting, in the Protector and Council. The Protector and Council were to have the power of peace and war, but a parliament was to be summoned immediately after entering upon a war, and any parliament so specially called could not be adjourned, prorogued, or dissolved, without its own consent, for five months after it had assembled. All legislation and taxation were to be by common consent of Parliament. Bills passed by the Parliament were to be presented to the Protector for his consent; but if that consent were not given in twenty days, the Parliament might then declare a bill law, unless it contained anything contrary to the provision of the Instrument of Government.[1]

In a speech addressed to the first parliament called under this constitution, Cromwell explained that the fundamental principles of the Instrument of Government, which the Parliament by itself could not infringe upon, were four: government by a single person and a parliament jointly, a limited duration of the Parliament, liberty of conscience in religion, and the check of either the Parliament or the Council on the Protector as regards the militia. But the liberty of conscience in religion, thus proclaimed by Cromwell as one of the fundamental principles of the new government, was not extended to the Roman Catholic or the Episcopalian; these were specially excepted from protection in the profession of their religion and exercise of their worship, together with "such as, under the profession of Christ, hold forth and practise licentiousness."

The Instrument of Government declared that the Christian religion, as contained in the Scriptures, was to be the public profession of the three nations, and that provision was to be made as soon as possible for a more equal and less irritating mode of payment of clergy than by tithes, but that in the meantime tithes were to be

---

[1] "Provided such bills contain nothing in them contrary to the matters contained in these presents." When Cromwell found the first parliament called under this new constitution refractory, he laid down, as is stated in the text, four fundamental principles not to be infringed without his consent; and the Parliament afterwards expressly assigned a negative to the Protector for all bills touching these four questions. Mr. Hallam's statement, therefore, that the Protector had no negative voice on the Parliament, requires qualification. (Constit. Hist. ii. 332.)

continued. A standing army of 10,000 horse and 20,000 foot was prescribed, and a constant yearly revenue was to be provided for maintaining these forces and a sufficient navy; and 200,000*l.* a year was assigned to the civil government. Till the first Parliament met, the Protector and Council were empowered to raise what money might be necessary for the support of the existing forces. Power was given them also to make laws and ordinances, till the meeting of the first Parliament; but these laws and ordinances were to be binding only until Parliament should make order concerning them.

Such were the principal provisions of this elaborate paper-constitution, which was destined soon to meet with difficulties too strong for it in practice, and which, having been violated in one essential point by Cromwell in little more than a twelvemonth after its establishment, was at the end of three years formally superseded by another. Doubtless, Cromwell hoped that he had now devised a constitution under which he might obtain the co-operation of the Presbyterians whom the Barebone's Parliament had scared, and which provided sufficient securities against the restoration of the royal family.

The fourteen members of the Council named, together with Sir Anthony Ashley Cooper, in the Instrument of Government, were Lord Lisle, Generals Fleetwood and Lambert, Sir Gilbert Pickering, Sir Charles Wolseley, Montagu, General Desborough, Walter Strickland, Henry Lawrence, Colonel Sydenham, Colonel Philip Jones, Richard Major, Francis Rouse (the late Speaker of the Barebone's Parliament), and General Skippon.

Three more members were added before the meeting
of the Parliament, Humphry Mackworth, Nathaniel
Fiennes, and the Earl of Mulgrave.[1]

A name more celebrated than that of any of Cooper's
colleagues in the Council occurs in the list of assistants
of the Secretary, Thurloe. John Milton was an assistant
in the department of Latin correspondence in the
Secretary's office, and gave the adhesion of his great
intellect and pure conscience to Cromwell's Protectorate.
The civil commotions and religious controversies of the
time had long since drawn him from the Muses; he
had been Secretary for foreign languages under the
Council of State of the Rump Parliament, and had been
employed by that Council to answer the Latin treatise
in which Salmasius had arraigned before the civilized
world the execution of Charles the First; and his Latin
answer to that great scholar had made his name widely
known, both for admiration and for obloquy. Shortly
after the installation of Cromwell as Protector, Milton
published, also in Latin, a second defence of the English
nation, in which he declared his approval of Cromwell's
recent acts, and counselled the Protector on the dangers
and the duties of his position. In this work he praises
several members of the new Council by name; but
Cooper is not among those whom Milton mentions.
There is no trace of personal intercourse between Cooper
and Milton either now or after the Restoration, when
the poet's fame had made him an object of curiosity
among foreigners, and gained for him, in spite of

[1] The father of the poet, author of the "Essay on Satire" and the
"Essay on Poetry," who was ultimately created Duke of Buckingham-
shire.

political passions, the notice of accomplished men even of the Court of Charles the Second.

Sir Anthony Ashley Cooper was elected to the first Parliament assembled under the Instrument of Government by no less than three constituencies, Wiltshire, Poole, and Tewkesbury. He afterwards elected to sit for Wiltshire.

The election for Wiltshire on this occasion has been described by Edmund Ludlow, in a passage of his Memoirs, which was suppressed. Ludlow at this time held a military command in Ireland; but the republican party, acting in opposition to Cromwell, proposed him as a candidate for Wiltshire, with which he was connected by ancient lineage and property. The new scheme of representation gave ten members to Wiltshire. According to Ludlow's account, which perhaps ought not to be taken implicitly, Cavaliers united with the Presbyterian clergy and Cromwell's partisans in proposing a list of ten candidates, with Cooper at the head, and Ludlow's republican friends proposed him and nine others. The gathering for the election was so numerous, that it became necessary to adjourn from Salisbury Town-hall to the plain of Stonehenge. There Sir Anthony Ashley Cooper, and a Presbyterian clergyman named Adoniram Byfield, addressed the people on the necessity of electing members who would endeavour to reconcile conflicting interests and heal the divisions of the State. On a show of hands, the numbers appeared so nearly equal that a poll was necessary; and by the union, according to Ludlow, of Cavaliers, Presbyterians, and Cromwellites, and by the use of force and of all the influence which the Government could exert, Cooper was placed at the head of the poll, and all the ten anti-republican candidates were elected.[1]

The interval of eight months between the inaugura-tion of the constitution and the meeting of the new Parliament was well employed by Cromwell and his Council. They availed themselves largely of their power of making provisional ordinances to do many things which the Barebone's Parliament had either refused to do or had left unfinished. They repealed the engage-ment : a bill for that purpose introduced by Cooper in the Barebone's Parliament had been rejected. They issued an ordinance settling the terms of union of Scotland with the Commonwealth, which the sudden termination of the Barebone's Parliament had alone pre-vented that assembly from passing, as it had already passed an act for the union of Ireland. An ordinance was issued for the reform of the Court of Chancery, and two others for the appointment of a body of commis-sioners for the approval of clergymen presented to livings, and of commissioners in the several counties for the ejection of unworthy ministers. Sir Anthony Ashley Cooper was appointed one of the latter commissioners for Wiltshire and Dorsetshire.[2] Peace was now made with Holland, and beneficial treaties were concluded

---

[1] This account is given in the first of a series of suppressed passages of Ludlow's Memoirs, which I found, in Locke's handwriting, among the Locke papers in the Earl of Lovelace's possession. See Appendix III. Mr. Martyn, in unaccountable departure from facts, states that Sir A. A. Cooper's election for Wiltshire was opposed by Cromwell (i. 165); and Lord Campbell has incorrectly followed Mr. Martyn in placing Cooper's estrangement from Cromwell before the election of this parliament.

[2] Wood, Ath. Oxon. (Bliss) iv. 71.

with Portugal, Denmark, and Sweden. The failure of a royalist conspiracy for assassinating Cromwell had rallied sympathy around him, and depressed the hopes of the friends of the royal family ; and when Cromwell met the Parliament which assembled on the third of September, 1654, under the provisions of the Instrument of Government, he might have fairly hoped that the recollections of the Rump and Barebone's Parliaments, the proofs which he and his Council had already given of energy and wisdom, and the natural desire for an end of change would ensure for the new constitution its sanction and co-operation.

Any such hopes, however, were doomed to speedy disappointment. Notwithstanding all the efforts which Cromwell and his Council had made to secure a majority, and notwithstanding many advantages which they possessed for procuring favourable returns, a large majority of the Parliament showed themselves immediately determined to dispute Cromwell's authority and the new constitution, instead of acknowledging the Instrument of Government as the foundation of their own legislative powers. The largest party in the Parliament were Presbyterians. A considerable number of Republicans also were returned. The Republicans, headed by Sir Arthur Haselrig, Scot, and Bradshaw, the celebrated president of the court which had condemned the late King to death, immediately offered an opposition ; and, to perplex Cromwell and promote their own aims, the Presbyterians aided the Republicans.

Cromwell having opened the Parliament with a speech, his friends proposed the day after that this speech should be taken into consideration, with a view to an address thanking him for the new government. But the Republicans and their Presbyterian allies would not admit this new government to be an accomplished fact. They claimed the right to discuss every provision of the Instrument of Government, and contended that it was for them, elected by the people, now to proceed to settle the constitution as they pleased. Instead of adopting the proposal to thank Cromwell, they resolved by a small majority to discuss the Instrument of Government in Grand Committee, or, in modern parliamentary phrase, in a Committee of the whole House, with a view to its being altered as they might think proper, and then passed into an act. The first clause, which declared the government to be in "one person and the people assembled in Parliament," was warmly debated in committee for four days; and when the committee broke up on the fourth day, it was expected that a proposal which had been made by Hale, now a judge, and which he intended as a compromise, would be carried by a large majority, to declare the government to be in "the Parliament and a single person, limited and restrained as the Parliament should think fit." Cromwell determined to make an attempt by force to prevent further discussion of the Instrument of Government.

As the members came to the House on the morning of the twelfth of September, they found the doors locked and guarded by soldiers, and were told that the Protector was coming to the Painted Chamber and commanded their attendance there. Cromwell arrived in state about ten o'clock, by which time there was a full

attendance of members. He made a long speech, re-
minding them with many reproaches that they were all
bound by the indentures of their returns not to alter the
government as settled in a single person and the Parliament, and ended by announcing that he should exact a
pledge not to interfere with the government as so settled
from every member before he re-entered the House.
When the members left the Painted Chamber, they
found the doors of their House still locked and guarded,
and an officer in the lobby with a paper containing the
following declaration, which each member was required
to sign : " I do hereby freely promise and engage to be
true and faithful to the Lord Protector and the Commonwealth of England, Scotland, and Ireland, and shall not,
according to the tenour of the indenture whereby I am
returned to sit in this present Parliament, propose or
give my consent to alter the government as settled in
one person and a parliament." Within an hour about a
hundred members had signed the paper. The Speaker
was then sent for; he came and signed it, and then
went into the House and took the chair. About forty
more members signed during the day. It was then
voted that by signing this declaration a member was
not bound to all the forty-two clauses of the Instrument
of Government, but only to the first clause, which vested
the government in a single person and a parliament.
This vote brought in more signatures ; and, in the end,
about three hundred of the four hundred and sixty
members signed the paper, and returned to the House.[1]

[1] Mr. Martyn continues his extraordinary misrepresentations of Sir
A. A. Cooper's course at this period by stating that he took a leading

The House now returned to the discussion of the Instrument of Government, admitting only that the government should be composed of a single person and a parliament; and though all the leading members of the Republican party were excluded by their refusal to sign the declaration which had been imposed, Cromwell found the Parliament hardly more manageable than before. They continued to discuss the Instrument of Government, clause by clause, in Grand Committee, for nearly three months. Several changes were made in it, unpalatable to Cromwell; the power to declare war was placed in the Protector and Parliament, instead of the Protector and Council, as had been provided by the original Instrument, and the election of future Protectors was also given to the Parliament instead of the Council. One change which was proposed by Cromwell's friends, and which Cromwell himself is said to have greatly desired, to make the Protectorship hereditary in his family, was rejected by the largest majority which occurred in the course of these discussions.

When the battle was concluded in the Grand Com-

---

part in the opposition, refused to sign the declaration, and was excluded from the parliament (i. 167). Lord Campbell follows Mr. Martyn, and, as usual, states the case strongly. " When the Parliament met, he strongly co-operated with the party who were beginning to inquire into the validity of the 'Instrument of Government.'..... This made the Protector resolve by a strong hand to exclude all such refractory spirits as Sir A. A. Cooper . . . Shaftesbury absolutely refused to sign the declaration. Thus excluded, he intrigued against Cromwell." Lord Campbell proceeds to say: " The Protector, finding his opponent so troublesome, soon after made a bold attempt to gain him over by appointing him a member of the Council of State, with promises of further advancement." Very little inquiry would have shown that Sir A. A. Cooper was made a member of the Council of State eight months before this parliament met, and that he was not excluded from the parliament, the Journals making frequent mention of his name.

mittee, it was fought over again in the House, which went through all the clauses as reported from the Grand Committee. At last the Instrument of Government, as altered by the Parliament, was embodied in a bill; and then it was resolved that, if the Protector did not agree to every clause, the whole should be void and of no effect. The object of this was, of course, to force Cromwell into accepting all the alterations. Five days after this resolution was passed, the House had sat five lunar months; and Cromwell, interpreting as lunar months of twenty-eight days the five months during which the original Instrument of Government had provided that a parliament should not be dissolved without its own consent, dissolved this Parliament on the very day on which five lunar months of its existence were completed. All its discussions and alterations of the Instrument of Government now went for nothing, for the bill had not been passed, and the original Instrument continued to be the constitution of the Commonwealth.

No provision had been made for revenue when the Parliament was dissolved; and the Instrument of Government had empowered the Protector and Council to issue ordinances for raising money only until the meeting of the first Parliament. In this respect Cromwell set his constitution at nought, and an ordinance was issued shortly after the dissolution of the Parliament for raising money monthly by assessment.

The dissolution took place on the twenty-second of January, 1655. On the twenty-eighth of December, 1654, Sir Anthony Ashley Cooper, who had hitherto regularly attended the meetings of the Privy Council, attended

for the last time. What led to his retirement from the
Council, and his separation from Cromwell, ending in
decided opposition to him, there are no means of determining. It is probable that differences of opinion arose
between Cooper and Cromwell in the course of the discussions on the Instrument of Government; and Cooper
probably found it difficult to maintain his position as a
supporter of Cromwell in face of the decided opposition
of his Presbyterian friends. It does not appear probable,
however, that there was an open rupture, or that Cooper
made overt opposition to Cromwell during the sitting of
this Parliament. On the twenty-seventh of November,
he was a teller, with Richard Cromwell, in a division on
one of the clauses of the Instrument of Government. It
is true that Ludlow states that Cooper opposed Cromwell
during this Parliament, but the same passage of Ludlow's
Memoirs contains other obvious inaccuracies, and this
statement, if not entirely inaccurate also, is probably an
exaggeration. Until Cooper had ceased to attend the
Privy Council, he could not have opposed Cromwell in
Parliament, even though dissatisfied with his proceedings; and there was only a short interval of three weeks
between his last attendance in Council and the dissolution of the Parliament.[1]

---

[1] Ludlow's statement occurs in the second of the suppressed passages
in Appendix III. Ludlow says that Cooper was turned out of the
Council because he opposed Cromwell in this parliament, and that
Colonel Mackworth was appointed member of the Council in his place.
There is no entry in the Council book, which I have inspected in the
State Paper Office, of Cooper's dismissal; and according to the Instrument of Government, a dismissal could only have taken place on a
specific charge of misconduct, after inquiry by a committee jointly
appointed by the Council and the Parliament. He was not succeeded
by Colonel Mackworth, who was appointed a member of the Council

One reason which has been assigned for his estrangement from Cromwell is that he wished to marry Cromwell's daughter Mary (who was shortly afterwards married to Lord Falconbridge), and was refused. This story is perhaps no more than a piece of idle gossip. It is however so far possible, that Cooper was now a second time a widower. If Cooper quarrelled with Cromwell before the end of 1654, the quarrel was very soon after Cooper became a widower, and so soon as to render this explanation of the cause of quarrel improbable.

Sir Anthony Ashley Cooper's second wife, the daughter of the Earl of Exeter, to whom he was married

April 27, 1654, six months before Cooper ceased to sit. This passage in Ludlow is, therefore, very inaccurate. There is no evidence even of Cooper having resigned his seat in the Council; and I should infer from a list, already referred to, of payments to members of the Council up to the end of 1655, that Cooper, though he had ceased to attend, was then still a member of the Council. Ludlow mentions in the same passage Sir A. A. Cooper's unsuccessful love of Mary Cromwell as the reason for his quarrelling with the Protector. This story is also mentioned by A. Wood (Ath. Oxon. iv. 71, Bliss's edition), and in Oldmixon's " Lives of the Chancellors." (i. 148.) The authority for the story is weak. Lord Campbell has adopted the gossip as true, and amplified it considerably; and, forgetting that he had previously explained the quarrel with Cromwell by Cooper's disappointment at not receiving the Great Seal, now ascribes it, without a word of doubt, to disappointed love. " This gracious demeanour roused in the bosom of Sir Anthony the ambitious project of forming an alliance with the Protectoral house, and, having been some time a widower, he *actually demanded in marriage* the musical, glib-tongued Lady Mary, afterwards united to Lord Fauconberg. *Probably on account of his dissolute morals, he met with a flat refusal.* Thereupon he finally broke with Oliver, and *became a partisan of the banished royal family. When he had only twice or thrice sat in the Council of State, he sent in his resignation;* alleging that ' the government by one person was against his conscience.' " Cooper had been a regular attendant at the Privy Council from his appointment in December 1653 to December 28, 1654, more than a year. He did not become a partisan of the banished royal family for nearly five years after this date. I do not know what is Lord Campbell's authority for the fact of Cooper's resignation, with the reason alleged under marks of quotation.

in 1650, died some time in the year 1654. There were no more children by this marriage than the two sons who have been mentioned, one of whom died in childhood, and the other, Anthony Ashley, lived to succeed his father.

In the course of the year 1656, Cooper married a third wife, Margaret, daughter of the second Lord Spencer of Wormleighton, and sister of the third lord, who was created Earl of Sunderland by Charles the First, and had fallen fighting for the Royal cause at Newbury.

The son of this Earl of Sunderland, a boy at the time of Sir Anthony Ashley Cooper's marriage with his aunt, rose to be the chief Minister of Charles the Second before the close of Shaftesbury's career. It has been already mentioned that Halifax was the nephew of Shaftesbury's first wife. Shaftesbury's connexion with both Halifax and Sunderland was rendered closer by the marriage of Halifax with Sunderland's sister. In the last years of Shaftesbury's career, Halifax and Sunderland divided political ascendency; and, seven-and-twenty years later, Shaftesbury fled for his life, to die in a foreign land, from a government of which his two nephews were the chiefs.

The third wife of Sir Anthony Ashley Cooper lived to share all the honours and troubles of his future career. She had no children, but she reared with a mother's care her husband's son by his second wife, and afterwards with the same care watched over the delicate boyhood of that son's son, the future author of the "Characteristics." She was a woman of strong religious feelings. It was her habit to rise at five in the morning and spend two or three hours in private devotions.[1] Though Shaftesbury's character did not agree with hers in this respect, they lived on terms of. the warmest affection. A letter written by Lady Shaftesbury to her nephew Sunderland two years after her husband's death, shows how deeply she still mourned his loss.[2] There must have been virtues and amiable qualities in one so loved by such a wife.

[1] Rawleigh Redivivus, p. 13. Locke dedicated to Lady Shaftesbury a translation which he made of three religious Essays of Nicole. Locke's translation of these Essays was published for the first time in 1828 by Dr. Haucock. As this small volume is not generally known, I extract a passage of Locke's dedication to Lady Shaftesbury : " I thought I could not find in all France anything fitter to be put into your hands, than what would make you see so rare and extraordinary a sight as a draught of some of your own virtues. For if to be constantly humble in a high station, if to appear little to yourself in the midst of greatness, is a mark of the sense of one's own weakness ; if to be beloved of all that come near you be a demonstration that you know how to live at peace with others; if to be constant and frequent in acts of devotion be the best way of acknowledging a Deity : it is certain your ladyship is in reality what the author has here given us an idea of."

[2] This letter is among the Domestic Papers of 1685 in the State Paper Office. Lady Shaftesbury writes to the Earl of Sunderland to beg him to make her excuses for not attending the coronation of James the Second :—

" 31st March, 1685.

"Because I think the shortest troubles are the best, I will, my Lord, only just tell you why you read this note from your disconsolate aunt, not make it longer by apologies for doing it. It seems, my Lord, that in observance to forms I was to have a letter concerning the coronation as well as those that are fit to observe the orders they bring with them, which I am so utterly incapacitated for, that I concluded at first, and indeed do think still, that it so answers itself, I needed to take no notice of it; but, if I am mistaken, I ask so much friendliness from your Lordship as to do for me what is proper in this case to be done by, my Lord, your afflicted, most faithful, affectionate, humble servant,

" M. SHAFTESBURY."

CHAPTER V.

Cooper now in opposition to Cromwell—He falls back on the Presbyterian party—Elected for Wiltshire to new Parliament—Prevented by the Council from taking his seat—Is one of the sixty-five who sign a letter to the Speaker protesting—Afterwards signs Remonstrance—The Humble Petition and Advice—Cromwell refuses to be King—House adjourned from June 26, 1657, to January 20, 1658—Cromwell's Peers or "Other House"—Cooper not one—The £500 fine for composition, imposed by Long Parliament in 1644, remitted by Cromwell—Cooper's friendship with Henry Cromwell, and letter to him—Cooper and the other excluded members take their seats on meeting of Parliament, January 1658—Formidable opposition to Cromwell and the new Constitution—Debates about the "Other House"—Cooper's speeches—Cromwell dissolves the Parliament, February 4—Cromwell's death.

In the absence of any positive information on the subject of the differences which arose about this time between Sir Anthony Ashley Cooper and Cromwell, it might be conjectured that Cromwell's dissolution of the last Parliament was disapproved of by Cooper. It does not appear that the proceedings of that parliament, however much they may have been irritating and disappointing to the Protector, furnished sufficient cause for a dissolution, which immediately rendered it necessary to trample on Cromwell's own constitution in order to raise money. The changes which the Parliament had made in the Instrument of Government were, after all, not extensive ; all the essentials of the original constitution promulgated by Cromwell and his officers had been retained. Moderate men generally thought that Cromwell should have accepted the alterations made by the Parliament, and borne with its provocations, rather than again peril the settlement of the Commonwealth; and there is no doubt that the dissolution of the last Parliament lost Cromwell many supporters.[1]

Cooper never returned to his seat in the Council of State. We know nothing at all of his proceedings during twenty months which intervened between the dissolution of the last Parliament and the assembling of another on the seventeenth of September, 1656. But when this Parliament assembled, Cooper was regarded by Cromwell as an opponent.

The Royalists became very active in intrigues and conspiracies after the dissolution of January 1655; but Cooper had no connexion now or for some time after with this party. The restoration of the heir of the late King could only have been regarded at this period as a remote possibility by any but the zealous adherents of his family. Cooper fell back on the Presbyterian party, and in the two next parliaments was one of the leaders of the opposition which the Presbyterians and Republicans combined to wage against Cromwell and his successor.

Sir Anthony Ashley Cooper was again elected by the county of Wiltshire to serve in the second Parliament elected according to the provisions of the Instrument of Government, which met in 1656. But this time Cromwell would not permit him to take his seat.

[1] Ludlow, ii. 512.

The Instrument of Government had provided that, for the first three Parliaments called under its provisions, all members elected must obtain a certificate of approbation from the Council, in order to be permitted to sit. This provision, designed to secure an observance of the qualifications enjoined for members, was stretched on the present occasion to exclude a large number of members whose opposition Cromwell feared. The number of members to whom the Council refused certificates of approbation is variously stated; there is no doubt that it exceeded a hundred, and probably it was not far below two hundred. Soldiers at the door of the House prevented the entrance of all who could not produce the Council's certificates. Sir Anthony Ashley Cooper was one of the excluded. About ninety other names of excluded members are known; among them are Sir Arthur Haselrig, Scot, and Weaver, leaders of the Republicans; and Morrice, Colonel Birch, Alexander Popham, Serjeant Maynard, and Sir Harbottle Grimstone, members of the Presbyterian party. Another name in the list is that of the Earl of Salisbury, who had sat in the Rump Parliament, and who, in the subsequent reign of Charles the Second, was a zealous member of the Opposition of which Shaftesbury was the leader.

Sixty-five of the excluded members, among whom was Cooper, signed a letter to the Speaker, complaining that they had been forcibly prevented by soldiers from taking their seats. This letter was presented in the House by Sir George Booth, a distinguished member of the Presbyterian party, who had not been excluded. The House resolved that the Council should be desired to state their reasons for what they had done. The Council said that the Instrument of Government had imposed on them the duty of judging whether the members returned possessed the prescribed qualifications; that the same Instrument had provided that the members to be elected should be " such and no other than such as were persons of known integrity, fearing God, and of good conversation ;" that they had examined all the returns according to their duty, and had not refused certificates of approbation to any who appeared to them to come within the above description; and that for those whom they had not approved " his Highness had given orders to some persons to take care that they should not come into the House." An overpowering majority of the members who had been allowed to sit resolved to be content with this insolent reply, and to refer the excluded members to the Council.

A Remonstrance, addressed to the people, couched in the strongest language, was afterwards drawn up, and printed with the names of ninety-three of the excluded members appended to it. This Remonstrance declared that whoever had advised the Protector's late proceeding was a capital enemy of the Commonwealth : that all who should sit and vote in the mutilated assembly were adherents of the capital enemies of the Commonwealth, and betrayers of the people's liberties ; that the assembly which now sat was not the representative body of England ; that their votes and acts were null and void ; and that a free Parliament alone could set aside the laws in times of danger, and justly provide for the future government of the Commonwealth. The paper concludes by declaring that those who sign it are ready to expose their lives and estates to the utmost hazard for the service of the people, and to procure the assembling of a free Parliament. Sir Anthony Ashley Cooper's name is appended to this printed document. But there is reason to think that all the names which were printed had not been subscribed to it; and it may be inferred from the strong language of this Remonstrance that it was not openly circulated.

A few of the members who had been excluded afterwards made peace with the Council, and obtained admission into the House. But Sir Anthony Ashley Cooper, with the great majority, remained excluded during the whole of the first session of this Parliament.[1]

This session lasted nine months, till the twenty-sixth of June, 1657. Cromwell's measure of exclusion had at last obtained for him a manageable Parliament.

It is probable, from what took place in this Parliament, that Cromwell's principal reason for assembling it was to procure a change in the constitution, involving

---

[1] Dr. Lingard, who is generally most accurate in details, has stated incorrectly that Sir A. A. Cooper became Cromwell's intimate adviser after this exclusion from Parliament. (xi. 80, note.) A little discussion in which Cooper's name was mixed up took place on December 22, 1656, during his enforced absence from this Parliament. A Captain Arthur petitioned for payment of moneys laid out by him for the Parliament in the beginning of the Civil War, and said he had been betrayed and taken prisoner by Cooper. One member, Mr. Robinson, suggested that Sir A. A. Cooper should satisfy the petitioner; another, Mr. Butler, replied, "Sir A. A. Cooper has done you good service, and the petitioner doth not say his sufferings were by him." The matter was dropped. Captain Arthur's complaint would probably refer to the time when Cooper was on the King's side. (Burton's Diary of Cromwellian Parliaments, i. 204.)

the creation of a second chamber, and the substitution
of the title of King for that of Protector.

The House had, however, sat some months before any
step was taken in promotion of such a design. But on
the twenty-third of February, 1657, Sir Christopher
Pack, an alderman and one of the members for the city
of London, suddenly presented to the House a document
elaborately drawn up, bearing the title of "The Humble
Address and Remonstrance of the Knights, Burgesses,
and Citizens now assembled in the Parliament of the
Commonwealth," and moved that it should be received
and read. This was an address to Cromwell, stating
that the nation could never become settled while it was
left uncertain who would succeed him after his death,
and praying him to assume the title of King, and to call
henceforth a parliament consisting of two houses, and
to govern the Commonwealth in future according to the
laws of the nation, subject to such alterations as were
proposed in this document, which was to supersede the
Instrument of Government. Apparently, nothing could
have been more undignified than the mode in which
this proposal to revive royalty was brought before the
Parliament. Sir Christopher Pack was probably selected
to present the address on account of his connexion
with the city of London, and that it might seem not to
come from Cromwell himself. But the worthy alderman
was no orator, and if there were any design to blind the
Parliament as to Cromwell's connexion with this address,
the execution was not successful. Sir Christopher
uttered a few confused words, of which all that could
be understood was that he had found somewhere, or

that some one had given him, a paper which he thought worthy of consideration, and which he begged the House to receive. Though the motion came before the House without notice, the contents of the paper were probably generally known, and a scene of violent disorder ensued. The small minority of Cromwell's opponents in the assembly made up by violence for their want of numbers. It was irregular to present such a document to the House without leave previously obtained, and some members endeavoured to snatch the paper from Sir Christopher. By the violence of opposing members he was jostled down the House as far as the bar, when his friends rescued him and carried him back to the Speaker's chair. After a warm debate, it was decided by a hundred and fifty-four votes against fifty-four that the paper should be read. It was then debated day by day till the twenty-seventh of March. A motion made at the outset that it should be discussed in Grand Committee was rejected by a hundred and eighteen votes to sixty-three. But the House discussed separately the various clauses of the address. The clauses constituting another House to be nominated by the proposed king, and to be approved by "this House," were passed without a division. The substitution of the title of King for that of Protector was carried by a hundred and twenty-three votes to sixty-two. When the whole paper had been gone through, the words " Address and Remonstrance " in the title were changed for " Petition and Advice," and a clause was added, providing that unless Cromwell consented to everything contained in it, no part of it should take effect. On the thirty-first of March, the "Humble Petition and Advice" was presented to Cromwell for his consent.

Cromwell refused to accept the title of King. There is no doubt that he desired it, and that he had encouraged the preparation of the address by which the Parliament asked him to assume that title. But unforeseen difficulties had arisen. His chief officers, including his two sons-in-law Lambert and Fleetwood and his brother-in-law Desborough, were vehemently opposed to the title of King, and a strong adverse feeling, fanned by the officers, appeared in the army. Cromwell took five weeks to consider what course he would adopt, and ultimately refused to be made King.

By Cromwell's refusal to consent to the clause which conferred the title of King, the whole of the Petition and Advice fell to the ground. But the House took it again immediately into consideration, substituted the title of Protector for that of King, and with this alteration again presented it to Cromwell for his consent. Now, however, the Petition and Advice was passed only by a majority of three, a large number of its former supporters absenting themselves, discontented with Cromwell's refusal of the kingship. Cromwell gave his consent to the Petition and Advice, as altered, on the twenty-fifth of May, 1657.

The Petition and Advice, which now superseded the Instrument of Government, made several changes in the constitution of the Commonwealth. 1. The Protector was empowered to nominate his successor during his lifetime. 2. The Parliament was to consist of two Houses. "The other House," as the new second chamber is always called in the Petition and Advice, was to be composed of not more than seventy nor less than forty members, who in the first instance were to be nominated by the Protector and approved by the Commons' House, but who, after the first nominations, were not to be admitted to sit and vote but by the consent of the other House itself. 3. The number of members of the House of Commons and the distribution of the representation were to be newly arranged by the Parliament then sitting. It was expressly declared in the Petition and Advice that nothing contained in it dissolved the existing Parliament. 4. It was provided that no members henceforth returned to Parliament were to be excluded, except by judgment and consent of the House itself; and that forty-one commissioners were to be appointed by act of Parliament to try elections. 5. The members of the Council, who, as under the Instrument of Government, were not to exceed twenty-one in number, were to be appointed in future with the consent of the Council and of the two Houses of Parliament, and were not to be removed but by consent of Parliament. 6. After Cromwell's death, the commander-in-chief of the army and all field officers by land or generals at sea were to be appointed with consent of the Council. The Chancellor, Keeper, or Commissioners of the Great Seal of England, the Treasurer or Commissioners of the Treasury, the Admiral, the Chief Governor of Ireland, the Chancellor, Keeper, or Commissioners of the Great Seal of Ireland, the two Chief Justices and the Chief Baron in England or Ireland, the Commander-in-Chief of the Forces in

Scotland, such officers of state there as by act of Parliament in Scotland are to be approved by Parliament, and the judges in Scotland hereafter to be made, were to be approved by both Houses of Parliament. 7. The disposal of the standing forces was to be in the Protector, acting with the consent of both Houses during the sitting of Parliament, and, while Parliament was not sitting, in the Protector acting with the consent of the Council. 8. A revenue of 1,300,000*l.* per annum was settled for the support of the Government, of which 1,000,000*l.* was for the army and navy, and the remaining 300,000*l.* for the expenses of the civil government; and it was stipulated that no part of this money should be raised by a land-tax.

An "Additional and Explanatory Petition and Advice" was afterwards passed, before the House adjourned, which prescribed, amongst other things, an oath to be taken by the members of both Houses, by which they bound themselves to be faithful to the Protector, as chief magistrate of the Commonwealth, and to abstain from all designs against his person or lawful authority.

The House adjourned, under an act specially passed for the purpose, from the twenty-sixth of June, 1657 to the twentieth of January, 1658; and a clause in the act commanded the attendance on that day of all members who had been elected to the Parliament, and were qualified according to the Petition and Advice.

On the twentieth of January, 1658, two Houses of Parliament assembled.

Cromwell had nominated sixty-three members of the newly-created second House. The nomination of this

assembly, which was designed to be a body superior to
the other House, and which would naturally provoke
comparisons with the old House of Lords, was necessarily a difficult task; and it is not astonishing that
Cromwell was not successful. As on the occasion of'
his naming the Barebone's Parliament, he did his best
to procure the services of men of birth and station.
Seven English peers were called to the new House, the
Earls of Warwick, Manchester, and Mulgrave, Viscount
Say and Sele, Lords Falconbridge, Eure, and Wharton;
but of these only Lord Falconbridge, who had married
Cromwell's daughter, and Lord Eure consented to sit.
Lord Broghill, an Irish peer, afterwards Earl of Orrery, a
restless intriguer through the whole period of the Civil
War and of the Commonwealth, and afterwards in the
reign of Charles the Second, and now a zealous supporter
of Cromwell, eagerly accepted a nomination. One Scotch
peer, the Earl of Cassilis, was nominated, and did not
sit. Lord Lisle, the eldest son of the Earl of Leicester,
the two sons of Lord Say and Sele, Montagu and
Howard, were on the list, together with most of Cromwell's councillors and several of his officers. Whitelocke, St. John, and Glyn represented the law. Of his
own family, Cromwell named his two sons, Richard and
Henry, his brother-in-law Desborough, and son-in-law
Fleetwood, besides Lord Falconbridge: Lambert had
now quarrelled with him. Three of the members who
had been excluded from sitting in the Parliament in the
former year were named, Popham, Sir John Hobart, and
Sir Arthur Haselrig. Popham and Haselrig scorned the
proffered honour; and it is difficult to understand how

Cromwell could have expected Haselrig's acceptance.
Pride, Barkstead, Hewson, Goffe, Berry, and Thomas
Cooper, colonels in the army, who had originally pursued various trades, and were not men of fortune or
social position, threw ridicule on this assemblage, and the
number of the more distinguished nominees who refused
to accept their nominations reduced this new "other
House" to about forty of Cromwell's personal adherents.
The debates in the two subsequent Parliaments, of which
full reports have been preserved, show the general contempt felt for this assembly, and the large share which
this part of the new constitution had in creating difficulties for Cromwell and his successor.

Sir Anthony Ashley Cooper's name is not in the list
of Cromwell's "peers," as they came to be called. It is
clear that Cromwell had now no hope of gaining him.
It is stated, probably with truth, that Cromwell was
wont to say of Sir Anthony Ashley Cooper that he
found no one so difficult to manage as that Marcus
Tullius Cicero, the little man with three names.[1] It
would seem, as was usually the case with Cooper, that
his political opposition to Cromwell was not attended
by personal enmity. In January 1658, the fine of five
hundred pounds which had been imposed on Cooper by
the Long Parliament as a composition for delinquency,
when he came over from the King's side, appears to have
been discharged by order of Cromwell on Cooper's petition.[2] A letter written by Cooper to Henry Cromwell,
the Protector's son, in the year 1657, has been preserved,

[1] Martyn's Life, i. 168.
[2] MS. memorandum among Lord Shaftesbury's papers.

the language of which indicates the greatest intimacy.
Henry Cromwell was at that time Lord Deputy in
Ireland, and Cooper addressed to him, on September 10,
1657, the following quaint and cordial letter :—

"MY LORD AND FATHER,—I hear from my brother
Moore [1] that your Lordship blames me for not answering
a letter of yours about some business. I really profess
I received none such, or else you mought have been
assured of an answer, for there is no person in the world
more desires to retain your Lordship's affection and
good opinion. You have many love his Highness' son,
but I love Henry Cromwell, were he naked, without all
those glorious additions and titles, which, however, I
pray may continue to be increased on you.

"My Lord, I must yet this once trouble you in the
behalf of my Lord Moore, for whom you have already
done so great favours. He has now prepared his business fit for your last act of perfecting your goodness to
him, his Highness having referred it wholly to your
Lordship and the Council there. 'Tis not possible he
should buy any way but in land until his act pass, and
he have some for sale ; besides, the land he offers lies
so about Dublin, that it cannot but be convenient for
the State. If it be as they inform, I wish it in your
Lordship's possession on any pretence, and there will
be enough officious to get it confirmed yours ; but that
is only a fancy of my own on the sudden.

"My request for myself is that you love me, and ever
believe there is no manner of expression enough to tell
you how really cordial and unchangeably I am, my Lord,

---

[1] Viscount Moore of Drogheda, who had married a daughter of Lord
Spenser of Wormleighton, sister of Sir A. A. Cooper's third and present
wife : he was created Earl of Drogheda after the Restoration.

your Excellency's most devoted humble servant and
dutiful son,

"ANT. ASHLEY COOPER." [1]

When the Parliament met on the twentieth of January,
1658, under the new constitution of the "Petition and
Advice," Cooper and the other excluded members of the
year before took their seats in the House of Commons;
and they took the prescribed oath of fidelity to the Protector as chief magistrate of the Commonwealth, binding
them to abstain from all designs against his person or
lawful authority.

The addition of the excluded members made the
House of Commons altogether unmanageable for Cromwell. They had had no voice in the framing of the
Humble Petition and Advice, and they denied its
legality. On the day of meeting, the Black Rod summoned the members of the House of Commons to "the
Lords' House," and there Cromwell addressed the two
Houses in a speech beginning with "My Lords and
Gentlemen of the House of Commons." No exception
was taken at the moment to the use of the word "Lords"
on these two occasions, but two days after a message
was announced by the Serjeant from "the Lords," and
the whole question of the title, powers, privileges, and

---

[1] This letter is printed from Thurloe's State Papers, vi. 506. It
escaped Mr. Martyn, who appears to have searched the Thurloe
Papers, and who makes the following statement: "Through the whole
collection of Secretary Thurloe's papers there is no mention made of
Sir Anthony but in two letters, wherein he is suspected among others
to be well-affected to the King, and to have remitted money to him."
(Life, i. 164, note.) I have not been able to find either of these two
alleged letters; and I have no doubt that any such suspicions were
without foundation.

expediency of "the other House," was opened by the excluded members. The message was brought by two judges. Should the messengers be called in, was the first question. Some opposition made to this, lest it should be a recognition of the title "Lords" was over-ruled, and the messengers were called in, gave their message as from "the Lords," and withdrew. Then came the question, should the messengers be recalled, and told that the House would return an answer by messengers of their own. Some were for giving no answer at all, till the whole question of the other House had been considered ; others were for saying that they would return an answer to the other House by mes-sengers of their own, to show that they did not recognise the title "Lords ;" others again were for sending answer simply that they would consider of the message. But it was carried on a division by seventy-five votes to fifty-one that the Speaker should inform the messengers that the House would send an answer by messengers of their own. It was understood that the whole question of the other House would be debated in debating the answer to be sent.

This had taken place on Friday, the twenty-second, and on Monday, the twenty-fifth, Cromwell sent to both Houses to attend him in the Banqueting House, and addressing them this time, " My Lords and Gentlemen of the two Houses of Parliament," made a long speech on the difficulties of public affairs, and the necessity of union. But it was of no use. The House of Commons, on the twenty-eighth, appointed a Committee to attend Cromwell and inform him, among other things, " that

this House will take the matters imparted to them by
his Highness in his speech at the Banqueting House
into serious and speedy consideration ;" and Cromwell
highly resented that the House of Commons should
take upon itself to answer singly a speech which he had
addressed to both Houses.   Still it was of no use.   The
House resolved to enter on no private business for a
month, that they might devote themselves entirely to
the consideration of the Government.   They proceeded
to debate the message from the other House, and this
debate went on from day to day till the fourth of
February, when Cromwell, seeing yet no probability of
an answer being returned to the " Lords' " message, dissolved the Parliament.

A member of this Parliament made copious notes of
the debates, which have been preserved and published.[1]
Sir Anthony Ashley Cooper took an active and leading
part in the opposition to the new constitution and the
new House of Lords.   Five speeches of his are reported
in the debates on the message from the other House,
and summaries are given of very many more of his
speeches in the following Parliament under Richard
Cromwell's short Protectorate.   Though all these reports are little more than skeletons of argument, and
the reporter has not taken pains with the language or to
preserve the speaker's style, they yet bear unmistakeably
the impress of that nervous and subtle oratory, of some

---

[1] In the work known as the Diary of Thomas Burton, edited by J.
T. Rutt, 4 vols. 1828.   Mr. Carlyle has raised doubts as to whether
the member was Burton, member for Westmoreland, and suggests that
it was more probably a Mr. Bacon (Cromwell's Letters and Speeches,
ii. 545).   The matter is not clear, one way or the other.

of whose efforts finished reports have been handed down
to us, and which, in the stormy days of the reign of
Charles the Second, rendered Shaftesbury so formidable
a leader of opposition.

The first position taken by Cooper in these debates
was that the House had to consider, not only what
answer they should return, but whether they should
return any answer at all. "Some," he said, "are neither
for another House nor for the title ; and if you put the
question to return an answer to the other House, you
tacitly admit such a House without further debate." [1]
The next day he seconded a motion of Sir Arthur
Haselrig's to have the question considered in Grand
Committee, that is, in a Committee of the whole House,
in which every member might speak on the same motion
any number of times, and every vote of which would
have to be reported to and re-affirmed by the House.
This motion was not carried, and the debate then turned
on what the first question to be decided should be,
the substance of the answer to be given or the title by
which the other House should be addressed.   Cooper
made a speech in support of first considering the title,
which is thus quaintly reported : " I apprehend nobody
speaks of that notion which I have in my head.   Your
order is very nice.   You have a message from the Lords,
brought by the judges from the Lords.   Unusual causes
produce unusual effects, and nothing so ordinary to
philosophers as to meet with such.   I would rather have
us consider from whom that message is, and we can
better tell what answer to return." [2]   After a long day's

[1] Burton's Diary, ii. 378, January 23.   [2] Ib. ii. 401, Jan. 30.

debate, the House decided that the title should be first considered. Haselrig then again tried to obtain a Committee of the whole House, and Cooper again supported him. He followed the Solicitor-General, Ellis, who had made a learned argument to show that, though the words "House of Lords" did not occur in the Humble Petition and Advice, it was clearly intended that "the other House" should be a House of Lords. Cooper's speech is thus reported. "I move to be turned into a Grand Committee for three or four days. There is a great deal more in it than appears. Admit Lords, and admit all. It is fit that laws should be plain for the people. We know what advantage the supreme magistrate and the other House always get by the learned's interpretation of them."[1] By "admit Lords, and admit all," Cooper doubtless meant that the admission of the name would involve the admission of a House of Lords according to the old constitution, for such is his argument in a second speech on this question of a Grand Committee, the last and the longest of his speeches in this short session. He is then reported as follows, February 3:—

"I am not of their opinion, that say there is nothing in the name, and that, if you could get over that, the fact would not stick; but better abstain from that than the people suffer. You are now upon the brink and border of settlement, and, if you go further, it may be you cannot stand. There is nothing but a compliment to call a man Lord; but if one call himself lord of my manor, I shall be loth to give him

[1] Burton, ii. 419, Feb. 2.

the title, lest he claim the manor. The gentlemen
of the long robe will tell you there is much in names.
The word King, they know, carries all. Words are the
keys of the cabinet of things. Let us first take the
people's jewels out before you part with that cabinet.
If we part with all first, when you come to abatement,
it is a question how you will redeem them. It was told
you by a learned gentleman that the writ makes them
no more than the Instrument[1] makes them, for the
Instrument makes them not peers for life, as the writ
does not. It is very clear. We are told it revives the
old Lords' House. I would fain know where the words
of revival be. The gentlemen of the long robe say
nothing of a revival."

Then with abrupt transition he answers another argument, that there must be some mode of address from the
one House to the other.

" There must be a way of address. I see no such
necessity, by the last Instrument. You passed laws
without the peers' consent after so many days. The
negative voice was denied the King. You know it was.
Thus laws passed without the King's concurrence. Consider, let us not lay foundations that we may repent.
They must be extant for the future." [2]

On the day on which this last speech was made, the
House divided on the question whether the motion for a
Grand Committee should be put, and the numbers were
equal. The Speaker was about to give his casting vote,
which would probably have been with the Noes, when

---

[1] The Humble Petition and Advice.
[2] Burton, ii. 435, February 3.

Mr. Fagg, member for Sussex, stood up and asserted that he and another member, Colonel Grosvenor, had entered the House before the question was put, but that their votes had not been counted. Mr. Fagg's vote was allowed, and added to the Ayes, so that the first question was carried. But the main question was immediately afterwards negatived by ninety-three votes to eighty-seven. It was therefore decided not to go into Grand Committee. Sir Anthony Ashley Cooper was one of the tellers for the Ayes in the division on the main question.

On the day following this close division, Cromwell, dissatisfied with the small majority, dissolved the Parliament. This was Oliver Cromwell's last Parliament. Seven months after the dissolution, on the third of September, 1658, he died.

The Petition and Advice had empowered Cromwell to declare, during his lifetime, his successor in the Protectorship; and soon after this power was confirmed, he had nominated in writing his son-in-law Fleetwood. But differences afterwards arose between Cromwell and Fleetwood, and now, on his death-bed, Oliver verbally nominated his eldest son Richard his successor, in the presence of Fiennes, the first Commissioner of the Great Seal, Thurloe, and three other witnesses. The paper in which Fleetwood had been more formally appointed was at the same time searched for by Cromwell's desire, but could not be found. Fleetwood, however, afterwards waived all claims arising out of this document, if it should be found; and Richard took his father's place without dispute.

From the dissolution of the Parliament in February till Oliver Cromwell's death in September we have no information about Cooper; but we find him again a member of the Parliament soon called by Richard Cromwell, and there waging as fierce a war as he had waged under Oliver against the Petition and Advice and its House of Lords.

CHAPTER VI.

1658—1659.

Richard Cromwell proclaimed Protector—The military commanders jealous of his civilian advisers—A Parliament called for January 27, 1659—Members for England and Wales elected under old constitution —Scotch and Irish members according to Instrument of Government, but not to sit till approved—Cromwell's peers summoned by writs of old House of Lords—Cooper elected for Wiltshire and Poole—Sits for Wiltshire—Debates on bill for recognition of Richard Cromwell s Protector—Cooper's many speeches—The "Other House"—Question of transacting with it—Cooper's long speech against time—Cooper's taunts against one of Cromwell's peers for changes—His abuse of Cromwell—House of Commons agrees to transact with other House during this Parliament—Unsuccessful attempt to settle revenue on Richard Cromwell—Message to other House as to a day of humiliation—Discussions thereon—Quarrel between Richard Cromwell and the military chiefs—Resolutions of House of Commons against the army—Richard Cromwell orders dissolution of Council of Officers—Fleetwood and Desborough rally the army, and force Richard Cromwell to dissolve Parliament—Fall of Richard Cromwell.

THE Council assembled immediately after Cromwell's death, and unanimously resolved to recognise his death-bed nomination of his eldest son Richard as his successor. His brother-in-law Fleetwood, the Lieutenant-General of the army, cordially concurred in this decision, declaring that, if the written instrument by which he had been nominated should hereafter be found, he would regard it as null. Desborough, the brother-in-law of Oliver, and the next in position to Fleetwood of the military commanders, while his

superior in energy and influence, also zealously supported in the Council Richard's succession. On the
following day Richard Cromwell was proclaimed Protector in London, without the slightest sign of opposition. The support of Fleetwood and Desborough had
carried that of the army. No opposition appeared in
any part of the Commonwealth, in England, Scotland,
or Ireland. Henry Cromwell, who governed as Deputy
in Ireland, gave a willing support to his brother. Monk,
the Commander-in-Chief in Scotland, declared his more
important adhesion. Addresses of congratulation came
in succession from all the counties and cities of the
three countries, and from the army.[1] The Royalists and
Republicans, who had both hoped that the death of
Cromwell would make an opening for their respective
causes, saw with surprise the tranquil succession of
Richard; and for a few months it seemed as if the
feeble Richard, succeeding by a doubtful title to an
usurped power, was to retain it free from the troubles
and difficulties which had ever vexed and thwarted the
great mind of Oliver.

The support of the army had placed Richard where
he was. From the army came the first sign of trouble;
and the army ultimately displaced him. The military
chiefs, who had zealously supported his succession to
the Protectorship, thought that, as he was a civilian, he
ought to relinquish the command-in-chief of the army,
and wished him to transfer it to Fleetwood. The army
generally approved this idea. Richard, counselled by

[1] Phillips's Continuation of Sir R. Baker's Chronicle, pp. 635, 636, ed. 1684.

Thurloe, Fiennes, St. John, Pierpoint, and other civilians, and following also the advice of Monk, resisted the proposals of the officers, and determined to retain in his own hands the command of the army.[1] Fleetwood, Desborough, and their friends, now became jealous of the influence of Richard's civilian counsellors, and complained that they themselves were treated with ingratitude. Richard hoped that by calling a Parliament, which the wants of his treasury rendered absolutely necessary, he should bring to his side a power which would hold in check the rising turbulence of the military chiefs.

Writs were issued for a Parliament to meet on the twenty-seventh of January, 1659. Some difficulties had presented themselves to the Council as regards the election of this Parliament. The last Parliament had not made a new scheme of representation, as the Humble Petition and Advice had enjoined. How then were the members of the House of Commons to be elected—according to the scheme of the extinct Instrument of Government, or according to the old law of England? But under the old constitution, Scotland and Ireland were not united with England, and there was no law for the election of Scotch and Irish members to a common Parliament. The Council determined that the members for England and Wales should be elected according to the old law of the land, and that thirty members, the

---

[1] Other leading advisers of Richard Cromwell were Dr. Wilkins, afterwards Bishop of Chester, Lord Broghill, afterwards Earl of Orrery, Colonel Philip Jones, and George Montagu, second son of the Earl of Manchester (Ludlow, ii. 632 ; Pepys's Diary, i. 104 ; Clarendon State Papers, iii. 421, 423).

number prescribed by the Instrument of Government, should be elected severally for Scotland and Ireland according to the provisions of that constitution, but that they should not be admitted to sit till the consent of the members for England and Wales was given. With regard to the "other House," a question arose as to the way in which they were to be summoned, and it was determined to summon them by the same writs as had been in use for the House of Lords, under the old constitution. Those whom Oliver Cromwell had nominated members of the "other House" were summoned, without any addition.[1]

The reason for reverting to the old constitution for the election of the English members was doubtless that it gave more scope for the exercise of government influence than the more popular scheme of representation which had been provided by the Instrument of Government. Richard Cromwell soon found trouble, where he had sought help. An indefatigable Opposition, composed of Republicans and Presbyterians, among the latter of whom many were now looking to the restoration of the royal family, and some were secretly in correspondence with the royal exile, endeavoured to reopen the whole question of the constitution and Richard Cromwell's power; and in three short months, Fleetwood and the army suppressed the Parliament and drove Richard Cromwell from the Protectorate.

Sir Anthony Ashley Cooper was returned to this Parliament for Wiltshire and for Poole. For Poole there was a double return, which was decided in his

---

[1] Ludlow, ii. 616.

favour; and he elected, after this decision, to sit for Wiltshire.[1]

The same member whose reports enabled us accurately to trace Cooper's course in the last session of Oliver Cromwell's last Parliament, continued to take copious notes in the present one; and we find Cooper a constant and leading speaker in opposition. The Diarist records Cooper's first coming into the House, on the fifth of February, as if he were a man of much consequence.[2]

A few days after the Parliament met, a bill for the recognition of Richard Cromwell's title was proposed to the House of Commons by Thurloe, the Secretary of State. The introduction of this bill led to protracted discussions, in which every objection that casuistry could suggest was employed by the opponents of the Government. The bill having been read a second time without a division, a debate was immediately opened by Haselrig on the question of going into committee, which lasted from the seventh of February to the fourteenth. The validity of the Humble Petition and Advice,

[1] Comm. Journ. March 30, 1659 ; Burton, iv. 308.
[2] Burton, iii. 80. Attention was called this day (Feb. 5) to Ludlow's sitting in the House without taking the prescribed oath, and a debate arose, which was interrupted by a member noticing the presence of a man named King, who had been sitting in the House not having been elected a member, and distributing pamphlets among the members. It was moved to send King to the Tower ; several members, and among others Sir A. A. Cooper, suggested Newgate, arguing that to send him to the Tower would be to give him too much importance. It was resolved to send him to Newgate. He was discharged two days after, being adjudged mad. The debate about Ludlow was not resumed, and he managed to continue to sit without taking the oath. (Memoirs, ii. 619.) Later, on the same day, a motion was made to appoint a Committee about the maintenance of clergymen in Wales. Cooper spoke, and is thus reported : " There is a vast treasure arising out of these revenues. I never heard of any account. I have passed through Wales, and found churches all unsupplied, except a few grocers or such persons that have formerly served for two years."

enacted by a Parliament from which a large number
of members had been excluded, was again impugned. It
was argued that Cromwell's nomination of his son
Richard by word of mouth on his death-bed, and not
by a written instrument, was insufficient, even if the
validity of the Humble Petition and Advice were admitted. Abuse and derision were lavished on the so-
styled House of Lords. It was contended that the bill
should confirm the people's rights and the privileges of
the House of Commons at the same time that it confirmed the Protector's title, and a preliminary resolution
limiting the Protector's powers and securing the House
of Commons in the two points of the "militia" and the
" negative voice " was called for. Verbal questions were
raised, such as those which had made so large a part of
the discussions on the Instrument of Government in
1654 : it having been proposed, for instance, to "recognise " Richard Cromwell as Protector, the Opposition
contended that the word " recognise " implied a power
independent of the Parliament, and proposed to substitute " declare ;" by way of compromise, the Government party added "declare" to "recognise," and
withdrew the word " undoubted " before " Protector," to
which the Opposition had made great objections.[1] Such
were the topics urged by a multitude of speakers, chiefly
Republicans, during an eight days' debate. Cooper
warmly supported the proposal for a resolution saving
the rights of the Parliament, and suggested the passing
of another resolution, such as had been passed in

[1] Some members objected to "recognise," as a French word.
Ludlow says that some proposed to "agnize." (Memoir, ii. 634.)

discussing the Instrument of Government in 1654, that nothing should be binding till the whole bill was passed. Cooper's speech is thus reported:—

"You have the same state of things now before you as you had in the Parliament of 1654, our judgments differing. A recognition was then proposed. It was said that it was not consistent with the care, wisdom, and gravity of this House, to pass the interest of the single person but with the interest of the people. At length a previous vote was agreed upon, that nothing in that should be of force, unless the whole did pass. That which is now proposed is thought impracticable, but it was not so then.

"You are now upon a Petition and Advice which it is told you is a law, and if you say so, the judges will say so. Never was so absolute a government. If the Florentine and he that sate in the great chair of the world [1] had all met together, they could not have made anything so absolute. Is there not another House sitting that claims a negative over you? When you have passed this, what is wanting? Nothing but monies.

"State the case. The Petition and Advice is necessary to stand. A Parliament is freely chosen, and we

---

[1] Machiavel and Pope Alexander the Sixth. There is doubtless an omission here, as "all" must refer to more than two. The omission may be supplied from a speech of Mr. Hobart, later in the debates, and from a passage in Slingsby Bethel's "Narrative" of this Parliament. Mr. Hobart is reported as saying, February 28: "For this Petition and Advice, if Pope Alexander and Cardinal Cæsar Borgia and Machiavel should all consent together, they could not lay a foundation for a more absolute tyranny." (Diary, iii. 543). Bethel, in his Narrative of the proceedings of this Parliament, printed in the sixth volume of the Somers Tracts speaks of the Opposition party as "showing that if Pope Alexander the Sixth, Cæsar Borgia, and their cabal had all laid their heads together, they could not have framed a thing more dangerous and destructive to the liberty of the people than is the Petition and Advice."

own it. We go home by some necessity of state. Then
does not the Petition and Advice outlive us ? This may
happen, and produce inconveniences to us ; to the Protector none. Is not this security to him that he shall
be put in the great *magna charta* ?

" If the Petition and Advice by piece-meal comes to
be confirmed, we may not feel the smart of the Petition
and Advice in this man's time. It may happen in
another's. It may not sound well in after ages, to have
things so uncertain and liable to disputes. The laws
left doubtful, we have not been faithful to his Highness.

" I move to assert his authority together with the
liberty of the people. This will be security and indemnity to all. Put the case, that you should vote him
Chief Magistrate only, and then leave him to the ancient
laws to expound what that means. Shall we not leave
him to those ancient doubts and disputes which have
cost us so much blood ?

" Englishmen's minds are free, and better taught in
their liberties now than ever. A Parliament cannot
enslave the people. It may happen in after ages that
the people may claim their liberties over again. I
would have the addition and the question go all together. We have left a bone of contention to posterity,
I fear. We may rise before all be perfected, for some
reason of state. It is not against the orders of the
House to put them together. I would have them put
together. Let them go hand in hand." [1]

Later, he made a short speech against the word
" recognise," arguing that it would take in the whole
Petition and Advice : " The word recognise goes to
things, and not to persons. I appeal to the long-robe

[1] Burton, iii. 227, Feb. 11.

men, if recognise take not in all the laws, Petition and
Advice, and all powers given by that."[1] And again, it
having been urged that to carry a preliminary restriction
in the interest of the people would really be doing
nothing, as unless a clause to the same effect were
carried in committee, nothing would be secured in the
bill, Cooper replied that there would be no record in the
Journals of a clause proposed in committee and rejected :
" Votes will remain on our books when we are gone, and
it will appear that we had also care of the people. You
will have it committed, and nothing appear. I would
have both appear on our books together."[2]

On the fourteenth of February, immediately after this
last short speech of Cooper's, two resolutions were
adopted by the House. The first, "that it be part of
this bill to recognise and declare his Highness, Richard,
Lord Protector, to be the Lord Protector and Chief
Magistrate of England, Scotland, and Ireland, and the
dominions and territories thereunto belonging," was
carried on a division by 223 votes to 134. After this
resolution was carried, Mr. Trevor, one of Richard
Cromwell's party, who became Secretary of State under
Charles the Second, offered a resolution "that before
this bill be committed, this House do declare such additional clauses to be part of the bill as may bound the
power of the Chief Magistrate, and fully secure the
rights and privileges of Parliament and the liberties and
rights of the people; and that neither this nor any other
previous vote that is or shall be passed in order to this
bill shall be of force or binding to the people until the

---

[1] Burton, iii. 276, Feb. 14.   [2] Ibid. iii. 286, Feb. 14.

whole bill be passed." This resolution, which was
intended as a concession to the Opposition, was passed
without a division, Thurloe alone saying " No " to it.

The consideration of the additional clauses was begun
on the seventeenth.[1] The Opposition were for beginning
with the limits of the Protector's power, and more particularly with the question of his veto, or negative voice;
the Government party contended, on the other hand,
that the question of the other House should be first
settled. Cooper, as usual, sided with the Opposition :—

" The bounding the single person is the most proper
thing in debate, and I apprehended we had now been
upon the Chief Magistrate's limitations. It is objected
that men cannot vote unless they know whether there
shall be another House. That objection is made as if
we were constituting a new commonwealth. If that
should be, then, unless you know what power your
single person shall have, how will you declare the power
of the other House, for this will still lie in your way ?
I have not heard that debated yet, whether we are upon
the footing of the Petition and Advice, or on a new
foundation, or on the old Constitution. I think we are
yet to be supposed to be upon the foot of the old Constitution, unless something appears to the contrary.

[1] On February 16, a motion was made by Mr. Bulkeley, a supporter
of Richard Cromwell's Government, to accuse Henry Nevil, the well-
known Republican, and author of "Plato Redivivus," of atheism and
blasphemy. The object was to prove Nevill disqualified to sit, the
existing law requiring that members should be " persons fearing God
and of good conversation," and thus to get rid of an Opposition member. Many defended Nevill, and objected to such a charge being made
on hearsay : among others Cooper, who said: "A motion of this nature
ought to be made clearly out. To make a man an offender for a word
is hard. Manifest and open offences may be punished with more
severity. I would have the charge clear, that the defence may also
be clear and certain." (Burton, iii. 300.) In the end, after an
animated four hours' debate, the matter was dropped.

Therefore, I would not have us surprised in a vote. We may by this put a limitation upon this that we mean not of, and, instead of bounding the Supreme Magistrate, be rather bounding the liberty of parliaments." [1]

It was decided by an overwhelming majority, 217 to 86, that the question of the other House should be taken first.

The next day it was resolved without a division that it should be part of the bill to declare that the Parliament consisted of two Houses. Then came the question of the powers of the second House. A discursive debate arose on this question. Various members of the Opposition contended for the rights of the old House of Lords, at any rate for the rights of those of its members who had not forfeited for delinquency. Some of the Government party, by way of avoiding this question, proposed that it should at once be resolved that the members of the other House should not be hereditary; others proposed to take into consideration the powers of the other House, and to begin with the judicial powers. Cooper spoke for determining first whether the other House should consist of the old Lords or of Cromwell's nominees, before entering into the question of their powers:—

"If you would have us all of one mind, your question must be as clear as may be. The first question ought to be, whether there be a right or no: for where there is a right (in all the actions of a man's life) there is a duty; and then matter of convenience or inconvenience

[1] Burton, iii. 335, Feb. 18.

is out of doors. Two rights are offered to be in being :
one of the old Lords; the other of the other House, or
new Lords, who have already a vast power in their
hands, and dangerous to the people. Some tell you the
right of one House, some of another. I offer it to you
that it is not fit, and if it may not be dangerous, to
prejudge or preclude either of their rights, before you
agree to the persons. If there be a right, then all their
boundaries must be offered to them, whether they will
pass them or not ; and I have seldom found men in
power to part with it on easy terms. It is therefore
necessary to be decided, how far we are to deliberate
and restrain them in this point. Seeing great rights are
claimed on both sides, let me be satisfied in that point
first, before I can give my vote. The consideration of
the persons is most natural. One while it is argued for
right, *pro* and *con*, and persons differ ; and then they
fly off to conveniency. Matter of right and conveniency
are two different things. Therefore, now take into consideration these two claims. Consider first whether the
old Lords or new Lords have a right or no, and then go
on to bound them."[1]

[1] Burton, iii. 418, Feb. 22. On the previous day, Cooper had
joined in urging the release from prison of George Villiers, Duke of
Buckingham, on the engagement of his father-in-law, Lord Fairfax.
This Duke, who became very celebrated in the next reign, and closely
connected in politics with Shaftesbury, both in the so-called Cabal
ministry and afterwards, had been sent to the Tower by Oliver Cromwell in August, 1658, as a royalist intriguer ; and he was now a prisoner in Windsor Castle. Cooper said he had "not so much as a
correspondence with this person," with whom in the next reign he
was so intimately associated. He urged strongly the claims of Fairfax
on the gratitude and respect of the Parliament. "Let it not be thought,
whatever is in our hearts, that we shall have ingratitude to that
person that offered the petition. The care that Lord Fairfax will have
of him in his family will be beyond all security you can care for. You
may well trust him." Buckingham was released, on his engagement
on his honour at the bar of the House, and on Lord Fairfax's engagement in £20,000, for his quiet behaviour and abstinence from intrigues
against the Government. (Burton, iii. 370.)

One of the Court party now proposed that the question should be, whether the House would transact with the other House now sitting, as with a House of Parliament: and on this question a discussion lasted for nine days. Arthur Annesley, the future Earl of Anglesey, a leading member of the Presbyterian party, proposed an addition to the question of a clause saving the rights of the old Peers. Cooper spoke zealously both against the proposal to transact and against Annesley's saving clause :—

"As to the old Lords, it is the way to destroy their rights which you take to pursue them. This is a saving that destroys the right. You bar their claim utterly by this, whereas you know not but their claim may come in more clearly. You make them and their interest your everlasting enemies. A few new men, but in the room of old men, what will the nation say? Let us consider what we can say to posterity. The remaining part of that famous Long Parliament would in the issue have rendered their designs famous. Your laws and liberties are all gone. Two negatives are in one hand. An army is in your legislature, and 1,300,000*l.* per annum for ever. To say that a law made under force shall be a good law, and binding in reason, is against all reason. That about the Bill of Sales is but *argumentum ad hominem.* If our neighbours say we look well, that will not satisfy; we must examine if we be well. I have sat sixteen years here, ventured my life and bought lands, and my friends and interest have done so. I always hoped, whenever you came to settlement, you would confirm all these sales. True, a possessory title of Chief Magistrate was never questioned in Parliament, but this is upon another foot, the Petition and Advice.

Now are you satisfied of that claim? Is there that
done that will pass 40*l.* per annum, and yet are passing
three nations into the hands of some few persons to
them and their heirs for ever? If there be a necessity
upon us now, where will the necessity be afterwards?
Where will be our posterity? You might have had as
good a government three hundred years ago. What are
you at present but a House of Parliament and a single
person? Is there any such difference than when the
Parliament was in 54? You must either transact, it is
said, with them, or you must not transact at all. There
is no such need. Are we bound to this or that other
House? We are not bound. It may be they will sit
without us. I had rather they did so and raised money,
than that we should so bind ourselves as to be but
bailiffs and servants to them. It is but a shoeing-horn
to tell us the right of the old Lords is preserved by this.
I cannot consent to transact, because it is against the
rights of others, the rights of this House, and the rights
of the nation. If you think you have no need of bounds
nor approving, pass your question singly, and then I
am sure you are bound for ever. If you will put it, put
it singly. It shall have my negative."[1]

And again :—

"It is impossible to save the rights of others, if you

[1] Burton, iv. 50, March 7. On March 4, Cooper had made a short
speech on the same subject : "I would not have things misrepresented
to the House. I was here last Parliament, and the constitution of the
other House was disputed all along, and their co-ordinate power
denied still, else we had not been so soon dissolved." (iv. 14.) On
February 24, he had made a long speech, on a proposal by Thurloe,
the Secretary, to equip a fleet for support of a mediation by England
in the war between Sweden and Denmark, objecting to leaving the
question in the hands of the Protector and Council, as was proposed,
and claiming the power of peace and war for the Parliament. It was
ultimately referred to the Protector to prepare a fleet, with a proviso,
"saving the interest of this House in the militia and in making of
peace and war." (Burton, iii. 465, 493.)

own these upon that foot that they are. You cannot alter
one bit of it without their consent. Their number is to
be but seventy. If sixty already, how can that clause
of yours be practised or put in execution? Now this
may be mended, but when you have once owned them,
you must stay their leisure. If these would give their
places to old Lords, there is one negative upon you still;
so you put two bars before their rights—to bring in
the old Lords upon the Petition and Advice : upon that
foot, I should for ever abhor them, and myself for doing
it. Upon this new foot, you cannot restore them;
though I honour them as much as any man, and wish
they were restored, but rather never see a Lord than
have them on such a foot. I would have the question
put singly, that we may not be surprised in our votes."[1]

Almost immediately after this speech, Annesley's proviso was put to the vote, and was carried by a majority of
seven. The main question for transacting was then about
to be put, when the Commonwealth men, seeing how
close the last division had been, called attention to the
Scotch and Irish members, and required that their right
to vote should be inquired into and decided upon before
any further proceedings were taken. The Court party
opposed this, but were obliged to give way; and it was
not until the twenty-eighth of March that, the right of
the Scotch and Irish members having been affirmed
after very long debates, the question of transacting with
the other House was resumed.[2]   Then another proposed

---

[1] Burton, iv. 83, March 8.
[2] Cooper had been active in the discussions on the right of the Scotch
and Irish members, doing of course all he could, as an opponent of the
Government, to prevent their being recognised. He spoke on March
9, 18, and 22, on this question. On March 9, a motion being made by
Mr. Bulkeley, during the debate about the Scotch and Irish members,

addition to the question was discussed, the effect of which would have been to postpone the transacting with the other House until it had been approved and bounded by that House. Cooper supported.this addition.

"I have observed the fortune of the old Peers, that the saving of their rights is the asserting of the rights of these, which is the most destructive to them that can be. It is clearly a putting others in their place, and is setting up a thing that is quite contrary. The saving of their rights is the clear proscription of their rights. You are upon the greatest piece of prerogative that ever was. At once you give him a whole negative in this other House. You give him the greatest prerogative that ever Prince had. While you have an eye to the other House, you overlook one whole negative, and reserve but half a negative to yourself. I think that those additions of bounding and approving do well suit with the new Constitution, and reach not the old."[1]

This proposal was rejected, and then the House came to the main question. Scot now moved to insert the words "during this present Parliament," and this

to declare any attempt either on the person of the Protector or on the House to be high treason, Cooper urged the postponement. "I like the thing very well, but it comes not in seasonably. Be the thing never so good, it ought not to break in upon this debate. Divert not upon this question." On March 16, he warmly supported a motion for releasing Major-General Overton from imprisonment in Jersey, and annulling the warrant under Cromwell's hand by which he had been committed in 1655. "I would not only have the warrant voted illegal, but the causes expressed, that it may appear upon your books, which will not appear by the warrant. I would have it further added, as another cause, that he was sent where a *habeas corpus* will not reach him. I am clearly of opinion, and all the long-robe at the Committee of Guernsey are of that opinion, that a *habeas corpus* lies not to Jersey. I would have a precedent. The case of Berwick differs much from it. They are a part of England, and send burgesses hither." (Burton, iv. 158.)

[1] Burton, iv. 284, March 28.

motion was supported by Cooper in a long speech, which was regarded by the Diarist as one against time. " Sir Anthony Ashley Cooper," he says, " made a long speech till the House was fuller of those of his party, and moved to second the motion that they be but for this Parliament, and would have them bounded in time."[1] This speech was afterwards printed in full, and separately published, and, if it was delivered as printed, was a very elaborate oration, intended to pro- duce a great effect. It is a very fierce attack on the existing order of things, on Oliver Cromwell, and on "the other House;" and some individuals among Crom- well's Lords are singled out for bitter personality. The whole speech may be read at the end of the volume :[2] one extract will here suffice :—

" What I shall speak of their quality, or anything else concerning them, I would be thought to speak with distinction, and to intend only of the major part; for I acknowledge, Mr. Speaker, the mixture of the other House to be like the composition of apothccaries, who mix something grateful to the taste to qualify their bitter drugs, which else, perhaps, would be immediately spit out and never swallowed. So, Sir, his Highness of deplorable memory to this nation, to countenance as well the want of quality as of honesty in the rest, has nominated some against whom there lies no other reproach but only that nomination ; but not out of any respect to their quality or regard to their virtues, but

---

[1] Burton, iv. 286. The Diarist remarks that ncither Haselrig nor Vane was in the House on this occasion, but that Haselrig came in at one o'clock and Vane later. The opponents of the Government had endeavoured, just before Cooper made his long speech, to obtain an adjournment of the House for an hour, but had not succeeded.
[2] Appendix IV.

out of regard to the no-quality, the no-virtues of the
rest; which truly, Mr. Speaker, if he had not done,
we could easily have given a more express name to this
other House than he hath been pleased to do : for we
know a house designed for beggars and malefactors is
a house of correction, and so termed by our law; but,
Mr. Speaker, setting those few persons aside, who, I
hope, think the nomination a disgrace—and their ever
coming to sit there a much greater—can we without
indignation think of the rest? He, who is first in their
roll, a condemned coward; one that out of fear and
baseness did once what he could to betray our liberties,
and now does the same for gain.[1] The second, a person
of as little sense as honesty; preferred for no other
reason but his no-worth, his no-conscience; except
cheating his father of all he had was thought a virtue
by him, who by sad experience we find hath done as
much for his mother—his country. The third, a Cavalier,
a Presbyterian, an Independent; for the Republic, for
a Protector, for everything, for nothing, but only that
one thing—money.[2] It were endless, Sir, to run through
them all; to tell you of the lordships of seventeen
pounds a year land of inheritance; of the farmer lordships, draymen lordships, cobbler lordships,[3] without one

[1] Nathaniel Fiennes, second son of Viscount Saye and Sele, who had,
in the beginning of the Civil War, surrendered Bristol to the King's
army without making any defence, and had been condemned to death
by a court-martial, but pardoned by the Earl of Essex, the General-in-
chief. He was now first Commissioner of the Great Seal, and one of
Richard Cromwell's chief advisers. His father and a younger brother,
John, were also named by Cromwell members of the House of Lords :
the father did not sit.

[2] Supposed to be Lord Broghill, after the Restoration created Earl
of Orrery; a poet and play-writer, as well as a versatile and ambitious
politician.

[3] Colonel Pride, one of the lords, had been a brewer, and is said to
have begun as a drayman; and Colonel Hewson, another lord, had been
a shoemaker.

foot of land but what the blood of Englishmen has been the price of. These, Sir, are to be our rulers, these the judges of our lives and fortunes ; to these we are to stand bare, whilst their pageant lordships deign to give us a conference on their breeches. Mr. Speaker, we have already had too much experience how insupportable servants are when they become our masters. All kinds of slavery are miserable in the account of generous minds ; but that which comes accompanied with scorn and contempt stirs up every man's indignation, and is endured by none whom nature does not intend for slaves as well as fortune."

It has been suggested that this speech was too strong to have been either spoken or at the time published ;[1] but there is a multitude of speeches equally strong reported in the Diary which has been so often quoted ; and as to publication, there would have been no obstacle a month later, after Richard Cromwell's fall ; indeed it is probably then that the speech was published. As a composition, the published speech is remarkable ; and, like the published speeches of Shaftesbury's later career, it gives manifold proofs of the author's literary ability. The strong language against Oliver Cromwell, from one who had for a time acted with him and been of his Council, is either revolting inconsistency, or to be taken as a proof that he had conscientiously given his support to Cromwell in the hope of obtaining through him a settlement of the nation under a good government, and had afterwards conscientiously withdrawn from him, because unable to approve his measures. It has been

---

[1] By the editors of the old " Parliamentary History."

seen that there is no certain knowledge of the causes of Cooper's separation from Cromwell. It is difficult to understand how Cooper, with all his changes, could have ventured to reproach any one else as " a Cavalier, a Presbyterian, an Independent ; for the Republic, for a Protector, for everything," even though his conscience acquitted him of liability to be justly assailed in return with the culminating taunt,—" for nothing, but only that one thing—money." Cooper's pecuniary disinterestedness could not be called in question. It may be fairly said that such vehement reproaches could not have been publicly uttered by one who had been a tool or flatterer of Cromwell, or under personal obligations to him, for very many would be eager to retort upon him and expose his own political changes ; and there is no sign in the copious reports of the Diary of Cooper's being twitted by any of his numerous adversaries in the House with inconsistency or ingratitude. In one of his speeches in this Parliament he had openly expressed his regret at Cromwell's violent dissolution of the Rump, declaring his belief that "the remaining part of that famous long Parliament would in the issue have rendered their designs famous." How easy would it have been for any Government supporter to reproach him in reply with having accepted, soon after this dissolution, a nomination to the Barebone's Parliament, and having then again soon after aided in establishing the Protectorate ! And, had he been so reproached, how natural a defence that, regretting Cromwell's conduct, he had thought it his duty as a good citizen to give aid in making the best of the situation, and 1 ad aided Cromwell as long as his conscience permitted, but no longer!

The additional words proposed by Scot and supported by Cooper, for limiting the recognition of the other House to the term of duration of the present Parliament, were carried ; and after an unsuccessful attempt, which Cooper also supported, to strengthen the limitation by further words, "and no longer unless confirmed by Act of Parliament," the question of transacting with the other House was at last brought to an issue, and the following resolution was affirmed on the 28th of March by 198 votes to 125: "That this House will transact with the persons now sitting in the other House as a House of Parliament during this present Parliament, and that it is not hereby intended to exclude such peers as have been faithful to the Parliament from their privilege of being duly summoned as members of that House."

No sooner had the question of the "other House" been disposed of, and it had been settled to transact with them, than Mr. Bulkeley, one of the constant supporters of the Government, proposed, on the twenty-ninth of March, a bill for settling taxes for the life of Richard Cromwell, Protector, and for a certain time after his death. The proposal was strongly opposed, and by none more strongly than Cooper. He opposed the introduction of the bill, but unsuccessfully: a few days later he proposed by way of amendment a resolution that after the end or other determination of the Parliament, no law of excise should be of force, and no excise should be levied. His speech on this occasion is thus reported :—

" Will you settle this revenue, and not in the body
of your government, to see what your money shall go
to support ? It is not yet said what hand you shall
have in anything. Once declare money, they may go
on without you.

" The money [that] is paid already, I would have
you put no discountenance upon it. Make a previous
vote, that after this present parliament none shall pre-
sume to levy this duty. That will keep it afoot this
parliament; and in the mean time, you may settle it.
Nobody can complain why they want money if we be
dissolved. If you have not time to grant it, and be
willing to it, you are excused.

" I shall offer this previous vote; and he read it
and put it to the table. He said it was not his own,
but Mr. Nevill's. 'Resolved and declared, that no law
for excise shall be of force, nor excise levied, after the
end or other determination of this parliament.'"[1]

Such a resolution, but even more extensive in its
terms, applying not only to excise, but also to customs
and all other imposts, was passed without a division ;
and the object of the Government in proposing the bill
was thwarted. The resolution was, that after the termination of the Parliament no tax of any sort could
be levied under any previous law or ordinance, unless
it had been expressly sanctioned by this House. This
was intended as a check on dissolution, and probably
accelerated it.

Four days later, on the fifth of April, the House
resolved on a declaration for a day of fasting and
humiliation through the three nations; and it was

[1] Burton, iv. 324, April 1.

settled after a renewed short discussion about the
" other House," that its title should be " A Declaration
of the Lord Protector and both Houses of Parliament."
It then became the subject of the first "transaction"
with the "other House;" but not till after much discussion as to the mode in which the "other House"
should be communicated with, and the appointment of a
committee to consider the forms. The House resolved,
on the recommendation of the committee: 1. " That
such messages as shall be sent from this House to the
other House shall be carried by members of this House;"
and 2. " That such messages as shall be sent from the
other House to this House shall not be received, unless
brought by members of their own number." The second
resolution was carried against the Government by 127
votes to 114. The message was at last sent up on the
fourteenth of April, entrusted to one member, Mr. Grove,
the original mover for a day of fasting. The Diarist
accompanied him to the " other House," and thus reports
what passed this day on that subject :—

"I came late and found the House in debate about
Mr. Grove's going to the other House with the Declaration for the fast. Mr. Grove desired instructions
whether we might stay for an answer.—*Mr. Bodurda.*
It is not rational that he should come away without an
answer. I only know two cases where a messenger
does not stay for an answer: 1. when a herald goes to
proclaim war, 2. when an apparitor comes to serve a
citation ; he claps it upon the door and runs away for
fear of a beating.—*Mr. Salway.* I perceive they are not
sitting in the other House ; most of them are at Wal-

lingford House.[1]—It seems so they were, and not above
four in the House, but they were gathering up their
numbers while we were debating.—The question was
put, that Mr. Grove, when he hath delivered his message to the persons sitting in the other House shall
return to this House without staying for any answer.
The question was misput; it ought not to have been
put with a negative in it.—Mr. Speaker declared for the
Noes, Mr. —— for the Yeas, and that the Yeas go out.
Sir Arthur Haslerig and others moved that the Noes
go out, because it was not new, but the Yeas went out.
Yeas, 100, Lord Falkland and Sir Arthur Haslerig,
téllers; Noes, 144, Mr. Annesley and Sir Coplestone
Bampfield, tellers. So it passed in the negative.—Sir
Arthur Haslerig said he had the worst luck in telling
of any man, and so it proved.—Mr. Grove, attended by
above fifty members, *quorum* myself, carried the Declaration to the other House accordingly. After a little
stay at the door, for the Lords were reading a bill, Mr.
Grove was called in. He and all the members stood
bare, by the walls, while the Lord-keeper Fiennes and
most of the Lords came down to the bar. We made
one leg, and then went up to the high step; and before
Mr. Grove ascended, we made another leg. He delivered
his message, *his verbis*, without giving them any title,
for so was the sense of the House. 'The Knights,
Citizens, and Burgesses, assembled in the House of
Commons, have commanded me to present this Declaration for a public fast to you, wherein they desire
the concurrence of this House.' The Lords were bare
all the time, and we withdrew, with two legs. After a
little stay we were again called in, and ascended the

---

[1] Wallingford House was then the residence of Fleetwood, and a
council of officers constantly met there; many of the chief officers were
peers. Wallingford House was on the site of the present Admiralty.

step with the same ceremony; all the Lords bare, sitting in their places, except Lord Fiennes, who was covered, but who stood up bare and returned their answer. 'The Lords'—and then made a pause, as if it had been mistaken—'this House will return an answer to you by messengers of their own.' Whereupon we withdrew with the same ceremony. It seems, after we were all gone out, one of the Lords called to Mr. Grove and told him they desired our excuse for making us stay so long, for they had read half the Declaration before they knew that we stayed. Else they would have despatched us sooner.—Mr. Grove reported this in effect to the House at our return; only he left out that passage, that they said 'The Lords' while we were delivering the message."[1]

There was a little discussion the next day as to the entry to be made in the Journals of Mr. Grove's report.

" Mr. Speaker. I desire to know what part of the report which Mr. Grove made yesterday you would have entered in your Journal. The whole narrative was read.—Lord Falkland. If you enter all, you will be laughed at for your reward.—Mr. Grove. If you enter all, enter also that there was such a crowd that I could not go in, and had like to have gone without my cloak. —Colonel White. Enter all, save that part of the colloquy between Mr. Grove and the single member, that being no act of the other House.—Mr. Speaker (and it was the sense of the House): Leave it to the Committee appointed to peruse the Journal, to insert what they think fit." [2]

---

[1] Burton, iv. 426—428.
[2] Ibid. 434, April 15. The entry in the Journals, April 14, is short: "Mr. Grove brings answer from the persons sitting in the

While the House of Commons was engaged in these solemn discussions of forms, grave questions of substance were rapidly developing, comparatively unheeded, into danger. The gathering of peers at Wallingford House, noted by the Diarist, was a gathering of the military Lords hostile to Richard Cromwell's command of the army. The many parliamentary victories of the Government over its Republican and Presbyterian opponents availed it nothing; and the fatal blow now came to Richard Cromwell from the military magnates, so numerously represented in the House of Lords, for which his government had borne so much labour and odium in the House of Commons. A large party of officers, headed by Fleetwood and Desborough, had early shown jealousy of Richard Cromwell as Commander-in-chief. The parliamentary Opposition, though generally vanquished by numbers, had necessarily weakened the Government; and as the Government became weaker, Fleetwood's party became bolder. A general Council of officers had regularly sat at Wallingford House by Richard Cromwell's permission; and they now passed resolutions in offensive language, recommending the transfer of the chief command of the army to some fit person in whom they could confide. Fleetwood was the person designed. There was an understanding between

other House that, in obedience to the commands of this House, he had delivered to them in the other House the declaration for the public fast, for their concurrence thereunto; that a little time after himself and other the members of this House who accompanied him to declare his message and went with him into the other House were withdrawn, they were called in again, and received this answer from them in the other House, that they would send an answer by messengers of their own."

the Wallingford House officers and the Republican party, who merged for the time their differences and mutual distrust in sympathy of opposition to Richard Cromwell.

The Protector appealed to the Parliament. After a warm discussion, on the eighteenth of April, it was resolved : " 1. That, during the sitting of the Parliament, there shall be no General Council or meeting of the officers of the army, without the direction, leave, and authority of his Highness the Lord Protector and both Houses of Parliament; 2. That no person shall have or continue any command or trust in any of the armies or navies of England, Scotland, or Ireland, or any the dominions or territories thereto belonging, who shall refuse to subscribe, that he will not disturb or inter- rupt the free meetings in Parliament of any of the members of either House of Parliament, or their freedom in their debates and counsels." These votes were sent up to the other House for their concurrence. The " Lords" promised to send an answer by messengers of their own, and resolved by a majority of one to debate the resolutions offered for their concurrence. Richard Cromwell did not wait for the decision of the House of Lords, but, acting on the advice of his Council, ordered the dissolution of the military Council at Wallingford House. This, however, was an act of boldness which he had neither strength of character nor power in the army to maintain. Fleetwood and Desborough appealed to force, counted their regiments against Richard's, and demanded a dissolution of the Parliament ; and Richard had no alternative but to comply.

On Friday, the twenty-second of April, the House of Commons met in alarm, and after an uneasy sitting adjourned to the following Monday. On the evening of Friday a dissolution was proclaimed; and the doors of the House were locked, and guards placed round the approaches to prevent the members from again meeting.[1]

This was the end alike of Richard Cromwell's Parliament and of Richard Cromwell's Protectorate.

---

[1] Ludlow's Memoirs, ii. 631—642; Sir R. Baker's Chronicle, p. 641, ed. 1684; Comm. Journ. April 18—22; Burton's Diary, iv. pp. 448 and sqq.; Guizot, Protectorat de Richard Cromwell, &c., i. 112—129.

THERE were two parties among the officers who had
combined at Wallingford House, under Fleetwood and

Desborough, to force Richard Cromwell to dissolve the Parliament. Fleetwood and Desborough themselves did not design to depose the Protector or abrogate the Petition and Advice: Fleetwood was husband of Richard's sister, and Desborough of his aunt. Their object was to take away from Richard the immediate command of the army, and make Fleetwood commander-in-chief. But a majority of the officers who met at Wallingford House were Republicans, and wished to establish a commonwealth, without any single person at the head having a share in the legislative power. When the officers assembled, after the forced dissolution, to deliberate on what was next to be done, this difference of opinion became manifest. Fleetwood and Desborough found that they could not stop where they wished. The Council of officers would not listen to their pleadings for continuing Richard Cromwell as Protector. It was proposed to revive the authority of that remnant of the Long Parliament whose sittings Oliver had forcibly discontinued in April 1653. This proposal found great support outside Wallingford House. The superior officers of the army in London and its neighbourhood assembled in St. James's Chapel to discuss the position of affairs, and Doctor Owen and other Independent ministers, attending to consecrate their deliberations by prayer, improved the occasion by dwelling on the glories of the old Rump. Lambert, whom Cromwell had deprived of his commission, but who, though not an officer of the army, had been deeply engaged in the late cabals of Wallingford House, and who now received the command of a regiment, exerted his powerful influence among the officers to promote the restoration of the Rump. The inferior officers declared themselves for this measure. A petition for the recall of the Rump was presented from the city. Fleetwood and Desborough were obliged to yield. A communication was opened with a few of the most influential members of the Rump. A committee, of which Lambert was the chief member, deputed by the officers of Wallingford House, had several conferences with Vane, Haselrig, Ludlow, and Salwey, in order to obtain their consent to certain conditions on which the officers proposed to invite those members of the Long Parliament who had sat after the execution of the King and till April 1653, to resume the sovereign authority. These conditions were an indemnity for all military and political acts since the dissolution of the Rump, a liberal provision for Richard Cromwell, an effectual reformation of the Church and the law, and the institution of a senate, similar to the second House of the Petition and Advice, for a check on the representative assembly in making provision for the future government of the commonwealth. It is clear that four individuals could not undertake to bind the whole body; they objected to the proposal of a senate; they promised to use all their influence to procure an ample indemnity and a decent provision for Richard Cromwell, and as to these points they anticipated no difficulty; as regarded the reformation of the law and the Church, the members of the Rump were not likely to be less zealous than the officers of the army.

Ultimately a declaration, inviting those members of the Long Parliament who had continued to sit after the execution of Charles the First to resume the sovereign authority over the three nations, was drawn up by the council of officers, and presented by Lambert to Lenthall, the old Speaker. On the seventh of May Lenthall once more took the chair of the Rump in the old Parliament House at Westminster, and thus the power of the army re-established an authority which, just five years before, the power of the army wielded by Oliver Cromwell had broken.[1]

Forty-two out of about a hundred and sixty members entitled to sit under the limitation imposed took their seats in Westminster on the seventh of May.[2] This was just more than enough to make a House, and as many as could be mustered in London on so short a notice. About ninety on the whole in the end took their seats. Some of the members whom the army had excluded in 1648 endeavoured, on the first day of meeting, to enter and sit also, but a military guard kept them out.

The first care of the new rulers was to appoint a Committee of Safety, in order to carry on the necessary duties of administration, and provide against danger from the Royalists, to whom the late confusions had

---

[1] Ludlow, ii. 642—651 ; Sir R. Baker's Chronicle, p. 642.

[2] It is Ludlow's statement that there were now 160 members of the Long Parliament still living of those who had sat after the execution of the King. (Mem. ii. 645.) But Ludlow is not always accurate, and this number is possibly an exaggeration. No more than 122 ever voted between the execution of Charles I. and the ejection of the Rump in April 1653. See note at p. 91 ; also Hallam's Const. Hist. ii. 325, and Bisset's History of the Commonwealth, i. 23.

given encouragement. This committee was composed in nearly equal proportions of officers of the army and republican members of the House. It consisted of Fleetwood, Desborough, Lambert, Sydenham, John Jones, and Berry, officers of the army, and Haselrig, Vane, Ludlow, Salwey, and Scot: Fleetwood, Sydenham, and John Jones were also members of the House. This committee was to continue only until a Council of State was organized; and no time was lost in electing a Council of State.

Cooper, who had so vigorously co-operated with the Republicans in the last two Parliaments, immediately endeavoured to gain admission to the revived Rump as a member, on his never-adjudicated petition for Downton at the beginning of the Long Parliament. His case was referred, two days after the Rump was reconstituted sovereign, together with the case of Lord Fairfax, to a revived committee for examining the cases of all members who had not sat since 1648.[1] But Cooper did not succeed at present in gaining admission: the reason why is not known. It was possibly a reason of form, at least ostensibly, and there were suspicions of Cooper's sincerity as a Republican which may have influenced the adverse decision.[2]

---

[1] Comm. Journ. May 9, 1659.
[2] Ludlow, in one of the suppressed passages in the Appendix III. says that the Committee, in Cooper's case, "alleging their powers were at an end, it was referred to them to search their books, and state matter of fact in relation thereto." He also says that Cooper having many friends in the House, those who suspected him managed to get the question referred to the Committee, as the best way of putting him off.

There was no delay in proceeding to appoint a Council of State, and Cooper was elected a member. It was first resolved that this council should consist of thirty-one members, twenty-one of whom were to be members of the House, and ten to be chosen from without. The House began, on the thirteenth of May, by electing seven who were not of their body. Lord Fairfax, Lambert, Desborough, Berry, Bradshaw, Sir Anthony Ashley Cooper, and Sir Horatio Townshend, were proposed and agreed to without a division. The remaining twenty-four members were elected by ballot on the fourteenth and sixteenth. They were Haselrig, Vane, Ludlow, Fleetwood, Salwey, Morley, Scot, Wallop, Sir James Harrington (the author of "Oceana"), Colonels Walton, John Jones, and Sydenham, Algernon Sydney, Henry Nevill, Chaloner, Downes, Oliver St. John (Chief Justice), Colonel Thompson, Whitelocke, Colonel Dixwell, Reynolds, Berners, Sir Archibald Johnstone of Warriston, and Sir Robert Honywood. The last three were not members of the House. The officers of the army were in a minority in the Council.

The election of Cooper and of Sir Horatio Townshend, a young Norfolk baronet of great possessions, whose father had been a Cavalier, but who, having lately come of age, had acted, like Cooper, with the Republican party in the last two Parliaments of the Protectors, is said by Ludlow to have surprised and disconcerted some of their colleagues. They were the two last proposed of the seven first elected from persons out of the House; it was at the close of a sitting,[1]

---

[1] Comm. Journ. May 13.

and it may be that the House was in some degree
surprised into electing them. "Which two motions,"
says Ludlow, "being upon the rising of the House made
on a sudden, before any could recollect themselves to
speak against them, there being also an unwillingness
to disoblige those of whom there was any hope, were
consented to."[1] Cooper had been proposed by Mr.
Love, a Republican, and Townshend by Nevill, who
was unquestionably of the same party. Ludlow further
states that several of the Wallingford House officers
alleged that Cooper and Townshend were "assured
to Charles Stuart's interest, and that they would give
intelligence to him of all that passed," and that they
kept away from the Council by reason of distrust
of these two colleagues; and that endeavours were
consequently used by some friends of Cooper and
Townshend to persuade them to resign, or at any
rate not to attend the Council.[2] With Cooper, any
such endeavours, if made, were ineffectual. Ludlow
says that Townshend was persuaded to forbear from
sitting. Cooper, on taking his seat in the Council,
took an oath of fidelity to the Commonwealth as constituted, as he had previously taken the engagement
and as later he took it again, and as he had taken oaths
of fidelity to the Constitution under the Protectors;
and whatever suspicions may have been entertained
by some of his colleagues, there is no pretence for
saying that he broke his oath by correspondence with
the exiled Charles or intrigues in his interest.

[1] No. 3 of Suppressed Passages of Ludlow in Appendix III.
[2] No. 4 of Ludlow's Suppressed Passages.

Thomas Scot, a leading Republican member, accused Cooper and Whitelocke, in the Council, of correspondence with Hyde, the companion in exile and chief counsellor of Charles. Both indignantly denied the charge, which Whitelocke says was made on the authority of " a beggarly Irish friar beyond the seas ;" and both were believed by the Council. Whitelocke, himself a sufficiently supple politician, insinuates, as he records this incident, that Cooper's solemn denial was not necessarily true. " Sir A. A. Cooper," he says, " made the highest professions that could be of his innocence, and the highest imprecations of God's judgments upon him and his posterity, if ever he had any correspondence with the King or with Sir Edward Hyde or any of the King's ministers or friends, and his expressions were so high that they bred in some the more suspicion of him ; but at this time he was believed, and what' followed afterwards is known."[1]

There is every reason to believe that Cooper's solemn denial was true. Eighteen years later, in a letter written to Charles the Second and appealing to his gratitude and clemency for release from imprisonment, he denied all correspondence with the King and his party before the Restoration, as solemnly as he now denied Scot's accusation in the Council of State ; and how could he venture on a falsehood in this matter to Charles ? " I had the honour," wrote Shaftesbury to Charles the Second in 1677 from the Tower, " to have a principal hand in your restoration ; neither did I act in it but on a principle of piety and honour. I never

[1] Whitelocke's Memorials, p. 679, May 18, 1659.

betrayed, as your Majesty knows, the party or councils
I was of. I kept no correspondence with, I made no
secret addresses to your Majesty; neither did I
endeavour to obtain any private terms or articles for
myself or reward for what I had done or should do."
Published letters of Royalist agents, the best possible
witnesses, prove that on the very eve of the Restoration,
when Cooper's part was decidedly taken, and he was
acting with the Presbyterians to bring in the King, he
was working independently of the Royalists, and in a
manner which did not satisfy them. Lord Willoughby
wrote to Hyde, February 24, 1660: "Sir William
Waller and Sir Anthony are his Majesty's fast friends,
but whether the Presbyterians will not be high in
them, as to the proposals when they come to be made,
is the only doubt."[1] Brodrick, a very active Royalist
agent, wrote about the same time that he perceived no
desire in Cooper to be mentioned to Hyde as offering
services, such as he was empowered to offer from Charles
Howard, the future Earl of Carlisle, and from Sir
Robert Howard.[2]

At this time, a twelvemonth before the Restoration,
immediately after the fall of Richard Cromwell, Cooper
separated himself from the general Presbyterian body

[1] Clarendon State Papers, iii. 689.
[2] Ibid. 681, Feb. 26, 1660. Brodrick wrote under the assumed name
of Hancock ; and after suggesting that power should be given to
Charles Howard and Robert Howard to make promises to Monk
and his party, he adds : "Sir A. A. Cooper endeavours the same way
earnestly, but I do not perceive any desire in him to be mentioned
by Hancock." Mr. Hallam has fallen into error in speaking of
Sir Anthony as a correspondent of Hyde (Const. Hist. of England,
ii. 378, note); the letter in the Clarendon State Papers which he
refers to was written by another Cooper, a Royalist agent.

to promote the new republic, as he had separated himself before from his Presbyterian friends to sign the engagement, enter the Barebone's Parliament, and take office under the Protectorate. When the leading Presbyterians generally discountenanced the Republicans, and were looking to Charles in exile, and many of them were joining to prepare the movement which soon ended in Sir George Booth's abortive rising, it was very natural that there should be suspicions of Cooper among the Republicans, and hopes of him among the Royalists; and these hopes again would increase the suspicions. Cooper was the only Presbyterian in the Council. Townshend was the young heir of a deceased Royalist. Published letters of Royalists again give aid to prove that Cooper disappointed royalist hopes and rejected royalist overtures. Brodrick wrote to Hyde, on May 23, that Cooper had engaged to raise three or four hundred horse in Dorsetshire for a contemplated rising for the King, but had not yet left London.[1] Now this Brodrick is described by Lord Mordaunt, the King's best agent, in a letter written June 7, as a very indiscreet and dangerous person, and given to drink. Brodrick's statement about Cooper was probably an exaggeration of his own hopes: for Mordaunt having been asked by Hyde whether he continued to have a good opinion of Cooper, replied, June 16: "Sir A. A. Cooper is rotten, and sits; he never knew he had a letter, being shy when taxed by Sir George Booth."[2] Thus we learn that the King had been led by

---

[1] Clarendon State Papers, iii. 478.
[2] Ibid. 488, 490.

his agents in London to write himself to Cooper, and a subsequent letter of Hyde gives information of Cooper's refusal. "I am sorry," Hyde wrote to Lord Mordaunt, July 3, "Sir A. A. Cooper hath so much disappointed your expectations, which no doubt is not for the reason he gives, for he is too wise to think it possible that the King would write to any subject to assist him, whose estate he had given away as forfeited, nor doth he believe himself a delinquent of that magnitude."[1] It is clear enough that Cooper repelled or evaded the royalist overtures, and would not encourage Sir George Booth. By "Sir A. A. Cooper is rotten, and sits," was, of course, meant that Cooper was good for nothing, and sat in the Council of State.[2]

The following letter was written by Monk, who was at this time Commander-in-chief of the forces in Scotland, to Cooper, as a member of the Council of State, early in June, and it is interesting as being the beginning of their intercourse, and as showing that

---

[1] Clarendon State Papers, iii. 512.

[2] Mr. Martyn, who says that he follows Stringer, states most erroneously that Cooper never sat in this Council. Martyn refers also in support of his statement to a tract called "England's Confusion," printed in the Somers Tracts (vol. vi. p. 521), by which he says it appears that neither Sir A. A. Cooper nor Sir H. Townshend ever sat or acted in the Council. But the tract does not say so; it describes all the members of the Council abusively, except Cooper and Townshend, saying of the latter that he was "a gentleman of too good estate to be hazarded with such a crew," and of Cooper that he was "a gentleman too wise and honest to sit in such company." Townshend probably never sat in the Council; Cooper did. The Minutes of this Council preserved in the State Paper Office begin only on August 11. Then Cooper was absent from the Council, in Dorsetshire, and afterwards he was charged with having abetted Sir George Booth's rising. But after he was acquitted of this accusation he attended the Council constantly till the revolution made by Lambert and Fleetwood in October; and there is no doubt that Cooper had frequently sat in the Council between May and August.

Monk regarded Cooper as an active and influential member of the Council. Similar letters were written by Monk to other members of the Council and to the Speaker, who read the letter received by him to the House :[1]—

"HONOURABLE SIR,—It is some trouble to me that, the first time I should have occasion to write to you, it must be to request a favour at your hands. But I hope you will please to pardon this my incivility and boldness, and place me in the list of your friends; for I can assure you I shall be as ready to serve you as any friend you have. Understanding that there is a committee appointed by Parliament for the presenting of officers to be continued in the several regiments in England, Scotland, and Ireland, and knowing the officers here were, upon the first motion, most desirous that the Long Parliament might be recalled to return to their former station, I make it my request to you, that you will be assisting that there may be no alteration amongst the officers belonging to the forces here; for I shall desire you to find credit herein, that you may be confident that there is not any you can employ will be more ready to serve the Commonwealth than they. But in case my request for the whole cannot be granted, I shall entreat that the officers of my own regiment of horse and foot, and Colonel Talbot's regiment (a list whereof

---

[1] Comm. Journ. June 9, 1659. Sir A. Haselrig was commissioned to prepare an answer, which may be read in the Journals, June 10. The answer was rather curt, but, though compliance was not promised, Monk's desire was in fact complied with, the Parliament and the Council attaching great importance to his support. Mr. Martyn says that Cooper's exertions in Monk's favour caused jealousy, and led to his being accused by Scot in the Council of holding correspondence with the King and Hyde. (Life, i. 204.) But Scot's accusation was prior to the date of Monk's letter.

I have sent enclosed), may be continued: they have usually quartered nearest me, and so are best known to me. I shall also desire you will acquaint as many members of the House as you shall think fit to engage in this business, by doing which you will very much oblige,

"Your humble servant,

"GEORGE MONK.

"Dalkeith, 4th June, 1659.

"For the Hon. Sir Anthony Ashley Cooper,

"One of the Council of State, at Whitehall."

Cooper apart, the new Council was a discordant body; and divisions and jealousies soon appeared among the army party and Republicans, both in Council and Parliament, which strengthened royalist hopes, and led in a few months to another military subjugation by Lambert. The weak and distracted state of the Council and the Parliament, in the month of June, is graphically described in two royalist letters printed in the Clarendon State Papers. "The confusions now," writes Major Wood, June 3, 1659, "are so great that it is not to be credited ; the chaos was a perfection in comparison of our order and government; the parties are like so many floating islands, sometimes joining and appearing like a continent, when the next flood or ebb separates them that it can hardly be known where they will be next."[1] A more particular account of the divisions in the Council at this time is given in a letter of June 7 from Lord Mordaunt, who describes the members as follow. 1. John Jones, Fleetwood, and Berry, for restoring

[1] Clarendon State Papers, iii. 479.

Richard Cromwell; 2. Salwey, Vane, Lambert, and Haselrig for the Petition and Advice and an executive of seven—Haselrig, however, not always with the three others, and he and Salwey more Presbyterians than anything else; 3. Ludlow, Nevill, Sir James Harrington, and Mildmay, Republicans, "who lead the House as to plurality of voices," but want interest in the army; 4. Overton, R. Fox, and Fifth Monarchy men.[1]

Extensive preparations were made by the royalist party for a general rising in England and Wales on the first of August: the Presbyterian gentry entered largely into the project, and it was the policy of the Royalists to give prominence to the Presbyterian element. Shortly before the first of August, Charles moved secretly from Brussels to Calais, in order to be ready to cross if the rising succeeded. But the Council of State obtained timely knowledge of the design, and prevented risings in many parts of the country. Several who had undertaken to move failed at the last moment. The principal rising was in Cheshire, under Sir George Booth, and the Parliament despatched a force under Lambert, by whom Booth was easily defeated.

Shortly after this unsuccessful rising, Cooper was arrested in Dorsetshire by a Major Dewey on suspicion of correspondence with Sir George Booth. The arrest was on a statement by a boy from Wales, named Nicholas, that he had carried a letter to Cooper from Sir George Booth. Major Dewey wrote to the Council

---

[1] Clarendon State Papers, iii. 483.

of State on August 21, reporting the arrest of Cooper
and the statement of the boy Nicholas. The Council
reported the matter to the Parliament, which approved
of Dewey's proceedings, and directed the Council to
institute an investigation. The Council then ordered
Dewey to release Cooper, and wrote to Cooper desiring
his attendance. They appointed a committee to conduct the inquiry, which consisted of the following
members :—Whitelocke, Bradshaw, Sir Henry Vane,
Walton, Morley, Salwey, Johnstone of Warriston,
Nevill, Desborough, Sir James Harrington, Downes,
Reynolds, Chaloner, Haselrig, Berners, and Berry.
This committee reported to the Council, and the
Council, on September 12, unanimously resolved:—
" That it be humbly reported to the Parliament that
upon the examination taken before the Council or
otherwise, in the business of Sir A. A. Cooper, referred
to the examination of the Council by order of Par-
liament, it doth not appear to them that there
is any just ground of jealousy or imputation upon
him, and Mr. Neville is desired to make this report."
The Parliament adopted the report of the Council
without a division. The members present in the
Council who unanimously acquitted Cooper, were Sir
H. Vane (chairman), Colonel Thompson, Berners,
Johnstone of Warriston, Nevill, Walton, Sydenham,
Haselrig, Scot, Dixwell, Bradshaw, Desborough, Fleetwood, and Downes.[1] The Committee was so composed

---

[1] Minutes of the Council of State in the State Paper Office from
August 25 to September 12, 1659. M. Guizot, who had not seen these
Minutes, has hazarded an assertion that Cooper, though acquitted, was
justly accused : " Accusé à bon droit de complicité dans l'insurrection,

that its verdict, adopted unanimously by the Council and the Parliament, may be taken as an entire acquittal of Cooper. Ludlow, carried away by his bitter feeling, has given an unfair account of the judgment, stating that "upon examination of a boy which brought, as was supposed, a letter from Sir George Booth before his rising, to Sir A. A. Cooper, it was found that he dismissed the boy with much civility, in token of consenting to what was done."[1] This may have been the evidence on which he was accused, but the acquittal was entire and unqualified.

Lambert's easy victory over Sir George Booth was, within two months, followed by another easy victory of Lambert over the Parliament itself. The Rump failed, as Richard Cromwell and his Parliament had failed, to satisfy the demands of the army and its officers. The Rump, immediately after its restoration, had, on the indication of the officers of the army, appointed Fleetwood commander-in-chief, but limited his commission to one year; and instead of authorizing him to issue commissions to the officers nominated by the Parliament, they resolved that the commissions should be signed by the Speaker, and that the officers should come to the House to receive them from his hands. The army had submitted to these arrangements, but most reluctantly. Soon after the suppression of Sir George Booth's insurrection of August, fifty

Sir Antoine Cooper, sur le rapport de Nevil, fut déclaré innocent." (Protectorat de R. Cromwell et Rétablissement des Stuart, i. 211.) There is no known evidence on which to dispute the justice of the acquittal.

[1] No. 5 of Suppressed Passages of Ludlow in Appendix III.

officers of the brigade which had served under Lambert's orders, met at Derby and prepared a memorial praying that Fleetwood should be made commander-in-chief of the army without limitation of time, Lambert major-general, Desborough lieutenant-general of the horse, and Monk major-general of the foot, and that no officer of the army should be dismissed from his command except by a court-martial. The memorialists complained that the Parliament had not shown enough energy in suppressing the late rebellion, and had not sufficiently punished those engaged in it or sufficiently rewarded those who had suppressed it; and they pressed for settlement of the government in a representative assembly and a senate. The memorial came to the knowledge of Haselrig, who immediately brought it before the House, and moved that Lambert and some others should be seized and sent to the Tower. This motion was not persevered in; but a resolution was passed, "that to have any more general officers in the army than are already settled by the Parliament is chargeable and dangerous to the Commonwealth;" and by another resolution Fleetwood was charged "to communicate the order of this House to the officers of the army, and to admonish them of their irregular proceeding, and to take care to prevent any further proceedings therein by the soldiers."[1] A council of officers now met at Wallingford House, where great anger was expressed, and it was resolved to prepare an address to the Parliament which should not be open to the objections made against the former memorial. This

1 Comm. Journ. Sept. 23.

address was presented by Desborough and other officers on the first of October; and the House took it into consideration. They were proceeding with the consideration of it, when, on the twelfth of October, Colonel Okey communicated a letter which he had received, signed by Lambert, Desborough, and seven other officers, inviting him to get signatures to the address among the soldiers of his regiment. This roused the indignation of the Commonwealth party. They had just received intelligence that Monk favoured the Parliament against the army. Encouraged by this news, they determined to proceed vigorously. The doors of the House were ordered to be locked, and votes were passed depriving Lambert, Desborough, and the other officers who had signed the letter to Okey of their commission, revoking Fleetwood's commission as commander-in-chief, and placing the government of the army in seven commissioners, Fleetwood, Ludlow, Monk, Haselrig, Walton, Morley, and Overton. There had lately been much suspicion of Lambert that he designed to make himself Protector, or even King, and it was probable that, when the House met the next day, a motion would be carried to send him to the Tower.[1]

The next day Lambert filled the approaches to the House with soldiers, and prevented the meeting of the

---

[1] Carte's Collection of Letters, ii. 203, 225, 246, 265. These letters of royalists mention that Lambert was distrustful and jealous of Fleetwood, that Vane and Thurloe favoured Lambert's ambition, and that Fleetwood was believed to be inclined to restore Charles. Hyde, writing to Ormond, says he had heard that Lambert was saved from the Tower by only three voices (p. 265).

Parliament. During the thirteenth and fourteenth the rival troops of Lambert and the Parliament stood in hostile attitude in the immediàte neighbourhood of the Parliament House in Westminster, but no collision occurred, and Lambert triumphed without bloodshed or even a blow.[1]

The friends of the Parliament mustered strong in the Council on the afternoon of the fourteenth, Lambert, Desborough, and Berry being absent, and it was re-solved, " That those persons that do exercise the chief power and command in the army, and all others con-cerned, be ordered to withdraw the guards about the Parliament House and Westminster and parts adjacent, to the end the Speaker and members of Parliament may return to the free exercise of the legislative power and their duty." The Council met again next morning, when the serjeant-at-arms reported that he had given the order of the day before to the Council of officers, "and delivered it to the Lord Lambert, General Des-borough, Colonel Berry, and Lord Fleetwood, and, being withdrawn, was again called in and had this answer, that they had received the order of the Council and would take a convenient time to consider of it."[2] When this report was given, the Parliament had been

---

[1] There is a very valuable and interesting letter of Mordaunt in Carte's Collection, ii. 244, describing the positions and proceedings of the opposed troops with much minuteness.

[2] Minutes of Council of State in State Paper Office, October 13-15. M. Guizot is in error in describing the order of the Council of State of the 14th for Lambert's forces to retire as a compromise of the Parlia-ment party with Lambert. (Protectorat de Richard Cromwell, &c. i. 228.) He also in the same passage erroneously describes the Parlia-ment party as acquiescing in the result: some Republicans gave in to Lambert, others stood out against him.

vanquished and the military revolution was complete. The Council adjourned to the afternoon, when Fleetwood was present, and it was then proposed that, in consequence of the condition of affairs, the Council should adjourn till the end of November. This proposal was negatived.

Cooper was present at these meetings of the Council of State of the fourteenth and fifteenth of October, and in this conjuncture he stood by the Council of State and by the Rump against Lambert and his party. The Council of State continued to hold sittings till the twenty-fifth, when a new Committee of Safety superseded it : but Cooper did not sit again after the afternoon of the fifteenth ; nor did Haselrig, Bradshaw, Walton, or Nevill. Bradshaw, the celebrated President of the High Court of Justice which tried and sentenced Charles the First, died a few days afterwards, having attended the council in spite of illness to protest against the military revolution. Scot and Reynolds appear to have attended the council till it ceased to sit on the twenty-fifth ; but they opposed Lambert. Vane, Salwey, and Harrington left the Republican party on this occasion, and sided with Lambert and the new Committee of Safety.

Lambert and the officers acting with him had, indeed, on the thirteenth of October, immediately after the interruption of the Parliament, nominated a rival temporary Council of State, consisting of ten persons, Fleetwood, Lambert, Whitelocke, Vane, Desborough, Harrington, Salwey, Berry, Sydenham, and Johnstone of Warrington. These, however, continued to attend the sittings of the old Council of State till it expired on the twenty-fifth. The council of officers had also, on the thirteenth, appointed Fleetwood commander-in-chief of the army, Lambert major-general, Desborough commissary-general of the horse, and Fleetwood, Lambert, Vane, Desborough, Ludlow, and Berry commissioners for the nomination of all officers of the army.[1] On the twenty-sixth of October, they nominated a Committee of Safety of twenty-three members, viz. Whitelocke (who was made keeper of the Great Seal), Fleetwood, Lambert, Desborough, Steel (Chancellor of Ireland), Vane, Ludlow, Sydenham, Salwey, Walter Strickland, Berry, Lawrence, Harrington, Johnstone of Warriston, Alderman Ireton, Tichborn, Hewson, Clark, Bennet, Colonel Lilburne, Holland, Henry Brandriff, and Robert Thomson, and they at the same time published a declaration, in which they pronounced all the votes of the Rump Parliament passed on and after the tenth of October to be null and void, proclaimed their desire to give full liberty to all the people of England, to make a complete reformation of the law, and to maintain a faithful ministry by some better means than tithes, and declared that they had no intention of setting up a military or arbitrary government, but that, having appointed in the first instance a Committee of Safety, they designed to prepare a suitable form of government without a single person, kingship, or House of Lords.[2]

Cooper was now, with some other members of the displaced Council of State, indefatigable to overturn the

[1] Sir R. Baker's Chronicle, p. 661.
[2] Ibid. p. 662; Ludlow, ii. 715.

new Committee of Safety and restore the power of the Rump. There acted with him of the late Council Scot, Haselrig, Colonels Morley, Reynolds, and Walton, Wallop, Nevill, and Berners.

The hopes of Lambert and Fleetwood soon received a heavy blow from Monk, who commanded the army in Scotland; he announced decided hostility to the revolution. They had hastened after the event to seek the support of Monk; and he replied in terms of strong disapproval. Monk wrote at the same time to the Speaker, declaring his intention to expose himself and his army to the utmost hazards for the restitution of the Parliament. He immediately proceeded to prepare his army to move. The Committee of Safety sent off Colonel Talbot and Dr. Clarges, Monk's brother-in-law, to Monk, to endeavour by explanations to persuade him to come to terms with them; and shortly after, in order to be prepared for the failure of these negotiators, they despatched Lambert to the North with a force of 12,000 horse and foot. Talbot and Clarges arrived at Edinburgh on the second of November. Monk accepted the proposal to treat, and appointed Major Knight, Lieut.-Colonel Clobery, and Colonel Wilks commissioners for this purpose. He instructed his commissioners to insist on the restoration of the Parliament; but if the members should refuse to sit, then, and then only, he authorized them to discuss some other form of government. The commissioners proceeded to York to treat with Lambert, and, on finding that he had no power to treat for the restitution of the Parliament, they went on to London. There the terms of a treaty were soon

arranged by them with Fleetwood in disregard of
Monk's instructions as to the restoration of the Parliament. This treaty was concluded on the fifteenth
of November, and provided for the meeting on the
second of December of a general Council nominated
from the army and fleet to determine a new form of
government, and for the prompt summoning of a new
Parliament according to whatever might be the resolutions of the proposed general Council.

The day after Monk's commissioners had made the
arrangement with the Committee of Safety, Cooper and
Haselrig had a meeting with them and endeavoured to
persuade them to recede, but entirely without success.
Cooper has himself narrated the course of events
and his own active proceedings from the establishment of the Committee of Safety on the twenty-
fifth of October to the sixth of February, 1660, when
the Rump, which had in the meantime been restored on
the twenty-sixth of December, admitted the secluded
Presbyterian members, and made the way clear for a
new Parliament and the restoration of Charles. It is
only a fragment of a narrative which remains, both
beginning and ending in the middle of a sentence. It
is clear from internal evidence that this narrative was
composed or refashioned after the Restoration ; it may
be another portion of the Autobiography of Shaftesbury's old age.[1]

---

[1] Clarges is always called Sir Thomas Clarges in the narrative : and
he was knighted by Charles at Breda, in May, just before the Restoration. The tone with regard to Monk is hardly what would have been
Cooper's tone at the time of these events or very soon after : and the
general tone of the narrative is that of justification for posterity.

"[General Monk was commander-in-chief[1]] in Scotland, and expected no great good to himself from so great a change, acted without the least communication with him. He, therefore, to secure himself and his interest, forthwith new-models his army, cashiers such officers as he suspected, and puts in their room absolute creatures of his own; with this army he marches towards the borders of England, and is there faced by a stronger army under the command of General Lambert, but neither of them being willing to put all to a venture, they remained in that posture whilst General Monk sends three officers, Colonels Wilks, Clobery, and Knight, to General Fleetwood and the rest of the Committee of Safety at Westminster, to treat with them, and to know what terms they might expect from them.

" In the meanwhile, myself and some others that were of that Council of State which was turned out by Lambert, constantly and privately met, turning every stone to recover our lost power, and hearing of these Commissioners sent up from General Monk, Sir Arthur Haselrige and I, after several attempts, at last procured a meeting from them at the Fleece Tavern, in Covent Garden, where at first they told us they had the day before made a full agreement with General Fleetwood and, therefore, were not then capable of answering any of our expectations ; but we laid before them the great uncertainty their General underwent in joining with these men, the best he could expect was to be gently

This fragment of a narrative I have found among the papers at St. Giles; but it is not in Shaftesbury's handwriting. Mr. Martyn has given a paraphrase of it in his Life (i. 209—230), but he has interwoven some errors. A similar account also is given in Locke's Fragment of a Memoir, with some variations, errors, and interesting additions, all most likely arising out of conversations with Shaftesbury and Stringer.

[1] The words in brackets are supplied, as indicated by the context, to complete the first sentence.

laid aside, and then ruined with some more artifice and caution than other men; that if, on the other hand, he declared for the restoring of the Parliament, he was fully assured to be generalissimo of all their forces, neither had he any competitor. Besides, we told them our cause was not so desperate, for we had a great correspondence and interest with the inferior officers and common soldiers of every troop and company they had in their army about London. Besides, we had Portsmouth at our devotion, and Sir Charles Coote had assured us of six thousand men out of Ireland upon the first notice; Vice-Admiral Lawson, who commanded the fleet now in the mouth of the river, was our firm friend; and that my Lord Fairfax, who had the greatest interest of any man amongst the soldiers, utterly abhorred the present proceedings. Upon these discourses we found Clobery and Knight very glad that there was so fair a prospect of a better way than they were in, and assured us they would do their best to cause General Monk to break off the treaty, to refuse the terms offered, and to declare for restoring the Parliament. But Colonel Wilks persisted.

"Whilst these Commissioners were returning to Monk, we were not idle, but Sir Arthur Haslerig and Colonel Morley went to Portsmouth, which town I had undertaken to them should be delivered into their hands, the Governor, Colonel Whetham, being my friend and very long acquaintance. I was left with a commission for general of those forces we expected every day should revolt from them about London.[1] This matter was not carried so secretly, but that some uncertain and dark

---

[1] Substantially the same story is told in Locke's fragmentary Memoir, and it is there mentioned that Shaftesbury "would often tell it laughing that, when he had his commission, his great care was where to hide it." (Works, ix. 275.)

discourse of it came to the Committee of Safety. So that Colonel Cook was sent by General Fleetwood to bring me prisoner to him, which he did, using me very civilly, as also did the General himself, who was naturally an obliging man. I quickly found upon discourse with him that they were in a mistake, and apprehended I was to command the forces in the West against them, which I assured him upon my word and honour was not so. Then the General demanded of me my word that I would act nothing to their prejudice, which I refused to give, declaring that I was of the Council of State, and greatly trusted by the Parliament whom they had turned out, and resolved to do all I could for their restitution; that they might give losers leave to speak, since they were well assured we had no power to act anything with; the army was wholly at their devotion; and they could not find, perhaps, another way to lose it than by using me and others of their old friends and commanders scurvily; that I knew their apprehension of me lay in the West, because of the interest I had there; that, being their prisoner, and to obtain my liberty, I would give him my parole not to depart the city without his leave. This the General accepted, and I was released; but before the next day they had better intelligence, and gave order for the reseizing me at any rate, which was executed accordingly,[1] and at ten

---

[1] There is an error here in Locke's narrative: he describes Lambert as coming in to the Committee of Safety after Fleetwood had released Cooper on his parole, and pressing for his arrest. Lambert was at this time in the North with his army, watching Monk. Martyn also erroneously places Lambert in London at the time of the restoration of the Rump. Locke tells an amusing minute story of the attempt to arrest Cooper, which he would probably have derived from Shaftesbury himself, and which may be true: "Sir A. A. coming home to his house in —— Street in Covent Garden, one evening, found a man knocking at his door; he asked his business: the man answered, it was with him, and feil a discoursing with him. Sir A. A. heard him out, and gave him such an answer as he thought proper, and so they

o'clock at night a party of soldiers broke suddenly into
my house, frighted my wife and my only child, lying
then sick of the small-pox; broke open all the trunks,
boxes, and closets, ran their swords into the hangings,
but lost their labour, and found me not, I being upon
notice removed some minutes before, and continued
unknown and secret in the city, until, by the assistance
of several officers that were of our party, I had got the
Tower delivered into my hands; and all the army they
had about London, both horse and foot, drawn up in
rank and file in Lincoln's Inn Fields (without their field-
officers and captains), declaring all for the restoration
of the Parliament, which the Monday following was
restored in triumph; and one of the first things they
did that day was to appoint me and some others Commissioners for the present command of their army and
forces.   Whereupon I, with the other Commissioners,
caused several clerks to be set to work, and that night

---

parted; the stranger out of the entry where they stood into the
street, and Sir A. A. along the entry into the house; but guessing by
the story the other told him that the business was but a pretence, and
that his real errand he came about was something else, when he parted
from the fellow he went inwards, as if he intended to go into the
house, but, as soon as the fellow was gone, turned short, and went out,
and went to his barber's which was but just by; where he was no
sooner got in, and got upstairs into a chamber, but his door was beset
with musketeers, and the officer went in too with others to seize him;
but not finding him, they searched every corner and cranny of the
house diligently, the officer declaring he was sure he was in the house,
for he had left him there just now; as was true, for he had gone no
further than the corner of the Half Moon Tavern, which was just by,
to fetch a file of soldiers that he had left there in the Strand out of
sight, whilst he went to discover whether the gentleman he sought
were within or no; where doubting not to find him safely lodged, he
returned with his myrmidons to his house, sure, as he thought, of his
prey; but Sir A. A. saw through his made story, and gave him the
slip.   After this he was fain to get out of the way and conceal himself
under a disguise; but he hid himself not lazily in a hole; he made
war upon them at Wallingford House, incognito as he was, and made
them feel him, though he kept out of sight." (Locke's Works, ix.
277.)

dispatched orders, and sent them to every field-officer
in Lambert's army; wherein, after a preamble of the
miraculous restoration of the Parliament, and the returning of the London army to their duty, they were required
upon pain of cashiering immediately to march the regiments to such quarters and posts as were therein assigned
them, which were carefully designed far enough distant
from each other or from the place wherein they then
lay. Those orders had their effect, and Lambert's army
vanished in an instant, not one entire regiment disobey-
ing the order. The same order we sent that night to
every county in England and place where their single
and dispersed troops lay, such as were not in regiments,
and therefore we ventured the boldlier, and required
them instantly to disband, and sent orders and authorities to some confiding persons that were near, to see it
done. These also had the effect we intended, so great
was the consternation upon this sudden and unexpected
revolution."

Though Shaftesbury, writing from his own point of
view, may make himself a little too prominent and
important, this account contains nothing at variance
with other published accounts of authority; what he
says of his own proceedings is indeed substantially confirmed by other statements, and several confirmatory
additions may be made to this narrative. Cooper's and
Haselrig's fruitless conference at the Fleece Tavern, in
Covent Garden, with Monk's commissioners, was on the
sixteenth of November; and on the nineteenth he and
eight other members of the late Council of State wrote
to Monk, thanking him for his opposition to the Committee of Safety and support of the late Parliament,

and assuring him of their zealous co-operation.[1] A few days later, the same nine, acting always as the Council of State, passed a commission constituting Monk commander-in-chief of the forces of England and Scotland. The eight who thus acted with Cooper have been already named : Scot, Haselrig, Colonels Morley, Reynolds, and Walton, Wallop, Nevill, and Berners. Cooper, Scot, Berners, and Weaver addressed a long letter to Fleetwood, bearing date December 16, and soon after printed, in which they boastingly owned an unsuccessful attempt to get possession of the Tower; declared that they had acted " by authority from the Council of State, who at the passing of that resolve had the sole legal power from the Parliament of ordering, directing, and disposing of all the garrisons and forces of this Commonwealth, both by sea and land," and resented the endeavour to arrest Cooper.[2] Cooper did secure the Tower eight days later, on the twenty-fourth. "The Speaker," says Whitelocke, " with Cooper, Reynolds, Weaver, and Berners, went to the Lord Mayor, and discoursed with him and the Sheriffs touching the Parliament's meeting again speedily, and found them to like well of it; from him they went to the Tower, and secured that."[3] Clarendon describes the surprise and grief of the Committee of Safety when they heard of the defection of Admiral Lawson, who brought his squadron into the Thames, and declared for the Parliament. "It broke," he says, " the heart of the Committee of Safety:" they sent

---

[1] The substance of the letter is given in Baker's Chronicle, p. 673. Scot signed it first of the nine, as President.

[2] This letter is printed in Appendix IV.

[3] Memorials, p. 691, December 24, 1659.

down Vane and two other intimate friends of Lawson,
to remonstrate with him; and these, "when they came
to the fleet, found Sir Anthony Ashley Cooper and two
others, members of Parliament, who had so fully pre-
possessed him, that he was deaf to all their charms, and
told them that he would submit to no authority but
that of the Parliament."[1]   A doggrel ballad of the time,
which celebrated the fall of the Committee of Safety,
recognises Cooper as one of those who chiefly contributed to the event, in co-operation with Monk.[2]

The first act of the Parliament on its restoration was
to appoint seven Commissioners, of whom Cooper was
one, to take temporary command of the army until the
return from Portsmouth of Haselrig, Morley, and Walton,
three of seven who had been made Commissioners for
the army by the Parliament on October 12, just before
Lambert's revolution, and the only three of those seven
who had opposed the Committee of Safety.   Cooper's
six colleagues in this temporary commission were
Alexander Popham, Colonel Thompson, Scot, Colonel
Okey, Colonel Alured, and Colonel Markham.   It was
these Commissioners who executed the prompt dispersion
of Lambert's forces which Cooper has related.   Their

[1] Clarendon, Hist. of Rebellion, xvi. 106.

[2]   "Sir Ashley Cooper, Scot, and more,
    Such honest hearts there are good store,
    The famous Lawson and the Fleet,
    And London lads in every street,
    Who vow to make subverters stare
    At Tyburn in the open air
    For doing what no King did dare,
      And thus vows our brave George."

This is from a ballad called "The Noble English Worthies," to be
found in Wright's "Political Ballads of the Commonwealth," vol. iii. of
the Percy Society's Publications.

power lasted only for two days, for Haselrig, Morley, and Walton returned on the twenty-eighth. A letter of one of the Royalist agents, Brodrick, addressed to Hyde, proves that Cooper's proceedings were a mystery as well as a disappointment to the Royalists. Brodrick couples him with another Presbyterian, Popham, who had undoubtedly been actively engaged in Sir George Booth's rising. "Alexander Popham," writes this active agent on December 30, "was in recompense chosen one of the seven generals to take care of the army in the absence of Haselrig, Walton, and Morley, expected two days after, so that his dignity lasted double the time of Bibulus's consulship, and to us appeared twice as ridiculous. Sir A. A. Cooper seems very eager in establishing these people, but the friends of both these great men find plausible excuses for every action of them."[1]

The care of the government of the Tower was also entrusted by the Parliament, on the very day of its meeting, to Cooper, Weaver, Scot, and Berners.[2] Their functions ceased on the seventh of January, when Colonel Morley was appointed Lieutenant of the Tower.

A Council of State, consisting of thirty-one members —twenty-one members of the Parliament, and ten not belonging to it—was appointed on the second of January, to continue till the first of April. Cooper was elected by the largest number of votes among the ten not belonging to the Parliament.

Now, at last, Cooper obtained recognition of his claim to sit for Downton, on his old petition of 1640. Once

---

[1] Clarendon Papers, iii. 637.   [2] Comm. Journ. Dec. 26.

more his case was referred with that of Fairfax to a
Committee; and this time the Committee reported that
he was entitled to the seat.[1]   The House immediately
adopted the report, and Sir Anthony at once took his
seat, on the seventh of January, and once more subscribed the Engagement.   Shortly after, he was made
colonel of Fleetwood's regiment of horse, Fleetwood
having been deprived of it.   His commission was given
him by the Speaker at the clerk's table.[2]

Cooper, now admitted to sit, was at once a leading
man in the Parliament. He had probably now made
up his mind to endeavour to obtain the restoration
to the House of the Presbyterian members who had
been secluded before the King's execution, and he
soon separated from Haselrig, Nevill, and other Republicans. A letter of the royalist Lord Mordaunt,
of January 14, describes him as the leader of a
party of some twenty-three opposing another party
of about sixteen led by Nevill.   "The present com-
plexion of the Parliament," writes Mordaunt to Hyde,
"is very pale; Sir Arthur Haselrig undermined by
Cooper, Morley, and Weaver, and from a Rodomont
is reduced to a pitiful rogue. : . . Cooper yet hath his
tongue well hung, and words at will, and employs his
rhetoric to cashier all officers, civil as well as military,
that sided with Fleetwood and Lambert; and Morley
rebukes all the sectaries. Thus these two garble the
army and state. . . . The parties in the House are
diametrically opposite: the three-and-twenty with
Cooper, who acts Cicero ; and some sixteen with Nevill,

[1] Comm. Journ. Jan. 5 and 7, 1660.   [2] Ibid. Jan. 18.

who represents Anthony."[1] It may be gathered from this letter that Cooper had not the confidence of the Royalists, and that they made no pretension of right to complain of his having deceived them.

Monk was now on his way from Scotland to London. He had crossed the Tweed on the first of January, after receiving news of the discomfiture of the Committee of Safety and the re-establishment of the Rump. He made a slow march with his army to London, which he entered on the third of February.

Shaftesbury's narrative is now resumed: he claims to have cleared the way for Monk by the dispersion of Lambert's forces effected by himself and the other temporary Commissioners for the army, immediately after the re-assembling of the Rump :—

"The way being thus cleared before them, General Monk marches up with his small army to London, and by the way in Yorkshire is caressed by General Fairfax, and is met before he comes to London with addresses from the persons of quality, Presbyterians, and other men of sober principles from all parts of England, who with one voice began to intimate their desires of restoring him their lawful Prince, and ancient government. This at first was but modestly intimated, and not boldly spoken out, and was as civilly and darkly returned by him; yet every one departed from him extremely well satisfied of his good intentions, and much the rather because his lady, that came with him, did not spare to declare her passion for the King's cause (which was most real and sincere in her); besides, her

---

[1] Clarendon State Papers, iii. 650.

brother, Sir Thomas Clarges (a very understanding and industrious gentleman), did apparently influence the General all he could that way. These proceedings, by that time the General came to London, had given such an alarm to Sir Arthur Haselrig, Mr. Scot, and the rest of that party, that they began already to cast about how they might deliver themselves from so dangerous a person; divers of them made a tender to me of the generalship, if I would declare, and march their army against him, which had been no difficult undertaking, his army being small and his horse very bad, and our army being highly and particularly disgusted with him and his; because all along their march through England they had taken upon them a distinguishing name of 'Coldstreamers,' as if they had done some mighty thing more than the rest, whereas they had only fared harder, until we had opened to them the way to better cheer. But, however, I had given General Monk my word to be his friend, and therefore could not break it; besides, I assured myself he was doing that that I and all good men prayed for, and therefore was not to be disturbed, but rather assisted by all that sincerely wished the public good. This rendered me with them in the same state as General Monk, or rather worse, inasmuch as principles are less reconcilable than interests. The General had very wisely for himself caused all the regiments to march out of London, to remote and distant quarters, the day before his army came into the town; so that there was no apparent opposition to him, but that he was master of his own actions, or at least might have been so if he pleased. Yet the jealousy grew so strong every day more and more with those that aimed at maintaining the oligarchy, that they resolved to put the General upon some action that might lose his interest in the city, and by consequence in the nation; the old army (all but those he called Coldstreamers, that he brought up with him) being sufficiently disobliged, not only by that form of distinction these had so cheaply purchased, but also by the plain distrust he had shown of them, in removing them so far from London and dispersing their quarters; for, if they could reduce his interest within the compass of that small army, and that the Presbyterians and Cavaliers would look on and become unconcerned in him, they knew how easily and speedily to do his business.

" In order to this, Sir Arthur Haselrig and his party caused a meeting to be summoned in the Council Chamber of such persons as they liked best, as well members of the Council of War as members of their Council. Sir Arthur himself was created General, and as soon as he came they locked themselves up and set guards at the doors, with express orders that none whatever should be suffered to come so much as near them. Of all this, myself and several others that were members of both Councils, and such as were looked upon as General Monk's friends, had not the least notice.[1] But they had not been sitting half an hour, before an officer of the army, meeting me and Mr. Weaver in Fleet Street, stopped the coach we were in, and asked me whether I knew of the Council of War now sitting in the Council Chamber at Whitehall, which, he said, was certainly met upon very important affairs, because of the locking their doors and the orders they had given, both which he, then being in the outward room, saw and heard. Upon this, Mr. Weaver and I made haste to Whitehall, and found no access was to be

---

[1] It is here omitted to be said, but it is clear from what follows, that Monk himself was summoned to the meeting; its object, indeed, being to prevail upon him to act with Haselrig and his party against the City.

had to them, although Mr. Weaver was of the Council
of State as well as I, and the respect the officers that
guarded the doors bore us had allowed us to knock and
call at several of the doors; so that we were forced with
shame to retire to the Lady Monk's lodgings, whom we
found extremely apprehensive of their designs, assuring
us her husband knew nothing of this sudden calling
them together. She was not satisfied until she had
caused us to return with her to the Council door, where
she knocked very hard, and called aloud that she had
business of great consequence to impart to her husband;
but neither her authority nor her artifice could get them
within to open the doors or give one word of answer.
After this second repulse, we waited on my Lady back
to her lodgings, and stayed there till the General came,
which was until it was past two of the clock in the
morning; he brought with him as much confusion and
disturbance in his face as ever was seen in any man's of
his courage and resolution. He told us all was nought,
and that this was plainly a designed and packed meeting; and that he saw they meant to ruin him, for they
had taken a pretence from a ridiculous attempt of some
apprentices and others in the City some days before,
and had expressly ordered him to pull down, that very
morning, all the gates, portcullises, and chains of the
City of London, and to send prisoners to the Tower ten
of the principal citizens. His lady and we laid before
him the certain ruin such an action would bring upon
him; that it would lose him the hearts of all the honest
and sober party, and deliver him up into the hands of
those that perfectly hated him. He replied that, be it as
it would, he could not now do other than to obey their
orders, which was indeed punctually performed the
same morning: so that the next day the Parliament
thought themselves in a capacity to use him as they

pleased; and accordingly, instead of making him General of all their forces, as he was promised and did expect, they pass one of their acts, all in the same day, by which they placed the command of their armies and forces in five Commissioners, or any three of them, whereof he had the honour to be one, and Sir Arthur Haselrig and three more of Sir Arthur's sure friends were the others."

The five Commissioners appointed were Monk, Haselrig, Morley, Walton, and Alured. Cooper was proposed as one, but his name was rejected by thirty votes against fifteen.[1] Shaftesbury's narrative proceeds :—

" The same evening, General Monk returned to his lodgings at Whitehall, where his lady, Sir Thomas Clarges, myself, and some other of his friends represented to him the condition he was in, and the neglect the Parliament had put upon him, so that his ruin was near at hand, if he did not take some vigorous course to prevent it. And we prevailed upon him so far, as that he returned with his forces the next morning into the City, and there demanded of those sitting at Westminster a full and free parliament, in a letter signed by himself and fourteen of the chief field-officers of his Coldstreams ; that afternoon repairing to Guildhall, where he gave the Lord Mayor and Court of Aldermen an account of what he had done, and made an apology for what he had been forced to do some days before. The merit of his present action did easily expiate for that great affront he had put upon them, insomuch as he was followed home to his quarters with the greatest acclamations imaginable; and through the whole City there was such expression

---

[1] Comm. Journ. Feb. 11, 1660; Ludlow's Memoirs, ii. 831.

of joy, both by ringing of bells, bonfires, roasting of
rumps, and all other ways that men's fancy could invent,
that the like has not been seen or heard peradventure
in any age."

Mr. Martyn adds, perhaps on Stringer's authority,
what is very likely, that Cooper, Popham, and other
Presbyterians, helped to reconcile Monk with the City
authorities after he had angered them by acting on the
instigation of Haselrig's party; and the same writer
tells from Stringer the following story of Cooper on this
occasion. As Sir Anthony and Popham were returning
home, the mob, all for the City and against the Rump,
surrounded their carriage, crying out, "Down with the
Rump!" Sir Anthony put his head out of the window,
and said, "What, gentlemen, not one good piece in a
rump?" The mob was pleased with the joke, and,
recognising friends, followed the carriage with cheers.[1]
To return to Shaftesbury's narrative:—

"This so frightened and alarmed the Parliament, that
they immediately vote a filling up of their House, and
are now willing to impart the power they can hold no
longer within the narrow bounds of their own number
to some others of their friends; but they passed withal
the strictest qualifications imaginable, that none but
such as were zealous men of the party might get
amongst them. So that they made appear to the world
that their design was to have continued a legislative
power in themselves, their friends, and their posterity,
and never settle a government that might be equal and
just to the people; whose security could lie in nothing
so much as that their representatives should, in a short

[1] Martyn's Life, i. 226.

distance of time, annual or biennial, be accountable to
them, and now eligible by them. Neither was General
Monk without his apprehensions that matters might
go too fast for him, and overset him; and he at last
not finding his own account, he refused divers of the
worthiest aldermen and citizens, that addressed to him
to have their militia raised, and care taken to have the
best men put in the head of them, which himself might
nominate. He treated at the same time with all sorts
of men, and appointed a select number of several sorts
to confer together, and consider what they had to offer
concerning the present posture of affairs; intermixing
them as he thought fit, sometimes two, sometimes three
parties together, keeping the world in great uncertainty,
and (if myself and others that were nearest him were
not mistaken) himself too. But he must suddenly come
to some issue or another, for the Lord Fairfax, a man of
great courage, resolution, and integrity, with the greatest
part of the gentry and ministers of the North, who were
all not a little influenced by Mr. Bowles, a Presbyterian
minister at York, a man of great wisdom and reputation, and fit for the management of the greatest affairs;
these, with the entire Presbyterian party, had declared
for a free Parliament, or the re-admitting the secluded
members. The same declaration was also made by
Sir Charles Coote, Sir Theophilus Jones, Sir Henry
Ingoldsby, and others in Ireland, to whose courage,
fidelity, and conduct was owing, not only all that was
done there, but much of what was done in England; for
we should have hardly ventured to have made an opposition to the Committee of Safety; neither would General
Monk have broken his treaty with General Fleetwood,
if we had not had assurance from them of considerable
aid and assistance by Sir Charles Coote, who was sent
over on purpose to us.

" The General was now removed to Alderman Wale's house, next door to Drapers' Hall, where, as I was waiting on my Lady, Colonel Markham came to me, and told me he just then came from the General, and as he went in unto him, he met coming out Sir Arthur Haselrig and Mr. Scot, whom he overheard saying they would secure Sir Anthony Cooper before to-morrow noon. But he thought they had been tampering with him, and feared they had come to some agreement; upon this I presently went to the General, told him what I had heard, and pressed him to deal clearly with me; and after some dark discourse, I got from him a direct acknowledgment that he was come to a full agreement with them, and had engaged to return the next morning to his lodgings at Whitehall, and to support their interest and obey their commands; he did not deny to me that they had promised him to be sole General of all their forces; he promised me they should do me no wrong, and that he would take upon himself to make all friendship betwixt me and them, and to take care of my interest as his particular friend. This being about five o'clock in the afternoon, I left him and told him I would wait on him at supper and desired some more discourse upon this subject with him after supper. So I went immediately to my Lady Monk, and gave her an account of the whole matter, and desired her to send for her brother Clarges, as I would for Colonel Clobery and Colonel Knight, that we might altogether make our utmost effort upon the General; which we did that night, and it was near three o'clock in the morning before he yielded to us, when we obtained from him a resolution to restore the secluded members to their places that very morning, and a commission to Sir Thomas Clarges and myself to summon them together, and so cause them to attend him at the Prince's lodgings

in Whitehall by nine o'clock that morning, from whence
he would cause them to be restored with honour and
safety to their places in the Parliament-house. Sir
Thomas and myself lost no time; before eight o'clock
that morning we had got together to Mr. Annesley's
house in Drury Lane a considerable number of the
secluded members, and before nine brought them to the
great room in the Prince's lodgings in Whitehall; and
all this happened to be without giving the other party
the least notice or alarm, inasmuch as that Sir Arthur
Haselrig came to wait on the General, thinking he was
returned to Whitehall upon their treaty of the day before; but as soon as he came into the aforesaid great
room, and saw so considerable a number of the old
secluded members, he changed his colour and grew extremely pale, and in great passion came up to me, and
told me this was my doing, but it should cost blood; I
replied, his own if he pleased, but Sir Anthony Cooper
would not be secured that morning. The General just
then came out, who told Sir Arthur that challenged him
of his promise that [it was necessary for the public peace
to restore these members, who had declared they intended
no alteration of the government; and since there was no
method of issuing summonses but by writs in the name
of the keepers of the liberty of England by authority of
Parliament, it could not be apprehended that any other
government would be introduced]."[1]

The admission of the secluded members took place
on the twenty-first of February. Cooper, now colonel
of a regiment of horse, commanded the guard appointed
to escort them into the House.[2] This had been Cooper's

[1] The words between brackets are supplied from Martyn's narrative;
the fragment found among Lord Shaftesbury's papers ending in the
middle of a sentence.
[2] Coke's Detection, ii. 95. Independent testimonies to the important

object since the last restoration of the Rump, which he had had so large a share in effecting; and he and his followers in the Rump now finally separated from their former republican coadjutors, Haselrig, Scot, Nevill, and others. The Presbyterians were now in an overwhelming majority in the Parliament. A new Council of State was immediately appointed, in which none but Presbyterians and friends of a restoration were named. It need not be said that Cooper was one. The others were Monk, Popham, Pierpoint, Crewe, Colonel Rossiter, Knightly, Colonel Morley, Lord Fairfax, Sir Gilbert Gerard, St. John, Sir John Temple, Widdrington, Sir John Evelyn, Sir William Waller, Sir Richard Onslow, Sir William Lewis, Montagu, Sir Edward Harley, Colonel Norton, Annesley, Holles, Colonel Thompson, Trevor, Sir John Holland, Sir John Potts, Colonel Birch, Sir Harbottle Grimstone, Swinton, Weaver, and Serjeant Maynard.

Monk was appointed Commander-in-chief, and Cooper received from him commissions to be Governor of the Isle of Wight and Captain of a company of foot in that island.[1]

It was soon settled, after the admission of the secluded Presbyterian members, that the Long Parliament should

part which Cooper had in persuading Monk to restore the secluded members, and to his influence at this time with Monk, may be found in Bishop Kennet's Register, pp. 59, 61, 62; Baker's Chronicle, ed. 1684, p. 687; and Gumble's Life of Monk, p. 261; and see the last of the suppressed passages of Ludlow in Appendix III.

[1] Wood, Ath. Oxon. ed. Bliss, iv. 70. The captain's commission, dated February 25, is in Lord Shaftesbury's possession; but I have not been able to find the commission of governor. There is, however, no doubt that Cooper was at this time Governor of the Isle of Wight, and his commission as such was temporarily renewed in the name of Charles II. on the Restoration.

expire on the seventeenth of March, and that a new Parliament should be called for the twenty-fifth of April. On the thirteenth of March it was resolved without a division, "that the engagement, appointed to be taken by members of Parliament and others in these words, 'I do declare and promise that I will be true and faithful to the Commonwealth of England, as the same is now established, without a King or House of Lords,' be discharged and taken off the file ;" and "that all orders, enjoining the taking of the said engagement, be, and are hereby, vacated and expunged out of the Journal Book of Parliament, and that Mr. Prynne, Serjeant Maynard, and Colonel Harley do see the same expunged accordingly."

The following letter from Montagu, afterwards Earl of Sandwich, who had the command of the fleet, addressed to Cooper, is a proof of his activity at this time as a member of the Council of State :—

" SWIFTSURE, OFF GREENHITHE,
" <i>March</i> 24, 1659.

" SIR,—This evening I have received your commands concerning an establishment for the navy, which I shall obey as soon as I possibly can. I suppose it will necessarily require Monday's time, and Tuesday's perhaps, to inform myself and consider about it; after which you shall receive a further account from

" Your most humble servant,
"E. MOUNTAGU."

The foiled Republicans now bethought themselves of an expedient, to play Monk against the Presbyterian leaders, and offer him their support if he would take the Crown himself. There is no doubt that such an offer was now made to Monk by Haselrig, Scot, and other Republicans. This is stated in the account of events preceding the Restoration appended to later editions of Sir Richard Baker's Chronicle, which, though ill-written and clumsily put together, has value, as being known to have been written with much assistance from Sir Thomas Clarges, Monk's brother-in-law; and the statement is confirmed by many passages of the despatches of the French Ambassador, M. de Bourdeaux. The idea was absurd: Monk treated the applicants civilly, and tried to keep them in good humour, but never entertained the project. Clarges gave Cooper information of what was passing. The following is an extract, from a narrative inspired, if not written, by Clarges himself:—

"The Council of State sitting at the time of this private conference, and within two chambers of the place where it was transacted, he (Clarges) sent in to the Council to Sir Anthony Ashley Cooper, and informed him of what he knew, and what he further suspected; upon which it was agreed, that, as soon as the General should depart from them and come into the Council, he should move that all clerks and attendants that were not Councillors should withdraw, and the doors be locked, and then declare that he had had information of a dangerous design in some seditious persons, who were continuing to make disturbances in the nation, and that they had proceeded so far as to make some indecent overtures to him, of which he desired that the Council might receive a full discovery, that thereupon

they might apply themselves to prevent the consequences of it. But the General, being unwilling to
expose those men to ruin, though they deserved not his
favour, because his purposes were designed to be effected
by the most peaceable ways, told the Council that there
was not so much danger in agitation as they apprehended, but that it was true some had been with him
to be resolved in scruples concerning the present transactions in Parliament, but they went away from him
well satisfied." [1]

The despatches of Bourdeaux entirely bear out the
account given in the foregoing extract. Bourdeaux
writes that there are different opinions about Monk's
object, but always gives his own opinion that he intends

[1] Phillips's Continuation of Baker's Chronicle, ed. 1684, p. 693.
This is probably a fair and correct account of an incident which has
been wonderfully exaggerated and enlarged in the Locke Memoir of
Shaftesbury, and in Martyn's Life. The story, as there told, is as
follows : that Haselrig and Scot had a zealous coadjutor in Bourdeaux,
the French Ambassador, who represented that he was instructed by
Cardinal Mazarin to urge Monk to make himself King and offer him
aid from France; that Monk consented; that Monk's wife, who, being
concealed behind the curtains, had overheard the conversation, sent
Clarges to inform Cooper; that Cooper immediately summoned the
Council of State, declared what he had heard, conjured Monk to
restore Charles, and obtained from him the requisite assurances, and
various changes among officers of the army and governors of forts
likely to make the restoration of Charles more secure. The account in
the Locke Memoir ends thus: "The French Ambassador, who had
the night before sent away an express to Mazarin, positively to assure
him that things went here as he desired, and that Monk was fixed by
him in his resolution to take on himself the government, was not a
little astonished the next day to find things taking another turn.
And indeed this so much disgraced him in the French Court that he
was presently called home, and soon after broke his heart." There is
no such despatch in the French Archives, which I have carefully
examined. M. Guizot has fairly published all that is material in
the despatches of Bourdeaux of this period in the Appendix to his
Life of Monk (Documents Historiques, Nos. 45—52, March 15 to
April 2, 1660), and in the Appendix to his History of Richard
Cromwell and the Restoration (Documents Historiques, vol. ii.
Nos. 33—36, March 25 to April 5, 1660).

to restore Charles; he speaks of the offer made to Monk
by the Republicans, and mentions surmises that he desired to make himself king; he makes no mention of
communications between himself and Haselrig's party.
Convinced that Monk meant to restore the King, he
endeavoured to induce him and the Presbyterians to
avail themselves of the aid of France, and employ France
to mediate the conditions of restoration; for this purpose
he tried to flatter Monk, through Clarges, and made
strong professions of Cardinal Mazarin's friendship for
him, and readiness to serve him. In playing this
game, Bourdeaux appears to have a little exceeded his
instructions, and practised some diplomatic finessing.
Anxious to secure for France the honour of mediation
and all the influence which would flow from it, and fore-
seeing a strong desire to avoid French interference, he
endeavoured to ingratiate himself with Monk by flattering messages, offering the aid of the French Government
to obtain for him from Charles all that he could desire
of profit or honour, and stating that the French king
was so completely his friend that he would even aid him
for his own elevation to the throne. "It has seemed
to me suitable," says Bourdeaux, writing to Cardinal
Mazarin, "to dispose him by these marks of esteem to
a better reception of the other proposals with which
I might be charged."[1] This crafty insinuation of
Bourdeaux, designed to aid the acceptance of an offer
of French mediation for the restoration of Charles, is
apparently the sole foundation for the story of his active
concurrence in the scheme to make Monk king. His

[1] March 29, 1660; Guizot's Monk (Documents Historiques, No. 50).

instructions from Mazarin were no more than to convey
to Monk general expressions of friendship and support
in his designs, which were believed to be for the restoration of Charles. It was of course the object of Bourdeaux
to stand well with Monk, to be prepared for all con-
tingencies, to do the best for French influence, and to
use flattery as well as other means for gaining knowledge of Monk's plans. He writes that in his interviews
with Monk he could extract nothing from him ; and the
statements of Bourdeaux in the above-quoted despatch,
and in another to Mazarin of April 5, describing an
interview with Monk,[1] tally sufficiently with the account
derived from Clarges.[2] It may be safely stated, then, that
Monk did not entertain the idea of making himself
king, that the French Ambassador did not act in such
a scheme, and that the story of Cooper's foiling Monk's
design for the kingship is an extravagant exaggeration.[3]

Another alarm and difficulty arose for those who were
now endeavouring to bring about a restoration of the
old monarchy from an insurrection headed by Lambert.
The re-established Rump had made Lambert a prisoner
in the Tower, on his refusing to find bail for twenty
thousand pounds. The Republican leaders were engaged

[1] No. 52 of Appendix to Guizot's Monk.
[2] Baker's Chronicle, p. 695.
[3] This story, soon after its publication in the Locke Memoir, was
satisfactorily refuted, without aid from the French Archives, by George
Granville, Lord Lansdowne, nephew of Sir John Grenville or Granville,
who negotiated with Monk for Charles, in his " Vindication of General
Monk." (Works, vol. ii. pp. 159 seqq.) It is stated in a despatch
of Bourdeaux of July 1, 1660 (in the archives of the French Foreign
Office), that Clarges had told Lord St. Albans that parties anxious to
make the restored King quarrel with France had urged him (Clarges) to
say that Bourdeaux had charged him to persuade Monk to make himself
Protector, and keep Charles out. Bourdeaux adds, that Clarges had
already publicly denied this at the Hague.

in a plan for freeing him by finding the bail required by
the Council of State, in order that he might head an
insurrection; but before this plan could be executed,
Lambert acted for himself, and made his escape on the
sixth of April. He raised a few troops in the midland
counties, but could make no resistance to a small force
sent against him by Monk under Colonel Ingoldsby.

The following letter was written by Cooper to
Montagu on April 23; and there is no stint in his
rejoicing at Lambert's defeat :—

" MY LORD,—Your Lordship's letter brings that account
of the fleet, and so satisfactory as might be expected
from it, since put under the conduct of such a general.
I hope you did not mistake the expression in my letter
about transposing your officers, as if it had any reflexion
of not approving what your Lordship had done, being only
to give you notice timely of this alteration about sending
the ' Worcester ' into the Straits, lest, when your officers
are fixed, it might be disobliging to remove them back.

" This morning the certain news of Colonel Lambert his
being taken came to the Council. There appeared with
him six troops of horse in Daventry fields in Northamp-
tonshire, Colonel Okey, Axtel, Creed, Sir Arthur Haselrig's son and others. But when Colonel Ingoldsby came
up, the kind men without showing much courage rendered themselves. Thus God has blasted the wicked in
their reputations and bloody designs, and I hope will
bless us with a happy settlement, which is the prayer of,

" My Lord,

" Your most faithful and humble servant,

" ANTHONY ASHLEY COOPER." [1]

[1] The latter half of this letter is printed in Bishop Kennet's Register,

In the meantime, Cooper and the Presbyterian leaders were pursuing their design of a restoration of Charles on conditions. Lord Mordaunt, writing to Hyde on April 19, mentions Sir Anthony Ashley Cooper as a member of a Presbyterian "cabal," then meeting constantly, of which the Earls of Bedford, Northumberland, and Manchester, Lord Wharton, Holles, Annesley, Pierpoint, Popham, Sir William Lewis, and Sir Gilbert Gerard, were among the members. The object of these Presbyterian leaders was to propose the restoration of Charles on terms very similar to those which had been offered in 1648 to his father in the Isle of Wight, and they were discussing how the chief offices of state should be distributed. They are described as fearing that Monk would spoil their plans, and recall the King without conditions.[1] This fear was realized.

When the Convention Parliament of two Houses for England and Wales, according to the old constitution, met at Westminster on the twenty-fifth of April, Monk had arranged his plans with the King through Sir John Grenville. Lord Lansdowne, in his "Vindication of Monk," in which he refutes the story of Cooper's thwarting Monk's aims on the Crown, describes Cooper as acting with the Presbyterian leaders independently of Monk, and proposing with them a negotiation which Monk's prompt action cut short. Cooper had been returned to the new House of Commons for Wiltshire. The Act of the expiring Long Parliament by which the summoning of this Convention had been

p. 120. I have been enabled to complete the letter from a copy preserved at St. Giles's among Lord Shaftesbury's papers.

[1] Clarendon State Papers, vol. iii. pp. 705, 729.

settled, had prescribed qualifications for its members
designed to exclude old royalists, and had contained a
clause saving the rights of such members of the old
House of Lords, and such only, as had been always
faithful to the Parliament. With Monk's countenance
and support these restrictions were disregarded, when
the Parliament met. The disappointment and dismay
of the Presbyterians were great.[1] Pepys records the
reproaches of Montagu, who thought the Presbyterians
too exacting, but "shook his shoulders when he told me
[Pepys] how Monk had betrayed them, for it was he
that did put them upon standing to put out the lords
and other members that come not within the qualifications, which he did not like; but, however, he had done
his business, though it be with some kind of baseness."[2]
The Presbyterians could now no longer control the movement, and had nothing to do but to make a virtue of
necessity. Sir John Grenville appeared in both Houses
on the first of May, and presented the King's letters
to the two Speakers and his famous Declaration, dated
from Breda. On the twenty-third of May Charles landed
at Dover, and on the twenty-ninth, his birthday, he
entered London, a restored King, and restored without
conditions. The two Houses had sent Commissioners to
Breda to invite him to return. Cooper was one of the
twelve deputed by the Commons. The other eleven
were Lords Fairfax, Falkland, Bruce, Castleton, Herbert,
and Mandeville, Sir Horatio Townshend, Sir George

---

[1] See the Despatches of Bourdeaux, May 10, 21, Nos. 59 and 60,
Appendix to Guizot's Monk.
[2] Diary, April 29, 1660, vol. i. p. 61.

Booth, Sir John Holland, Sir Henry Cholmley, and Denzil Holles.

On his journey to Breda on this occasion Cooper met with an accident by the upsetting of his carriage, which caused an internal abscess that was never cured. That Shaftesbury constantly suffered from this malady during his later years of political eminence has been made notorious by the foul gibes of vile lampooners. This misfortune brought him advantage by leading, in the year 1666, at Oxford, to the acquaintance of John Locke, who quickly became his intimate friend, and an inmate of his house; whose friendship was a chief help and solace of his troubled life, and whose great name is inseparably associated with Shaftesbury's to bring him honour.

We have now gone through twenty years of Sir Anthony Ashley Cooper's public life, which began before he was of age : he began as a Royalist, and he is now a Royalist again. The intervening time has been full of change and revolution, and he has changed often, influencing public changes or following in their wake. His course has been that of a restless, excitable, eager, impulsive man, not content to be idle or let his talents long lie hid under a bushel; full of desire to govern men and control events, and full of confidence in himself. Such a man is prone to quit a party if he does not have his own way: such a man is often the most hopeful in the outset, and the first to despair. Every politician's life is a public target, and satire and malice have not spared Cooper's changes. Lord Macaulay has latterly given new life and prominence to

the sparkling satire of Butler and Dryden's reckless
and venomous invective.[1] The author of "Hudibras" was
an honest and consistent Royalist, and it was but natural
that he should misinterpret Cooper's actions, and suppose
interested calculation and unprincipled scheming where
the friendly and charitably disposed and well-informed
may see the working of an ardent temperament on an
active intellect. Admirable as is Dryden's satire for
keenness and his verse for vigour, the malice and falsehoods of one who was himself unrivalled for apostasy,
and who had chosen the ignoble task of reviling Shaftesbury to please his royal master, should receive reproba-
tion. Dryden, who bespattered Cromwell's grave with
fulsome flattery in the first days of his son's Protectorship, when it seemed strong and durable, and who, in a
short twelvemonth, flattered the restored Charles and
vilified Cromwell; Dryden, who slavered the Lord
Treasurer Clifford with praise in one dedication, and in
another, a few years after, lauded his successor, Danby,
as the repairer of Clifford's mismanagements;[2] Dryden,
who, when he addressed his venal dedication to Clifford,
praised the acts of the Cabal, and afterwards denounced
them when hope of other profit inspired him against
Shaftesbury; Dryden, who could describe Charles the
Second as a liberal patron of arts and letters when he
wrote to please James, and sneer at him as neglecting

---

[1] In his Essay on Sir William Temple; where Macaulay speaks only
of Dryden's "Absalom and Achitophel," and does not mention the
fiercer and coarser invective of "The Medal."

[2] Compare Dryden's dedication of his "Amboyna" to Clifford in
1673 with his dedication of "All for Love" to Danby in 1678.
Presents of money were received and expected in return for these
eulogistic dedications: and this mode of flattery was a part of Dryden's
means of living.

and degrading genius when to James had succeeded William;[1] Dryden, who when Charles the Second, who had befriended ｟him and whom he had flattered, lay cold in the grave, endeavoured to load his memory with the opprobrium of his own licentious playwriting, the willing servility of a coarse nature to degraded tastes;[2] Dryden, who, fresh from ridicule and abuse

[1] In the "Threnodia Augustalis," an ode on the death of Charles II. by Dryden, "servant of his late Majesty and the present King," there are these flattering lines:—

> "Amidst the peaceful triumphs of his reign,
>   What wonder if the kindly beams he shed
> Revived the drooping Arts again,
>   If Science raised her head,
>   And soft Humanity, that from rebellion fled!"

In his Address to Sir Godfrey Kneller, published in 1694, Dryden wrote:—

> "Apelles' art an Alexander found,
> And Raphael did with Leo's gold abound,
> But Homer was with barren laurel crowned;
> Thou hadst thy Charles a while, and so had I,
> But pass we that unpleasing image by."

[2] In a reply to Jeremy Collier's reproaches for his immoral playwriting, Dryden wrote, in his very last Epilogue, composed a few weeks before his death, for a representation for his own benefit:—

> "Perhaps the parson stretched a point too far
> When with our theatres he waged a war.
> He tells you that this very moral age
> Received the first infection from the stage;
> But sure a banished court, with lewdness fraught,
> The seeds of open vice returning brought.
> The poets, who must live by courts or starve,
> Were proud so good a government to serve;
> And mixing with buffoons and pimps profane,
> Tainted the stage for some small snip of gain.
> Thus did the thriving malady prevail,
> The court its head, the poets but the tail.
> The sin was of our native growth, 'tis true,
> The scandal of the sin was wholly new.
> Misses there were, but modestly concealed;
> Whitehall the naked Venus first revealed,
> Who standing as at Cyprus in her shrine,
> The strumpet was adored with rites divine."

But Dryden's licentious writing is not confined to his plays. Lord Macaulay, who, in his early Essay on Sir William Temple, assailing

of Roman Catholic priests, and from expounding in matchless verse the tenets of Protestantism, became a Roman Catholic when it seemed likely that James would establish the Roman Catholic religion, and when to adopt that religion was the way to the King's heart: it is this Dryden who has arraigned Shaftesbury for political venality, treason, and apostasy, and who by the power of his verse and the fame of his poetry has been mainly instrumental in blackening Shaftesbury's name for posterity. A careful examination of Shaftesbury's public career and private life and character reveals many misstatements and exaggerations in Dryden's attacks. Change of opinion is not necessarily wicked or dishonest. In times of successive revolution, patriots who desire public quiet and orderly rule may accept and endeavour to make the best of several successive forms of government. In France, do we not know of honourable men who have been successively Royalists under Charles the Tenth, Royalists under Louis Philippe, Republicans, supporters of the Second Empire? In our own land and in our own time, in happy absence of revolution, have not foremost statesmen and whole political parties, in the short space of one generation,

---

Shaftesbury, calls as a witness Dryden's "gorgeous satiric muse, who comes sweeping by in sceptred pall, borrowed from her more august sisters," has in his later "History of England" given a scathing sketch of Dryden's character. "Self-respect and a fine sense of the becoming," says Macaulay the historian, "were not to be expected from one who had led a life of mendicancy and adulation." And after rebuking the impurity of Dryden's plays, he proceeds to reprobate justly the grossness of his translations. "He made the grossest satires of Juvenal more gross, interpolated loose descriptions in the tales of Boccaccio, and polluted the sweet and limpid poetry of the Georgics with filth which would have moved the loathing of Virgil." (History of England, ii. 200.)

completely changed their political creeds? It is beyond
doubt that Shaftesbury never sought or made pecuniary
profit out of his politics: Dryden's charge of venality is
false. Shaftesbury was born to wealth and high social
station. If he was ambitious, public ambition is not a
sin; it is indeed recognised in others as the useful spur
of noble minds to public service. Shaftesbury may have
been headstrong, impatient, volatile; but he was not
mercenary, he was not self-seeking; and no imputation
or even suspicion lies on him, in any part of his career,
of trickery or falsehood.

CHAPTER VIII.

1660.

AT the time of the Restoration, Sir Anthony Ashley
Cooper was close on completing his thirty-ninth year.
He was at once specially recommended by Monk to
the notice of the restored King, and received an early
mark of favour. While Charles halted at Canterbury
for a couple of days before making his triumphal entry
into London, he gave Garters to Monk, Montagu, and
a faithful Royalist, the Earl of Southampton; he conferred on Morrice, a relative of Monk, who had more
than any one else of his confidence during the last few
eventful months, the office of Secretary of State; and
he made Cooper a member of the Privy Council.[1]

[1] Continuation of Clarendon's Life, 13. Clarendon says that it
was hoped and believed that, as Cooper's wife was a niece of the Earl

Q 2

Cooper afterwards appeared at the head of his regiment of cavalry, which had been Fleetwood's, in the army assembled at Blackheath when the King approached the capital. Like all who had been implicated in any of the irregular proceedings of the past period of civil wars and revolutionary governments, he availed himself of the King's promise of pardon from Breda, to all who within forty days should properly demand it, and were not afterwards excepted by Parliament, and he received a formal pardon on the twenty-seventh of June. Further pardons were granted to him under the Great Seal on the tenth of February and the eighth of June, 1661.[1]

In the distribution of offices and honours which followed the Restoration, great pains were taken to attain an appearance of equality between those who had steadily clung to the Royal fortunes and old adversaries who had now mainly contributed to effect the Restoration. To Monk both King and people gave pre-eminence of merit, and he was for the moment the nation's idol; he was re-appointed Lord General, was appointed Master of the Horse, a Groom of the Bedchamber, and Lord-Lieutenant of Ireland, with the understanding that he should perform the duties of this last office by deputy, and was created Duke of

of Southampton, "his slippery humour would be easily restrained and fixed by the uncle." This early nomination of Cooper to the Privy Council is doubtless the explanation of a statement by eulogistic biographers that Charles showed his high admiration of Cooper by placing him in the Privy Council above his brother, the Duke of Gloucester, and above Monk. (Rawl. Rediviv. p. 49, and "Brief Account" in Harleian Miscellany, vol. v. p. 368.)

[1] These pardons are among the papers in Lord Shaftesbury's possession at St. Giles's.

Albemarle. Hyde, the King's chief adviser in exile, was made Lord Chancellor and a Peer, with the title of Baron Hyde; he became Earl of Clarendon later, at the Coronation. The office of Lord Treasurer was given to the Earl of Southampton, but it was first, at his request, put into commission, that the Treasury might be brought into some order before he assumed the charge, which he did in September. The offices of Lord Chancellor and Lord Treasurer having been given to Royalists, the office third in rank in the kingdom, that of Lord Privy Seal, was given to Viscount Saye and Sele, one of the survivors of the Presbyterian leaders of the beginning of the Civil War. Ormond, one of the King's most devoted and distinguished followers, was made Lord Steward; he was raised from the rank of Marquis, to be a Duke in the Irish Peerage, and was made an Earl in the Peerage of England. The Earl of Manchester, the Lord Kimbolton of 1641, was Lord Chamberlain; the Duke of York was appointed Lord High Admiral; Montagu, who had been the friend and servant of Cromwell, and one of his peers, and who had served under every government of the Commonwealth, was created Earl of Sandwich and appointed Master of the Wardrobe. Of the two Secretaries of State, one, Nicholas, was an old servant of the King and of his father; the other, Morrice, was a Presbyterian, and the particular friend of Monk. The Privy Council, comprising the King's two brothers and all surviving Privy Councillors of Charles the First, consisted at the outset of this reign of thirty members, of whom twelve had been opponents of the Royal cause;

viz. Monk, the Earls of Northumberland, Leicester, and Manchester, Viscount Saye and Sele, Lord Roberts (appointed Lord Deputy in Ireland, but who shortly after, on the death of Lord Saye and Sele, exchanged that office for the Privy Seal), Montagu, Morrice, Arthur Annesley, Denzil Holles, Charles Howard, and Sir Anthony Ashley Cooper.

Hyde continued to be the King's chief adviser. The name of Prime Minister was then known only as that of a French institution, and the name and office were regarded with dislike, founded partly on aversion to a French example, and partly on jealousy of inter-ference with the constitutional functions of the Privy Council. Charles, whose indolence and love of pleasure made him peculiarly dependent on Clarendon's labori-ousness, had the vanity of wishing to be thought to do everything himself, and loved to call himself his own *Premier Ministre.*[1] There was not then, as now, an united Ministry, dependent for existence on the con-fidence of the Parliament, and governing the King's policy; each Minister held his office at the King's pleasure, and was entirely the King's servant. There was no necessary unity of sentiment or action among the Ministers; high officers of State, and also sub-ordinate officials, often opposed in Parliament measures promoted by the King, and retained their offices; a Minister would be dismissed singly by the King on account of personal displeasure.

---

[1] M. de Bourdeaux mentions in a despatch of June 7, 1660, in the archives of the French Foreign Office, that Charles trusted a great deal to Hyde, but did not like him to be called Prime Minister.

The Privy Council being too numerous for matters requiring secrecy and despatch, a small Committee of that body was appointed, consisting of those who had most of the King's confidence and favour; and this Committee was his constant council of advice. Such a Committee of the Privy Council had existed before the Civil War.[1] It was called the Committee for Foreign Affairs, and, in common conversation, the King's Cabinet or Cabal. This Committee for Foreign Affairs is the origin of the present Cabinet. It was in the nature of things that it should become more important than the Privy Council itself. Its encroachments on the functions of the Privy Council gave rise to frequent complaints during the reign of Charles the Second. Twice during his reign, after the fall of Clarendon in 1667, and after the fall of Danby in 1679, Charles was so far moved by the popular outcry against Prime Minister and Cabinet as to promise publicly that he would be governed entirely by the advice of his Privy Council, and have no secrets from that body. But on both occasions the promise was almost immediately broken. In truth, a chief minister and a small council of advice were necessities for the Sovereign. Thus it happened that, in the interval between the Restoration and the Revolution of 1688, the Cabinet,

---

[1] Clarendon minutely describes such a Committee of the Privy Council in 1640. "These persons," he says, "made up the Committee of State (which was reproachfully after called the *juncto*, and enviously then in the Court the Cabinet Council), who were upon all occasions, when the Secretaries received any extraordinary intelligence, or were to make up any extraordinary despatch, or as often otherwise as was thought fit, to meet: whereas the body of the Council observed set days and hours for their meeting, and came not else together except specially summoned." (Hist. of Rebellion, ii. 99.)

notwithstanding all the opposition and obloquy which
it created, came to assume a regular form and recognised position in the State, and both Cabinet and
Prime Minister have long been practically important
parts of our Constitution.

Hyde, then, without the name of Prime Minister,
and holding a position materially different in many
respects from that of the Prime Minister of to-day,
became the chief director of public affairs; and he continued ostensibly to hold this position until his hard
fall in 1667. His first colleagues in the Committee
for Foreign Affairs, were Southampton, Monk, Ormond,
Lord Colepepper, and the new Secretaries of State,
Nicholas and Morrice. Hyde, Ormond, Colepepper,
and Nicholas, had formed the King's council of advice
in exile. Colepepper, who was also appointed Master
of the Rolls, died within a few months after the
Restoration. The Duke of York was called a little
later to the meetings of the Cabinet, and afterwards
Sheldon, the Bishop of London.[1] Thus, in the first
Cabinet of the Restoration, the Royalist party predomi-
nated; Monk (who was not a politician, and did not
shine in council) and Morrice being the only two there
of the King's new friends. The King called which of
his Privy Councillors he chose to this Committee, and,
when he chose, ceased to call them; some were sometimes called in for the discussion of a particular
measure, sometimes to aid the King in opposing his
usual Cabinet. The active supremacy of the King
must never be forgotten in judging the statesmen of

[1] Pepys's Diary, ii. 30, 155.

this period. Charles the Second continually had secrets from his Cabinet and Prime Minister, which he entrusted to favourites who were not even Privy Councillors. Most of the labour of administration fell on the chief Minister, and public odium fell on him for miscarriages; but a policy for which he was blamed had sometimes been determined on by Charles without his knowledge or against his remonstrances, in concert with other Ministers, or even with household parasites and mistresses. This soon became apparent under Clarendon's ostensible chief ministry. The Earl of Bristol, who had been one of Charles's Secretaries of State while he was in exile, but who, having embraced the Roman Catholic religion, was excluded from office and from the 'Privy Council on the Restoration, and the Duke of Buckingham, a friend of Charles's youth, who in May 1662 was appointed a Privy Councillor but had no office, came to possess the King's ear and know all his secrets, and used their influence against Clarendon. Sir Charles Berkeley, a servant of the Duke of York, afterwards created Earl of Falmouth, gained a great ascendency with the King by agreeable personal qualities and by forwarding his pleasures. Bennet, afterwards Earl of Arlington, who succeeded Nicholas as Secretary of State in 1662, joined with Berkeley against Clarendon, who had hoped to play Bennet against Berkeley; and all who wished to thwart Clarendon with the King found an eager patron in the favourite mistress, Lady Castlemaine, who nightly held a rival Cabinet in the palace.

The Convention Parliament, which had recalled

Charles, was not dissolved until the twenty-second of December, 1660. The resolution passed by the Lords, when they first met, for excluding all peers created since the commencement of the Civil War, was, after the King's return, rescinded in prompt obedience to a royal message, and the new peers were admitted to sit. Two days after the King's entry into London, he gave his assent to a Bill declaring the two Houses then sitting to be a legal parliament. It is obvious that a parliament which had not been legally convened, if the stamp of law were required, could not thus invest itself with legality; but the expedient was useful for the moment; and all the acts of this Convention were afterwards submitted for confirmation to the parliament which assembled in the following year under the forms of the Constitution. The oaths of allegiance and supremacy were administered to the members of both Houses. Sir Anthony Ashley Cooper, now a member of the Privy Council, was one of the representatives of the new Government in the House of Commons. The others were Morrice, Arthur Annesley, Holles, Charles Howard, and Sir Heneage Finch, the Solicitor-General. Cooper at present held no office besides that of Privy Councillor; he was not appointed Chancellor of the Exchequer and Under Treasurer till nearly a year after the Restoration, nor till after he had been made a Peer, which was not till the Coronation.

A few slight notices of Cooper's speeches in the Convention Parliament are furnished by some extracts printed in Cobbett's " Parliamentary History " from a

manuscript Diary of one of the members.[1] It would
seem, from the extracts there published, that Morrice
and Finch took the leading part in the debates in
behalf of the Government.

The question of pardon and indemnity was the first
which called for settlement. The Commons had begun
upon a Bill with this object before the King's arrival,
and he- seized the earliest occasion to urge them to
expedite its progress. It was yet some time, however,
before the Bill passed the two Houses; so many questions arose about exceptions.

Charles, in his Declaration sent from Breda, in which
he offered a general pardon, had guarded himself by
speaking of such exceptions as might be made by
Parliament; and in his letter to the House of Commons
which accompanied that Declaration, he had clearly
indicated his expectation that Parliament would exact
an atonement for his father's death. It is clear, both
from previous declarations and from addresses which
he afterwards made to the House of Lords, that the
wish of Charles was, that all who had joined in the
sentence on his father or who had signed his death-
warrant, should suffer the extreme penalties of high
treason. The Commons by no means carried out this
intention. They began by resolving that of the surviving judges of Charles the First who sat when
sentence was passed upon him, seven only should be

---

[1] It is stated that the Diary was communicated to the editors of
the "Parliamentary or Constitutional History of England" by the
Rev. Dr. Charles Lyttelton, Dean of Exeter (vol. iv. p. 73). It would
be of interest to know where this manuscript Diary now is. The Dean
was afterwards Bishop of Carlisle.

excepted for life and estate.[1] The remainder of such
surviving judges of the King were to be visited with
penalties not extending to life, to be determined by
a future Act. The seven to be excepted for life and
estate were selected: General Harrison, Say, Colonel
John Jones, Scot, Holland, Lisle, and Barkstead. A
proclamation was then published by the King, at the
request of the two Houses, calling upon all the late
King's judges, who sat when sentence was passed, to
surrender on pain of being excepted for life and estate.
Nineteen surrendered in consequence of this proclamation. There were eleven who failed to surrender;
and the Commons, before the Bill left them for the
House of Lords, added these eleven to the seven previously selected to be excepted for life and estate.
Had they surrendered, their lives would have been
secure, so far as depended on the intentions of the
House of Commons. Having thus dealt with the
living judges who had sat when sentence was passed,
the Commons proposed, with regard to their associates
now dead, that Bradshaw, the President of the Court,

---

[1] Commons' Journals, May 14, 1660. This resolution has been
misdescribed by Mr. Hallam and other writers, who have made an
unjust charge of inconsistency and breach of faith against the
Commons. Mr. Hallam erroneously says that "the Commons voted
that not more than seven *persons* should lose the benefit of the
indemnity, both as to life and estate," and then proceeds to represent
all their subsequent exceptions, whether for life and estate or for
minor penalties, as infractions of this first resolution. (Constit. History,
ii. 414.) The resolution was strictly confined to *those then living of
the King's judges who had sat when sentence was given*, and limited to
seven the number of such judges to be excepted *for life and estate*.
The Commons were, therefore, quite free both to except for life and
estate others who were not in the category of surviving judges who sat
when the sentence was passed, and to except for minor penalties others
in that category beyond the number of seven. The same mistake
occurs in Mr. Lister's Life of Clarendon, ii. 16.

Cromwell, Ireton, and Pride should be attainted by
Act of Parliament, and that the estates of the remainder
should be mulcted by another Act. The Commons then
further excepted for life and estate seven individuals
who were not among the King's judges, but who had
been prominently accessory to his death. These were
Coke, late Chief Justice of Ireland, who had acted
as solicitor for the trial; Brompton and Dendy, two
officers of the Court, the two persons who were on the
scaffold in disguise when the sentence was executed;
Hewlet, who was accused of having been the King's
executioner; and Hugh Peters, who had preached many
violent sermons instigating to the King's death. They
excepted for minor penalties to be regulated by a future
Act the survivors, and the estates of such as were dead,
of those judges who had not been present when sentence was passed, but who had sat on previous days
of the trial; and among the living were Lord Monson,
Harrington, the author of "Oceana," and Robert Wallop.
They likewise excepted for minor penalties, to be prescribed by a future Act, twenty individuals who had
no direct part in the King's trial, but had .been prominent actors in the late revolutions, among whom
were .Speaker Lenthall, Sir Harry Vane, Oliver St.
John, Sir Arthur Haselrig, Desborough, Lambert, and
Fleetwood.[1]

---

[1] With reference to this exception of twenty for minor penalties
under a future Act, Mr. Hallam makes another unjust charge of
inconsistency against the House of Commons. The House resolved on
June 8, that "the number of twenty and no more, other than those
already excepted, or who sat as judges on the late King's Majesty,
shall be excepted out of the Act of General Pardon and Oblivion, for
and in respect only of such pains and penalties and forfeitures (not

Such were the exceptions from pardon in the Bill
sent up from the House of Commons to the House
of Lords. A wiser policy, at this moment of general
reconciliation, and when so many who were now in
the councils of the restored King had been as much
guilty of high treason in the eye of the law as his
father's judges, would have spared the lives of all,
and confined itself to measures necessary for future
security. This was the intention of Monk, and the
first advice which he gave to the King. This was the
opinion strongly expressed by several of the Presbyterian
leaders, including the Earl of Northumberland. This
was the earnest desire of Fairfax, who had effectively
contributed to the Restoration. This was the wish and
hope of Sir Anthony Ashley Cooper. Ludlow mentions
as a proof of Monk's treachery that, on Lord Saye and
Sele's suggesting to him before the Restoration that
some who had had a principal part in the King's execution should be put to death, he replied in anger, "Not
a man; for if I should suffer such a thing, I should be
the arrantest rogue that ever lived."[1] Mrs. Hutchinson
brands Cooper as a vile traitor, because, before the Restoration and before the meeting of the Convention Parliament, he had strongly protested to her husband
that, if the popular enthusiasm brought back the King,

extending to life) as shall be thought fit to be inflicted on them by
another Act." Mr. Hallam represents that they broke their resolution
by ordering a prosecution of Milton for his books (Const. Hist. ii.
414, note). But the resolution of June 8 did not preclude such a
prosecution: John Goodwin was ordered to be prosecuted at the same
time for a book of his. These orders were made on June 16, while the
House was engaged in selecting the twenty to be dealt with under the
resolution of June 8.
[1] Ludlow's Memoirs, iii. 11.

not a hair of any man's head nor a penny of any man's estate should be touched for what had passed.[1] Cooper's or Monk's language would not lose force in either Ludlow's or Mrs. Hutchinson's description. But even admitting the words as described, there is clearly passion and prejudice in both judgments. It does not require an extraordinary charity to see in both statements evidence of an intention which deserved praise, and which, certainly so far as Cooper was concerned, was frustrated by events beyond his power of control. If Monk could not impose the condition, how was Cooper to accomplish his desire?

If any were to die, it cannot be said that the Commons desired an immoderate number of victims. Nor can we reprobate the feelings which led the son of the murdered King to demand even a larger expiation of his father's death. The Lords altered the bill so as to give effect to the King's wishes. They proposed to except for life and estate, in one comprehensive clause, all who had sat on the King's trial at the time when sentence was passed, and who had signed the death-warrant. They went further, and excepted for life and estate Vane, Lambert, Haselrig, Axtel, and Hacker. They also determined to except for life and estate four of the members of the High Courts of Justice which had condemned to death four members of their own body, the Duke of Hamilton, the Earls of Holland and Derby, and Lord Capel; and they gave to the nearest relation of each of these peers the choice of one expiatory victim. The King had

---

[1] Memoirs of the Life of Colonel Hutchinson, near the end, where the last restoration of the Rump, and the re-admission of the secluded members, are briefly spoken of.

thanked the Lords for excepting all his father's judges ;
but all these additional exceptions for life were against
his expressed wishes.   The Lords' amendments were
not acceptable to the Commons, and it was with much
difficulty that the two Houses came to an agreement.
The Commons objected to excepting for life and estate
the regicides who had surrendered in obedience to the
King's proclamation calling on them to do so on pain
of being excepted. They argued, justly, that the natural
interpretation to be put on the proclamation was, that
the lives of those who surrendered should be spared.
It is probable that the Commons, on the one hand, and
the King and Lords, on the other, had concurred in this
proclamation with different meanings.   The Commons
had clearly intended it in the sense in which they now
argued that it should be taken ; they had previously
selected seven who should be excepted for life, and
resolved that all the rest should be subjected to penalties
not extending to life : and they proposed by the proclamation to frighten them into surrendering for these
minor penalties, on pain of being excepted for life if
they did not surrender.   The King and the Lords, on
the other hand, who were not bound by the preliminary
resolutions of the Commons, and who were for excepting all the King's judges for life, must be supposed to
have concurred in the proclamation, understanding it in
the sense in which they now argued that it should be
taken, and which the words may be made to bear, that
those who surrendered should have the benefit of a trial,
while those who did not surrender should be visited,
without trial, with the extreme penalties of high treason.

The meaning given to the proclamation by the Commons was that which the public generally assigned to it. If the words of the proclamation were only ambiguous, those who had surrendered should have been allowed the benefit of the ambiguity. Yet it was with very great difficulty that the Lords were prevailed upon to recede one step. After three conferences between the two Houses, the following compromise was agreed upon.

The nineteen regicides who had surrendered were to remain in the bill, as the Lords had placed them, excepted for life and estate; but a proviso was introduced declaring that, if on trial they were sentenced to death, the sentence should not be carried into effect without a special Act of Parliament passed for their execution. The Lords abandoned their proposal of the victims to avenge the deaths of the peers executed under sentences of the Commonwealth High Courts of Justice. The Commons consented to the exception of Hacker and Axtel for life. Vane and Lambert remained in the bill as excepted for life; but the two Houses agreed to present a joint address to the King, praying him to spare their lives. Haselrig's life was spared; and he was placed in the bill with others to be visited with penalties not extending to life, which should be fixed by a future Act. Arthur Annesley, Sir Anthony Ashley Cooper, and Colonel Birch spoke for Haselrig in the Commons, where it was voted to disagree with the Lords' amendment in his case; and Monk afterwards successfully exerted his influence in the Lords to obtain their acquiescence in the vote of the Commons.

Lambert, Vane, Haselrig, and Axtel had been four of the twenty, not judges of the late King, whom the Commons had in the first instance selected for minor penalties, under a future Act; the remaining sixteen of these twenty were now, instead of being reserved for subsequent legislation, declared disqualified from holding any office; and the same disqualification was imposed on all who had been members of any High Court of justice.

Three months had been consumed in discussion; and at last, on the twenty-ninth of August, the royal assent was given to the Act of Pardon, Indemnity, and Oblivion. Cooper does not appear to have taken a prominent part in the discussions relative to the Bill of Indemnity; his name does not occur in any of the various Committees appointed during its progress. Twice he is reported in the Diary already referred to as having spoken on the side of leniency. On one occasion he opposed a clause which had been moved for making all officers who had served under the Protectorate refund their salaries; saying that "he might freely speak, because he never received any salary, but he looked upon the proviso as dangerous to the peace of the nation; adding, that it reached General Monk and Admiral Montagu after the House had given them thanks, and thousands besides." Cooper on this occasion closed the debate, which had lasted above two hours, and was very animated; and the clause was rejected by 180 votes to 151.[1] The other speech reported of Cooper's was on the Lords' amendment

[1] Parl. Hist. iv. 78, July 4.

excepting Haselrig for life. "Sir A. A. Cooper was for executing nobody but those who were guilty of the King's blood, and said he thought this man not considerable enough, and moved to put him with the rest." Haselrig's life was saved by 141 votes to 116.[1]

On the twelfth of September the Parliament was adjourned for two months, and during this adjournment took place the trial of those individuals who had been excepted for life and were in custody.

A Special Commission was appointed for these trials ; and, to give greater solemnity, all the chief Ministers and most of the members of the Privy Council were named Commissioners. The whole number of the Commissioners was thirty-four, and among them, of those who had been adversaries of Charles and of his father, were Monk and Montagu, now Duke of Albemarle and Earl of Sandwich, Lords Manchester, Saye and Sele, and Roberts, Denzil Holles, Arthur Annesley, Sir Harbottle Grimstone, Secretary Morrice, and Sir Anthony Ashley Cooper. Sir Orlando Bridgman, the Lord Chief Baron of the Exchequer, a royalist lawyer, presided. Twenty-eight individuals in all were tried by this Court, and all were found guilty. Ten of them were immediately executed : Harrison, Scrope, Clements, Scot, Carew, Jones, Coke, Hacker, Axtel, and Hugh Peters. The rest were respited, in accordance with the provision of the Act of Indemnity that those who had surrendered in obedience to the royal proclamation should not be executed unless an Act were expressly passed for their execution. A bill for this purpose was passed by the

_____
[1] Parl. Hist. iv. 109, August 24.

Commons in the next Parliament, but was dropped in
the House of Lords, by the wish of Charles himself, and
by the management of Clarendon; and the eighteen
now respited ultimately escaped execution.

Shaftesbury's share in this trial of the regicides has
been generally condemned, not only by enemies, but also
by persons otherwise not unfriendly to his memory.
This much is clearly unjust in the censure lavished on
Shaftesbury, that he has been visited with reproach
from which others similarly situated have gone free.
Even if a distinction can be allowed between Shaftesbury and such of his fellow-judges,—Manchester, Roberts,
Holles, and others,—who had not only had no part in
the execution of Charles the First, but had kept aloof
from all succeeding governments and had reappeared in
public life only for the Restoration, how can Monk and
Montagu be distinguished from Shaftesbury? Montagu
especially had been Cromwell's favoured friend; he had
been long, as Cooper was for a short period, one of
Cromwell's Council of State; he had been, what Cooper
had not been, one of Cromwell's Peers. But, in truth,
no fundamental difference can be shown in favour of
the Presbyterian noblemen and gentlemen who had
carried on war against the King, and were now sitting
with Cooper and Montagu in judgment on authors and
abettors of his execution. All had been, according to
the law, guilty of high treason,—Manchester, Roberts,
Saye and Sele, and Holles, not less than Monk, Montagu,
and Cooper; and none of these who now sat as judges
were less rebels by law than the regicides whom they
judged. The law of high treason, however, apart, there

is a distinction between complicity in the King's trial and execution, and all those other acts of war against his authority and person, and of support of *de facto* revolutionary governments, of which many who now sat as judges on the regicides had been guilty. This distinction was taken by common consent at the Restoration. It was part of the compact between King and people, that amid general pardon, indemnity, and oblivion, there should be expiation for the execution of Charles the First. None of those who, having helped to bring about the Restoration, sat as judges on this occasion, had had part in the trial, or approved the execution. Cooper was as clear of that offence as Holles or Grimstone. If he acknowledged the government which afterwards stood between the nation and anarchy, he did so unfettered by previous connexions, and did what might be done, and was done, by many good citizens, supporting an existing authority when none other was probable. If he served under the Protectorate of Cromwell, gave him independent counsel, and was on terms of familiar friendship with the great Protector and his family, he did not thereby become an approver of the King's execution, any more than do those who now admire Cromwell as a great man, and deem him worthy of a statue among English sovereigns at Westminster.

Another broad and obvious distinction, which was also taken at the Restoration, was between those who, like Vane, Lambert, and Haselrig, had opposed the royal family to the last, and those who had done service in the Restoration. The Restoration, like most great political acts, was a compromise. The members of the

Government formed on this eventful occasion had each and all to make concessions of opinion and sacrifices of feeling. Royalists forgave Presbyterians and Cromwellites ; the King placed old adversaries of his father and of himself in high offices around him; and it was required of the Presbyterian leaders to concur in exceptions from pardon, and join in the trial for their lives of some who had brought Charles the First to the scaffold, and had in arms resisted the Restoration. It is known that the Presbyterian leaders, and Cooper in the number, had endeavoured in the first instance to prevent all exceptions for life, and afterwards, when they were unsuccessful in this, to reduce the number of such exceptions as much as possible. It would have been far better if those who had kindled the Civil War, or who had adhered to the governments of the Commonwealth, could have been absent from this trial; but then it would have appeared as a pure Royalist vengeance ; the nation would not have seemed united.

As regards Cooper, amid all the obscurity which still exists as to the details of his career during the Commonwealth, there are two written passages which are safe guides to the conclusion that he was clear of approval of the execution of Charles the First and clear of treachery or servility in the restoration of Charles the Second. One passage is that in which Hyde, writing confidentially to Charles nearly twelve months before the Restoration, declares it impossible that Cooper should think himself so great a delinquent as that his estate would be forfeited if Charles were restored to his father's throne.[1] The other

---

[1] Clarendon State Papers, iii. 512.

passage is that in which Shaftesbury, writing in 1677 from a prison to which an arbitrary act of power had consigned him, solemnly calls the King to witness, in a letter which he would expect to be read by many enemies, and saying what none could judge better of the truth of than the King himself, that he had acted in the Restoration as a patriot and a man of honour, had betrayed no associate, held no private correspondence with the King, made him no private addresses, and never endeavoured to make terms for himself or obtain a reward for his co-operation.

When the Convention Parliament again assembled after the recess, an Act was passed for the attainder of Cromwell, Bradshaw, Ireton, and Pride, and of the King's surviving judges who had fled. Some debate arose on a proposal to allow just debts, legacies, and funeral expenses out of the forfeiture of the estates. This was supported by Finch, Annesley, and Holles ; the last observing that " he had as great an abhorrence of that black crew as any one." Prynne vehemently took the other side. Cooper appears to have argued for the exceptions. He said, " There was reason to allow settlements before marriage or as far in retrospect as 1647."[1] Both Houses concurred in a resolution that the bodies of Cromwell, Bradshaw, Ireton, and Pride should be exhumed, carried to Tyburn, there hung up for a time, and then buried under the gallows ; and this resolution was executed as regards the bodies of the first three on the next thirtieth of January. In the first session of the next Parliament,

[1] Parl. Hist. iv. 156, Dec. 4.

an Act was passed for pains and penalties on those
who had been excepted from the Act of Indemnity
for minor penalties by future legislation; and on the
thirtieth of January, 1662, Lord Monson, Sir Henry
Mildmay, and Robert Wallop, three of the King's
judges who had sat on previous days of the week,
but not when sentence was given, were carried through
the streets on hurdles, pinioned, and with halters round
their necks, from the Tower to Tyburn and back
again. It has been already stated that a bill, afterwards introduced to authorize the execution of those
of the King's judges who had surrendered themselves,
was not proceeded with; it had passed the House
of Commons, but was stopped in the Lords. Vane
and Lambert were brought to trial for their lives in
1662, by order of the House of Commons, notwithstanding that in the Convention Parliament both
Houses had presented an address to the King, desiring
that in any event their lives might be spared, and
the King had acceded to this desire. Vane was
executed; Lambert's life was spared by the exercise
of the King's prerogative. The executions in England
ended, in 1662, with three of the King's judges who
had fled to Holland and were given up by the States.
In Scotland there had been three other executions;
the three victims were the Marquis of Argyle, Guthrie
a clergyman, and one Gowan, of whom Burnet says
that "the man was inconsiderable, till they made
him more considered by putting him to death." All
the expiations by life, for the death of Charles the
First and the past rebellion, have now been enumerated.

During the recess of the Convention Parliament,. which continued till the sixth of November, Sir Anthony Ashley Cooper was named member of a Council of ten appointed to superintend the plantations or colonies, and also member of a very numerous Council for trade. It is clear from many papers preserved at St. Giles's, that Shaftesbury gave great attention to the business of these two councils, and later chapters will contain proofs of his official diligence in these matters.

There appears to be a mistake in the statement made by some biographers, that Cooper was appointed after the Restoration Governor of the Isle of Wight. The commission previously given him by Monk for that government may possibly have been renewed temporarily under the royal authority. But there is no doubt that the second Lord Colepepper was appointed Governor of the Isle of Wight in 1662, on the surrender of the Earl of Portland's patent from Charles the First.[1] An act granting a supply for the disbanding of the army had received the royal assent before the adjournment, at the same time as the Act of Pardon and Indemnity; and Cooper soon ceased to hold a cavalry colonelcy.

When the Convention Parliament met again in November, the two questions which chiefly engaged its attention were revenue and the Church. The House of Commons had already agreed, before the adjourn-

---

[1] Lord Campbell erroneously states that Cooper was made Lord Lieutenant of Dorsetshire at this period. He never obtained this office. In "Rawleigh Redivivus" it is said that he received it in 1672, but this is a mistake.

·ment, to a vote to settle a revenue of 1,200,000*l.* a year on the King for his life. The ways and means were now to be provided; these were derived from an increase of excise duties, an increased tax on wine licences, and the post-office. The Court of Wards and all military tenures of knight-service were abolished, and the King was recompensed for the loss of revenue from the Court of Wards with one-half of the new excise duties. In the passing of this measure Cooper had a part. "Sir A. A. Cooper spoke against the Court of Wards and for the excise." [1] He had suffered grievously in youth from the Court of Wards.

As regards the Church, a measure was passed without difficulty for restoring to their livings such of the ejected Episcopal clergymen as were still alive, and for confirming Presbyterian incumbents in all cases where the ejected clergyman was dead, or where the actual incumbent had been presented on a legal vacancy. But though this measure was now passed without difficulty, the next Parliament refused to confirm it; and the Act of Uniformity made general havoc with the Presbyterian clergymen whose titles were thus legalized. The Presbyterian party had high hopes, immediately after the Restoration, of such a settlement of the Church establishment as would be agreeable to their own views of discipline and economy; and a bill for this purpose was early introduced under the title of "An Act for the maintenance of the true Reformed Protestant Church and for the suppression of Popery, superstition, profaneness, and other disorders and inno-

[1] Extract from MS. Diary in Parl. Hist. iv. 148, November 21.

vations in worship and ceremonies." On the sixth of
July this bill was read a second time, and referred to
a Committee of the whole House, which was ordered
to meet for matters of religion every Monday. The
difficulty of reconciling the views of the royalist Episco-
palians with those of the Presbyterian party, by which
this bill had been brought forward, soon became apparent; and the result of the deliberations in Grand
Committee was to adjourn the Committee for three
months and recommend an address to the Crown,
desiring his Majesty to call a number of divines to
advise with him on matters of religion. Brief reports
of two discussions on this bill in Committee of the
whole House are given in the Parliamentary History
from the Diary already mentioned; and in one of
them Sir Anthony Ashley Cooper appears urging the
postponement of the question: "Sir A. A. Cooper said,
our religion was too much mixed with interest, neither
was it ripe enough now to handle that subject, and
moved that this debate be now laid aside, and the
whole Committee adjourned for three months." After
a long debate, which lasted till the very unusual hour
of ten at night, the Committee having "sat an hour
in the dark before candles were suffered to be brought
in, and then they were twice blown out, but the third
time they were preserved, though with great disorder,"
the vote which has been mentioned, and for which
Cooper spoke, was come to.[1] The King now called
a meeting of Episcopal and Presbyterian divines; and

[1] Parl. Hist. iv. 79, 82, July 9 and 16. There is clearly some
mistake in the Parliamentary History in giving the same vote as
carried at the end of both these debates.

a Declaration, drawn by Hyde, was submitted to them
and issued during the recess, well adapted for conciliation of the Presbyterians. But the Declaration was
necessarily provisional and subject to the future decision of Parliament; and it further avowed the King's
intention of submitting the Liturgy of the old Church
to revision by a synod equally composed of Episcopalian and Presbyterian divines, and of asking the
advice of Convocation on all matters of ceremony and
discipline with a view to future legislation. It also
repeated the promise contained in the Declaration from
Breda of "liberty to tender consciences, and that no
man should be disquieted or called in question for
differences of opinion in matters of religion, which do
not disturb the peace of the kingdom;" with the addition, also contained in the Declaration from Breda,
which implied the necessity of legislative sanction, that
"we shall be ready to consent to such an Act of Parliament as upon mature deliberation shall be offered to
us for the full granting of that indulgence." The
Declaration gave high satisfaction to the Presbyterians :
Dr. Reynolds, a leading Presbyterian divine, immediately after accepted the bishopric of Norwich ;
Richard Baxter refused indeed a bishopric, but seriously considered the proposal. When the Parliament
re-assembled in November, the House of Commons
immediately thanked the King by acclamation ; but
an attempt made by Presbyterian members to pass
an Act confirming the Declaration was not successful.
This bill was opposed by the Government, and also
by some Presbyterian members, among others Serjeant

Maynard; and it was rejected on the second reading by a majority of twenty-six. It is difficult to elicit from the scanty and somewhat confused information which exists what were the exact reasons for rejection of this bill; but some members appear to have stated that it went further than the Declaration, and others urged waiting for a synod, as had been intended in the Declaration.[1] The King's government probably opposed the bill with the intention of consulting Convocation, and with the desire, through the constitutional mediation of that body and of a legal Parliament, to give legal effect hereafter to the various conciliatory concessions of the Declaration. The King himself seems really to have desired an extension of the basis of Church communion so as to comprehend the Presbyterians and a general toleration of other sects, including Roman Catholics.

This Convention Parliament was dissolved on the twenty-seventh of December. It was "beginning," says Pepys, "to grow factious."[2] There had been, a fortnight before, a debate on grievances raised by Sir Walter Erle on a money-bill, according to old custom. "Sir Walter Erle moved to do somewhat for the good of the people, in lieu of those great payments, and complained of some disorders in the army. He said that soldiers had come into some houses he knew of, and, calling the people 'Roundheads,' had done much mischief." Sir John Northcote seconded the motion. Colonel King, Mr. Stevens, and Mr. Bamp-

[1] Parl. Hist. iv. 141, 152, November 6 and 28.
[2] Pepys's Diary, i. 169.

field complained of the power of Lord Lieutenants.
Sir George Booth complained of great abuses abroad.
Here was an array of old Presbyterian members
grumbling already. Sir Heneage Finch, Colonel Charles
Howard, and other ministerial members, urged that
the remedy would be the settlement of the militia;
a bill proposed for this purpose had been rejected.
Sir Anthony Ashley Cooper appeared also in defence
of the King's government. "Those things," he said,
"had no approbation from his Majesty, but checks;
and he moved for a law to know how to walk by
a rule, but to pass over such things as could not be
justified." [1]

[1] Parl. Hist. iv. 160—162, December 13.

CHAPTER IX.

1661—1664.

Meeting of new Parliament—Cooper made Lord Ashley at the Coronation—Appointed Chancellor of the Exchequer and Under Treasurer
— Violent policy of the new Parliament — The Corporation,
Uniformity, and Militia Acts—Lord Ashley's opposition to these
measures—The King and Clarendon endeavour to check the violence
of the High Church party—Bill for confirming Presbyterian
ministers in vacant livings – Dispensing clause proposed in the
Uniformity Bill by Clarendon on the King's recommendation—
Refused by the Lords—Charles promises a three months' suspension
of the Act of Uniformity, but cannot fulfil his promise—King's
marriage—Sale of Dunkirk—King's Declaration of Indulgence,
December 26, 1662, advised by Bennet, Bristol, and Lord Ashley—
Dispensing Bill presented to House of Lords by Lord Roberts by
the King's desire—Lord Ashley warmly supports the Bill —
Clarendon opposes it — Despatches of the French Ambassador,
M. de Comminges—Clarendon's inaccuracies—The Dispensing Bill
dropped—Proclamation for banishing Jesuits and Roman Catholic
priests—Conventicle Act—Lord Ashley grows in favour with the
King—His ability and influence—Bristol's attack on Clarendon—
Lord Ashley and others work against Clarendon with encouragement from the King—Testimonies to Lord Ashley's assiduity and
ability.

THE Convention Parliament having been dissolved, a
new Parliament was immediately called. This met for
the first time on the eighth of May, 1661, and continued in existence for eighteen years.

When the new Parliament assembled, Sir Anthony
Ashley Cooper was no longer a commoner. He had,
within the preceding month, on the occasion of the
Coronation, been raised to the Upper House with the
title of Baron Ashley of Wimborne St. Giles. This

was one of several honours conferred at the same time
on Royalists and on old adversaries who had obtained
the King's pardon and favour. Of the former class,
Hyde, who had previously been created Baron Hyde,
was promoted to be Earl of Clarendon; Lord Capel,
for his father's services and death, was raised to be
Earl of Essex; Sir John Grenville was created Viscount
Lansdowne and Earl of Bath; Lord Brudenell was
made Earl of Cardigan, and Sir Frederick Cornwallis
Baron Cornwallis. The old adversaries who had contributed to effect the Restoration now rewarded were,
Charles Howard, who became Earl of Carlisle; Arthur
Annesley, who had lately inherited the Irish peerage
of Viscount Valentia, Earl of Anglesea; Crewe, Baron
Crewe; Holles, Baron Holles; Sir Horatio Townshend,
Baron Townshend; Sir George Booth, Baron Delamere;
and Sir Anthony Ashley Cooper, Baron Ashley.[1]

A few days after the meeting of Parliament, on the
thirteenth of May, Lord Ashley was appointed Chancellor of the Exchequer and Under Treasurer. The
place of Chancellor of the Exchequer had been held up
to this time by Clarendon, and the duties of Under
Treasurer had been discharged by the Lord Treasurer,

---

[1] Lord Campbell says that Shaftesbury always took to himself the
whole merit of the Restoration, representing Monk as his tool, and "in
the preamble to his patent of peerage he introduced a statement that
this 'happy event was chiefly brought about by the efforts of our right
trusty and well-beloved Sir Anthony Ashley Cooper.'" There is no
such passage in the patent. The following is a correct translation of
an extract from the patent: "After very many endeavours of bringing
a remedy to these evils, undertaken with as much prudence as
possible, at length by his counsels, in concert with our beloved and
faithful George Monk, knight, &c., &c. he did a service worthy to be
remembered, and most grateful to us, in the great business of restoring
us to our kingdom, and delivering his country from the bitter servitude
under which it so long groaned."

the Earl of Southampton, in pursuance of letters patent, specially authorizing him to discharge them. Lord Ashley probably owed this appointment in some measure to his connexion by marriage with the Earl of Southampton : his wife was Lord Southampton's niece.[1] Lord Ashley held the office of Chancellor of the Exchequer until he was made Lord Chancellor in November 1672. He ceased to be Under Treasurer when, after Lord Southampton's death, the Treasury was put into commission in 1667, he himself, as Chancellor of the Exchequer, being one of the Commissioners.

The new House of Commons, elected while the nation's fit of exuberant revived loyalty was not yet over, presented a large majority of enthusiastic Royalists and High Churchmen. They began by voting that the League and Covenant, and the Acts for erecting a High Court of Justice for the trial of Charles Stuart, for subscribing the Engagement, for establishing a Commonwealth, and for renouncing the title of the present King, and for security of the Protector's person, should be burnt by the common hangman in Westminster Hall. They required every member to take the Sacrament kneeling. They restored the bishops to the House of Lords. They passed an Act for the punishment of any one who should call the King a heretic or papist, or should assert either that the Long Parliament was not dissolved or that Parliament possessed legislative

---

[1] Lady Ashley, the third wife, married in 1656 (see p. 121), was daughter of Lord Spencer of Wormleighton, by Penelope, sister of the Earl of Southampton. Mr. Hallam has made a mistake in speaking of Sir Philip Warwick as Chancellor of the Exchequer; he held the subordinate office of Secretary of the Lord Treasurer. (Const. Hist. ii. 423, note.)

authority independently of the King. They also passed
an Act declaring the sole right of governing the militia
to be in the King. Old royalists were in ecstacies. A
few days after the meeting of the Parliament, Daniel
O'Neil, an old servant of the King, wrote to Archbishop
Bramhall. " The Parliament will settle the militia upon
the King and his heirs, a step never yet made towards
the perpetual peace of these nations. In a word, there
is nothing relative to the good of the kingdom and his
Majesty's satisfaction but this Parliament is prepared to
do." [1] But moderate men, who desired conciliation and
tranquillity, shook their heads. Roger Pepys, member
for Cambridge town, told his relative the diarist that
things were basely carried on in Parliament by the
young men, that did labour to oppose all things that
were moved by serious men. " They are the most pro-
fane swearing fellows that ever he heard in his life,
which makes him think they will spoil all, and bring
things into a war again if they can." [2]

Three measures of the utmost practical importance,
and containing much mischief, were passed in the first
session of this Parliament, which lasted, with an intervening adjournment from July till November, until
May 1662. These measures were:

1. The Act for the government of Corporations,
which appointed commissioners empowered to remove
all officers in corporations at their discretion, and required all who were retained, or who were hereafter
appointed, to renounce the League and Covenant as

---

[1] Rawdon Papers, p. 150, May 23, 1661.
[2] Pepys's Diary, i. 212, July 31, 1661.

an unlawful oath, take the oaths of allegiance and
supremacy, and declare on oath their belief of the
unlawfulness of taking up arms against the King on
any pretence whatever, and their abhorrence of the
traitorous doctrine that arms may be taken up by his
authority, against his person or against those commissioned by him; and which also provided with regard
to future officers, that no man should be eligible who
had not within the year before his election taken the
Sacrament according to the rites of the Church of
England. By this Act, all Dissenters from the Church
were excluded from municipal offices:

2. The Act of Uniformity, which enacted that the
Book of Common Prayer and of Ordination of Ministers,
as revised by the Convocation in a spirit anything but
favourable to Nonconformists, should be used in all
places of public worship, and that all beneficed clergymen should, on some Sunday before the feast of St.
Bartholomew, August 24, in 1662, read the service
from it, and at the close of the service declare their
" unfeigned assent and consent to everything contained
and prescribed in it," on pain of deprivation; that no
person should administer the Sacrament or hold ecclesiastical preferment who had not received episcopal
ordination; and that all incumbents, dignitaries, officers
in universities, public schoolmasters, and even private
tutors, should subscribe a renunciation of the Covenant
and a declaration of the unlawfulness of taking up
arms against the Sovereign, the same tests as had been
inserted in the Corporation Act. Here, then, was a sad
substitute for that Act for confirming the King's

gracious Declaration of October 1660, which had nearly
been passed by the Convention Parliament; rigorous
exclusion took the place of conciliation and comprehension :

3. The Act for ordering of the military forces, which
enjoined on all lord lieutenants, deputy lieutenants,
and all officers and soldiers, the same tests as were
contained in the Corporation and Uniformity Acts,
excepting the renunciation of the Covenant.

There was a more vigorous opposition to these Acts
in the House of Lords than in the House of Commons.
In the Upper House much opposition was offered,
though unsuccessfully, by a small band of noblemen
of the old Presbyterian party, including Lord Ashley,
and reinforced by the Earl of Southampton. Lord
Ashley is stated by Mr. Martyn, probably on the
authority of that portion of Stringer's manuscript
which cannot now be found, to have argued strongly
and wisely against the Corporation Bill :—

"Lord Ashley set forth the ill consequences of the
bill in various instances; viz. the injustice it might
do to the wealthiest, the most able, and the most
conscientious members of their respective corporations; the fixing these in the hands of perhaps the
most profligate persons in them, at least the dividing
of the people into parties; and he showed that, as it
would be a restraint upon those who had a regard
to their oaths and their country, it was the most
effectual method which could be contrived for lodging
the executive power of the Government in the hands
of such persons as could make no difficulty of sub-

jecting the whole nation to an absolute tyranny of both Church and State."[1]

Of the Uniformity Bill Mr. Martyn states that "the Earl of Southampton and Lord Ashley were remarkably strenuous against several clauses, and the former, being told that it was believed he had spoken three hundred times against the bill, answered that he was so firmly persuaded of the fatal consequences of it, that he would have spoken three hundred times more to have prevailed." And again, it is stated by the same writer that the Earl of Southampton and Lord Ashley, with others, warmly opposed the Militia Act.[2] These statements of Mr. Martyn as to Lord Ashley's opposition to the measures of 1662 are generally confirmed by the well-known and valuable pamphlet bearing the title of a "Letter from a Person of Quality to a Friend in the Country," published in 1676, which is printed in Locke's Works, but which is without doubt erroneously ascribed to Locke.[3] They are further confirmed by

---

[1] Martyn's Life, i. 255.   [2] Ibid. pp. 260, 262.

[3] I make this assertion positively, on the authority of an unpublished letter of Locke in the possession of Mr. E. A. Sanford of Nynehead Court, Somersetshire, from which Mr. Sanford has kindly given me permission to print an extract. Locke's letter is addressed to the Earl of Pembroke, and was written December 3, 1684, soon after he was deprived of his studentship in Christchurch, Oxford. "I have often wondered, in the way that I lived and the make I knew myself of, how it could come to pass that I was made the author of so many pamphlets, unless it was because I of all my Lord's [Shaftesbury's] family happened to have been most bred amongst books. This opinion of me I thought time and the contradictions it carried with it would have cured, and that the most suspicious would at last have been weary of imputing to me writings whose matter and style have, I believe (for pamphlets have been laid to me which I have never seen), been so very different that it was hard to think they should have the same author, though a much abler man than me. . . . And it is a very odd fate that I did get the reputation of no small writer without having done anything for it. For I think two or three copies of verses

the whole tenour of Shaftesbury's subsequent political life.

The violent legislation of the High Church and Royalist party was displeasing to Charles, who felt that his promises from Breda were substantially, if not literally, broken; and it was displeasing also, though perhaps in a less degree, to his honest but prejudiced adviser, Clarendon. The opposition made, before the Act of Uniformity was passed, to the confirmation of the Act of the Convention Parliament for confirming Presbyterian ministers in vacant livings was strongly resented by both King and Chancellor, and no historian has done justice to this conduct. The following is from a letter written by Doctor, afterwards Sir Peter, Pett to Archbishop Bramhall, on the eighth of February, 1662:—

" There have been great animosities lately, and heats in the House of Lords, about the bill for the confirmation of ministers that passed in the last Parliament in England, save only as to those livings where Lords had the *jus patronatus*, which the Commons in this Parliament would have had the Lords join with them in exploding. At first all the bishops in the House of Lords were against it, and most of the Protestant lords temporal. But my Lord Chancellor was resolved to oblige the Presbyterians by keeping the Act from being repealed, and at last got seven of the bishops to join with him, five of which I have not forgot the names of, and they were the Bishops of London, Nor-

of mine published with my name to them have not gained me that reputation. Bating these, I do solemnly protest in the presence of God that I am not the author, not only of any libel, but not of any pamphlet or treatise whatever in part good, bad, or indifferent."

wich, Exeter, Lincoln, Worcester.[1] The Duke of York was likewise brought over by his father-in-law, and the Earl of Bristol was vehement in the thing, and all the Popish lords. The Presbyterian ministers sent Calamy, Baxter, and Bates, that day to the Chancellor to give him thanks. Some of the Commons, going to the King' the day before to desire him to express himself positively against the confirmation of the ministers, he said he had promised them at Breda the continuance in their livings; whereupon they said that the Commons might possibly, many of them, be tempted not to pass the bill intended for enlarging of his revenue, if his Majesty would favour the confirmation of the Presbyterian ministers; to whom the King answered that, if he had not wherewith to subsist two days, he would trust God Almighty's providence rather than break his word."[2]

These facts, which rest on unexceptionable authority, place the conduct of the King and of Clarendon in a new light, and are much to their credit. But they did not succeed in procuring confirmation of the Act.

Again, no historian has noticed the fact that a very earnest effort was made by the King and Clarendon, while the Bill of Uniformity was in the Lords, to introduce a clause enabling the King to dispense with its provisions. Such a clause was presented by Clarendon to the House of Lords on March 17, as "recommended from the King."[2] Notice was taken the next day of this recommendation, probably by Bristol, as an infringement of the privilege of Parliament, but

[1] These five bishops were Sheldon, Reynolds, Ward, Sanderson, and Morley.
[2] Rawdon Papers, p. 137.

a motion made for a resolution saving the privilege of
the House was negatived. The bill was recommitted
on the nineteenth, with a reference to the Committee
of "the proviso sent from the King." But the Committee did not adopt the clause. Archbishop Bramhall's correspondent, Sir Peter Pett, and Pepys both
mention Clarendon's eagerness in advocating this clause,
which was violently opposed by Bristol.[1] The Duke
of York warmly supported Clarendon. "The Presbyterians and other Nonconformists," says Pett, "would,
as I am credibly informed by a knowing person, have
offered to the King as great a revenue for their toleration as he will have from chimneys, if the aforesaid
proviso would have passed among the Lords and
Commons and had the royal assent." It is strange
that Clarendon in his "Life" makes no mention of this
memorable incident.

The Act of Uniformity received the royal assent
on the nineteenth of May, 1662. Three months only
remained for the Presbyterian clergy to make their
choice between conformity and loss of their preferments. An attempt was made in the interval to work
on the King to obtain by proclamation, or by order of
the Privy Council, or in some other way, some relief
from the provisions of the Act, or at least an extension
of time. Charles promised a three months' suspension
of the Act; but he was unable to fulfil his promise.
The bishops denied his power to suspend, and declared

[1] Rawdon Papers, pp. 141, 143 ; Pepys's Diary, i. 336, March 21,
1662. This clause, the terms of which have not before been published,
is printed from the Rolls of the House of Lords in the Appendix VI.
It is not given in the Lords' Journals.

that they must and would execute the Act. Monk and
Manchester, on this occasion, warmly urged the suspension prayed by the Presbyterian ministers, but they
were overruled by Clarendon and the King's other
Royalist advisers, and especially by the zeal of Bishop
Sheldon.[1]   When St. Bartholomew's Day came, two
thousand Presbyterian clergymen obeyed conscience
and quitted the Church.

After the close of the session of 1662 came two
events of importance, with neither of which, however,
was Lord Ashley specially connected, — the King's
marriage with the Princess Catharine of Portugal, by
which Bombay and Tangier became British possessions ;
and the sale of Dunkirk to France, from want of money,
for four hundred thousand pounds.   In October, Sir
Henry Bennet, better known by the title which he
afterwards acquired of Earl of Arlington, replaced
Nicholas as Secretary of State, and Bennet's influence
soon became prejudicial to the supremacy of Clarendon.

Under the influence of Bennet, Bristol, and Ashley,
the King issued, on the twenty-sixth of December, 1662,
while Parliament was not sitting, an important declaration as to the Act of Uniformity.   He declared his
desire to exempt from its penalties "those who, living
peaceably, do not conform themselves thereunto through
scruple and tenderness of misguided conscience, but
modestly and without scandal perform their devotions
in their own way," and, "without invading the freedom
of Parliament, to incline their wisdom next approach-

---

[1] Burnet's Own Time, i. 331; Pepys's Diary, ii. 30, Sept. 3, 1662 ;
Clarendon's Continuation of Life, i. 159.

ing session to concur with him in making some such
Act for that purpose as may enable him to exercise
with a more universal satisfaction that power of dispensing which he conceived to be inherent in him."
This was intended for the benefit of Roman Catholics
as well as Protestant Nonconformists, and so was promoted by Bristol, who had opposed the dispensing
clause proposed to be inserted in the bill.   Bennet
wrote to the Duke of Ormond that this Declaration,
before it was published, was read twice over to Clarendon, who not only approved, but applauded it.   Clarendon, however, also wrote to Ormond to deny this
statement.[1]   It was not his act, he said, and he would
have nothing to do with it.

On the meeting of Parliament in February 1663, a
bill was immediately presented to the House of Lords,
not by Clarendon, but by Lord Roberts, the Lord Privy
Seal, bearing the title, " An Act concerning His Majesty's
Power in Ecclesiastical Affairs," which was to enable
the King by letters patent under the Great Seal, or in
such other way as he might think fit, to dispense with
the Act of Uniformity, and "with any other laws or
statutes concerning the same or requiring oaths or
subscriptions, or which do enjoin conformity to the
order, discipline, and worship established in the Church
of England, and the penalties in the said laws imposed,
or any of them."[2]   The High Church party in the
House of Commons were no less eager to denounce

---

[1] See the two letters of Bennet and Clarendon in vol. iii. of Lister's
Life of Clarendon, pp. 231—233.
[2] The bill is printed for the first time in the Appendix VI. from
the Rolls of the House of Lords.

the Declaration of December; and on the very day on which Lord Roberts's bill was read a second time in the House of Lords, the Commons voted an address to the King, strongly deprecating the passage in his Declaration which proposed indulgence to Nonconformists. The Lords, having procured a list of all ecclesiastical laws which might be dispensed with under the measure introduced by Lord Roberts, adopted, on the fifth of March, a resolution restricting the operation of the bill to the Act of Uniformity. The bill was ultimately dropped. It was opposed by Southampton and Clarendon, and zealously supported by Lord Ashley.

The account given by Clarendon in his "Life," of the proceedings in the House of Lords with reference to this bill, is inaccurate; and, though there is no doubt that he was against the bill, his opposition in the House of Lords does not appear to have been nearly so strong as he represents it. The correspondence of the French ambassador, the Count de Comminges, contains some reliable particular information. The Count wrote, on March 9, that Clarendon had excused himself from attending the House of Lords on account of illness, that it was thought he would not go again until matters were satisfactorily arranged, and that he had wished to be absent from deference to the King's opinions in favour of the bill, which he could not advocate without injury to his conscience. On March 12, Comminges writes that the Chancellor had been that day to the House of Lords and obtained a month's delay for the bill, which would give time for the arrangement of the matter. "He appeared," says the

Count, "to take no side in the matter; he managed well his master's reputation, the designs of the Parliament, and his own conscience, which he believes concerned."[1] On this day, the twelfth, the Lords went into committee on the bill; and also on the day following, when the Grand Committee, or Committee of the whole House, appointed a sub-committee, after which there is no further mention of the bill. This tallies well enough with the statement of Comminges. Clarendon most incorrectly says, in his "Life," that the bill was never committed; that indeed "it was agreed there should be no question put for the commitment, which was the most civil way of rejecting it, and left it to be no more called for." The bill had been ordered to be committed on the twenty-fifth of February; the Lords went into Committee of the whole House upon it, the Lord Chamberlain (Manchester) being appointed Chairman, on the twenty-seventh, and again on March 5, 6, 12, and 13. On April 9 Comminges wrote that "Clarendon, who had acquired great credit in the House of Commons at the beginning of the session by his opposition to the bill, has now almost quite lost it by the ambiguous manner in which he has twice lately spoken: his friends lose heart, and his enemies decry him to the King."

Of Lord Ashley's vigorous support of the bill there is no doubt. Mr. Martyn gives a short account of his arguments:—

"Lord Ashley took notice of the fatal consequences

---

[1] Archives of French Foreign Office.

of the Act of Uniformity ; that by it great numbers of
ministers were reduced to beggary ; that many Pro-
testants were running into other countries, to the prejudice of trade and the dishonour of the kingdom ;
that the Reformers in King Edward the Sixth's reign
had acted in a different manner ; for they had, like wise
and good men, contrived the doctrine and discipline of
the Church so as to enlarge the terms of communion ;
that they had set open the doors, and by gentle means
persuaded and invited all they could into the Church,
thinking that the enlargement of their body would
redound to the honour of their religion."[1]

Clarendon represents Lord Ashley as the keenest and
ablest supporter of the bill.

" The Lord Privy Seal," he says, " either upon the
observation of the countenance of the House or adver-
tisement of his friends, or unwilling to venture his
reputation in the enterprise, had given over the game
the first day, and now spoke not at all ; but the Lord
Ashley adhered firmly to his point, spake often and
with great sharpness of wit, and had a cadence in his
words and pronunciation that drew attention.   He said,
it was the King's misfortune that a matter of so great
concernment to him, and such a prerogative as it may
be would be found to be inherent in him without any
declaration of Parliament, should be supported only by
such weak men as himself, who served his Majesty at a
distance, while the great officers of the Crown thought
fit to oppose it ; which he more wondered at because
nobody knew more than they the King's unshakeable
firmness in his religion, that had resisted and vanquished
so many great temptations, and therefore he could not

, [1] Martyn's Life, i. 285.

be thought unworthy of a greater trust with reference to it than he would have by this bill."[1]

The bill, as has been said, was shelved in Committee, and this fresh endeavour of the King to procure toleration led to fresh measures of severity. The two Houses voted an Address to the King for a proclamation for the banishment of Jesuits and Roman Catholic priests, and the King assented to their prayer. A severe measure against Dissenters' meetings for prayers was introduced, and became a law in the following session of 1664. This Act, commonly known as the Conventicle Act, declared all meetings of more than five, besides members of the family, for any religious purpose not according to the Book of Common Prayer, to be seditious and unlawful conventicles, and punished attendance at such meetings by a fine of five pounds or three months' imprisonment for the first offence, a fine of ten pounds or six months' imprisonment for the second, a fine of a hundred pounds or transportation for seven years for the third, and added a hundred pounds to the fine for every offence after the third. One of Clarendon's many inaccuracies is a statement that the Conventicle Act was one of the reasons why Bennet and Ashley urged the bill for indulgence brought in by Lord Roberts.[2] This Conventicle Act was a subsequent measure, passed a year later.

The failure of the bill which Lord Roberts had introduced by the King's desire caused Charles much disappointment, and sensibly estranged him from Cla-

---

[1] Clarendon's Continuation of Life, p. 247.   [2] Ibid. p. 245.

rendon and the bishops. Lord Ashley rose in favour
and influence with the King. Clarendon mentions that
Lord Ashley and Lord Roberts were now called to attend
the meetings of the Cabinet. Pepys, whose political
gossip is always valuable, records on May 15, 1663 :—
"It seems the present favourites now are my Lord
Bristol, Duke of Buckingham, Sir H. Bennet, my Lord
Ashley, and Sir Charles Berkeley, who among them
have cast my Lord Chancellor upon his back, past ever
getting up again." And he goes on to speak of Lord
Ashley in particular. "Strange to hear how my Lord
Ashley, by my Lord Bristol's means (he being brought
over to the Catholic party against the bishops, whom he
hates to the death, and publicly rails against them, not
that he is become a Catholic, but merely opposes the
bishops), is got into favour, so much that, being a man
of great business and yet of pleasure and drolling too,
he, it is thought, will be made Lord Treasurer on the
death or removal of the good old man." The "good old
man" was Southampton. Clarendon was not yet fallen
past rising again, and it will be seen that he and Ashley
came to be on cordial terms before Clarendon's fall, more
than four years afterwards. The Count de Comminges
also notices Lord Ashley's growing reputation, and his
present antagonism to Clarendon. He thus wrote, April
9, 1663: "Lord Ashley, Chancellor of the Exchequer,
who was formerly of Cromwell's Council, and who in my
opinion is the only man who can be set against Clarendon for talent and firmness, does not shrink from
speaking his opinions of Clarendon with freedom, and
contradicting him to his face. He has gone so far that

he has made the King perceive that Clarendon's alliance
with the Duke of York was very prejudicial to him, and
as he is very acute and a very good courtier, and is
perfectly well in the King's graces, it is suspected with
sufficient probability that Lord Bristol and Secretary
Bennet and Morrice and all the rest of that clique may
well give trouble to the Chancellor, and place him in a
disagreeable position."

A foolish and violent attempt of Bristol to impeach
Clarendon for high treason, made in the House of Lords
towards the close of the session of 1663, tended to
Bristol's own injury, and to the revival for a time of
Clarendon's influence. Bristol's charges were referred
by the Lords to the Judges, who advised that his proceeding was irregular, and that that the charges did not
involve treason. The King sent a message to the Lords,
in which he stated that Bristol's charges against the
Chancellor contained several statements which he knew
of his own knowledge to be untrue, and many scandalous reflections on himself and his relations which he
regarded as libels against his person and government.
The King banished Bristol from his presence. Lord
Ashley appears to have taken part in a discussion on
the opinion given by the Judges in order to maintain
that the Judges' opinion was not a law for the Lords,
but only advice and information ; "and this," says
Pepys (mentioning that Lord Ashley told him so),
"the Lords did concur in."[1] This may have led to his
being thought to favour Bristol's proceeding against the
Chancellor, of which there is no direct or better evidence.

[1] Pepys's Diary, iv. 200.

As the next meeting of Parliament drew near, it was rumoured that Bristol intended to revive his charges, and Pepys was told that Lord Ashley and Lord Lauderdale, the Secretary of State for Scotland, " open high against the Chancellor."[1] But the matter was not again brought forward.

M. de Ruvigny, who had succeeded the Count de Comminges as French Ambassador, wrote on February 4, 1664, that the great enemies of Clarendon were Bristol, Lauderdale, and Ashley; and he adds that Clarendon's old friend Ormond is joined to them, though Clarendon cannot believe it. In a later letter from Ruvigny it is mentioned that Clarendon had persuaded Ormond to come over to London from Ireland, that he might converse with him and receive his confidence as against " the cabal of Lord Lauderdale, which has swindled him (*escroqué*) out of knowledge of all the affairs of the kingdom." Ruvigny proceeds to say that Lauderdale is " united with Ashley, Lord Roberts, and some others, who spare no pains to ruin Clarendon in the free convivial entertainments which are of daily occurrence. They do not scruple to speak of him with freedom in the presence of the King, who has had his own witticism (*mot*) like the rest in the excitement of conviviality, thus giving free scope to all his guests, each of whom has spoken part of what was on his mind."[2]

Pepys's description of Lord Ashley as "a man of great business, and yet of pleasure and drolling too," has been quoted; and some other notices of him occur

[1] Pepys's Diary, ii. 279, Feb. 1, 1664.
[2] Archives of French Foreign Office.

in Pepys's Diary.   Pepys went to him on business on
the twenty-seventh of May, 1663, and wrote down : " I
find my Lord, as he is reported, a very ready, quiet, and
diligent person."   The Russian Minister Resident took
as high a measure of him as the French Ambassador,
Comminges.   Pepys writes, June 6, 1663 : " Sir John
Hebden, the Russia Resident, did tell me how he is
vexed to see things at Court ordered as they are by
nobody that attends to business, but every man himself
or his own pleasures.   He cries up my Lord Ashley
to be almost the only man that he sees to look after
business, and with the ease and mastery that he wonders
at him."[1]

Lord Ashley had now thrown himself, heart and soul,
with all the ardour of his nature, into administrative
duties. His latest biographer, Lord Campbell, unable now
to taunt him with turbulence, ridicules him for diligence
and regularity in public business.   " After the Restoration," says Lord Campbell, " his conduct for the next
seven years seems wholly inexplicable, for he remained
quite regular, and seemingly contented.   He had a little
excitement by sitting as a Judge on the trial of the regicides, and joining in the sentence on some of his old
associates.   These trials being over, he seemed to sink
down into a Treasury drudge."   The duties of a
Chancellor of the Exchequer two hundred years ago
may not have been so numerous and arduous as now ;
but the office was a high office of state, and the station
of Privy Councillor was one of greater responsibility
and dignity than it is in the present day.   To speak

---

[1] Pepys's Diary, ii. 169.

contumeliously of Shaftesbury as a mere Treasury drudge, because, with brilliant talents, he was a laborious Chancellor of the Exchequer, is unworthy of a serious biographer.[1]

[1] Two letters of this period written to Lord Ashley, preserved among Lord Shaftesbury's papers, may be printed here. The first is from the Princess Elizabeth of Bohemia, soliciting his good offices for a pension: her mother, the ex-Queen of Bohemia, aunt of Charles II., had died in London in February 1662. The Princess had entered the Protestant nunnery of Herfort or Herworden in Prussia, and she became ultimately its Abbess.

"*Herfort, Sept.* 13, 1662.

"My Lord,—The kindness you have expressed to the Queen my mother, and my brothers, since their being in England, makes me hope you will continue the like to me, in reference of the pension which his Majesty has been pleased to confirm upon me, there being none of her Majesty's children at the present more in need of this benefit than myself, nor anybody in the world that shall be more sensible of your goodness and more desirous to appear,

"My Lord,
"Your affectionate friend to serve you,
"ELISABETH.

" For the Lord Ashley Cooper,
Chancellor of the Exchequer to His Majesty at London."

The other letter is from the Secretary, Sir Henry Bennet, soon to be made Lord Arlington, praying Lord Ashley's aid for confirmation of a possession, the King having, it appears, been bribed with a share in the property; and Shaftesbury has docketed this letter, " Papers for my justification." Shaftesbury declared always that he had never jobbed for grants for himself; and this declaration has never been discredited.

" My Lord,—I have sought your Lordship this day to beseech you to move in the House of Lords the obtaining an order for the quiet possession of Wildmore Fen to the proprietors, wherein his Majesty hath accepted of a share, and upon the same account to procure my Lord Treasurer to be favourable to it; and this to be done to-morrow, if Mr. Attorney be present, otherwise that your Lordship would defer it till another day.

"I am, my Lord,
" Your Lordship's most humble servant,
"HENRY BENNET.

"*May* 11, 1663."

CHAPTER X.

Lord Ashley's position at the beginning of 1664—Attention to revenue
and trade—Dutch war—Opposed by Clarendon, Southampton, and
Ormond and supported probably by Ashley—Appointed Treasurer
of Prizes—Clarendon's hostility to the appointment—Affectionate
letter to his wife, February 26, 1665—Grant of Carolina to Lord
Ashley and seven others—The Plague—The King visits Lord Ashley
at Wimborne St. Giles's—Session of Parliament at Oxford, October 1665—Appropriation Clause in Supply Bill unsuccessfully
opposed by Clarendon and Ashley—The Five Mile Act—Opposed
strongly by Southampton and Ashley but prosecuted by Clarendon
—Bill for general imposition of oath against endeavouring change
in Church or State opposed by Ashley—Letter to his wife from
Oxford, November 23, 1665—Beginning of acquaintance with Locke
—Friendship of Locke and Shaftesbury—Session of 1666–67—
Complaints of expenditure and misappropriation—Act against
importation of Irish cattle—Supported by Ashley—Earl of Ossory's
insult and apology—Discussion with Viscount Conway—Rumoured
possible Lord Lieutenant of Ireland—Secret treaty between Louis
XIV. and Charles II.—Dutch fleet enters the Thames and burns three
men-of-war at Chatham—Peace of Breda—Death of Earl of Southampton—Office of Lord High Treasurer put in commission and Lord
Ashley one of the Commissioners—Clarendon's account of the
appointment of the Commission—Proceedings of the Commissioners—Sir William Temple and Lady Fanshawe blame Shaftesbury
for their economies—Clarendon removed from the Chancellorship
—Lord Ashley unjustly accused of conspiring against Clarendon—
Opposes the impeachment of Clarendon without specific treason
assigned and falls into disgrace with the King for supporting
Clarendon—Clarendon's exile—Lord Campbell's misstatements—
Charge of licentiousness against Shaftesbury.

THE end of the last chapter has brought us to the
beginning of 1664. The subject of this biography is
now Lord Ashley, a Peer, a Privy Councillor, and Chancellor of the Exchequer. His abilities and independence,

the favour of the King and his intimacy with Arlington, Lauderdale, Bristol, and others, who in various ways thwarted Clarendon and menaced his ascendancy, have made him already formidable to the too jealous and imperious Chancellor. In the House of Lords he has distinguished himself by strenuous and eloquent opposition to all the measures of Church exclusiveness and oppression of Protestant Dissenters which were enacted after the Restoration. He was very diligent as a Minister, and gave the greatest attention to all matters of revenue and trade. Papers of his have been preserved which show his minute care and industry in collecting details as to the Exchequer, the customs and excise, the navy, the merchant companies, and all branches of our trade, manufactures and revenue.[1] In the study of details he did not lose sight of principles, and some of his views were in advance of the time. He was an enemy of monopoly, and said that "the restraining of a general trade was like the damming of increasing waters, which must either swell them to force their boundaries, or cause them to putrefy where they are circumscribed."[2]

In the session of Parliament from March 16 to May 17, 1664, the Conventicle Act, already mentioned, was passed,[3] the famous Triennial Act of the Long Parliament, making a new parliament every three years compulsory on the King, was repealed, to please

[1] Martyn's Life, 289—293.
[2] Ibid. 292 ; and see in Appendix I. of the second volume Shaftesbury's memorial addressed to the King, probably in 1669, and Mr. Martyn's account of his recommendations in 1672 for a Council of Trade, paraphrased from a paper of Shaftesbury's.
[3] See p. 270.

Charles, and a report of a Committee on the complaints of our merchants against the Dutch, followed by an address of both Houses to the King couched in very strong language, gave a sanction and intensity to national jealousy and irritation, which paved the way for the war with the Dutch declared by England in the following year.

It is well ascertained that Clarendon, Southampton, Ormond, and other old advisers of Charles were against this war, and were overborne by, the popular feeling and the warlike animosities of the Duke of York and of Monk, Duke of Albemarle.[1] Bristol, Arlington, and others, with whom Ashley was latterly more or less associated, were promoters of the war; and Sir William Coventry, the Secretary of the Duke of York as Lord High Admiral, and Clifford, the future Lord Treasurer, were conspicuous in the House of Commons for hostility to the Dutch. There is no authentic information of Ashley's sentiments or line of action. But it may be inferred from the opinions of those with whom he was now most friendly, and from his zealous attention to

[1] M. de Ruvigny wrote, September 12/22, 1664 : " The King, Chancellor, and Treasurer are against making war, but allow themselves to be carried away by the crowd." (Archives of French Foreign Office.) In an anonymous memoir on the origin of the war in the same archives, which was furnished from England, the Earl of Bristol is said to have first recommended the war. It is there said that Bristol having no office or hope of any, formed intimate relations with Thurloe, Ashley, Trevor and other Cromwellites, the most skilful men in England, and that Thurloe showed Bristol Cromwell's papers, and told him that Cromwell had had two great objects, one to make himself King, and the other to destroy the power of Holland. Later, it is said in this memoir, the Parliament, the City of London, and the Council were for the war, but Clarendon, Southampton, and Ormond kept the King in suspense ; he was, however, at last carried away, yielding to the importunities of the Duke of York and of Monk, and goaded by libels and insolent discourses of the Dutch.

English trade, that he was, like all the younger statesmen, on the side of war. The war, indeed, was regarded by the nation, which had become infuriated by Dutch insults, injuries, and cruelties to English merchants in all parts of the globe, as necessary for upholding the honour and preserving the commerce of England.

In a session which began on November 24, 1664, and ended on March 2, 1665, the House of Commons enthusiastically voted a very liberal supply of two millions and a half sterling, and war was declared against Holland on February 22, 1665.

It is the more probable that Lord Ashley was a supporter of the war with Holland, as, when war was determined on, he was appointed by the King, and evidently to the great annoyance of Clarendon, Treasurer of Prizes. Clarendon says that Ashley's appointment contained a proviso that he was to be accountable to the King and to no one else, and was to make payments in obedience to the King's warrant under his sign manual and by no other warrant, and was to be exempt from accounting into the Exchequer. To this arrangement Clarendon says that he made great opposition, desiring that the proceeds of prizes should go into the Exchequer and be available solely for the expenses of the war; but the King was immoveable, and Lord Ashley's appointment was made as originally proposed.[1] Clarendon's narrative of this incident is so obviously tinged by asperity towards Ashley, that many of its details must be regarded with distrust; but his substantial statement

---

[1] Continuation of Life of Clarendon, 575—581.

that the King reserved power over the distribution of the proceeds of prizes is correct.

The following is the substance of what regards Lord Ashley in Clarendon's statement about this appointment. A servant of Lord Ashley came to him one evening with the appointment signed, and desired from his master that the Chancellor's seal might be put to it that night. Clarendon bade the messenger tell Lord Ashley "that he would speak with the King before he would seal that grant, and that he desired much to speak with himself." The next morning Clarendon saw the King, and remonstrated; he represented the proposed proceeding as unprecedented, and as opening the way to frauds on the King himself, who would have no check if the receivers of prizes were exempted from accounting to the Exchequer; he further described it as a slight to the Lord Treasurer, "there being another Treasurer much more absolute than himself, and without dependence on him." The remonstrance produced no effect. "He [Clarendon] found that the King had not been surprised in what he had done, which, he said, was absolutely in his own power to do, and that it would bring prejudice only to himself, which he had sufficiently guarded against. However, he seemed willing to decline anything that looked like an affront to the Treasurer, and therefore was content that the sealing it might be suspended till he had further considered." Lord Ashley now went to Clarendon, and "seemed to take it unkindly that his patent was not sealed." Clarendon answered "that he had suspended the immediate sealing it for three reasons, whereof one

was that he might first speak with the King, who, he
believed, would receive much prejudice by it; another
that it would not consist with the respect he owed to
the Lord Treasurer, who was much affronted in it, to
seal it before he was made acquainted with it; and in
the last place, that he had stopped it for his, the Lord
Ashley's, own sake; and that he believed he had neither
enough considered the indignity that was offered to the
Lord Treasurer, to whom he professed so much respect,
and by whose favour and powerful interposition he
enjoyed the office he held, nor his own true interest, in
submitting his estate to those incumbrances which such
a receipt would inevitably expose it to; and that the
exemption from making any account but to the King
himself would deceive him; and as it was an unusual
and unnatural privilege, so it would never be allowed in
any court of justice, which would exact both the
account and the payment or lawful discharge of what
money he should receive, and if he depended upon the
exemption he would live to repent it." Lord Ashley,
according to Clarendon, sullenly replied " that the King
had given him the office, and knew best what was good
for his own service, and that except his Majesty re-
stricted his grant, he would look to enjoy the benefit of
it; that he did not desire to put an affront upon the
Lord Treasurer, and if there were any expressions in his
Commission which reflected upon him, he was content
they should be mended or left out; in all other respects
he was resolved to run the hazard." Southampton, the
Lord Treasurer, whom Clarendon describes as much
hurt, would not interfere, " but sat unconcerned, and

took no notice of anything." It is not improbable that Clarendon misrepresented or exaggerated Southampton's feeling. The end of it was that "within a short time the King sent a positive order to the Chancellor to seal the Commission, which he could no longer refuse, and did it with the more trouble, because he very well knew that few men knew the Lord Ashley better than the King himself did, or had a worse opinion of his integrity."

The question here at issue was one like several others that arose during this reign, a question of power and old prerogative against reason and public advantage. That Clarendon was right in his view of this matter, so far as concerns public expediency, we who live in days when prerogative has long since been wholesomely reduced and regulated, can have no doubt. But the King cannot be unreservedly blamed for insisting on the exercise of a power which he thought rightfully his. Personal bias and irritation probably made Clarendon on this occasion the opponent of royal prerogative, which in other similar instances he upheld. Lord Ashley was doubtless stimulated by his own advantage in his resistance to Clarendon's opposition to the proposed arrangement. The dangers to Ashley himself, pictured by Clarendon's imagination, were never in the least realized.

During this war, and in the straits of the Government for money, the question of the justice and necessity of appropriation of prize-moneys to the needs of the war was often raised. There was a body of Commissioners of Prizes, and one of these was Sir William

Coventry, Lord Ashley's brother-in law, who was Secretary to the Lord High Admiral, and one of his Council,
a man of great ability, and the real administrator of the
Admiralty for the first eight years of the reign of
Charles the Second. Pepys mentions a proposal by Sir
W. Coventry to the Duke of York, April 3, 1667, to
devote 3,700*l.* worth of prize goods to payment of a
debt for the war, when "the Duke of York, Sir George
Carteret, and Lord Berkeley saying, all of them, that
my Lord Ashley would not be got to yield it, who is
Treasurer of the Prizes, Sir W. Coventry did plainly
desire that it might be declared whether the proceeds of
the prizes were to go to the helping on of the war or no,
and, if it were, how then they could be denied."[1] Another
entry of Pepys in his Diary shows the worthy Secretary
of the Admiralty astonished at Lord Ashley's not
quailing before the great man of his office. "With
Sir W. Warren, who tells me that, at the Committee of
the Lords for the Prizes to-day, there passed very high
words between my Lord Ashley and Sir W. Coventry
about our business of the prize ships, and that my
Lord Ashley did snuff and talk as high to him as he
used to do to any ordinary man, and that Sir W.
Coventry did take it very quietly; but yet for all did
speak his mind soberly and with reason, and went
away saying he had done his duty therein."[2] An order

---

[1] Pepys's Diary, iv. 4.
[2] Ibid. iii. 173, March 21, 1666. These statements by Pepys of
differences between Ashley and Coventry are the more interesting,
as Clarendon, in his story of Ashley's appointment to be Treasurer of
Prizes, speaks of him as "fast linked to Sir Harry Bennet and Mr.
Coventry in a league offensive and defensive, the same friends and the
same enemies."

from the King to stop the sale of some prize goods asked for by the Duke of York for the use of the navy, is stated by Pepys to have made Lord Ashley very angry.[1] Pepys dined with Lord Ashley on the twenty-third of September, 1667, and took an opportunity before dinner of looking over his prize accounts. "We were put in my Lord's room before he could come to us, and there had an opportunity to look over the state of his account of the prizes, and there saw how bountiful the King hath been to several people; and hardly any man almost, commander of the navy of any note, but hath some reward or other out of them; and many sums to the Privy Purse, but not so many, I see, as I thought there had been; but we could not look quite through it. But several bedchamber men and people about the Court had good sums, and, among others, Sir John Minnes and Lord Brounker have 200*l.* a-piece for looking to the East India prizes, while I did the work for them."[2] No imputation was ever made against Lord Ashley himself for misappropriation of funds; the distribution was under the King's orders. The accounts of the prizes were inspected by the Commission appointed in 1668 for examination of public accounts, and no charge of any sort was made against Lord Ashley.

A letter written by Lord Ashley a few days before the close of the session of 1664–5, to his wife in the country, gives a pleasing glimpse of him in his family

---

[1] Pepys's Diary, iii. 376–8, January 16 and 19, 1667.
[2] Ibid. iv. 201. The proceedings of the Commissioners of Prizes, in three folio volumes, are preserved in the British Museum. (Harl. MSS. 1509–11.)

relations. His only son, who had just completed his
thirteenth year, was now going to Oxford to begin his
studies there, it being then customary to enter the
Universities at so early an age. The son was entered
at Trinity College. "My brother Robert," mentioned
in the following letter, was Lady Ashley's brother,
Robert Spenser[1] and "My lady" is the widow Lady
Spenser of Wormleighton, the mother of Lady Ashley,
whom her son Robert would be going to fetch away
from St. Giles's. "My Lord Northumberland" was one
of the survivors of the leaders of the Presbyterian party
at the beginning of the Civil War, who had concurred as
a venerable member of that party in the Restoration.
The Earl of Northumberland recovered from the illness here spoken of; he died in October 1668. Lady
Ashley's nephew, the Earl of Sunderland, had lately
married a niece of Lord Northumberland; and Lord
Northumberland's eldest son was married to a cousin
of Lady Ashley, a daughter of the Earl of Southampton,
the Lord Treasurer, and Lord Ashley's intimate friend.
"My brother Chicheley" was Mr., afterwards Sir
Thomas, Chicheley, of Wimpole in Cambridgeshire,

---

[1] Robert Spenser, brother of the Earl of Sunderland who fell at Edge-
hill, and uncle of the Sunderland who was minister to Charles II. and
James II., was created a Scotch peer, with the title of Viscount Teviot,
by James II. in 1686. A mention of him in one of the Countess of
Sunderland's, his sister-in-law's, charming letters to Lord Halifax, shows
him in strong opposition to Shaftesbury's politics in the days of the
Popish Plot and Exclusion Bill. "My brother Spenser," says Lady
Sunderland, "was yesterday in town ; he had a mind to see his sister
[Lady Shaftesbury], and sent her to meet him at Southampton House
[Lord Russell's]. He would not go to my Lord Shaftesbury's, because
of his proceedings against the Duke [of York]. My Lord Russell asked
him why he would come to his. He might have told him, ' You are but
a blind follower.' " (July 8, 1680. Lady Russell's Life and Letters,
edited by Miss Berry, 1819, p. 354.)

who had married a sister of Shaftesbury's first wife, one of the daughters of Lord Keeper Coventry, who had previously been the wife of Sir William Savile, and who by this first marriage was mother of the celebrated George Savile, Lord Halifax. The affectionate tone of this letter is very pleasant.[1]

"LONDON, *February* 26, 1665.

"MY DEAREST,—I received yours of the 23rd instant just now and write this by James Percivall. I have some hopes of seeing you Wednesday sevennight and coming the Monday after away with you for London. My brother Robert goes this week for Petworth, where he is like to find a sad house, for my Lord Northumberland is reported in great danger, but I hope he will be with you so as my lady will remove next week, for it will be not only inconvenient but dangerous to remove too great a company.[2] The safest road is Winchester and Guildford. If my lady be not well or able to travel, I beg she will not think of removing until she be well. My dearest, you gave my child the best thing that could be, but his extreme wilful disorders taken in eating always gives me great fears until he be removed to a place of other discipline. I have provided all things ready for him at Oxford, and desire you will borrow Sir Edward Hooper's or any other of my neighbours' coaches and

---

[1] This letter is printed from the papers at St. Giles's.
[2] The danger and inconvenience of too great a company was probably from the badness of the roads. Lady Russell, describing her journey in 1678 from London to Tunbridge Wells, writes : " I do really think if I could have imagined the illness of the journey, it would have discouraged me ; it is not to be expressed how bad the way is from Sevenoaks ; but our horses did exceeding well, and Spenser very diligent, often off his horse to lay hold of the coach." (Lady Russell's Letters, i. 38, ed. 1853.)

four horses who may in three days carry him and Mr. Craven to Oxford. Mr. Bergen shall not go with him, but to London with us. You may acquaint Laurence that I shall desire him to go along and see him settled. I intend his journey the same day with ours on this day fortnight; he may lodge at Clarendon the first night, at Hungerford the next, and at Oxford the third, no journey above twenty mile. I hope my niece's toothache is breeding, but pray tell her I beg she will resolve not to leave her son less than her husband was left. I hear she has taken a waiting woman, a house-keeper, and a chambermaid. If so, I am sorry for it. Mr. Constantine is my author. A chambermaid and a washmaid had been enough; let her not think I fiddlingly disturb her, but I love to speak early, as knowing what things will come to ; and I rely so much on her kindness to me that she will lay down all romance and take up discretion. I am extremely joyed with her behaviour towards her husband as you describe it. My brother Chichely[1] has given Colonel Fagg ten thousand pound for his place of Lieutenant of the Ordnance, and 'tis said he owes twice that sum before. We hear no more of that ill news of my Lord Berkley.[2] I had rather you had found treasure than

[1] Mr. Chicheley was appointed Commissioner of the Ordnance in November 1664, with Sir John Minnes, Lord Berkeley of Stratton, and Sir John Duncombe for colleagues. (Pepys's Diary, ii. 396.) He appears to have been extravagant ; and Lord Ashley speaks of him as in debt. Pepys mentions his dining with him in Queen Street, Covent Garden, March 11, 1668. "A very fine house, and a man that lives in mighty great fashion, with all things in a most extraordinary manner noble and rich about him, and eats in the French fashion all ; and mighty nobly served with his servants, and very civilly ; so that I was mightily pleased with it ; and good discourse. He is a great defender of the Church of England, and against the Act for Comprehension." (Diary, iv. 387.)

[2] This was probably Lord Berkeley of Stratton, so created in 1658, formerly Sir John Berkeley, whose account of his negotiations in 1647

pictures, but I satisfy myself in the portion I have in this
world, and that treasure God has given me in so faithful
and affectionate a wife, to whom I ever vow myself,

"A most sincere and truly affectionate husband,

"ASHLEY."

In the year 1663 a grant had been made by the King
of the province of Carolina, now part of another mighty
dominion, to nine individuals, of whom one was Lord
Ashley. The other eight were the Duke of Albemarle,
the Lord Chancellor, the Earl of Craven, Lord Berkeley,
Sir George Carteret, Sir John Colleton, and Sir William
Berkeley. The grant was renewed in June of this year,
1665, to all the original grantees, except Sir John
Colleton. Lord Ashley took a leading part in the
management of this grant. Locke, at his request, drew
up a constitution for the colony, which is dated 1669.
In 1670 another grant was made by the King of the
Bahama or Lucayo Islands, to the second Duke of
Albemarle (the famous Monk having died in the interval), Earl of Craven, Lord Berkeley, Lord Ashley,
Sir George Carteret, and Sir Peter Colleton. A large
volume of letters written by Shaftesbury about the
affairs of the two colonies of Carolina and the Bahamas,
showing his very great attention to them, is preserved
at St. Giles's.[2]

for Charles I. with Cromwell is published under the title of Sir John
Berkeley's Memoirs. He was now one of the Lord High Admiral's
Council and a Commissioner of the Ordnance, and was afterwards Lord
Lieutenant of Ireland. I do not know what ill news is here referred to.
    [1] See "The Fundamental Constitutions of Carolina" in Locke's
Works, x. 175, ed. 1812.
    [2] Two of these many letters are printed in Mr. Martyn's life, vol. ii.
p. 95. The letters are too numerous to insert in this work, and they
have no general interest.

The degree of Lord Ashley's favour at this period with the King is shown by the King's visiting him in September of this year, at his country house at Wimborne St. Giles. The plague was now raging in London, and the King and Court had been staying for some time at Salisbury. The only known notice of this royal visit to Lord Ashley is contained in a letter from Lord Arlington, who was with the King, to the Duke of Ormond in Ireland, written from Salisbury, September 11, 1665. "His Majesty is, God be thanked, perfectly well recovered, and is now in his coach gone to divert himself at my Lord Ashley's, whither I am following him, and from whence I shall be to send your Grace such a present as this the next week."[1]

On account of the plague, the Parliament was called to meet at Oxford in October, and there a short session was held, beginning on the ninth and ending on the thirty-first of October. In this short session, however, much business was got through. An additional supply of a million and a quarter for the war was granted, and a present of 120,000l. was voted to the Duke of York, whose valour and success in the first naval battle of the war, off Lowestoft, on June 3, had made him a popular hero. Clarendon gives a long account of a proviso introduced into the Supply Bill of this session, at the suggestion of Sir George Downing, and with the approval of the King, "to make all the money that was to be raised by this bill to be supplied only to those ends to which it was given, which was the

[1] Miscellanea Aulica, p. 361.

carrying on the war, and to no other purpose whatsoever,
by what authority soever." Though the object of this
clause seems to be very much the same as Clarendon
says he had in view when he opposed the conditions of
Lord Ashley's appointment of Treasurer of Prizes, he
now strongly opposed Sir George Downing's clause as
an encroachment on the King's prerogative, as well
as an impediment to the administration of finances.
Ashley, who at first had favoured the clause, was also an
opponent. The bill had passed the Commons and was
in the Lords, when, at the instance, Clarendon says, of
Lord Ashley, the King summoned a few of his chief
advisers to a meeting at Clarendon's lodgings, for the
reconsideration of the proviso. There were present with
the King the Duke of York, the Chancellor (who was
in bed with the gout, wherefore the meeting was in
his bedroom), Lord Southampton, Lord Ashley, Lord
Arlington, and Sir W. Coventry ; also the Attorney and
Solicitor-General to draft any amendments which might
be approved of, and Sir George Downing to defend his
proposal. " The Chancellor had never seen the proviso
which contained all the novelty (for all the other parts
of the bill were according to the course), and the
Treasurer had read it only an hour or two before the
meeting ; the Lord Ashley, therefore, who had heard it
read in the House of Peers, and observed what that
House thought of it, opened the whole business with
the novelty and the ill consequence that must inevitably
attend it, all which he enforced with great clearness and
evidence of reason, and would have enlarged with some
sharpness on the advisers of it. But the King himself

stopped that by declaring that whatsoever had been done
in the whole transaction of it had been with his privity
and approbation, and the whole blame must be laid to his
own charge, who, it seems, was like to suffer most by it."
The end of it was that the bill passed the House of
Lords with the proviso unaltered.[1] Clarendon inaccurately says that the King agreed to some "small
amendments, which would be as soon consented to in
both Houses as read," and that with such amendments
the bill was passed. The Lords made no alteration
whatever, and the amount of opposition made in the
House of Lords is probably much exaggerated by
Clarendon, for the bill, which was only sent up to the
House of Lords on the twenty-first of October, was
passed without any alteration, and without a division
at any stage, on the twenty-third. This is another
instance of conflict in this reign between prerogative
and public interest, and the influences and traditions
of office made Lord Ashley an opponent, as is still
frequently the case with parliamentary officials, of a
change which in an independent position he would
probably have supported. The King's need of money
and desire to conciliate Parliament induced him to
admit, in spite of Clarendon and Ashley, and contrary
to his own high notions of prerogative, the principle
of parliamentary appropriation of money voted, which
is now an uncontested and highly prized part of our
constitution.

The agreement of Clarendon and Ashley on the subject of this proviso for the Supply Bill may have helped

[1] Continuation of Life of Clarendon, 792—803.

to improve their relations and bring them to friendship for a time, for in the following January, Ruvigny writes that they were on the most confidential terms. "Bennet and Ashley," he wrote, "appear to be the two chief confidents of the Chancellor, which last year would have been incredible; so great is the force of ambition and interest."[1]

During the October session at Oxford, another Act, on which Clarendon and Ashley widely differed, was added to the list of persecuting measures against Dissenters. This is the Act known by the name of the Five Mile Act. By it Dissenting ministers were prohibited, under a penalty of forty pounds for every offence, from going, unless only in passing on the road, within five miles of any city, corporation, borough, town, or place where they had been ministers, or had preached, after the Act of Oblivion, unless they first took the following oath: "I do swear that it is not lawful, under any pretence whatever, to take up arms against the King, and that I do abhor the traitorous position of taking up arms by his authority against his person, or against those that are commissioned by him in pursuance of such commissions, and that I will not at any time endeavour any alteration of government either in Church or State." The Earl of Southampton, Lord Ashley, and Lord Wharton strongly opposed this measure in the House of Lords.[2] The courageous labours

---

[1] Ruvigny to De Lionne, January 9/19, 1666, in Archives of French Foreign Office. Ruvigny says of Bennet in the same passage that he "has as great a share in the King's pleasures as in business." He does not say the same of Ashley.

[2] Letter from a Person of Quality in Locke's Works, x. 203;

of Dissenting ministers at this very time, amid the
ravages of the plague in London, should, now at least,
have procured for them consideration, instead of
increased severity; and policy strongly counselled
measures for uniting the nation, instead of increasing
heartburnings, when England was at war with Holland,
and expecting that France would immediately declare
war as Holland's ally.

But not content with the Five Mile Act, some of its
supporters introduced into the Commons during this
session a bill for imposing on the whole nation the oath
not to take up arms against the King or endeavour to
make any alteration of government either in Church or
State.   The bill was rejected, but only by the small
majority of six.   It is a singular circumstance, which
has been noted, that in the majority were three members
who had appeared in the House that day for the first
time, Mr. Peregrine Bertie, a younger son of the Earl of
Lindsey, who took his seat that day as a new member,
and the two members who introduced him, his eldest
brother, Lord Bertie, and Sir Thomas Osborne, who soon
afterwards became celebrated as Lord Treasurer and
Earl of Danby.[1]   Had these three voted the other way,
the numbers would have been equal; and it is extraordinary that ten years later the same bill was proposed
and pressed by Lord Danby, and introduced into the

Martyn's Life ii. 302. Bishop Burnet dwells on Lord Southampton's
vigorous opposition (Own Time, i. 390-1).
[1] Letter from a Person of Quality in Locke's Works, x. 204; Hallam's
Constitutional History, ii. 475. Mr. Martyn has erroneously represented the bill of 1665 as having been defeated in the Lords, and has
indeed altogether misapprehended the story told by the " Person of
Quality." (Life, i. 302.)

House of Lords by the same Lord Bertie, who was then Earl of Lindsey and Lord Chamberlain.

Lord Ashley stayed a few weeks at Oxford after the prorogation, as appears from the following letter to his wife, who was at Wimborne St. Giles. He may have stayed there to be with his son. "My sister Cooper" is of course the wife of his brother George. The postscript shows fear of the plague at Oxford.

"OXFORD, *Nov.* 23, 1665.

"MY DEAREST DEAR,—I received a letter last night from my sister Cooper, which brought me the sad news of your being ill, and that you had sent for no advice. She very kindly and discreetly gave me a punctual account of the manner of your disease, which I have consulted Dr. Willis upon; he is one of the learnedest and most famed physicians in the world; he has given me the enclosed directions, and fearing you might not get the things so suddenly or well made, I have caused his apothecary to make them and have sent them to you by this bearer, my groom, with your oil of almonds and spirits of hartshorn. All this I have done lest Dr. Hurst be not in the country near you, for else I wonder you would not send for him, which I require you upon all the love you bear me immediately to do, and show him these directions, but I would not have you stay from using these things as soon as they come to your hand. Pray show them and this letter to my good lady your mother, who, I doubt not, will have care of you, for it very much adds to my affliction that 'tis not possible for me to come to you this week; but if you continue ill, I have Dr. Willis his promise to go with me to you. The Lord in mercy

---

[1] From Lord Shaftesbury's papers at St. Giles.

preserve my dear, and restore your health, is the most
hearty and humble prayer of,

" My dearest,
" Your most truly affectionate husband,
" ASHLEY.

" Pray, my dear, send up somebody that can purify
our linen, for the concourse of people frights us all
more than ever, though it abates well at London."

In June, 1666, Lord Ashley was again at Oxford, and
he, on this occasion, accidentally made an acquaintance
with John Locke, which rapidly ripened into an intimate
friendship.   Lord Ashley was now suffering much from
an internal swelling, the consequence of the accident
which befel him when he went over to Breda on the
eve of the Restoration, and he had been advised to
drink the mineral waters of Astrop.   Before arriving at
Oxford, he had written to a physician there, Dr. Thomas,
requesting him to procure some of these waters for him.
Dr. Thomas, being obliged to leave Oxford at this time,
entrusted the commission to Locke, who had lately
returned to Oxford from diplomatic employment in
Germany, and was now residing as a Student of Christ
Church and studying medicine.   Locke waited on Lord
Ashley, who was greatly pleased with his visitor; and
this visit was the origin of a life-long friendship between
these two celebrated men.   Lord Ashley went from
Oxford to stay at Sunning Hill and there drink the
Astrop waters, and Locke accompanied him.   Locke
was again his companion at Sunning Hill, in the year
following.   Afterwards he became an inmate of Lord

Ashley's house, and one of his family, and his constant
medical adviser. Recommended by Lord Ashley to the
young Earl and Countess of Northumberland, he went
with them to France in 1669.[1]   When in November,
1672, Shaftesbury became Lord Chancellor, he appointed Locke one of his Secretaries; and soon after
he made Locke Secretary of the Council of Trade and
Plantations, of which he was President from September
1672 to April 1676. In the year 1674, Shaftesbury
gave Locke a life annuity of a hundred pounds on easy
terms.[2]   The eager and restless politician and the calm
and high-minded philosopher remained on terms of
affectionate intimacy till Shaftesbury's death. Then, in
a time of arbitrary rule, came grief and injury to Locke
on account of his close connexion with the deceased
Shaftesbury. While in Holland, whither he had gone
from fear perhaps of staying in England, he was, in
1684, deprived of his Studentship at Christ Church, by
an order of Charles the Second, servilely obeyed by
the Dean and Chapter of that cathedral College. In
a letter to his friend, the Earl of Pembroke, at the
close of 1684, part of which has been before quoted,[3]
Locke, writing in a tone of depression, describes his
connexion with Shaftesbury, saying that it had been
much misunderstood, and that he had unjustly suffered
in consequence. He describes himself as having lived

[1] The old Earl of Northumberland had died in 1668. His son and
successor, with whom Locke travelled, died abroad in May 1670. His
widow, a daughter of the Earl of Southampton, and cousin of Lady
Shaftesbury, afterwards married Ralph Montagu, ambassador at Paris,
who became in time Duke of Montagu.
[2] See Shaftesbury's letter to Locke of November 23, 1674, printed
in the second volume, and Martyn's Life of Shaftesbury, i. 5.
[3] See note at p. 261.

in Shaftesbury's house as his medical adviser rather
than in any other capacity, and he says that, though
always treated kindly by Shaftesbury, he improved his
fortune but little, and found himself at Shaftesbury's
death without the means which he would probably have
acquired had he practised as a physician.[1] He goes on to
deny in the strongest and most unqualified language that
he had ever published any political or other pamphlet or
treatise whatsoever. This was in December 1684. He had
then published, he says, nothing but two or three copies
of verses, which had not gained him the reputation of a
poet.[2] And now, remaining in exile in Holland during the
whole of the reign of James the Second, he laboured at
his great work on the Human Understanding, which has
given him with posterity a rank very far above that
of any king or minion who in worldly power and pride
trampled on his living worth and intellect. After the
Revolution of 1688 Locke returned to England, and he
lived for sixteen years afterwards in ease of circumstances, honoured and famous. It is gratifying to read
authentic testimonies of his respect for the memory
of Shaftesbury. Le Clerc says that Locke "remembered
all his life with great pleasure the satisfaction which he
had in intercourse with Lord Shaftesbury, and when he
spoke of his good qualities did so not only with esteem,

---

[1] See Dr. John Brown's notices of Locke as a medical man in his
interesting Essay on Locke and Sydenham in "Horæ Subsecivæ."

[2] There are two poems by Locke, a short one in Latin with translation and a longer English poem, on Cromwell and his conclusion of the
war with the Dutch, printed in the State Poems (vol. i. part 2) from
an Oxford collection. Mr. Martyn prints some verses written by
Locke in 1672, addressed to Greenhill, the painter (Life, ii. 13), but
these were probably not published before 1684. There can be no
doubt that Locke had not the gift of poetry.

but even with admiration." Mr. Coste, who had been
an amanuensis to Locke, and was long a fellow inmate
with him of Sir Francis Masham's house at Oates, in
Essex, where Locke lived for the last fourteen years of
his life, says that Locke "loved to confirm his opinion
on any subject by that of the famous Earl of Shaftesbury, to whom he took a delight to give the honour of
all the things which he thought he had learnt from
his conversation." "I wish," also says Mr. Coste, "I
could give a full notion of the idea which Mr. Locke
had of that nobleman's merit. He lost no opportunity
of speaking of it, and that in a manner which sufficiently showed he spoke from his heart."[1]

The Dutch war, in which France and Denmark had
joined as the allies of Holland, the Plague which, lasting
fifteen months, caused a hundred thousand deaths, and
the Great Fire, which, as the Plague was dying out,
destroyed two thirds of London, were an accumulation of
misfortunes for England in the year 1666. The Parliament assembled in London in September of that year, and
the session lasted till February 8, 1667. There were now
great complaints of mismanagement, extravagance, and
misappropriation of funds voted for the war, and the
House of Commons insisted on a close examination of
accounts.[2] There was a calculation that rather more than
five millions and a half sterling had been at the disposal of Government for the war, and only 3,200,000*l.*
was accounted for. The Commons voted a supply of

---

[1] "The Character of Mr. Locke" by Mr. Peter Coste, printed in
Locke's Works, vol. x.
[2] Pepys's Diary, Sept. 21 and Oct. 10, 1666. The proceeds of prizes
were estimated at 300,000*l.*

1,800,000*l*., and endeavoured, first by a proviso in a money-bill, and then by a separate bill, to obtain a Commission to inspect the accounts of the war. Such an inquiry was averted for the present; but an Act for appointing such a Commission was passed a year later.

Lord Ashley made himself conspicuous during this session by eager support of a bill for prohibiting importation of Irish cattle into England. An attempt to pass such a bill had failed in the Oxford session of the previous year; but now the bill became an Act. Lord Clarendon, who opposed the bill, describes Ashley as second only to the Duke of Buckingham in violent support of it, and against probability, attributes the eagerness of both Ashley and Buckingham to personal hostility to the Duke of Ormond, a great Irish proprietor. " It grew quickly evident," says Clarendon, " that there were other reasons which caused so earnest a prosecution of it above the encouragement of the breed of cattle in England; insomuch as the Lord Ashley, who, next the Duke, appeared the most violent supporter of the bill, could not forbear to urge it as an argument for the prosecuting it, that, if this bill did not pass, all the rents in Ireland would rise in a vast proportion, and those in England fall as much, so that in a year or two the Duke of Ormond would have a greater revenue than the Earl of Northumberland, which made a visible impression on many as a thing not to be endured. Whereas the Duke had indeed at least four times the proportion of land in Ireland that descended to him from his ancestors that the Earl had in

England, and the revenue of it before the Rebellion was not inferior to the others. But nothing was more manifest than that the warmth of that prosecution in the House of Peers in many Lords did proceed from the envy they had of the Duke's station in one kingdom and of his fortune in the other."[1] It is enough that in a period of great depression of the value of land in England English proprietors, and especially those of the western counties, were anxious to obtain protection against competition of Irish cattle. The great fall of English rents was a sufficient moving principle for Ashley; and if the bias of self-interest sharpened his zeal, it is by no means clear that special circumstances did not counsel an exception to general rules of political economy, then indeed little understood or appreciated.[2] The opponents of the measure feared that the passing of it might inflame the Irish to rebellion; and Irish content was of greater importance, when England was at war with France, and a French invasion of Ireland was even a probability. The debates on this bill in the House of Lords were marked by very great acrimony. The Earl of Ossory, the Duke of Ormond's gallant but impetuous son, quarrelled during these debates both with the Duke of Buckingham and

[1] Clarendon's Continuation of Life, 967.
[2] Some notices in Pepys's Diary show very forcibly the depression of the agricultural interest in England. April 9, 1667 : "Several do complain of abundance of land flung up by tenants out of their hands for want of ability to pay their rents, and by name that the Duke of Buckingham hath 6,000l. so flung up." Jan. 1, 1668 : Pepys dined with Lord Crewe, when "they did talk much of the present cheapness of corn, even to a miracle, so as their farmers can pay no rent, but do fling up their lands." Jan. 31, 1668: Colonel Birch told Pepys of "the general want of money in the country, that land sold for nothing, and the many pennyworths he knows of lands and houses upon them with good titles in his county at sixteen years' purchase." See Lord Ashley's memorial to the King of 1669 in Appendix I. of the next volume.

with Lord Ashley, and he was on both occasions repri-
manded and ordered to make an apology.[1] Lord Ossory,
replying to Lord Ashley, said that he had spoken like
one of Cromwell's councillors. Lord Ashley complained
of this language, and the House required Lord Ossory
to stand up in his place and say "that he is very sorry
for the great offence he hath given to the House, and
humbly desires their pardon; and that he is very sorry
that any words of his should reflect on the Lord Ashley,
for which he desires the Lord Ashley's pardon."

Carte, in his Life of the Duke of Ormond, relates a
lively altercation in private between Lord Ashley and
Lord Conway, an Irish proprietor, who became Secretary
of State near the end of Charles the Second's reign,
during the discussions of the same bill.

" Upon the news of a French invasion and a powerful
army embarking at Brest, which was all the subject of
discourse, Lord Conway coming in before the House sat,
Lord Ashley asked him in the presence of twenty lords
how they would do to defend themselves in case the
invasion fell on Ireland. Conway replied they should
not so much as think of it, for when they had represented to the House that they should be disabled by the
bill from doing so, he [Lord Ashley] had answered they
never had been able to defend themselves, and when
they were in danger England ever had and ever must
defend them, and therefore they should leave that matter
to him, who had said those words, and to the Parliament
which believed him. Ashley replied with a very super-
cilious air : 'They knew better where to lay the blame,
and that was on those lords that had driven the English

[1] Lords' Journals, Nov. 19, 1666. Pepys's Diary, same date, iii. 339.

out of the seaports and corporate towns and filled them with Irish.' Conway's answer was as resolute, 'that there were no such lords in Ireland, nor was the matter of fact true, for the Irish in all their seaports and towns put together would not make up one reasonable street.'"

Carte goes on to say that Lord Conway, suspecting Lord Ashley of an ambition to be Lord Lieutenant of Ireland, took occasion, a few days after the passing of the Irish Cattle Bill, to say to him " that he wondered exceedingly to see his Lordship so injurious to Ireland, since no man was so likely in a short time to be Lord Lieutenant of that kingdom as himself, but he had now contracted an incapacity which was not usual; for the violence he had so lately shown would make the whole country believe he came to destroy them totally, so that they would be tempted to rebel and tear him to pieces." Ashley seemed, said Lord Conway, pleased with the insinuation, and vindicated himself from the charge of ill-will to Ireland. " He said that it was true they had done an unnatural act, but the fault was in the present governors of that country, who by their settlement, their book of rates, and other principles of government, endeavoured to divide the two kingdoms; whereas he desired they should be united and sit in one Parliament, and then all these acts would fall to the ground; and though he had exclaimed in the last session at Oxford against granting a liberty of conscience in Ireland, yet as he found it for the good of the kingdom in its present situation, he would befriend the country particularly in that point, and in all others as occasions offered." Carte proceeds, writing of course on Lord Conway's authority: "He [Lord Ashley] was so fond of the subject that he kept on the discourse and renewed his professions for an hour together, thereby convincing Lord Conway, who only proposed the matter in raillery, of his inclination to be at the head of that kingdom; for men of great parts and cunning are seldom bit in that way, unless they are betrayed by some passion or other."[1]

The close of the year 1666 found both England and France anxious to terminate the war. When the war began between England and Holland, Louis XIV. had at first viewed it with complacency, as likely, by giving to both occupation and impairing the resources of both, to prevent both from obstructing his designs on Spanish Flanders. Later, France was brought into the war as the ally of Holland under a clause in a treaty made between France and Holland in 1662. Tardily and ungraciously had France consented to fulfil the obligations of this treaty, in contracting which she had acted faithlessly towards England; and when at last she had declared war against England, she gave Holland no cordial or effective co-operation. Louis then soon became anxious to conclude the war, get rid of obligations which he was unwilling to fulfil, and be free to invade Spanish Flanders. At the close of the campaign of 1666, Louis found the King of England ready to treat for peace, while the States General made difficulties, hoping on their part to prevent Louis from embroiling himself with Spain and invading Spanish Flanders by keeping him engaged in war with England. In the spring of 1667, Louis succeeded in making a secret

[1] Carte's Life of Ormond, ii. 338.

arrangement with the King of England, by which the
latter promised to make no alliance, during the period
of one year, with any nation against France, or which
might possibly prejudice French interests, and to
make during the year a close alliance with France,
Louis promised in return to restore to England the
French conquests in the West Indies made in the
course of the war. This _secret arrangement was
made by letters written by the two Kings to Henrietta Maria, the Queen Dowager of England, the
mother of Charles and the aunt of Louis.[1] Shortly
after, negotiations for peace were opened at Breda
between England and Holland, but the Dutch refused
an armistice during the progress of negotiations. The
poverty of the English exchequer had led to premature
reductions in the English navy, and De Witt, with a
strong Dutch fleet fully prepared, saw his advantage
and determined to strike, while he yet could, a heavy
blow. The Dutch fleet under De Ruyter, in June,
entered the Thames, proceeded as far as Chatham, and,
there destroyed by fire three of our men-of-war. This
was a humiliating disaster for England. Peace now
soon followed. Louis XIV., secured by his secret
arrangement with Charles, had in the month of May
entered Flanders with an army of seventy thousand
men; and his rapid conquests terrified Holland into
acquiescence in a treaty of peace. Peace was concluded at Breda on the thirty-first of July, 1667.

The Earl of Southampton, the Lord High Treasurer,
had died in May, and that office was now put into Com-

[1] Mignet, Négotiations relatives à la Succession d'Espagne, iii. 58.

mission, at the King's instance and against the opinion
of Clarendon. The Commissioners were the Duke of
Albemarle (George Monk), Lord Ashley, who continued to
be Chancellor of the Exchequer, Sir William Coventry,
Sir John Duncombe, and Sir Thomas Clifford. Clarendon has given an account of this arrangement, in which
he describes the King at the time as being dissatisfied
with Ashley and unwilling to include him in the Commission, and further represents it as a humiliation for
Ashley that, being Chancellor of the Exchequer, he was
not made an indispensable member of the quorum. It
is clear from Clarendon's account that the King had
made up his mind to appoint a small number of Commissioners who should all be men of business, and not
to follow the custom of appointing a number of high
officials of state who would only give dignity to the
Commission and leave the work to the Chancellor of
the Exchequer. Clarendon, who was strongly opposed
to a Commission for the Treasury, but saw that the
King had made up his mind to it, perceived also that
the King "would not approve the old course in the
choice of Commissioners, who had always been the
Keeper of the Great Seal, and the two Secretaries of
State, and two other of .the principal persons of the
Council, besides the Chancellor of the Exchequer, who
used to be the sole person of the quorum." The Duke
of York agreed with the King in opinion, cited the case
of the Ordnance which had shortly before been placed
in Commission on the death of Sir William Compton,
and contended that, as in the Ordnance so in the
Treasury, business would be better done, " if fit persons

were chosen for it, who might have nothing else to do."
The King proposed Sir Thomas Clifford, who, being a
member of Parliament of small fortune, had been much
befriended by Arlington, and was now Comptroller of
the Household and a Privy Councillor, Sir William
Coventry, and Sir John Duncombe. The King thought
that these three would be enough for despatch of
business. Clarendon then suggested the necessity of
naming Ashley, because he was Chancellor of the
Exchequer, and urged the appointment also of the Duke
of Albemarle and some other person of high rank to
give lustre to the Commission. The King said, according to Clarendon, that "he did not care if he added the
General to them. The Lord Ashley gave him some
trouble, and he said enough to make it manifest that he
thought him not fit to be amongst them ; yet he knew
not how to put him out of his place ; but gave direction
for preparing the Commission for the Treasury to the
persons named before, and made the Lord Ashley only
one of the Commissioners, and a major part to make a
quorum; which would quickly bring the government of
the whole business into the hands of those three who
were designed for it, and Ashley rather chose to be degraded than to dispute it."[1] Such is Clarendon's story ;
but he is commonly so [inaccurate in details, and he is
clearly so carried away by prejudice against Shaftesbury,
that the true story probably is that the King's desire
was to associate working Commissioners, and not mere
ornamental cyphers, with Lord Ashley, Chancellor of the
Exchequer, of whom it is very likely that he at the

[1] Continuation of Clarendon's Life, 1082-8.

same time, from some recent irritation, spoke words of disrespect, which would not displease Clarendon.

The animosity of Clarendon against Shaftesbury is clear in every allusion which he makes to him; but it is not easy, in any case, to extract from this narrative anything to Shaftesbury's prejudice. The alleged degradation disappears when it is seen that the King designed to depart from the old precedents in the formation of the Commission. That the King, whose inclinations and affections were ever varying, and who was soon to treat his old and faithful servant Clarendon himself with heartless cruelty and ingratitude, was at the moment indisposed towards Shaftesbury and found him troublesome, may be taken as proof that Lord Ashley had shown independence of character and had not been the King's servile instrument either in politics or as Treasurer of Prizes. Pepys records Lord Ashley's unwillingness to obey orders of the King as to the disposal of prize goods; his motives may have been good or bad, regard for the public or self-interest, or perhaps even mere self-will.[1]   It also appears that Lord Ashley was not quite pleased with the new arrangement; it was not in human nature that he should be so. Sir George Carteret, who was Treasurer of the Navy, and was himself much displeased with the new Commission, ("and he hath reason," says Pepys, "for it will eclipse him,") told Pepys that "my Lord Ashley says they understand nothing, and he says he believes the King do not intend they shall sit long."[2]

[1] Diary, iii. 376-8, January 16, 19, 1667.
[2] Ibid. May 31, 1667, iv. 58.

Pepys however himself thought otherwise, and, being
a man of business, he thought the Commission a good
measure. A few days later, Pepys had to attend the
Commissioners, and was much struck with their busi-
ness-like way of proceeding.   Lord Ashley, Clifford,
and Duncombe were the only three present, with their
Secretary, Sir George Downing.   " I do like the way of
these Lords, that they admit nobody to use many words,
nor do they spend many words themselves, but in great
state do hear what they see necessary, and say little
themselves, but bid withdraw."[1]   Later, Mr. Pepys is of
opinion that Sir William Coventry is the leading man
in the Commission.   " I perceive Sir W. Coventry is
the man, and nothing done till he comes."[2]   But Lord
Ashley was not likely to allow himself to be led by
Coventry, and we may be sure, with his active and
eager character, his official experience, and his habits
of business, that he took a prominent part in the Commission. All, indeed, were active, as it had been
designed they should be.   Clifford's activity was afterwards shown in the memorable Stop of the Exchequer.
Some, indeed, regarded Ashley as the governing spirit
of the Commission.   Sir William Temple visited on
Shaftesbury his wrath for the refusal by the Commissioners of the customary gift of his plate when he
returned in 1671 from his embassy to Holland.[3]   The
charming Lady Fanshawe denounces Shaftesbury with
all an amiable woman's anger, as " the worst of men,"

---

[1] Diary, June 3, 1667, iv. 61.
[2] August 23, 1667, iv. 164.
[3] Le Clerc, Bibliothèque Choisie, vi. 364 ; Stringer's Fragment of
Memoir in Appendix III.; Mr. Wyche's MS. Vindication of Shaftesbury.

for a similar refusal by the Commissioners of his plate
to her husband, who had been ambassador to Spain.[1]
There is no doubt that this new Commission began by
endeavouring to introduce economy and order into the
finances; but this was a task beyond their strength.

A few months after this change at the Treasury
Clarendon ceased to be Chancellor. The great seal was
rudely taken from this illustrious and virtuous statesman on the thirty-first of August, 1667. The war with
Holland, which less than three years before had been
begun in national excitement against the judgment of
Clarendon, and which had lately brought disaster and
humiliation on England, had been terminated by treaties
with Holland and with France, concluded at Breda in
the previous month of July. It was necessary, the
King found, to do something to appease the general
discontent, and Clarendon was made scapegoat. In the
course of his administration he had, both in the exercise
of duty and by haughty and imperious ways, made
many enemies. Among the foremost of his adversaries
were Arlington and Coventry; they zealously urged his
removal, and were seconded by one still more powerful
with the King, the "lady," Lady Castlemaine. At this
time the King was deeply enamoured of another lady
at Court, the beautiful Miss Stuart, who firmly refused
his dishonourable proposals, and whom in the violence
of his passion he is said to have conceived the idea of
enabling himself to marry by divorcing himself on some
or other pretext from his Queen. She married the Duke
of Richmond; and among all the causes of Clarendon's

---

[1] Lady Fanshawe's Memoirs, p. 297.

fall none appears to have been more potent with Charles than his belief that Clarendon had hastened this marriage to foil his own designs on Miss Stuart. The subsequent persecution of Clarendon in Parliament was fanned by the King with spiteful eagerness, notwithstanding the Duke of York's most zealous efforts in his behalf.

There is no pretence whatever for accusing Shaftesbury, as has been done by Lord Campbell and others, of actively contributing to the fall of Clarendon. Clarendon has himself given a long and circumstantial account of his removal from the Chancellorship; he had no love for Shaftesbury when he wrote this narrative in exile; he mentions Arlington, Sir W. Coventry, Lady Castlemaine, and others as his enemies: he does not so mention Lord Ashley. Nor is Ashley mentioned by any other historian as having a share in this event. It is true that Ashley had on various occasions opposed Clarendon's policy and opinions, and especially in 1663 had actively concurred with Arlington, Bristol, and Roberts in promoting a bill for indulgence to Dissenters which Clarendon disapproved. The dislike manifested by Clarendon for Shaftesbury is not greater than that which he manifests for all the younger statesmen who came forward during his Chancellorship, and did not owe their positions to himself, and exercised an independent judgment; and the warmest admirers of Clarendon's character, which on the whole merits admiration, must allow that he was jealous, irritable, and imperious. It is also true that Ashley, like most of Charles's ministers and friends, attended the evening

receptions in Lady Castlemaine's apartment, which
Clarendon viewed with jealousy, and where Clarendon
and Southampton never appeared. The age and long
devotion of these two venerable statesmen, both to
Charles and to his father, empowered them to frown
on the mistress; their course deserves commendation,
and, had they acted otherwise, they would have deserved blame. But Ashley's was a very different
position. From an early period of his reign it was
Charles's custom to pass the evening in Lady Castlemaine's apartment, and there hold what Clarendon
always calls "the nightly conversation." All who
attended Charles in that apartment which custom
sanctioned were not debauchees nor lovers of Lady
Castlemaine nor unprincipled statesmen nor unscru-
pulous enemies of Clarendon. It has been seen that
in the beginning of the year 1666, the French Ambassador reported that both Ashley and Arlington were
on the best terms with Clarendon. And so far is it
from being true that Ashley was Clarendon's enemy
at the moment of his fall, that he really incurred the
displeasure of Charles and risked disgrace, and came
to be accounted a "Clarendonian" by opposition to
the proposed impeachment. There is a remarkable
entry on this subject in the Diary of Pepys, on December 30, 1667: "Sir G. Carteret and I alone did talk
of the ruinous condition we are in, the King being
going to put out of the Council so many able men,
such as my Lord Anglesey, Ashley, Hollis, Secretary
Morrice (to bring in Mr. Trevor), and the Archbishop
of Canterbury and my Lord Bridgewater. He tells

me that this is true, only the Duke of York do endeavour to hinder it, and the Duke of York himself
did tell him so : that the King and the Duke of York
do not in company disagree, but are friendly;. but that
there is a core in their hearts, he doubts, which is not
to be easily removed; for these men so suffer only for
their constancy to the Chancellor, or at least from the
King's ill-will against him."[1]   A few days later, on
January 5, 1668, Pepys mentions that the plan of dis-
missing a certain number of privy councillors is laid
aside.[2]   Ashley is mentioned in a despatch of Colbert
to Louis XIV., of November 15, 1668, as one of
Clarendon's party whom Buckingham had gained to
himself against Arlington.[3]   Clarendon himself mentions Ashley once in the narrative of his fall and persecution in such a manner as to imply that he was
an opponent of the measures of the House of Commons against him.[4]   Mr. Seymour, one of Clarendon's
opponents, the future Sir Edward Seymour, Speaker of
the House of Commons, "told the Lord Ashley," says
Clarendon, "that the people would pull down the Chancellor's house first, and then those of all the Lords who
adhered to him." Mr. Martyn states that Clarendon's
son, Laurence Earl of Rochester, acknowledged to the
grandson of Shaftesbury that his grandfather had
opposed the motion for sequestering and imprisoning
Clarendon on the impeachment by the Commons.[5]

---

[1] Diary, iv. 302.   [2] Id. iv. 314.
[3] Mignet, Négociations relatives à la Succession d'Espagne, iii. 58.
[4] Continuation of Life, 1189.
[5] Life, i. 329, note. This is stated doubtless by Martyn on Stringer's
authority. The statement is made also in Mr. Wyche's MS. Vindication of Shaftesbury.

Lord Ashley's name is not to be found among the signatures to the protest entered on November 20, 1667, signed by twenty-eight peers, including Buckingham, Arlington, Albemarle, Bristol, and Carlisle, against the vote of the House of Lords refusing to commit Clarendon on an impeachment without particular treason assigned. It may be taken for granted, then, that Lord Ashley was an opponent of the endeavour of the House of Commons to obtain the co-operation of the Lords for an impeachment on a general allegation of treason, and that his opposition was so conducted as to displease the King, bent on the ruin of his old and faithful minister.

The last years of Clarendon were passed in forced exile in France, and chiefly at Montpelier. In November 1667, he fled from England, in obedience to an order from the King, but leaving behind a manly vindication addressed to the House of Lords, which provoked an Act requiring him to surrender for trial before February 1, 1668, and dooming him, on failure of appearance, to banishment for life, to the penalties of high treason if he should return to England, and impossibility of pardon except by Act of Parliament. Clarendon was at Rouen when he heard of this Act; he started in haste for England to accept the trial to which he was dared; but a dangerous illness seized him at Calais, and the time prescribed by the Act had expired before he was able to leave his bed. There was nothing now for him but exile till death. He died seven years after at Rouen, in December 1674. The base ingratitude of Charles and the injustice of Claren-

don's contemporaries have been the gain of posterity;
for the fallen statesman beguiled the weariness of his
exile by the composition of those memoirs of the great
transactions in which he had borne so laborious a part,
which, with all their inaccuracies, natural enough in
one writing at a distance from his books and papers,
and with all their partisanship, from which no contemporary writer can escape, and even with their
vanities and weaknesses, easy to be forgiven in one
smarting in old age · and in lonely exile under the
world's cruellest injustice, will continue to delight, as
they have long delighted, as a narrative of a most
eventful period of English history, written in a style
fascinating by its freshness, and constantly elevated
by noble sentiments and principles.

It is unnecessary, after the preceding detailed statement, to go through the wearisome labour of exposing
all the fanciful misstatements of Lord Campbell in his
representation that Lord Ashley was prime mover of
Clarendon's disgrace. At the close of the last chapter
I commented on Lord Campbell's singular sneer at
Lord Ashley as being during the seven years which followed the Restoration a mere "Treasury drudge." Lord
Campbell writes, in the same passage : " Strange to say,
it was some years before he began seriously to try to
undermine Clarendon." He adds that Ashley relieved
the dulness of Treasury drudgery by deliberate dissi-
pation. " He considered himself bound regularly to
attend the King at Whitehall, to pay court to Lady
Castlemaine, and to cultivate with unwearied assiduity
his reputation for licentiousness, which he did so suc-

cessfully as even to rival that of his master. But he became tired of routine business and the life of a mere *roué*, and, seeing with satisfaction the King's growing dislike to Clarendon, he took every opportunity of widening the breach between them." All these specific statements are creations of the biographer's fancy ; and he further imagines that Ashley "spirited Lady Castlemaine to seek revenge" on Lord Clarendon because he had forbidden his wife to visit her, and that his zeal was whetted by hope of being made Chancellor. Shaftesbury's supposed dissolute morals and imagined long dream of the Chancellorship were pressed by Lord Campbell into his service to explain by conjecture why Cromwell refused him a daughter in marriage, which he may or may not have done, and why he quarrelled with Cromwell.[1]

There is no authority whatever for Lord Campbell's precise statements about Ashley's court to Lady Castlemaine and dissipated life. It is a remarkable fact, that in Grammont's minute scandalous chronicle of Charles's court from 1662 to 1669, Lord Ashley's name never appears. His letters to his wife, printed in this chapter, show a degree of conjugal affection and happiness certainly inconsistent with that character of extreme licentiousness which malicious, coarse, and shameless libellers have foisted on careless, copying biographers. I believe that a main cause of the reputation of licentiousness, which, once given, has stuck to Shaftesbury, is the good story, which may be true or false, of Charles having one day said to him, "Shaftes-

---

[1] See pp. 104 and 120.

bury, you are the wickedest dog in England."[1] The story is to the credit of Shaftesbury's wit, for he is said to have replied, "Of a subject, Sir, I believe I am." Charles's joking accusation, even if true, proves nothing. In a clever bitter tract, written against Shaftesbury towards the close of his career, when he was the mark of all eyes and the theme of every tongue, it is written that he is " temperate by nature and habit," but "rather chooses to invert nature itself than suffer a disappointment in his designs of revenge ;" and that "he accompanies, and carouses, and contracts intimacy and amity with the lewdest debauchees in all the nation that he thinks will anyways help to forward his private intrigues."[2] This is the casual testimony of an enemy bearing all the appearance of truth.[3]

---

[1] This story is variously told. Lord Campbell tells it more suitably for his purpose, but I do not know on what authority: "Shaftesbury, you are the most profligate man in my dominions." The story is told by Lord Chesterfield with the words, " the greatest rogue in England." (Chesterfield's Works, ii. 334, Lord Mahon's edition.)

[2] " The Character of a Disbanded Courtier," printed in Martyn's Life, ii. 362.

[3] Two letters to Lord Ashley of the period covered by this chapter may be printed here. The first is from Lauderdale about payment of a sum of money granted by the King, written to Ashley as Treasurer of Prizes. The letter is interesting as referring to one of those grants to statesmen and favourites, of which it is believed that Shaftesbury never received one. The journey alluded to was doubtless Lord Ashley's visit to Oxford, when he made Locke's acquaintance.

"WHITEHALL, *May* 30, 1666.

"MY LORD,—I have moved his Majesty this evening concerning payment of my privy seal of 1750*l*., which the King granted for my use a year ago, and which you know is not assigned nor paid. I desired that it might be paid out of the discoveries of prize wool and other goods, which is no part of Mr. Killigrew's discovery. This his Majesty was pleased very readily to grant at first word. I then asked his Majesty if he would allow me to signify so much to your Lordship, and the King commanded me to let your Lordship know so much from him, which I am sure he will tell you when he sees you. I do heartily wish you a good journey and a happy return.   You will please to order Mr. Kingdon to come and speak with

      " Your Lordship's faithfullest servant,

          " LAUDERDAILL."

The other letter is from the Dowager Queen of England, Henrietta Maria, about the payment of her pension, and it is printed *literatim*.

      "COLOMBE *ce* 14 *August,* 1667.

" My Lord Ashley, l'estime que je fais de vře personne me persuade que je reccucre dans les choses qui regardent mes affaires et assignations pour ma pention toutes les facilitations qui depandront de vos offices et ministere ce dont je vous en prie et en mesme temps de vous assurer que je rechercheray de mon coste les occations de vous temoygner mes ressentiments avec les mesme soings et que je suis avec toute sorte de verite

      " Vře bien bonne amie

        " HENRIETTE MARIE R.

" Pour milord Ashley."

APPENDICES.

APPENDICES

TO VOL. I.

APPENDIX I.

Fragment of Autobiography, from birth (1621) to 1639.[1]

WHOEVER considers the number and the power of the adversaries I have met with, and how studiously they have, under the authority of both Church and State, dispersed the most villanous slanders of me, will think it necessary that I in this follow the French fashion, and write my own Memoirs, that it may appear to the world on what ground or motives they came to be my enemies, and with what truth and justice they have prosecuted their quarrel ;[2] and if in this whole narration

---

[1] This fragment is printed from a copy at St. Giles's. With the copy are two pages of the original in Shaftesbury's handwriting, reaching only to the top of p. vi. So far the copy entirely agrees with the original. The rest of the original has not been found. There are possibly a few mistakes in the copy.

[2] The opening passage of this fragment makes it clear that Shaftesbury composed it in his old age. Mr. Martyn states that a work, of which this fragment was only the beginning, was entrusted by Shaftesbury, when he fled to Holland, to the care of Locke, who, after Shaftesbury's death and Algernon Sydney's execution, burnt it from fear of the court (Life, i. 3, 10). He gives no authority for these statements, and I am not aware of any. The story is probably a fable. There is no reference to any part of this story in any Life of Locke, nor in any of his published correspondence, nor in his letters existing at St. Giles's (among which, besides many to the grandson, the author of the "Characteristics," are some written shortly after Shaftesbury's death to his widow and his son), nor in any of the Shaftesbury papers, nor in the Locke papers which I have examined at the Earl of Lovelace's. It is not probable that Shaftesbury had regularly composed the work much beyond where this fragment ends. The only other possible parts of the work in existence are the two short notes for the year 1640, printed in Chapter II., the fragment of a narrative of events in 1659, printed in Chapter VII., and an account of the state

they find me false or partial in any particular, I give up the whole to whatever censure they will make.

My birth was at Wimborn St. Gyles[1] in the county of Dorsett, on the 22d day of July, 1621, early in the morning; my parents on both sides of a noble stock, being of the first rank of gentry in those countries where they lived. My mother's name was Anne, the sole daughter and heir of Sir Anthony Ashley, knight and baronet, lord of the manor and place where I was born: my father, Sir John Cooper, knight and baronet, son of Sir John Cooper, of Rockborn in the county of Hamshyre. I was christened by the name of Anthony Ashley, for, notwithstanding my grandfather had articled with my father and his guardians that he should change his name to Ashley, yet, to make all sure in the eldest, he resolved to add his name, so that it should not be parted with.

Sir Anthony Ashley was of great age, but of strong sense and health; he had been for wisdom, courage, experience, skill in weapon, agility, and strength of body scarce paralleled in his age, of a large mind in all his actions, his person of the lowest. His daughter was of the same stature, a modest and a virtuous woman, of a weaker mould, and not so stirring a mind as her father. Sir John Cooper was very lovely and graceful both in face and person, of a moderate stature, neither too high nor too low, of an easy and an affable nature, fair and just in all affairs.

Sir Anthony Ashley, although near fourscore, had married a young lady that was under twenty years of age, near of kin to the then great favourite, the Duke of Buckingham, from

of affairs on the opening of the parliament in March 1679, which appears in the second volume. But these were all possibly separate snatches of composition. The following short paper of "Queries," relating to this fragment, is among the papers at St. Giles's in Shaftesbury's handwriting; there is no trace of other similar notes or queries. "Queries:—1. Dr. Olivian was of the Palatinate or Bohemia. 2. The time of my grandfather's death; 3. of my mother's; 4. of my father's; 5. of Sir Francis Ashley's; 6. of Sir Daniel Norton's; 7. of my going to Oxford; 8. When Dr. Reynolds and Mr. Carvill were preachers at Lincoln's Inn. 9. The time of tucking freshmen."

[1] I generally follow the manuscript for the spelling of names. The same names are sometimes differently spelt in the same manuscript. For ordinary words I have thought it would be more agreeable to the reader that I should adopt modern spelling, but I have here and there retained or mentioned an old form which seemed worthy of note.

whom he expected great preferment, and from her children ;[1] but he failed of his expectation in the first, and his age, with virtue of the young lady, could not help him to the latter, so that recollecting himself he resolved, and did accordingly settle all his fortunes in his lifetime, that they should come after his decease to my mother and father for their lives, and after that to me, without his own or their power to alter it, for he grew every day more and more fond of me, being a prating boy and very observant of him.

It ought not to be forgotten that at my birth there was Doctor Olivian, a German, a very learned physician and greatly skilled in nativities, who took the minute of my birth and foretold great things from it, which he told several people then of, and me very often since, for he lived till I was past twenty and was always particularly kind and conversant with me.

I continued at Wimborn St. Gyles until my grandfather's death, which was in 1627, January 13th,[2] and so likewise until my mother's sickness, who falling ill of the small-pox, whereof she died in July, 1628, myself, one brother, and one sister, which were all the children my parents had, were removed for some months for fear of the infection to Rockborn and Whichbury ;[3] the disease following us causing our change of places. From thence afterwards we returned to Wimborn St. Gyles, and continued there until my father married a second time the widow of Sir Charles Moryson and daughter and co-heir of the Lord Viscount Camden, a lady beautiful and of great fortune, a discreet woman of a large soul, who, if she had not given some jealousy to both her husbands and confirmed it after by marrying the person, mought[4] have been numbered amongst the excellent.[5] This marriage caused our remove to Cashiobury, in Hertfordshyre, the jointure house of this lady by her first husband, living

---

[1] The name of this lady was Philippa Sheldon.

[2] January 13, 1628, according to the present mode of counting the year. It was then reckoned to begin on March 25.

[3] Rockborne is a parish in the hundred of Fordingbridge in Hampshire, close to the borders of Wiltshire and Dorsetshire. Whichbury, where Sir J. Cooper also had a house, is in Wiltshire, close to Rockborne; and Wimborne St. Giles in Dorsetshire is a few miles distant from Rockborne and Whichbury.

[4] The form mought is always used by Shaftesbury for might.

[5] Her third husband was Sir Richard Alford, knight.

there and at Wimborn St. Gyles by turns, as their business or their fancy required until March 1630,[1] when my father died at Cashiobury, where all his family then was.

From a little before my grandfather's death to this time, I had been under the instruction of one Mr. Guerden[2] as my tutor, who has since taken the degree of a doctor of physic, and has been of great practice in the city of London. Old Sir Anthony chose him for his being a noted Puritan, saying youth could not have too deep a dye of religion, business and conversation in the world would wear it to a just moderation. This man was moderately learned, a great lover of money, had neither piety proportionable to the great profession he made nor judgment and parts to support the good opinion he had of himself; but he served well enough for what he was designed for, being formal and not vicious. Upon the death of my father, the Easter term following, I made my first journey to London. I lodged at Sir Daniel Norton's lodging in Three Cranes Court, in Fleet Street, he being one of my guardians by my father's will, and after the term went down with him to Southwick, his house near Portsmouth in Hamshyre. Here Mr. Guerden left me and went not down; but I was then taught by Mr. Fletcher, who was tutor in the house to four sons of Sir Daniel's, a very excellent teacher of grammar.

My father's debts, which were very great, contracted by his loss at play—his only fault, and a very fatal one to our family[3]—had raised so many suits, and given the then Court of Wards and some near relations and neighbours hopes to

[1] Sir J. Cooper died March 23, 1631.

[2] There is a blank in the manuscript for this name. I supply it from the next autobiography.

[3] He was also generally extravagant. In a letter from Lady Elizabeth Harris (November 1734) to the Countess of Shaftesbury, wife of the fourth Earl, preserved among Lord Shaftesbury's papers, occurs this passage: "Why, when mention is made of Sir John Cooper's great debts from play, should not his very great hospitality, which was conspicuous (some old servants of the family have oft times told me he had no less than three houses, viz. St. Giles's, Rockborne, and, if my memory fails me not, Lediard, all furnished with servants, &c., and kept open house whenever he was at any of them), be remarked?" Lady Elizabeth Harris was a granddaughter of Shaftesbury, sister of the third Earl, the author of the "Characteristics;" she was mother of James Harris, the author of "Hermes." She took great interest in the biography of her grandfather, which the fourth Earl had engaged Mr. Martyn to prepare, endeavoured to procure materials, and wrote suggestions to the Countess.

advantage themselves in the confusion and disorder of so great an estate, insomuch that my grandfather's own brother, Sir Francis Ashley, the King's serjeant-at-law, one of more elocution, learning, and abilities than gratitude or piety to his elder brother's family; old Mr. Tregonwell, a near neighbour but no good Samaritan, one that never knew generosity or kindness but for himself, his horse, or his dog; Sir William Button, a miserable wretch; the Earl of Danby,[1] and others, on pretence of being creditors or sureties, but in truth having an eye on several parts of the estate which, if sold in haste, must become good pennyworths; these having by the help of Sir Francis Ashley found the way to engage to their party Sir Walter Pye, Attorney of the Court of Wards, a corrupt man who then swayed that Court, the Master, Sir Robert Naunton, being not the activest man, they quickly took the estate by order of the Court out of my father's trustees' hands and appointed these very men (except the Earl of Danby) and their friends commissioners to sell the land, who speedily despatched the matter, selling the most part to one another at their own rates : Rockborn, my father's seat, to Mr. Tregonwell; Damerham, Martin, and Lodyrs, the two first very near me, goodly manors, to Sir Francis, my uncle. This occasioned Sir Daniel Norton to go constantly to London every term, and he very often took me with him as thinking my presence, though very young, might work some compassion on the Court or those that should have been my friends. My father had appointed three trustees for me and my estate, Sir Daniel Norton, Mr. Edward Tooker that had married my father's sister, and Mr. Hannam, of Wimborn, a near kinsman; but Mr. Hannam, finding trouble, gave up the trust, not having kindness for our family to undergo either hazard or trouble for us. Sir Daniel and my uncle, Mr. Tooker, undertook it, and refused to convey the lands to such purchasers as the Court of Wards sold the land to by those commissioners of

---

[1] Henry Danvers, Earl of Danby, son of Sir John Danvers who had married, in the reign of Elizabeth, one of the daughters and co-heiresses of the last Lord Latimer; he was created by James I. Baron Danvers, and by Charles I. Earl of Danby. He died unmarried, 20th January, 1644. He was a soldier, and was the founder of the medical garden at Oxford. (Banks's Extinct and Dormant Peerages, iii. 225.) The title of Earl of Danby, which became extinct on his death, was revived in 1674 in the person of the famous Lord Treasurer Osborne, afterwards Duke of Leeds, whose mother was another co-heiress of Lord Latimer.

their own appointing, excluding them my father had only
trusted, and desired time to sell the land at better rates; and
in particular that I might be allowed to be a purchaser of
Rockborn, Pawlett, and the manors of Damerham, Martin,
and Lodyrs; I having an estate of my own from Sir Anthony
Ashley, my mother's father, for which I was not in ward.
This was pressed in open court, I being then present; the
Court refused, unless the purchasers, who were also present,
would consent. The argument for Pawlett[1] was that it was
ancient land of my family; for Rockborn that it was the seat
of the Coopers, near my other house, as also was Damerham
and Martin, and that they were all too good bargains to be
sold from the family. Mr. Blanchflower, a gentleman that
was esteemed very near and knew how to make the best of
his money, yet thought this so reasonable that he readily
consented, and declared that he aimed at no other advantage
but his debt and interest to be forthwith paid.[2] My uncle,
Sir Francis Ashley, who had bought Damerham, Martin, and
Lodyrs, and my neighbour, Mr. Tregonwell, who had contracted for Rockborn, positively refused, though very much
urged, to part with their bargains. Whereupon my trustees
were required by the Court to convey the estates to them,
which they refusing, the Court committed them to the Fleet,
and they were forced to convey before released.

Thus was my estate torn and rent from me before my face
by the injustice and oppression of that Court, near relations
and neighbours who, I may truly say, have been twenty
thousand pound damage to me; yet Mr. Tregonwell had not
good success in his hard dealing, for he was so greedy of a
good bargain that he looked not into his title, and this manor
proved entailed on my father's marriage with my mother, my
father having left this out of the fine he passed on all his
other lands when he conveyed them for the discharge of his
debts, not intending to sell the place of his father's bones,
especially when his other land would more than serve to pay
all. This blot was soon hit when I came to manage my own
matters; and Mr. Tregonwell's grandchild and myself came

---

[1] Pawlett or Paulett had been acquired by Shaftesbury's great
grandfather, Richard Cooper, part by purchase from Sir Amias Paulett,
and part by grant from Henry VIII., who took the manor from
Gaunt's Hospital at Bristol. (Collinson's Hist. of Somerset, iii. 100.)

[2] Mr. Blanchflower would be the purchaser of Pawlett.

to an agreement, I suffering him to enjoy his own and his lady's life in the manor, in which I designed to bury all animosity or ill will as well as lawsuits betwixt the families.

My trustees, notwithstanding their forced conveyance, yet preferred a bill against my uncle, they having sold the manors of Damerham and Lodyrs before to one for my use, and my uncle having bought it by a particular that now he endeavoured to avoid; for it consisting all of old rents, my trustees, to make it the easier purchase for me, had granted all the estates untilled to friends in waste to the value of some two thousand pounds, and my uncle, Sir Francis, bought it by the same particular as full stated, yet afterwards endeavoured to overthrow this trust, and to improve his great bargain in yet two thousand pounds more. Sir Francis Ashley, being opposed by my trustees in this design, and finding my separate estate, which came to me from his brother my grandfather and was not liable to wardship, to be the fund by which my trustees were enabled to give him this opposition, he most wickedly designs the total ruin of my fortune, and desires to be heard on behalf of the King to prove that the deed by which I claimed was not valid to preserve that land from wardship, and accordingly a day was set down for hearing the debate of this deed. Mr. Noy was then the King's Attorney, who, being a very intimate friend of my grandfather's, had drawn that settlement; my friends advised that I was in great danger if he would not undertake my cause, and yet, it being against the King, it was neither proper nor probable he would meddle in it for me; but weighing the temper of the man, the kindness he had for my grandfather, and his honour so concerned if a deed of that consequence should fail of his drawing, they advised that I must be my own solicitor, and carry the deed myself alone to him, which, being but thirteen[1] years old, I undertook and performed with that pertness that he told me he would defend my cause though he lost his place. I was at the Court, and he made good his word to the full without taking one penny fees. My Lord Cottington was then Master of the Wards, who, sitting with his hat over his eyes, and having heard Sir Francis make a long and elegant speech for the overthrowing of my deed, said openly, " Sir Francis, you have spoke like a good uncle." Mr. Attorney Noy argued for me, and my uncle rising up to reply

---

[1] A blank in the manuscript for the age.   This trial was in 1634.

(I being then present in court), before he could speak two words, he was taken with a sudden convulsion fit, his mouth drawn to his ear, was carried out of the court, and never spoke more.

I continued under the care of Sir Daniel Norton for several years until his death, which happened in 1635. He was a worthy and an honest gentleman, and had been in his younger days a very valiant, experienced, and fortunate sea-commander ; he had Southwick by my lady, who was heir of the Whites : she was a worthy and a shining woman, an excellent housewife, and mother of many deserving children, and was my godmother. Sir Daniel being dead, and I of that age as now to choose my own guardian, being above fourteen, my Lady Norton was desirous to continue me with her, and the rather because she might reasonably expect I might prove a husband for one of her daughters, there being a great friendship between her youngest daughter Elizabeth and me : and truly, if the condition of my litigious fortune had not necessitated me to other thoughts for support and protection, the sweetness of the disposition of that young lady had made me look no further for a wife. My uncle Tooker and Sir Walter Erle both also pretended to the care of me ; Sir Walter Erle's son, Mr. Thomas Erle, being of the same age with me, and there being the nearest friendship betwixt us was imaginable in our years, which increased as we grew older and never to expire but in both our deaths. But my being so very young was assisted with the troubles I had already undergone in my own affairs, having now for several years been inured to the complaints of miseries from near relations and oppressions from men in power, being forced to learn the world faster than my book, and in that I was no ill proficient : yet I had for my diversion both hounds and hawks of my own. I chose my uncle Tooker, my surviving trustee, for my guardian, he being most versed in my affairs, my nearest relation, and had the reputation of a worthy man, as indeed he proved ; he was a very honest, industrious man, an hospitable, prudent person, much valued and esteemed, dead and alive, by all that knew him. To his house in Salisbury my brother George, my sister Philippa, and myself removed from Southwick, where, and at Madington, a country house of my uncle's eight miles from Salisbury, we continued until, in the year 1637, I went to Oxford to Exeter College, under the immediate tuition of Dr. Prideaux.

During my residing with my uncle and my being at Oxford, my business often called me to London in the terms, where I was entered of Lincoln's Inn. Thus the condition of my affairs gave me better education than any steady, designed course could have done : my business called me early to the thoughts and considerations of a man, my studies enabled me better to master those thoughts and try to understand my learning, and my intermixed pleasures supported me and kept my mind from being dulled with the cares of one or the intentness I had for the other.

I kept both horses and servants in Oxford, and was allowed what expense or recreation I desired, which liberty I never much abused ; but it gave me the opportunity of obliging by entertainments the better sort and supporting divers of the activest of the lower rank with giving them leave to eat when in distress upon my expense, it being no small honour amongst those sort of men, that my name in the buttery book willingly owned twice the expense of any in the University. This expense, my quality, proficiency in learning, and natural affability easily not only obtained the goodwill of the wiser and older sort, but made me the leader even of all the rough young men of that college, famous for the courage and strength of tall, raw-boned Cornish and Devonshire gentlemen, which in great numbers yearly came to that college, and did then maintain in the schools coursing against Christ Church, the largest and most numerous college in the University. This coursing was in older times, I believe, intended for a fair trial of learning and skill in logic, metaphysics, and school divinity, but for some ages that had been the least part of it, the dispute quickly ending in affronts, confusion, and very often blows, when they went most gravely to work. They forbore striking, but making a great noise with their feet, they hissed and shoved with their shoulders, and the stronger in that disorderly order drove the other out before them, and, if the schools were above stairs, with all violence hurrying the contrary party down, the proctors were forced either to give way to their violence or suffer in the throng. Nay, the Vice-Chancellor, though it seldom has begun when he was present, yet being begun, he has sometimes unfortunately been so near as to be called in, and has been overcome in their fury once up in these adventures. I was often one of the disputants, and gave the sign and order for their beginning, but being not strong of body was always guarded from violence by two or three of the sturdiest youths, as their chief and one who always relieved them when in prison and procured their release, and very often was forced to pay the neighbouring farmers, when they of our party that wanted money were taken in the fact, for more geese, turkeys, and poultry than either they had stole or he had lost, it being very fair dealing if he made the scholar when taken pay no more than he had lost since his last reimbursement.

Two things I had also a principal hand in when I was at the college. The one, I caused that ill custom of tucking freshmen to be left off: the other, when the senior fellows designed to alter the beer of the college, which was stronger than other colleges, I hindered their design. This had put all the younger sort into a mutiny; they resorting to me, I advised all those were intended by their friends to get their livelihood by their studies to rest quiet and not appear, and that myself and all the others that were elder brothers or unconcerned in their angers should go in a body and strike our names out of the buttery book, which was accordingly done, and had the effect that the senior fellows, seeing their pupils going that yielded them most profit, presently struck sail and articled with us never to alter the size of our beer, which remains so to this day.

The first was a harder work, it having been a foolish custom of great antiquity that one of the seniors in the evening called the freshmen (which are such as came since that time twelvemonth) to the fire and made them hold out their chin, and they with the nail of their right thumb, left long for that purpose, grate off all the skin from the lip to the chin, and then cause them to drink a beer glass of water and salt. The time approaching when I should be thus used, I considered that it had happened in that year more and lustier young gentlemen had come to the college than had done in several years before, so that the freshmen were a very strong body. Upon this I consulted my two cousin-germans, the Tookers,[1] my aunt's sons, both freshmen, both stout and very strong, and several others, and at last the whole party were cheerfully engaged to stand stoutly to defence of their chins. We all appeared at the fires in the hall, and my Lord of Pembrook's son calling me first, as we knew by custom it would

[1] There is here a blank in the manuscript; the name is supplied by conjecture.

begin with me, I according to agreement gave the signal,
striking him a box on the ear, and immediately the freshmen
fell on, and we easily-cleared the buttery and the hall, but
bachelors and young masters coming in to assist the seniors,
we were compelled to retreat to a ground chamber in the
quadrangle. They pressing at the door, some of the stoutest
and strongest of our freshmen, giant-like boys, opened the
doors, let in as many as they pleased, and shut the door by
main strength against the rest; those let in they fell upon
and had beaten very severely, but that my authority with
them stopped them, some of them being considerable enough
to make terms for us, which they did, for Dr. Prideaux being
called out to suppress the mutiny, the old Doctor, always
favourable to youth offending out of courage, wishing with
the fears of those we had within, gave us articles of pardon
for what had passed, and an utter abolition in that college of
that foolish custom.

Being now grown up towards a man, several marriages
were proposed, and amongst others a half-sister of Mr. Rogers,
daughter of Sir Robert Banister by Mr. Rogers his mother.
Mr. Rogers was of the same county, a near neighbour, of a
noble family and estate, a proper handsome man, and indeed
a very worthy noble gentleman, and one that thought so well
of himself as gave him a value with others. The Earls of
Hertford had married into his family, which filled his sails
with no small vanity. This match Dr. Olivian, my great
friend, earnestly pressed me to, not only as it was every way
suitable and fit for me, but, as he positively affirmed, he saw
by his art there would be feuds and great danger to me if it
was not a match, and, if it were, he could assure me she
would prove a vast fortune, professing he had no concern in
it above mine; and I did truly believe so, but I told him I
could not see a possibility of her being so great a fortune or
having considerable addition to her present portion, since her
father had divers sons, and some married. He replied he
was sure of the thing, but could not tell me how it should be;
and this lady, after marrying my Lord Maynard, by the death
of her brothers and strange unequal humour of her father,
came to be a very great fortune indeed. But my uncle
Tooker, considering the great use I had of powerful friends,
advised me to make address to one of my Lord Keeper
Coventry's daughters; which with his assistance I did, and
was kindly received by my lord and his lady. And notwith-

standing I was very young and unexperienced in love affairs, yet the prudence and affection of the lady I addressed to overlooked that and made a judgment what I was like to be for a man or a husband rather than how good love-speeches I then made; for I did that very ill, was very talkative and good company to her sisters, but my love to her gave me that desire to seem excellent that I could say nothing, insomuch that her mother and they suspected that I was more inclined to one of them, but, that being cleared, all matters went successfully on, and we were married in February 1638.[1] But before our marriage the first part of Dr. Olivian's predictions began to have their effect; for Mr. Rogers, hearing where my address was, did, by the favour of my Lord Cottington, then a suitor to the elder sister, earnestly press to be admitted a servant to my mistress, but neither she nor her friends would admit it, but yet the offer and attempt was so open and avowed that it began a never reconciled feud betwixt us, he having offered me the highest injury, and merely out of malice.

My wife and I lived with my Lord Keeper at Durham House and Canbury,[2] and I very often went to my own house in the country, where, though young, I made it one part of my business to show Mr. Rogers in his stately and ambitious humour, which did easily disoblige those of best quality, and by degrees make others not so fond of him. The eastern part of Dorsetshire had a bowling-green at Hanley,[3] where the gentlemen went constantly once a week, though neither the green nor accommodation was inviting, yet it was well placed for to continue the correspondence of the gentry of those parts. Thither resorted Mr. Hastings of Woodland,

[1] February 1639.

[2] Durham House was in the Strand, overlooking the river. Canbury is Canonbury, in Islington, where there was a mansion at this time rented by the Lord Keeper from the Earl of Northampton. This mansion had been built in 1432 for the Prior of the Canons of St. Bartholomew. It was bought in the sixteenth century by Sir John Spenser, whose daughter and heir married the first Earl of Northampton. There was a tradition that the old house had been built for the Prior for a penny a day; this and the salubrity of Canbury are alluded to in a poem published in 1743 in the "Gentleman's Magazine:"

" Now Canbury's numerous turrets rise to view,
No costly structure, if the tale be true ;
Here city doctors bid the sick repair
Only too oft to die in better air."

[3] Hanley or Handley, near Cranborne and Wimborne St. Giles.

Sir Gerard Nappeir, Mr. Rogers, Sir William Uvedall, Mr. Carent of Woodyats, Mr. Okeden, Mr. Butler, father and son, and Mr. Edward Hooper of Boryds,[1] Mr. Ryves of Raynston, Mr. Holles, Mr. Chafin of Chettle, Mr. Hussey of Edmondsham, Mr. Ernley, Mr. Arney, Sir George Moreton, and myself, with several others. Here I omitted no opportunity, and it was often given, to show Mr. Rogers, where his coach and six horses did not a little contribute to their envy. His garb, his discourse, all spoke him one that thought himself above them, which when observed to them they easily agreed to. My family, alliance, fortune being not prejudiced either by nature or education, gave me the juster grounds to take exceptions; besides my affable, easy temper, now with care improved, rendered the stiffness of his demeanour more visible.

Mr. Hastings, by his quality, being the son, brother, and uncle to the Earls of Huntingdon, and his way of living, had the first place amongst us. He was peradventure an original in our age, or rather the copy of our nobility in ancient days in hunting and not warlike times; he was low, very strong and very active, of a reddish flaxen hair, his clothes always green cloth, and never all worth when new five pounds. His house was perfectly of the old fashion, in the midst of a large park well stocked with deer, and near the house rabbits to serve his kitchen, many fish-ponds, and great store of wood and timber; a bowling-green in it, long but narrow, full of high ridges, it being never levelled since it was ploughed; they used round sand bowls, and it had a banqueting-house like a stand, a large one built in a tree. He kept all manner of sport-hounds that ran buck, fox, hare, otter, and badger, and hawks long and short winged; he had all sorts of nets for fishing; he had a walk in the New Forest and the manor of Christ Church. This last supplied him with red deer, sea and river fish; and indeed all his neighbours' grounds and royalties were free to him, who bestowed all his time in such sports, but what he borrowed to caress his neighbours' wives and daughters, there being not a woman in all his walks of the degree of a yeoman's wife or under, and under the age of forty, but it was extremely her fault if he were not intimately acquainted with her. This made him very popular, always speaking kindly to the husband, brother, or father,

---

[1] Boryds, Boridge, or Boveridge.

who was to boot very welcome to his house whenever he
came. There he found beef pudding and small beer in great
plenty, a house not so neatly kept as to shame him or his
dirty shoes, the great hall strewed with marrow bones, full of
hawks' perches, hounds, spaniels, and terriers, the upper
sides of the hall hung with the fox-skins of this and the last
year's skinning, here and there a polecat intermixed, guns
and keepers' and huntsmen's poles in abundance. The
parlour was a large long room, as properly furnished ; on a
great hearth paved with brick lay some terriers and the
choicest hounds and spaniels ; seldom but two of the great
chairs and litters of young cats in them, which were not to be
disturbed, he having always three or four attending him at
dinner, and a little white round stick of fourteen inches long
lying by his trencher, that he might defend such meat as he
had no mind to part with to them. The windows, which
were very large, served for places to lay his arrows, crossbows,
stonebows, and other such like accoutrements ; the corners
of the room full of the best chose hunting and hawking poles ;
an oyster-table at the lower end, which was of constant use
twice a day all the year round, for he never failed to eat
oysters before dinner and supper through all seasons : the
neighbouring town of Poole supplied him with them. The
upper part of this room had two small tables and a desk, on
the one side of which was a church Bible, on the other the
Book of Martyrs ; on the tables were hawks' hoods, bells,
and such like, two or three old green hats with their crowns
thrust in so as to hold ten or a dozen eggs, which were of a
pheasant kind of poultry he took much care of and fed himself ;
tables, dice, cards, and boxes were not wanting. In the hole of
the desk were store of tobacco-pipes that had been used. On
one side of this end of the room was the door of a closet,
wherein stood the strong beer and the wine, which never
came thence but in single glasses, that being the rule of the
house exactly observed, for he never exceeded in drink or
permitted it. On the other side was a door into an old
chapel not used for devotion ; the pulpit, as the safest place,
was never wanting of a cold chine of beef, pasty of venison,
gammon of bacon, or great apple-pie, with thick crust extremely baked. His table cost him not much, though it was
very good to eat at, his sports supplying all but beef and
mutton, except Friday, when he had the best sea-fish as well
as other fish he could get, and was the day that his neigh-

bours of best quality most visited him. He never wanted a London pudding, and always sung it in with "my part lies therein-a." He drank a glass of wine or two at meals, very often syrup of gilliflower in his sack, and had always a tun glass without feet stood by him holding a pint of small beer, which he often stirred with a great sprig of rosemary. He was well natured, but soon angry, called his servants bastard and cuckoldy knaves, in one of which he often spoke truth to his own knowledge, and sometimes in both, though of the same man. He lived to a hundred, never lost his eyesight, but always writ and read without spectacles, and got to horse without help. Until past fourscore he rode to the death of a stag as well as any.[1]

Sir Gerard Nappeir had one of the best estates in the county, was a deputy-lieutenant, colonel of the western regiment, a good housekeeper, well versed in all his country business and employments, but had not a genius above that, and of a temper inclined to envy, not obliging, and to speak as ill as he could of the absent. Sir George Moreton, of the noble family of Cardinal Moreton, that wise and worthy statesman in Henry the Seventh's days ; he was of the shape and temper of his family, large, strong, stout, generous and plain-hearted, but wanting conduct had much worsted his estate, which from the Cardinal's time had always been one of the very best of the county. Sir William Uvedall was of a good family and fortune, and would have had a considerable regard in his country, had not those things which were good in him been drowned in his excessive covetousness ; he had got together and hid in house many thousand pounds, which were afterwards stolen from him by some that got intelligence

---

[1] This racy sketch of Mr. Hastings has been often separately printed, and is in the "Connoisseur," No. 81, August 14, 1755. It has been hitherto printed with some few inaccuracies and variations. The "my part lies therein-a" has been wrongly printed "my pert eyes," &c. and so written in the copy at St. Giles's. This is part of an old catch,

> "There lies a pudding in the fire,
>   And my part lies therein-a.
> When shall I call in, O !
>   Thy good fellows and mine-a ?"

I owe this piece of information to "Notes and Queries," 2d Series, vol. vii. p. 323. There is a portrait of this Hon. Henry Hastings at St. Giles's, and an engraving from the portrait in Hutchins's Hist. of Dorset, ii. 510.

of it. Mr. Carent was of a good estate, and of a very ancient family, a lean, tall old man, very worthy and honest. Mr. Hooper was a judicious, discreet country gentleman, of a good estate. Mr. Chafin was a personable, well-carriaged man of a good estate, wanted neither understanding nor value for himself, was an enemy to the Puritan party.

These were the men of most consideration and sway that resorted to that meeting; but in that eastern part of the county there were other men of power that came not to the meeting, Sir Walter Earl of Charborow, Mr. Hannam of Wimborn, both worthy and honest gentlemen, lovers of their country, and no admirers of Mr. Rogers his way. Sir Walter had been a Low Country soldier, valued himself upon the sieges and service he had been in ; his garden was cut into redoubts and works representing these places, his house hung with the maps of those sieges and fights had been most famous in those parts. They were both inclined to the Puritan. Sir Francis Fulford, Mr. John Tregonwell of Milton, and Mr. Thomas Tregonwell of Anderson, may be also reckoned among the eastern men, since their seats are much nearer Blandford than Dorchester. Sir Francis Fulford was of a very ancient and noble family in Devonshire, had an estate and lived most in our country. Colonel Bingham was of a very noble and ancient family that had been possessed, and left their names to many towns, in this county and Somerset ; he had now a good estate, and was a very honest, good man, and a Puritan. Mr. John Tregonwell enjoyed his nightcaps, his poached eggs, his chamber pleasures, and thought no further of the world. Mr. Thomas Tregonwell was perfectly his father's son. These two had the old man's estate almost equally divided, so that he that had least, which was the youngest, had near 1,700l. per annum.

The western side afforded several men of quality, the Earl of Bristol at Sherborn and his son the Lord Digby, Sir John Strangwaies of Abotsbury, Sir John Heal of Clifton, Sir Thomas Trenchard of Woolton, Mr. Coker of Maypouder, Mr. Angell Gray,[1] and divers others. The Earl of Bristol was retired from all business, and lived privately to himself; but his son, the Lord Digby, a very handsome young man, of great courage and learning, and of a quick wit, began to show

---

[1] Mr. Anchitell Grey, mentioned by Clarendon as a Dorsetshire royalist. (Hist. of Rebellion, ix. 17.)

himself to the world, and gave great expectations of himself,
he being justly admired by all, and only gave himself disadvantage with a pedantic stiffness and affectation he had
contracted.[1] Sir John Strangwaies was very considerable
both for estate and family, a wise, crafty, experienced man,
but extremely narrow in expenses, a great enemy of the
Puritans ;[2] Sir Thomas Trenchard, of a very noble family
and good estate, a very honest, well-natured, worthy man, a
favourer of the Puritans.[3] Sir John Heal had a very great
estate, was a personable, well-natured, honest gentleman, very
generous, kept a great house; his fault was only that he
loved the cup, and that way of over-caressing his friends.
Mr. Coker, of a very ancient family, and a most worthy, discreet gentleman, very knowing in the justice, government,

[1] Lord Digby, afterwards second Earl of Bristol, was now twenty-
seven. In four years from this time he was Secretary of State to
Charles the First. He succeeded to the title of Earl of Bristol in
1653. He became a Roman Catholic before the Restoration. He was
born in 1612, and died in 1677. Being an avowed Roman Catholic, he
was not admitted to office in Charles II.'s reign ; but he from time to
time exercised great influence over the King; and he was at times out
of favour and in opposition. In the violent debates of the House of
Lords in 1675 Bristol made an attack on Shaftesbury; the House
interfered and ordered Bristol to beg pardon, and resolved that what
he had said had made no impression on them to Shaftesbury's prejudice
(Lords' Journ. Nov. 20, 1675.) Shortly before, his son, Lord Digby,
had made a violent speech against Shaftesbury at a public meeting in
Dorsetshire (August 27, 1675), for which Shaftesbury brought an action
and obtained a thousand pounds damages.

[2] In 1644 Sir A. A. Cooper at the head of a parliamentary force stormed
and destroyed the house of Sir John Strangways, at Abbotsbury
(chap. iii. p. 62). Sir John died in 1666. His heir, Colonel Giles
Straugways, inherited Cavalier politics; he was member for Dorsetshire
in the Long Parliament of Charles the Second's reign, made himself conspicuous in support of the Court and in opposition to the Protestant
dissenters, and was made a member of the Privy Council in 1675.
Roger North in his "Examen" speaks of Strangways with great
admiration as Shaftesbury's great opponent in Dorsetshire, and as
having organized the opposition to Shaftesbury when Chancellor for
his having issued writs for the House of Commons.

[3] The Trenchards had been long seated at Woolton, Wolveton or
Wolverton, near Dorchester. This Sir Thomas was sixth in descent
from the Sir Thomas Trenchard who, in 1506, entertained at Wolverton Philip, king of Castile, driven by a storm into the port of
Weymouth. A grandson of his, Sir John Trenchard, was accused
with Russell and Sydney for the Rye House Plot, but escaped conviction, had afterwards another narrow escape for his life, having
joined Monmouth's rebellion, and ultimately became Secretary of
State under William III.

and affairs of the country, of a good estate. Mr. Gray wanted
neither discretion nor cunning, no friend to the Puritan, and
by consequence not in love with his neighbours of Dorchester,
who were totally devoted that way, being managed by their
parson, Mr. White, one of the wisest and subtlest of that
sort of men.

This was the state of Dorsetshyre at that time. The neighbour county of Somersett was then divided into two warm
factions, Sir John Stowel and my Lord Pawlett leading
the one side, Sir Robert Philips and Mr. John Coventry the
other. Sir John was one of a very ancient family, very great
estate, haughty and obstinate.[1] The Lord Pawlett was a
cunning, crafty old fox.[2] Sir Robert Philips was a very able,
well accomplished man, and Mr. Coventry being eldest son by
the last lady to my Lord Keeper,[3] had married a lady of the
family of Coles,[4] who had a very good fortune in that county.
He had besides the support of his father's greatness all that
nature or education could do for him, and was every way an
extraordinary person, and had continued so, if he had not
drowned much of that and his health in sacrificing to Bacchus.
This country evil began to spread itself into Dorsetshyre.
Mr. Rogers his ambition and his ill-will to me gave me the
alarm to provide against him and to prosecute my design to
make him to be understood by his greatest and most potent

[1] Sir John Stowel or Stawel was a zealous royalist, and a chief
promoter of the Western Counties' Association organized in 1645 for
effecting peace, through the clubmen. (Clarendon's Hist. of Rebellion,
viii. 258.) The part which he took in this Association is exactly
such as is wrongly ascribed to Shaftesbury in Locke's fragment of a
Memoir.

[2] The first Baron Pawlett, Paulett, or Poulett, created a peer by
Charles I., grandson of Sir Amias Pawlett.

[3] Lord Coventry, the Lord Keeper, was twice married; first to
Sarah, daughter of Edward Sebright, esq. of Besford in Worcestershire,
by whom he had a son, Thomas, who succeeded to his title, and a
daughter, Elizabeth, who married Sir John Hare of Stow-Bardolph in
Norfolk; and secondly to Elizabeth, daughter of John Aldersey, Esq.
of Spenstow in Cheshire, by whom he had four sons, John, Francis,
Henry, and William, and four daughters, Anne, married to Sir
William Savile, bart., and mother of the Marquis of Halifax, Mary to
Sir Henry Frederic Thynne, bart., Margaret to Sir A. A. Cooper, and
Dorothy to Sir John Pakington, bart. Sir John Coventry, whose nose
was slit by the courtiers in Charles the Second's reign, was the son of
the Mr. Coventry described by Shaftesbury in the text, the eldest son
of the Lord Keeper's second marriage.

[4] This name is usually spelt Colles: a known Somersetshire name.

neighbours, Sir John Strangwaies, Sir Gerard Nappeir, and Sir John Heal, that all justly thought themselves at least his equals, and were easily brought to apprehend him as one who expected to command us all, and valued himself to the Court as already doing so.

Matters thus standing in the West, my wife continuing at her father's house, my Lord Keeper's eldest son, Mr. Thomas Coventry, an honest fair direct man, carried me with him to see his house in Worcestershyre, where we stayed some time, and I grew in great respect in those parts for a pleasant easy humour, but especially in the town of Tewkesberry by an accident. They having invited their neighbour, my Lord Keeper's son, to a hunting in the chace near them and a dinner at their town after, all the neighbour gentry were called in to grace the matter, who failed not to appear and pay a respect not only to the town, but so powerful a neighbour. At the hunting I was taken with one of my usual fits, which for divers years had hardly missed me one day, which lasted for an hour, betwixt eleven and one, sometimes beginning earlier and sometimes later betwixt those times. It was a violent pain of my left side, that I was often forced to lie down wherever I was; at last it forced a working in my stomach, and I put up some spoonfuls of clear water, and I was well, if I may call that so, when I was never without a dull aching pain of that side. Yet this never abated the cheerfulness of my temper ; but, when in the greatest fits, I hated pitying and loved merry company, and, as they told me, was myself very pleasant when the drops fell from my face for pain ; but then, my servant near me always desired they would not take notice of it, but continue their diversions, which was more acceptable to me; and I had always the women and young people about me at those times, who thought me acceptable to them, and peradventure the more admired me because they saw the visible symptoms of my pain, which caused in all others so contrary an effect. At this hunting the Bailiffs[1] and chief of the town, being no hard riders, were easily led by their civility to keep me company, and being informed of my humour, we were very pleasant together, and they thought themselves obliged with my respect, as liking their company and being free with them.

---

[1] The chief officers of Tewkesbury were two Bailiffs, annually elected by the burgesses, twenty-four in number, from their own body.

On the other hand, I was ready to make them any return of their kindness, which quickly offered itself, for part of our discourse had been of an old knight in the field, a crafty perverse rich man, in power as being of the Queen's Privy Council, a bitter enemy of the town and Puritans as rather inclined the Popish way. This man's character and all his story I had learnt of them. At dinner the Bailiffs sat at the table's end; Sir Harry Spiller and myself, opposite to one another, sat near them, but one betwixt. Sir Harry began the dinner with all the affronts and dislikes he could put on the Bailiffs or their entertainment, which enraged and discountenanced them and the rest of the town that stood behind us; and the more, it being in the face of the best gentlemen of the country, and when they resolved to appear in their best colours. When the first course was near spent, and he continued his rough raillery, I thought it my duty, eating their bread, to defend their cause the best I could, which I did with so good success, not sparing the bitterest retorts I could make him, which his way in the world afforded matter for, that I had a perfect victory over him. This gained the townsmen's hearts, and their wives to boot; I was made free of the town, and the next parliament, though absent, without a penny charge, was chosen Burgess by an unanimous vote.[1]

During this time of my youthful days and pleasant humour I had one accommodation which was very agreeable, a servant that waited on me in my chamber, one Pyne, a younger brother of a good family, every way of my shape and limbs and height, only our faces and the colour and manner of our hair was not alike; mine was then a flaxen inclined to brown, soft, and turning at the ends; his was dark brown, thick, bushy, hard, curled all over. My stockings, shoes, clothes, were all exactly fit for him; my hat, though my head was long and big and his round and little, yet he wore his hair so long and so thick that it served him reasonably well, that being the only part of my clothes that he could not buy and fit me by his own trial. His great felicity was to wear my clothes the next day after I had left them off, so very often appearing in the same suit of clothes I had worn the day before. He had a strong mechanic genius, he quickly learnt

---

[1] For the parliament which met April 13, 1640, the fourth parliament of Charles I., which sat only three weeks, and is called the Short Parliament.

to trim me, and all the art of any tradesman I used, but
especially he was an excellent sempster ; he sewed and cut
out any linen for men or women, equal if not beyond any of
the trade, and he never went without patterns of the newest
fashions ; and, as soon as I alighted at any place, I was hardly
in the parlour before my man had got to the nursery or
laundry, and, though he was never there before, his confidence
gave him entrance, and his science in that art they had most
use of gave him welcome, and his readiness to teach and impart his skill and to put them and their ladies into the newest fashions gave him an intimacy especially with the most
forward and prating wenches, those he expected his best
return from, which was besides the usual traffic and commerce
of kisses (the constant trade betwixt young men and women),
the intelligence of all the intrigues of the family, which he
with all haste conveyed to me, and I managed to the most
mirth and jollity I could.   My skill in palmistry and telling
fortunes, which for my diversion I professed, was much assisted
by this intelligence, and gave me choice of opportunities which
some would have made worse use of than I did.

Thus I have set down my youthful time.   What follows is
a time of business which overtook me early, and the rest of
my life is not without great mixtures of the public concern,
and must be much intermingled with the history of the times,
and therefore it will be necessary to give you a state of them
as they then stood in the beginning of the year 1639.

Our Reformation in England was begun by Henry the
Eighth, a vigorous and haughty prince, who found himself
affronted by the Pope, and, resolving to avenge it, cast off his
power, and made himself head of the Church and was by act
of parliament acknowledged to be so as of ancient right, and
as annexed to his imperial crown and dignity, and that the
names of spirituality and temporality were but terms that did
distinguish his people, which under him made but one body ;
and that the king might by his letters-patent nominate and
present bishops without any other election : that all ecclesiastical laws, canons, and constitutions that are not expressly
founded in God's word, are but human laws, and may be
altered, enacted, or dispensed with as shall seem meet by the
King and his two Houses of Parliament.   The next thing he
attempted was to pull down the abbeys and priories, wherein
he disbanded the greatest and surest strength the Pope had,
they being his creatures and vassals.   Besides, with their

estates he secured the nobility and gentry to him and his design. Edward the Sixth, his son, reformed the doctrine; his first act of Parliament introduces communion in both kinds, his second act enables the king without election to constitute archbishops and bishops. In his third year he establishes by act of parliament a new liturgy in the English tongue, which being drawn up by men of great moderation and prudence, they retain as much of the old service and mass-book as would agree with the true doctrine and the Scriptures, not affecting a departure from what was before without evident and convincing reason, that they might give just scandal to none, but invite all to embrace the truth now in following the footsteps of the Apostles amongst the Jews. The chief of them, being Archbishop Cranmer and other eminent divines, in answer to certain queries the King put to them at Windsor, declare under their hands and seals that bishops and priests were not two things, but both one office in the beginning of Christ's religion; that there needeth no consecration by the Scriptures, for election or appointing thereunto is sufficient; that Christian princes may make or appoint a bishop or a priest, and that the people formerly did elect or appoint them; that the bishops or priests cannot excommunicate where the law forbids, and that such as be no priests may, when the law allows them thereunto.

This glorious Reformation was hardly settled when Queen Mary succeeds her brother, and makes a furious, bloody, and violent return of all things to the Romish Church; only the Church-lands were refused by the nobility and gentry to be restored notwithstanding.[1]

---

[1] This fragment here ends abruptly.

APPENDIX II.

Autobiographical Sketch from birth (1621) *to end of* 1645, *followed by a Diary from January* 1, 1646, *to July* 10, 1650.[1]

SIR ANTHONY ASTLEY[2] COOPER, baronet, was born at St. Giles Wimborne, in the county of Dorsett, A.D. 1621, on the 22d day of July, early in the morn, being the eldest child then living of his father and mother.

He was nursed at Cranborne by one Persee, a tanner's wife.

At six years old he lost his grandfather, Sir Anthony Astley. Presently after this, his father falling sick of the small-pox, he and his brother and sister, George and Philippa, he above four years younger and she just two years younger, were removed to Rockborne, a house of Sir John's in Hantshyre. His father recovering, his mother fell sick of the same disease and died, upon which the children were again removed to Whitsbury,[2] a house of Sir John's in the same county. Within two months after they were again removed to Giles Wimborne, where they continued above a year, when Sir

---

[1] Almost the whole of this Life and Diary is printed from an original manuscript of Shaftesbury, which goes as far as December 29, 1648. The small remainder to July 10, 1650, is printed from a copy at St. Giles's. The reader will see at p. xxxii. that the Autobiographical Sketch which precedes the Diary was written in January 1646.

[2] Spelt Astley always by Shaftesbury in this manuscript. The name of the Norfolk family of Astley is frequently spelt Ashley in books of the time, as in Ludlow and Clarendon. Hence confusion has in one instance arisen between Sir Anthony Ashley Cooper and Sir Jacob Astley. See p. xli. The name Cooper is once spelt Couper in this manuscript, and once Cowper; and I have seen it spelt both ways in other papers. The Earls Cowper descend from an intimate friend of Shaftesbury in later life, but apparently no relative, Sir William Cooper, whose name was always spelt Cooper.

[3] Whitsbury, Whichbury, also often spelt Whitebury.

John marrying the Lady Morrison, widow to Sir Charles, and eldest daughter and co-heir to the Lord Viscount Cambden, they were removed to Cashiobery in Hartfordshyre, where they continued two years; only one summer Sir John and his whole family dwelt at Giles Wimborne.

Sir John Couper, at the two years' end dying of a consumption, left his eldest son to Sir Daniell Norton, a kinsman, and Mr. Tooker, his brother-in-law; so that he was removed to Southwicke in Hampshyre, Sir Daniell's house, where he dwelt five years, only divers times he went with Sir Daniell to London.

Mr. Guerden, a fellow of Queen's College in Cambridge, since doctor of physic in London, was his tutor at Giles Wimborne and Cashiobery. But Mr. Fletcher was his tutor the first four years at Southwicke, and the last year one Mr. ——,[1] of Oriell College in Oxford, a master of arts.

Sir Daniel Norton dying, he removed from thence to his uncle Tooker's house at Sarum, where, and at his said uncle's house at Madenton, he lived one year.

Then, being sixteen years old, he went to Oxford, where he was of Exeter College; Doctor Prideaux, then rector of the College and doctor of the chapel, since Bishop of Worcester, being his tutor, and Mr. Hussey, since minister of Hinton Martin, being his servitor.

He went from Oxford but a little before his marriage, which was on Shrove Monday, being the 25th February, 1638,[2] he being under the age of eighteen, to Margarett, the daughter of Thomas Lord Coventry, keeper of the Great Seal, a woman of excellent beauty, and incomparable in gifts of nature and virtue.

After his marriage, he lived with the Lord Keeper at Durrham House and Canbury, till the Lord Keeper's death, which was in January, 1639,[3] after which my lady kept the house a year at these two places.

In March 1640 he was by a general and free election of the town of Tewkesbury chosen their first burgess for the parliament, in which short parliament he served them faithfully.[4]

---

[1] There is a blank for the name in the manuscript.
[2] February 25, 1639.
[3] January 1640.
[4] By first burgess can only be meant first on the return of two members. This parliament met April 13, and was dissolved on May 5, 1640.

For this happy parliament,[1] which was called the latter
end of the same year, he was chosen a burgess for Downton
in Wiltshyre, in the place of Mr. William Herbert, second
son to the Earl of Pembrooke, who was chosen knight also of
a county in Wales ; Mr. Gorge, eldest son to the Lord Gorge,[2]
was also returned ; but at the Committee for Privileges it
was clearly decided for Sir Anthony, yet no report yet made
of it.

My Lady Coventry leaving off the housekeeping, Lord
Coventry and his brother Sir Anthony kept house together
in Westminster, at Dorchester House.[3]

In 1641 he went to Stow to see his sister, the Lady Hare,[4]
and went through the most part of Norfolk.

1642. He about the end of March removed his lady to
Rufford in Notinghamshyre,[5] and returned to London, and so
into the West, and stayed not there, but returned by Croome,[6]
in Worcestershyre, where the Lord Coventry then was, to
Rufford.

He was with the King at Notingham and Darby, but
only as a spectator, having not as yet adhered against the
Parliament.

Only being named by ordinance a deputy-lieutenant for
Dorsett, he returned from Rufford; the whole family removed
to Thornehill in Yorkshyre, another house of Sir William
Savile's.

From Thornehill, the county being unquiet, Sir Anthony,
his lady, the Lady Savile, and the Lady Packington, her
sisters, removed to Bishop Aukland in Durrham, where they
lived some months ; only for some weeks they were forced

[1] The famous Long Parliament ; and it is important to note this
passage, written by Sir A. A. Cooper in January 1646, after he had
retired from military service, as it shows his continued devotion to
the Parliament.

[2] Lord George, Gorge, or Gorges, of a family anciently established
in Wiltshire and Dorsetshire, and the first and last Baron. See
Banks's Extinct and Dormant Peerages, i. 329, and Hutchins's Hist. of
Dorset, iii. 30. The name is also spelt George ; Sir S. d'Ewes so
spells it.

[3] Dorchester House was in Covent Garden.

[4] Elizabeth, daughter of first Lord Coventry, married to Sir John
Hare, bart., of Stow Bardolph, Norfolk, and Sir A. A. Cooper's
sister-in-law.

[5] The seat of Sir William Savile, his brother-in-law, married to a
daughter of Lord Coventry.

[6] Croome d'Abitot, the seat of Lord Coventry.

to retire to the city of Durrham and to Newcastle. They lived at Mr. Wren his house in Aukland parish. From hence, in the beginning of February, the county being much unquiet, the ladies with Sir Anthony took a journey through Stainmore and Westmoreland, Lancashyre, Chessyre, and North Wales to Shrewsbery ; by the way they went through the towns of Kendall, Lancaster, Preston, Lerpole,[1] Chester, Wrexham.

At Shrewsbery they lived some weeks, and then removed to Upton Crescett, in the same county, Mr. Crescett's house, where the Lady Thynne, their elder sister, was. From thence after some time they removed to Cause Castle, Sir Henry Thynne's house, in the same county.

1643. Sir Anthony left the ladies, and went into Dorsett to his house at St. Giles Wimborne, where he continued generally till, the Lord Marquess Hertford[2] coming into the county, he was employed for the treating with the towns of Dorchester and Weymouth to surrender, the commission being directed to him, Napper, Hele,[3] Ogle, which they effected, and Sir Anthony was by the gentlemen of the county desired to attend the King with their desires and the state of the county.

Sir Anthony was by Marquess Hertford made governor of the towns of Weymouth and Melcombe and the Isle of Portland, and the castles of Sandesfoote and Portland, colonel of a regiment of foot, and captain of a troop of horse.

[1] Liverpool.

[2] William Seymour, Marquis of Hertford, so raised from the rank of Earl in 1640, great-grandson of the Protector Duke of Somerset. Hertford had incurred the anger of James I. by marrying Arabella Stuart of royal blood, and had been committed to the Tower, whence he effected his escape. His wife soon died, and he made a second marriage with a daughter of the Earl of Essex, sister of the first parliamentary General-in-chief. This is the lady mentioned in the later Diary. On the breaking out of the civil war, Hertford was appointed Commander-in-chief of the King's western army, but he was soon superseded by Prince Maurice. Hertford's constancy and services to the royal cause were rewarded immediately after the Restoration by his being created Duke of Somerset with a reversal of the Protector's attainder : but he lived only a few weeks to enjoy his new honours. He died in October 1660. There is no ground for Mr. Martyn's statement that Shaftesbury was a relation of the Marquis of Hertford (Life, i. 138, 141).

[3] Sir Gerard Napper, Nappeir, or Napier, and Sir John Hele or Heal. See Autobiography, p. xvii.

He raised a full regiment of foot and a troop of horse at his own charge. Some months after this, Marquess Hertford's commission was taken away, yet Sir Anthony had a continuation of all his commands under the King's own hand, and he was made high sheriff of the county of Dorsett, and president of the council of war for those parts.

Notwithstanding, he now plainly seeing the King's aim destructive to religion and the state, and though he had an assurance of the barony of Astley Castle,[1] which had formerly belonged to that family, and that but two days before he received a letter from the King's own hand of large promises and thanks for his service, yet in February he delivered up all his commissions to Ashburneham, and privately came away to the Parliament, leaving all his estate in the King's quarters, 500*l.* a year full-stocked, two houses well furnished, to the mercy of the enemy, resolving to cast himself on God and to follow the dictates of a good conscience. Yet he never in the least betrayed the King's service, but while he was with him was always faithful. The first place he came to of the Parliament's quarters was Hurst Castle, where Captain Buchester was governor. From thence he went into the Isle of Wight, to Portsmouth, Chichester, and London, where he dwelt at Dorchester House in Westminster, and his lady came to him about the middle of March, whom he had not seen in a year before.

1644. After Weymouth was taken in[2] by the Lord General Essex, the Committee for Dorsett, going into the country, desired Sir Anthony's company with them, which he did;[3] and presently after they drawing in the forces of their county into a body, consisting of seven regiments of horse and foot, gave him a commission to command as Field Marshal General, with which they besieged Wareham, and having received an addition of a thousand horse and dragoons under

---

[1] In Wiltshire, whence the Ashleys of Wimborne St. Giles came. See Coker's Survey of Dorsetshire, p. 14.

[2] To "take in" a town was the usual phrase of the time for taking a town: it occurs again below in speaking of the taking of Abbotsbury. See note at p. 59 of the "Life."

> "I would say more, but death has taken in the outworks,
> And now assails the fort."
>   DENHAM, *The Sophy*, act v.

[3] Leave was given by the Parliament to Sir A. A. Cooper to go down into Dorsetshire July 10, 1644. (Comm. Journ.)

the command of Lieutenant-General Midleton, they starved
the enemy out of bestall, and had the town delivered upon
articles.

Sir Anthony was employed by the Committee and Council
of War to give the House a narrative of it, which he did at
the House of Commons' bar, and was the same day by an
ordinance of both Houses added to the Committee for
Dorsett.[1]

About the end of September the Committee drew all the
forces in Dorsett a second time into a body, consisting of ten
regiments of horse and foot, and gave Sir Anthony a commission to command them in chief as general of that brigade,
with which he took in Abotsbury by storm, and in it
Colonel James Strangwais; his whole regiment, all the
officers and soldiers, one troop of horse, all prisoners at
mercy. From thence he marched to Sturminster Castle,
where Colonel Radford was governor for the enemy, but he
quitted the garrison before he could get thither, so that he
marched to Shaftesbury, where the enemy were erecting a
new garrison, which he forced them to quit also. After this
he received orders to attempt the relief of Taunton, and a
commission from his Excellency the Earl of Essex to command in chief for that design, which, having received the
addition of some forces under the command of Major-General
Holborn and Commissary-General Vaudniss,[2] was by the
mercy of God happily effected, and in the way the enemy
for fear quitted their garrisons of Shute and Coxum Houses
in Devon.[3] This was in December.

1645. In May he received divers commissions from the
Committee of the West, the chief of which was to command
in chief the forces they designed to beleaguer Corffe Castle,

---

[1] It is not mentioned in the Commons' Journals that Sir A. A.
Cooper attended at the bar to make this statement; but it is recorded
that on the 14th August, 1644, he was added to the Committee for
governing the army in Dorsetshire, and his case as regards sequestra-
tion referred to the Committee at Goldsmiths' Hall. The Committee
reported in a few days, recommending that he should be permitted to
compound by a payment of 500l., and the House immediately adopted
the report. See chapter III. of "Life," pp. 59–61.

[2] Called Vandruske by Clarendon. (Hist. of Rebellion, ix. 9.)

[3] Coxum House, spelt Cokam in Sir A. A. Cooper's letter from
Taunton printed at p. 73 of the "Life," is Colcombe, where there had
been a castle, an old seat of the Courtenays. It now belonged to Sir
John Pole, owner also of the neighbouring house of Shute; they
were both near Colyton in Devonshire.

which forces he was to receive from Colonel Welden, who
then commanded in the West; but when Sir Anthony came
into the country, he found Welden blocked up by Goring,
so that being not supplied with men he was obliged to
return.[1]

In June he went with his lady to Tunbridge, where he
for six weeks drank the waters. In September his lady went
to Oxsted in Surrey, to her aunt Capell's,[2] where her mother
also was, and they both sojourned there.[3] In October he went
down into the country, and sat with the Committee constantly, most commonly as chairman.

In December he was employed by the Committee with
Colonel Bingham to the General, who lay then at Autree in
Devon, to obtain an assistance of force towards the besieging
Corff Castle, which they obtained.[4]

---

[1] Instructions from the Committee of Lords and Commons for the
Associated Western Counties to Cooper for the blockade of Corfe Castle,
dated May 17, 1645, are among the papers at St. Giles's. Mr. Martyn
states, at variance with the facts, that Cooper successfully accomplished the task, and adds : "Corfe soon surrendered, and received a
strong garrison for the Parliament, and for the better preservation of
the place Sir Anthony threw a troop of horse with a body of foot
into Lulworth." (i. 148.) This is all misstatement. Corfe did not
surrender till April 1646 : Sir A. A. Cooper was not there then; it
was surrendered to Colonel Bingham. Mr. Martyn's misstatement is
probably owing to his having misunderstood the passage in Cooper's
memoranda for the governor of Poole, printed at p. 68 of the "Life,"
where he says, "A few foot in Lulworth with a troop of horse will
keep Corfe far better than Wareham." But this means, keep Corfe in
check, Corfe being still besieged.

[2] Lady Capel, a sister of the second Lady Coventry, wife of Sir
Henry Capel, knight, of Hadham, Herts. She had been previously
married to Sir Thomas Hoskins of Oxted.

[3] No mention is made by Cooper of an unsuccessful attempt made at
this time to obtain a report on his election-petition for Downton. An
order was made by the House of Commons, on September 1, 1645, for
Sir Walter Erle to report on the subject; but apparently no report
was made. See chapter III. p. 76 of "Life."

[4] See Bankes's "Story of Corfe Castle," p. 215. Sir Thomas
Fairfax was now General in the place of the Earl of Essex, and was
now at Ottery St. Mary, Autree, or Ottree, as it is variously written in
books of that time, besieging Exeter. (Sprigge's Anglia Rediviva,
p. 151 and seqq. ; Bell's Fairfax Correspondence, i. 257, 263 ;
Clarendon's History of Rebellion, v. 288.) Cooper's mission to
Fairfax on this occasion was probably exclusively civil. He probably
ceased to act as a military commander after the new modelling of the
army which had taken place in this year ; he was not included in the
new model. See p. 75 of "Life."

In the end of this month he returned to Oxsted in Surrey.

This was writ in January 1645.[1] .

1646. *January* 1*st*. I was at Oxsted in Surrey, the Lady Capell's, whither I came out of the West, 26th December.

5*th*. I came to London; lodge at Mr. Tarver's in Holborn.

9*th*. I sealed a new lease to John Bates, of his house in Ely Rents for five years more than the twenty-one he had in his former, so that his term is to 1670; this was granted in regard he had built a considerable part of his house new. His rent is 5*l*. yearly.

I sealed another lease to John Hancock, which makes his old term full twenty-one years in another house of the same liberty; his rent 8*l*. yearly. This was freely granted him because he had been an old faithful servant to our family.

15*th*. I went to Oxsted, where my wife has been this half-year.

22*d*. I came to London to Mr. Tarver's. I entertained[2] Henry Shergall again.

24*th*. I paid Mr. John Collins 100*l*. borrowed of him by a bond dated the 5th day of August, 1645, and had the bond delivered up, which was by me cancelled : and 4*l*. for half a year's interest.

The aforesaid 104*l*. *was paid the day above-said, by me for the use of my master,*

John Round.

31*st*. I went to my aunt Capell's at Oxsted, where my wife has been this half-year.

February 4*th*. I came from Oxsted to London to Mr. Tarver's in Holborne. My cousin Norton came to my house at Holborne the 2nd day.

6*th*. Mr. George Skutt the elder, of Poole, had a bill from me to James Percivall for 5*l*. which he affirmed he lent me formerly, so that I owe him nor his sons nothing.

---

[1] January 1646. In printing the Diary which follows, I for convenience print the years according to the present mode of reckoning.

[2] "Entertained," took into service.

The 5th day I had a nerve and vein cut by Gell and two more, for which I was forced to keep my chamber twelve days.

February 9th. Mr. Skutt had a bill of exchange on James Percival for 100*l.*, which I received.

12th. I had another nerve and vein cut.

18th. I went to Aldenham in Hertfordshyre, to Sir Job Harbye's.

20th. I went to Northampton from Aldenham.

21st. I went to Warwicke to my Lady Rous[1] for my wife's jewels, which I had of her.

24th. I returned to Newport Pagnall.

26th. I returned to Aldenham to Sir Job Harbye's.

I went to see Latimers and Cheynes in Buckinghamshyre, but returned to Aldenham.

March 2nd. I went from Aldenham to Kenton Park in Middlesex, Mr. Carre Rawleigh's house.[2]

---

[1] The wife of Sir Thomas Rous, Bart., of Rous-Lench, Worcester shire, and daughter of Sir John Ferrers of Tamworth Castle, Warwick-shire.

[2] Carew Raleigh, the son of Sir Walter, had married the widow of Sir A. A. Cooper's grandfather, Sir Anthony Ashley. He was a member of the Long Parliament; he began as a Royalist, but afterwards left that party; he was a member of Richard Cromwell's parliament 1658-9, and was appointed Governor of Jersey by Monk. He was a man of no remarkable ability or reputation. He is lampooned with Cooper and Wallop in a Royalist satire on the Rump, printed in a " Collection of Loyal Songs, &c.," 1731, vol. ii. p. 57.

> " Ashley Cooper knew a reason
>   That treachery was in season,
> When at first he turned his coat
> From loyalty to treason.
>
> And gouty Master Wallop
> Now thinks he hath the ballop,
> But though he trotted to the Rump,
> He'll run away a gallop.
>
> There's Carew Raleigh by him,
> All good men do defy him,
> And they that think him not a knave,
> I wish they would but try him."

Carew Raleigh died in 1667, leaving no son. He was buried at West Horsly in Surrey with his father's head in his coffin. See Cayley's Life of Sir Walter Raleigh, ii. 215.

March 5th. I came from Kenton Park to London to Mr. Tarver's.

7th. I went to Oxsted and delivered my wife her jewels.

10th. I came to London to Mrs. Tarver's.

14th. I went to Oxsted to my wife.

17th. I came to London to Mrs. Tarver's.

21st. I came to Oxsted in Surrey.

23rd. I came to London to Mrs. Tarver's.

I and Mr. Matthew Hopkins signed and sealed interchangeably articles concerning my plantation in the Barbadoes, for which he is my agent.

26th. I went to Guildford, being part of my journey into the West to the quarter sessions in Dorsettshyre.

27th. To Winchester.

28th. To Allhollowes Wimborne, Walter Goddard's.

30th. To Salisbury, my uncle Tooker's, and in the way I was at Damerham Parva, at my court-keeping.

31st. I came to Walter Goddard's at Allholland.

April 1st. I was at the Court at Hinton Martin, and viewed Holt forest inclosures. Henry Andrews of St. Giles Wimborne, and William Cutler of Gussage, two boys of fifteen years old, bound themselves to me for seven years for the Barbadoes, to give them 5*l.* a piece at the term's end.

I came to Wimborne to Mr. John Hannam's.

2nd. I went to Rockborne to meet Mr. Carre Rawleigh, and came back to Allholland to Walter Goddard's.

6th. I came to Dorchester to the quarter sessions, lodged at Will. Patye's house.

7th. We began the quarter sessions, which was this time kept at Dorchester, and not at Sherborne, for security. The justices present were Mr. Whitaker who gave the charge, myself, Mr. Erle, Mr. Browne, Mr. Grove, Mr. Chettle, Colonel Sidenham, Mr. Robert Coker, Colonel Butler, Colonel Brodripp, Mr. Hussey, Mr. Floyre, Mr. Savadge.

8th. We ended the sessions. Nine hanged, only three burnt in the hand.

9th, 10th. We sat at the Committee.

11th. We sat in the Shire hall at Dorchester, by the ordinance for punishing pressed soldiers that run away of the 15th of January last; when three were condemned to die, two to run the gantelope, two to be tied neck and heels, one to stand with a rope about his neck. The judges were Sir

A. A. Cooper, Mr. John Browne, Colonel Sidenham, Lieut.-Colonel Coker, Mr. Savage, Mr. Christopher Erle, Colonel Herbert, Lieut.-Colonel Cary, Major George Skutt, Major William Skutt, Major Jerdan, Colonel Butler, Captain Arney, Captain Gulson, Captain Woodward, Captain Gold, Captain Batten, Captain Henry Culliford, Captain William Culliford, Captain Yeardly, Captain Wase, Captain Bachelor of the army; Mr. Loder, Judge-advocate.[1]

April 13*th*. We sat at the Committee.

14*th*. I and Mr. Thomas Erle went and dined with Mr. Churchill at Muston; from thence we went to Grange to Sir Gerard Naper's.

15*th*. I came to Allholland to Walter Goddard's.

21*st*. I went to Wimborne to a petty sessions, with Mr. Erle, Mr. Chettle, Mr. Hannam.

22*nd*. I went to Grange, to Sir Gerard Napper's to meet my brother John.[2]

23*rd*. I came to Blandford, whither the Committee was adjourned from Dorchester, Mr. Sheriff, Mr. Erle, Colonel Butler, Mr. Elias Bond, Mr. Chettle, Mr. Joy. The sequestrators of Blandford were ordered to pay Mr. Chettle 20*l.*, Mr. Bond 10*l.*, which was borrowed of them by the Committee, and for which Colonel Bingham and I gave our bills.

24*th*. We sat at the Committee at Blandford.

25*th*. I sat at the Committee in the morning, but in the afternoon I went to Allholland.

27*th*. I went to Blandford to the Committee, and returned in the evening to Allholland.

28*th*. I went to Tollard to Mr. Plott's, and met Mr. Erle and Mr. Grove.

29*th*. We all went to Salisbury.

30*th*. We all went to Farnham in Surrey.

May 1*st*. I and Mr. John Ryves came to Oxsted in Surrey.

4*th*. I came to London to Mr. Tarver's.

9*th*. I went to Oxsted.

13*th*. I came to London to Master Brough's in the Strand. My Lady Coventry and my wife came with me.

---

[1] The names are sometimes very difficult to read in this manuscript, and I cannot be sure that they are always correctly given.

[2] John Coventry, the eldest son of the Lord Keeper by his second wife.

May 16*th.* I sealed a bond of 1,000*l.* to Noell the scrivener, to pay the bills of exchange of Hopkins from the Barbadoes to the value of 500*l.*

18*th.* I gave my servant, James Percivall, two bonds wherein he owed me 70*l.*; this for his losses in coming in with me to the Parliament.

28*th.* I removed my lodging to my cousin Day's in Axe Yard, Westminster, my wife and her mother being gone out of the town.

30*th.* I went to Oxsted.

This month I borrowed 100*l.* on interest of Mr. Browne, Mr. Collins and myself bound.

I borrowed this month another 100*l.* of Mr. Strong, without bond. But he has bond since.

June 8*th.* I came from Oxsted to London, to my cousin Day's house.

12*th.* I went to Oxsted.

16*th.* I came to London to my cousin Day's house.

20*th.* I went in a coach with Sir John Packington and my brother, John Coventry, to Oxsted.

22*nd.* I came to London with them, and lodged at Mr. Bowes his house near Strand bridge.

25*th.* I went to Oxsted.

July 1*st.* I and my wife came to London to our own house in Holborne.

7*th.* I and my wife went to Oxsted.

9*th.* I dined at Limsfield with Sir Edward Gresham; there dined Sir John Eveling[1] of Godstone and his lady.

10*th.* I went to Somerhill to see my Lady Marquess Hertford, and lay that night at Tunbridge.

11*th.* I returned to Oxsted.

14*th.* I came to London to my house.

16*th.* I returned to Oxsted.

20*th.* In the afternoon I went with my Lady Capell, my cousin Edmund Hoskins and his wife, to Limsfield, to Sir Edward Gresham's, and to Titsey to my Lady Gresham; but we all returned at night.

22*nd.* In the afternoon I and my cousin Charles Hoskins went to Crauherst to Mr. Angell's, but returned at night.

27*th.* My wife miscarried of a boy. She had gone twenty

---

[1] Sir John Evelyn, cousin of John Evelyn of Wotton, whose Diary and other writings are well known.

weeks ; her brother John in jest threw her against a bed-staff, which hurt her so, that it caused this.

July 30*th.* I went to my house in London.

31*st.* I returned to Oxsted.

August 6*th.* I went from Oxsted to Farneham, being my first day's journey westward.

7*th.* I went from Farneham to Salisbury.

8*th.* I went with Mr. Thistlethwait, the High Sheriff, to meet the Judges, Judge Roles[1] and Serjeant Godbolt,[2] who were the two Judges for this circuit.

10*th.* I sat with Judge Godbolt on the Crown side, being the only justice there besides the Judge and clerk of assize in the commission of oyer and terminer. I was sworn this day a justice of the peace for the county of Wilts before Mr. Turner. The justices present this day were Mr. William Eyre the younger, Mr. Edward Tooker, Mr. Bennett, Mr. Joy, Mr. Hussey, Mr. Giles Eyre, Mr. Turner, Mr. Dove, Mr. Barnaby Coles, Mr. Francis Swanton. I am in commission for oyer and terminer this whole circuit.

11*th.* Sir John Danvers[3] came and sat with us. Seven condemned to die, four for horse stealing, two for robbery, one for killing his wife ; he broke her neck with his hands, it was proved that, he touching her body the day after, her nose bled fresh ; four burnt in the hand, one for felony,

---

[1] Judge Rolle, as the name is usually spelt, had been made a Judge of the King's Bench in 1645, and was made Chief Justice of the same court in 1648. He was a zealous Parliamentarian, and was one of the six Judges who accepted a commission from the Commonwealth, after the King's execution. He was one of the two Judges seized in their beds at Salisbury, in the Royalist rising headed by Penruddock in 1655, and had then a narrow escape for his life. He resigned his chief justiceship in 1655, to avoid a conflict with Cromwell. He died July 30th, 1656, at the age of sixty-seven. (Foss's Judges of England, vi. 472, Noble's Cromwells, i. 430.)

[2] Serjeant Godbolt was made a Judge of the Court of Common Pleas, April 30, 1647. He died in 1648. He took no active part in politics. (Foss's Judges, vi. 318.)

[3] Brother of the Earl of Danby, mentioned in the Autobiography, p. vii. Though under obligations to Charles I., he from the first took a zealous part against him, and was ultimately one of those who sat in judgment and signed the warrant of death. Lord Danby, who died without children in 1644, had marked his anger against his brother by leaving his estate to his sister. Sir John Danvers obtained from the Parliament a reversal of this will. He died before the Restoration. (Noble's English Regicides, i. 163.)

three for manslaughter; the same sign followed one of them, of the corpse bleeding.

August 12*th.* I and the Sheriff of Wilts begged the life of one Prichett, one of those seven condemned, because he had been a parliament soldier. I waited on the Judges to Dorchester.

13*th.* I sat with the Judges at assizes. Judge Roles gave the charge. Justices present, myself, Sir Thomas Trenchard, · Mr. Thomas Erle, in the commission of oyer and terminer; Mr. John Trenchard, Colonel Bingham, Colonel Sidenham, Colonel Coker, Colonel Butler, Mr. Chettle, Mr. Hannam, Mr. Hussey, Mr. Gallop, Mr. Savadge, Mr. Brodrip.

14*th.* The assizes continued ; five condemned to die, two women for murdering their children, one of them a married woman ; one for murder, one for robbery, one for horse stealing ; three burnt in the hand, one for manslaughter, two for felony. Chibbett condemned for horse stealing ; we the justices begged his reprieve, he having been a faithful soldier to the state.

15*th.* I waited on the Judges out of Dorchester, swore two of the committee for accounts, being a commissioner nominated for that purpose. I sat at the Committee ; we were a full Committee, Sir Thomas Trenchard, Mr. John Trenchard, Colonel Bingham, Colonel Sidenham, Mr. Chettle, all parliament men, being present. I got the parsonage of Abers for the repair of Harnham bridge, at Salisbury.

17*th.* I went to Wimborne to my cousin Hannam's.

I met my cousin Earle and divers other gentlemen at Brienston bowling green, where we bowled all day, and in the evening Mr. Earle and I went to Tollard, to Mr. Plott's.

18*th.* We went to Cobley Walk to course. I lay at the Falcon in Blandford this night, being going to Grange.

19*th.* I went to Grange and lay there.

20*th.* I came to Allholland to Walter Goddard's.

24*th.* I met at Brienston Bowling Green, and returned to Allholland.

27*th.* I met my cousin John Hannam and Mr. John Tregonwell, jun., at the Vine against Frampton's house, beyond the bridge at Blandford. I there declared to them and Frampton, who was sent to me from his mother, that I would not meddle in my cousin Frampton's trust as a trustee.

August 28*th.* I came to Madenton in Wiltshyre to see my uncle Tooker.

31*st.* I went to Stocketon to Mr. Topp's to dinner, but returned. I there sealed two bonds of 500*l.* each for my brother John Coventry, himself and Sir Gerard Napper bound with me, one bond to Mr. John Foyle, the other to Mr. William Whitaker of Shaftesbury, payable 1st of March next.

September 1*st.* I came to Salisbury to a petty sessions ; myself, Mr. Tooker, Mr. Bennet, Mr. Eyres of White parish, justices present.

2*nd.* I came to Allholland to Walter Goddard's.

3*rd.* I went to Dorchester and sat at the committee, lay at Will. Patye's.

4*th.* I sat at the committee in the morning, and went in the evening to Sir Gerard Napper's to Grange.

5*th.* I met the Eastern committee at Blandford, and came to Allholland to Walter Goddard's at night.

7*th.* I dined at Salisbury, and came to Winchester to bed.

8*th.* I came to Guildford.

9*th.* I came to Oxsted in Surrey.

10*th.* I came to my house in Holborne, where my wife and her mother were.

26*th.* I sealed a bond of 200*l.* for my brother John Coventry, payable the 1st of November, to one Mr. Rice, a woollen draper in Paul's Church Yard. For this and the two former bonds I have counter bonds from my brother.

28*th.* I came to Hartford Bridge.

29*th.* I came to Salisbury, by the way I went to Weyhill fair.

30*th.* I came to Walter Goddard's at Allholland Wimborne.

October 1*st.* I went to Shaftesbury to the council of war for Massey's brigade, and got them removed out of Dorset.[1] I lay at Shafston.

---

[1] Compare Ludlow's Memoirs, i. 181. The Parliament had ordered that this brigade should be disbanded, and it was endeavoured to get as many of the men as possible to enlist to serve against the rebels in Ireland. Ludlow and Alderman Allen, members for Wiltshire, acted in that county to execute the Parliament's orders. Ludlow says, "Though many of that brigade were glad of the opportunity to return home to their several callings, having taken up arms and hazarded their lives purely to save the public, yet divers idle and debauched

October 2nd. Colonel Fitzjames, Colonel Cooke, and I went a hunting in Rushmore Waste; we dined at Tollard, at Mr. Plott's. I came home to Allholland.

5th. I came to Salisbury.

6th. I came to Marleborough to the quarter sessions, where Mr. Hussey, judge,[1] myself and Mr. William Eyre the younger, Edward Tooker, Francis Swanton, George Joy, Mr. Bennet of Norton, Mr. How of Berwick were justices.

7th. We sat at the quarter sessions all the day.

8th. I sat at the quarter sessions part of the morning and went afterwards to Purton.

12th. I came from Purton to Marleborough, lay at the Bear.

13th. I came to Salisbury, lay at my uncle Tooker's.

17th. I came to Allholland Wimborne, to Walter Goddard's.

20th. I came to Salisbury, lay at my uncle's, being in my way to London with my sister Philippa Cowper.

21st. I came from Salisbury to Basingstoke to Mr. Spittle's.

22nd. I came to Stanes to the Vine at the bridge foot.

23rd. I came to my house in London in Holborne, next Hatton house, where my wife was.

This month I lent my dear friend and kinsman, Mr. Thomas Erle, 100*l.* on his note.

November. Mem.: This month the bond I stood bound with my brother John Coventry for 200*l.*, borrowed in September last, to one Mr. Price is paid and cancelled.

Mem.: The bond Mr. Collins stood bound with me for 100*l.*, borrowed in May last, to one Mr. Browne, is paid and cancelled.

Mem. : The note wherein Colonel Bingham and I stand engaged to Mr. Chettle for 20*l.*, which Colonel Bingham had for the service at Corfe, is acknowledged by Mr. Chettle to be satisfied.

persons, especially the foreigners, amongst them, not knowing how to betake themselves to any honest employment, endeavoured to stir up the brigade to a meeting; but not being able to effect that, some of them listed themselves to serve against the rebels in Ireland under Sir William Fenton and others there present to receive them, for which we had instructions from the Parliament; the rest dispersed themselves and returned home."

[1] By judge is meant chairman of the court of sessions.

My coachman, Anthony, was entertained by me the middle of this month.

I was bound with my brother John Coventry for 200*l.* to Mr. Browne. Mr. Collins was bound with us, who had my brother's and my counter bond, and I my brother's.

December. I was by both houses of Parliament made High Sheriff of the county of Wilts.[1]

I was by ordinance of Parliament made one of the Committee for Dorsett and Wilts for Sir Thomas Fairfaxe his army's contribution.

Mr. William Ayres, a bencher of Lincoln's Inn, died, a special friend of mine, and made me one of his executors in trust and gave me 10*l.* in plate.

16*th.* I and my wife and sister removed from my house at London towards Salisbury and came to Egham.

17*th.* We went to Basingstoke.

18*th.* We came to my house at Salisbury. I rented Mr. Hyde his house in the Close next to the Deanery.

1647. *January* 28*th.* I went towards London, lay at Basingstoke.

29*th.* I came to London to my house in Holborne.

February 17*th.* I came from London to Egham.

18*th.* I came to Andover.

19*th.* I came to my house in the Close at Sarum.

This term I had up and cancelled my bond of 1,000*l.* which I entered into to Mr. Noell the 16th of May last, for the payment of such bills of exchange as should be charged from Hopkins in the Barbadoes.

22*nd.* I went to Giles Wymborne to my house, and came back at night.

March 13*th.* The Judges came into Salisbury, Justice Roles and Serjeant Godbolt. They went hence the 17th day. I had sixty men in liveries, and kept an ordinary for all gentlemen at Lawes his,[2] four shillings, and two shillings for blew men. I paid for all. There were sixteen condemned to die, whereof fourteen suffered. George Philips condemned for stealing a horse; I got his reprieve, and

---

[1] Leave was given him to reside out of Wiltshire during his shrievalty. (See Commons' Journals, Dec. 1, 1646; Jan. 6, 1647.) In some biographies Sir A. A. Cooper is said to have been sheriff of Norfolk in 1646; but this is a confusion with Sir Jacob Astley, who was the King's sheriff of Norfolk in that year.

[2] So in the manuscript; Lawes's.

another for the like offence was reprieved by the judge.
There were more burnt in the hand than condemned.

March 29*th.* My wife miscarried of a child she was eleven
weeks gone with.

This month I raised the country twice, and beat out the
soldiers designed for Ireland, who quartered on the county
without order, and committed many robberies.

April 5*th.* I went to Glastonbury in Somerset, in my way
to Pawlett.

6*th.* I came to Pawlett.

7*th and* 8*th.* I kept my court there.

9*th.* I came to More Critchell in Dorset, to Sir Gerard
Napper's.

10*th.* I came home to Salisbury.

22*nd.* I went with Colonel Kern to More Critchell, Sir
G. Napper's.

23*rd.* I returned to Sarum.

24*th.* I was bound in three bonds for my brother, John
Coventry : 1st. to Gyles Eyre of White parish in the county
of Wilts esquire for 150*l.*, we two only ; 2nd, to Dorothy
and Anne Aubery, daughters of William Aubery of Meer in
Wilts esquire, for 390*l.*, we two alone ; 3rd, to Henry
Whitaker of Shafston in Dorset esquire for 500*l.*, we two
and Sir Gerard Napper. For all these I have his counter
bond.

30*th.* I and my wife and sister went to Gyles Wymborne,
and lay at Walter Goddard's at Allholland Wimborne.

May 1*st.* We dined at More Critchell at Sir Gerard
Napper's.

2*nd.* We returned to Sarum.

4*th.* I lay at Hartford bridge on my way to London.

5*th.* I came to London to my house in Holborne.

This Easter term I acknowledged a judgment to Mr. Boes [1]
for 360*l.* which I borrowed of him.

I likewise borrowed this term of my cousin Day 250*l.*,
for which myself, my brother George, and my brother John
Coventry stood bound.

June 1*st.* Myself, Sir Gerard Napper, Mr. John Churchill
of Glanvills Wooton in the county of Dorsett, were bound
with my brother John Coventry in two bonds of 250*l.* each,
the one to the Lady Sarah Kempe, the other to Mr. Roger

---

[1] Elsewhere spelt Bowes, p. xlvi.

Draper, both of Islington. Both bonds payable the 4th of December next. I have my brother John Coventry's counter bond for both these.

June 2nd. Myself and Sir Gerard Napper were bound with my brother John Coventry for 600*l.* to Mr. John Warr, jun. of Didlington in the county of Somerset : this bond payable the 3rd of November next. For this I have my brother John Coventry's counter bond.

I came to Bagshott this night.

3rd. I came to my house at Sarum.

14th. My wife, myself, and my sister began our journey to Bath, and came this night to Trubridge.

15th. We came to Bath, where my wife made use of the Cross bath for to strengthen her against miscarriage. We lay at Mrs. Bedford's by that bath.

17th. I came back to my house in Salisbury and dined at Madenton.

18th. We met at Wilton at bowls. I went with my uncle Tooker to Madenton that night.

22nd. I went to Bath to my wife.

28th. I came back to my house in Salisbury and dined at Madenton.

29th. I went to Walter Goddard's at Allholland.

July 1st. I came back to my house at Salisbury.

3rd. I went and dined at Allholland, but came back to Salisbury at night.

This month we had up the bond wherein myself was bound with my brother John Coventry to Mrs. Dorothy and Anne Aubery for 390*l.*, and we gave them two bonds, the one to Mrs. Dorothy for 150*l.*, the other to Mrs. Anne for 240*l.*; for both these I have my brother's counter bond. The first bond was dated April 24th.

16th. I went to my uncle Tooker's to Madenton.

17th. I went to my wife at Bath.

22nd. My wife and sister and myself came from Bath to my house at Salisbury.

Vide de hoc mense in proximo.

August 1st. My wife, sister, and myself went to Allholland in Dorset.

4th. We dined at Woodlands.

5th. We came back to Sarum.

14th. The judges came to Salisbury, Judge Godbolt and

Serjeant Wild.[1] They went hence the 18th day. Four condemned to die, one for a robbery, two for horse-stealing, one for murder. Yorke that was for the robbery, I got his reprieve. The justices present were Sir Edward Hungerford, Mr. Edward Tooker, Mr. John Ashe, Mr. Whitehead, Colonel Ludlow, Mr. William Eyre, Mr. Giles Eyre, Mr. Bennet of Norton, Mr. Joy, Mr. Aubery, Mr. Sadler, Mr. Hippesley, Mr. How of Wishford, Mr. How of Berwick, Mr. Dove, Mr. Stephens, Mr. Coles, Mr. Swanton, Mr. Goddard of Upham.

The last assize Sir John Danvers was present.

I kept my ordinary at the Angel, four shillings for the gentlemen, two for their men, and a cellar.

August 20th. I went to Hinton Martin, and lay at Walter Goddard's at Allholland.

21st. I came back to Salisbury by Damerham.

24th. I went a hunting to Cobley and from there to More Critchell to Sir Gerard Napper's.

25th. I heard Mr. Strong preach, and in the evening returned to Salisbury.

26th. I met the commissioners for the assessment for Sir Thomas Fairfax his army at the Devizes and came to Madenton at night. The commissioners present were myself, Mr. Tooker, Mr. Jenner, Mr. Dove, Mr. Bennett, Mr. Sadler, Mr. Hippesley, Mr. Edward Martin, Mr. Gabriel Martin, Mr. Jesse, Mr. Thomas Bayly, Mr. Brown, Mr. John Stephens, Mr. William Coles, Mr. Thomas Carter, Mr. Nicholas of Simley, Mr. Ditton, Mr. Read, Mr. Crouch.

27th. I came back to Salisbury.

In July last I settled my brother George's estate on him, who was some months since married to one of the co-heirs of Mr. Oldfield of London, sugar baker. I gave my brother freely 4,000l. for his preferment, and an annuity of

---

[1] John Wilde had taken an active part in the early proceedings of the Long Parliament, and had been recommended to the King for the appointment of Chief Baron of the Exchequer in the negotiations of February 1643. He was appointed Chief Baron of the Exchequer by the Parliament in October 1648. After the execution of the King he was a member of the Council of State. When Cromwell became Protector he did not re-appoint Wilde Chief Baron. He was, however, restored to that high office in January 1660, by the restored Rump; but he necessarily lost the office again on the restoration of Charles the Second. He died in 1669. (Foss's Judges of England, vi. 519.)

55*l.* per annum for one life, and cleared it of my sister's portion.[1]

September 2nd. I went to Warminster and sat on the Commission for Sir Thomas Fairfax his army's contribution. There were commissioners myself, Mr. Bennet of Norton, Mr. Carter, Mr. Crouch, Mr. Jesse. I lay there that night.

3rd. I came back to Salisbury.

14th. I went to Madenton to my uncle Tooker's.

15th. My uncle and I went to the Devizes, where we met the commissioners for Sir Thomas Fairfax his army. There were commissioners present, myself, Mr. Tooker, Mr. Alexander Popham, Mr. Bennet, Mr. Crouch, Mr. Carter, Mr. Bayly, Mr. Jesse, Mr. Martin the elder, Mr. Ditton, Mr. Read, Mr. Stokers, Mr. Brown, Mr. Manning. We came back to Madenton to bed.

16th. I came home to Salisbury.

17th. I went to Mrs. Lee her house at Fishwood[2] in Hamshyre.

18th. I came home to Salisbury.

27th. I went to Warmister, and sat in the Commission for raising money for Sir Thomas his army. There were commissioners myself, Mr. Bennet of Norton, Mr. Carter, Mr. Jesse. I lay there that night.

28th. I dined at Mr. Topp's at Stoketon, and came home to Salisbury.

October 2nd. I went to Totnam to Marquis Hertford, and lay there this night and the 3rd.

4th. I went to my own house at Purton to keep my court there.

6th. I went to Malmsbury to return up my money.

7th. I returned to Salisbury.

---

[1] There is very little information to be found about Shaftesbury's brother and sister, and very few traces, in Shaftesbury's later life, of his intercourse with them. The sister, Philippa, married Sir Adam Brown, Bart., of Betchworth Castle in Surrey, and died at a great age in 1701. (Aubrey's Surrey, ii, 307.) The brother, George, lived at Clarendon Park near Salisbury. He is probably the George Cooper who was made one of the commissioners of the Admiralty by the Rump Parliament on its second restoration, in December 1659, to which his elder brother prominently contributed. (Kennet's Chronicle, p. 35.) He is also probably the George Cooper who was member for Poole in the Convention Parliament of 1660. (Willis, Not. Parl. ii. 411.)

[2] So apparently in the manuscript.

October 8*th.* I came to Damerham and kept court there, and went that night to Allholland.

9*th.* I kept court at St. Giles Wimborne.

11*th.* I kept court at Hinton Martin.

12*th.* I returned to Salisbury.

19*th.* I went from Salisbury to Farneham.

20*th.* I came to Oxsted to my Lady Coventry's.

25*th.* I came to my house in Holborne at London.

30*th.* I went to Oxsted.

November 1*st.* I came to Alton in Hamshyre.

2*nd.* I came to Salisbury to my house.

6*th.* The bond wherein I was bound with my brother John Coventry, the one to Mrs. Anne, the other to Mrs. Dorothy Aubery, both dated 15th July 1647, the one for 150*l.*, the other for 240*l.*, were cancelled, and I delivered up my counter bonds.

8*th.* I came to Hartford bridge in my way to London and fell sick there of a looseness, and was forced to stay there till the 12*th.*

12*th.* I came to my house in Holborne at London.

The little ship called the *Rose*, wherein I have a quarter part, which went for Guinea, came to town this term (blessed be God!). She has been out about a year, and we shall but make our money.

27*th.* I went with my brother John Coventry to Oxsted, to see my Lady Coventry, and my sister Packington, who was lately delivered of her daughter Margarett.

29*th.* We returned to London to my house in Holborne.

This term I paid Mr. Bowes his 360*l.*, which I borrowed of him in Easter term last.

This term my cousin Wallop conveyed Ely Rents to me which he had in trust, being bought by me formerly of my father's estate for 1,800*l.*

December 2*nd.* I came from London to Bagshot.

3*rd.* I came to Andover.

4*th.* I came home to my house in Salisbury.

20*th.* I went to Tollard to Mr. Plott's.

21*st.* I went to Blandford and returned to Tollard.

22*nd.* I returned to Salisbury.

26*th.* My wife was delivered at seven o'clock in the evening of a dead maid child : she was within a fortnight of her time.

1648. *January* 11*th.* I went to Blandford to the quarter

sessions, where Mr. Hussey gave the charge. Sir A. A. Cooper, Sir Thomas Trenchard, Mr. Thomas Erle, Mr. John Tregunwell, Mr. Hannam, Colonel Sidenham, Colonel Coker, Colonel Brodrip, Mr. Hugh Windham, Mr. Chettle, Mr. Whitway, Mr. Arnold, Colonel Fitzjames, were justices.

January 14*th*. We sat there in a committee, the High-sheriff, Sir A. A. Cooper, Sir Thomas Trenchard, Mr. Erle, Colonel Fitzjames, Colonel Coker, Mr. Chettle, Colonel Brodrip, Mr. Hussey, Mr. Whitway, Mr. Bury.

15*th*. I returned to my house in Sarum.

21*st*. My brother John Coventry sealed a deed of all his lands to me, Sir Gerard Napper, Thomas Child, and Edmund Hoskins, Esqrs., for the payment of those debts we are engaged for him.

I paid Sir Gerard Napper 500*l*. I owed him on bond, and burned the bond.

I borrowed 500*l*. of Mr. William Hinton; my brother Coventry and uncle Tooker were bound with me; I gave them my counter bonds.

This month I bought of one Jeffery some tenements in Gussage, which cost me sixty and odd pounds.

This month, Mr. Hastings and Mr. Hooper, feofees in trust for my father's estate, conveyed to me the manor of Pawlett, for which I paid formerly to the Court of Wards 2,500*l*.

Mem.: I have purchased, not mentioned in this book, a tenement called Suddon Hill, which cost me 600*l*., and a tenement in Staffordshyre in Ilam, which cost me 200*l*.

February 8*th*. I went to Hinton Martin, lay at Allholland at Goddard's.

9*th*. I returned to Sarum.

11*th*. I had my writ of discharge from being Sheriff of Wiltshyre delivered me by my uncle Tooker, who succeeded me in my office.

14*th*. I fell sick of a tertian ague, whereof I had but five fits, through the mercy of the Lord.

March. I went and waited on the Judges at their lodging; the Judges were Judge Godbold and Serjeant Wilde.

7*th*. I dined with the Judges, but I sat not on the bench all this assize for fear the cold might have made me relapse into an ague.

April 4*th*. Mr. Swanton and I kept a privy sessions at Salisbury. Mr. Gyles Eyres sat with us this day.

5*th*. We continued our privy sessions.

April 6th. I went to Marlborough, in my way to Purton.

7th. I came to Purton.

10th. I returned to Chipenham by Malmesbury.

11th. I came to Sarum.

12th. I kept a court at Damerham Parva, and went to Walter Goddard's to All Saints Wimborne.

13th. I dined at More Critchel at Sir Gerard Napper's.

14th. I dined at Hinton Martin, where I kept a court, and came to Sarum.

17th. I and my wife and sister came from my house in Salisbury to Basingstoke, in our way to London.

18th. We came to Stanes.

19th. We came to London to my house in Holborne.

29th. I fell sick of a tertian ague, whereof I had but two fits, through the mercy of the Lord.

May 15th. My wife and I went to Oxsted in Surry, to see her mother, and stayed there till the

19th, when we returned to our house in Holborne.

June 22nd. I paid Mr. Strong the 100*l.* I borrowed of him on my bond in 1646. The bond was cancelled.

24th. My wife and I went to Stubbers[1] in Essex to my Lady Capell's.

27th. We returned to our house in Holborne.

July. Mem.: The bond wherein I was bound to Mr. Gyles Eyre, with my brother Coventry, is paid and cancelled. This bond was for 150*l.*, dated April 1647.

I was this month made a commissioner of the ordinance of Parliament for the rate for Ireland, for Dorsett.

I was this month by ordinance of Parliament made one of the commissioners for the militia, which they settled in Dorsettshyre by that ordinance.

August 1st. I went to Egham from London, on my journey westward.

2nd. I went to Stockbridge.

3rd. I went to Salisbury, and from thence to Madenton, my uncle Tooker's.

4th. I came to Wimborne St. Giles.

6th. I dined with Sir G. Napper at More Critchell, and heard Mr. Hussey preach.

10th. I went to Dorchester to meet the commissioners of

---

[1] So in manuscript; query Stebbing or Stubbing, where the Capels had property. (Morant's Essex, ii. 413.)

the militia, which was there settled. Present, Sir Thomas Trenchard, Mr. Erle, Mr. Trenchard, Mr. Dennis Bond, Mr. Chettle, Col. Sidenham, Col. Henley, Mr. Brown, Col. Buttler, Mr. Whitway, Col. Coker.

Received of Sir Anthony Ashley Cooper what was borrowed of him at Poole for the great occasions of the garrisons and buildings, two hundred pound, which I paid unto him again by two hundred pound he received of Mr. John Hoyle by my order. Witness my hand the 10th of August 1648.

R. Burie, Treasurer.[1]

This note was made to me the 10th of this month, when I had also delivered up and cancelled the bond Col. Bingham and I entered into for twenty pound for the State.

August 11th. I went with my cousin Erle to his house at Axmouth in Devonshyre.

13th. We went to church in the afternoon to Culliton, and visited Mr. Young there, but returned in the evening.

15th. I came to my house at Wimborne St. Gyles.

23rd. I went to Salisbury to meet Mr. William Hussey, Mr. Norden, Mr. William Eyres; we all met on commission directed to us out of Chancery, to hear and certify the cause betwixt Lowe and Sadler about Fisherton manors. We continued there on the commission till the 26th, and adjourned till the 12th of September.

26th. I returned to my house at St. Giles Wimborne.

29th. I went to Salisbury to the assize.

30th. The Judge, Mr. Serjeant Wilde, who came alone this circuit, came into Salisbury.

31st. We began the assize, where were present Sir John Eveline, Colonel Whitehead, myself, who were all three commissioners of oyer and terminer, Mr. William Hussey, Mr. Yorke, Mr. Stephens, counsellors; Mr. Norden, Mr. Joy, Mr. Bennet of Norton, Mr. William Eyres, Mr. Long, Mr. Coles, Mr. William Littleton, Mr. Dove, Mr. Sadler, Mr. Rivett. My uncle To ker, High-sheriff.

September 2nd. I sealed an assignment of a mortgage belonging to my cousin Ernley, I being a trustee of his wife's jointure, together with my uncle Tooker, Mr. Swanton,

---

[1] This is the original note by Bury, written in the little book which contains the manuscript of this Diary.

and Mr. Topp. My uncle keeps the writings and accounts about it.

I had a verdict against St. Johns for my common in Lydeard, myself the plaintiff, and 80*l.* damage given me. The last summer assize I had another verdict against him and Webb, myself the plaintiff.

September 4*th.* I returned to my house at St. Giles Wimborne.

11*th.* I borrowed of my servant James Berboons one hundred pound, myself and James Percivall bound to him for it.

12*th.* I came to Salisbury. Myself, Mr. Hussey, Mr. William Eyres, Mr. Norden, Mr. Ernley met on the commission betwixt Low and Sadler, and at the desire of both parties adjourned to the 11th day of December.

13*th.* I came to Bagshott.

14*th.* I came to my house in Holborne.

October 4*th.* My wife and I went to Oxsted in Surrey.

Mem.: I borrowed on my own bond of my cousin Charles Hoskins 200*l.*

10*th.* We came to Guildford.

11*th.* We came to Winchester.

12*th.* We came to our house in St. Giles Wimborne in the county of Dorsett.

19*th.* I went to Salisbury to join with my uncle Tooker in putting in our answer to my aunt Sanderson.

21*st.* I came back to St. Giles Wimborne.

26*th.* I went to Sutton on my way to London.

27*th.* I went to Stanes.

28*th.* I came to London and lodged at Mr. Guidett's house in Lincolnes inn fields.

November. This term I borrowed of my aunt Mrs. Alice Coventry 1,100*l.*, for which I gave her my own bond.

December 4*th.* My cousin Harbin, Mr. Chettle, and myself came from London in a hackney coach to Egham.

November 5*th.* We came to Basingstoke.

6*th.* We came to Stockbridge.

7*th.* To Salisbury.

8*th.* I came to my house at St. Giles Wimborne in Dorsetshyre.

December 11*th.* I went to Salisbury on the commission betwixt Lowe and Sadler.

12*th.* There being but three commissioners, Mr. Hussey, Mr. Norden, and myself, we could not proceed, but adjourned by consent of both parties to the 20th of March next, we to meet the 19th at night there. Mr. Kelaway and Mrs. Sadler desired it might be put off till then; Lowe pressed to hear it sooner.

December 21*st.* I went to Wimborne and dined with my cousin Hannam, and came home in the evening.

27*th.* I went to Shaftesbury to sit on the commission for the contribution for the army. There met commissioners Mr. Hussey, Colonel Bingham, and Mr. Bury.

28*th.* We sat on the business.

29*th.* I returned home.

1649. *January* 1*st.* I dined at my cousin Hannam's of Wimborne.

4*th.* I and my wife, my brother, and sister, dined at Sir Gerard Napper's at More Critchell.

9*th.* I went to the quarter sessions at Blandford. The justices present this session were myself, Mr. Chettle, Colonel Butler, Colonel Bingham, Colonel Sidenham, Colonel Brodrip, Mr. Hussey, judge of the sessions, Mr. Savadge, Mr. Whiteway, Mr. Hannam, Mr. Arnold.

10*th.* We sat at sessions.

11*th.* In the morning at sessions, in the afternoon myself, Colonel Bingham, Mr. Chettle, Mr. Whiteway, sat on rates.

January 12*th.* I returned to my house at St. Giles.

29*th.* I began my journey to London, and went to Andover.

30*th.* I went to Bagshott.[1]

31*st.* I came to London, and lodged at Mr. Guidett's in Lincoln's inne fields.

February. I was made by the States a justice of peace of quorum for the counties of Wilts and Dorsett, and of oyer and terminer for the Western circuit.

In Candlemas term I paid 200*l.* to my cousin, Charles Hoskins, which I had borrowed of him.

I mortgaged my manor of Pawlett to my aunt Mrs. Alice Coventry for 1,100*l.* I owed her.

March 3*rd.* I went to Oxsted in Surrey to wait on my wife's mother.

5*th.* I went to Guildford on my way home.

---

[1] The day of the execution of Charles I. The ordinance for the trial had been passed by the House of Commons on January 6th; the trial began on the 20th; on the 27th sentence was passed.

March 6th. I came to Rumsey in Hamshyre.

7th. I came to my house at St. Giles Wimborne in Dorsettshyre.

April 3rd. I went to Marleborough in my way to Purton for my rents.

4th. I came to Purton in North Wiltshire.

6th. I came to the Devizes in my way home, having called at Malmsbury to return my money to London.

7th. I came home to my house in St. Giles Wimborne.

April 10th. I went to Salisbury.

12th. I returned home.

May 2nd. Mr. Plott and I went to Poole to buy sack, and returned at night.

I was made by the States a commissioner in their act of contribution for the counties of Wilts and Dorsett.

June 19th. I went to my cousin Whitehead's at Fillery [1] in Hamshyre, in my way to London.

25th. I came to Hartford bridge.

21st. I came to London to Mr. Guidett's.

July 3rd. I came to Hartford bridge in my way home.

4th. I came to Salisbury.

5th. I came home.

10th. My wife, just as she was sitting down to supper, fell suddenly into an apoplectical convulsion fit. She recovered that fit after some time, and spake and kissed me, and complained only in her head, but fell again in a quarter of an hour, and then never came to speak again, but continued in fits and slumbers until next day. At noon she died; she was with child the fourth time, and within six weeks of her time.

She was a lovely beautiful fair woman, a religious devout Christian, of admirable wit and wisdom, beyond any I ever knew, yet the most sweet, affectionate, and observant wife in the world. Chaste without a suspicion of the most envious to the highest assurance of her husband, of a most noble and bountiful mind, yet very provident in the least things, exceeding all in anything she undertook, housewifery, preserving, works with the needle, cookery, so that her wit and judgment were expressed in all things, free from any pride or forwardness. She was in discourse and counsel far beyond any woman.

---

[1] So apparently in the manuscript.

July 19*th*. I went to Madenton in Wiltshyre, to my uncle Tooker's.

27*th*. I returned home.

August 16*th*. I was sworn a justice of peace for the counties of Wilts and Dorsett by Mr. Swanton. This was the first time I acted since the late King's death.

30*th*. I went to Andover in my way to London, with my uncle Tooker and sister.

31*st*. We came to Bagshott.

September 1*st*. I came to London to my cousin Day's house in Axe Yard, Westminster.

11*th*. I sold my land at Finderne in Derbyshire for 2,700*l*.

September 14*th*. I paid my uncle Tooker 200*l*. he had lent me in Easter term.

15*th*. I paid my cousin Rogers, my aunt Coventry's executor, 1,100*l*., and cancelled my mortgage of Pawlet and bond for performance of covenants ; and I went to Oxsted in Surrey, to my wife's mother.

17*th*. I came to Guildford.

18*th*. To Winchester.

19*th*. To my house at St. Giles Wimborne.

October 2*nd*. I went to Marlborough.

3*rd*. I sat at sessions in the morning, where were present ten justices ; myself, Mr. Swanton, Mr. Littleton, Mr. Joy, Mr. Sadler, Mr. Hippesly, Colonel Ayres of Hurst, Lieut.-Colonel Read, Captain Martin, Mr. Shute. In the afternoon I went to Purton.

4*th*. I went to Malmsbury.

5*th*. I came to Salisbury.

October 6*th*. I came home to my house.

22*nd*. I, my brother, and cousin Day went to Winchester, in our way to London.

23*rd*. We came to Farnham.

24*th*. We came to London. I lodged at my cousin Day's.

27*th*. I went to my brother's house at Bow, and lay ere.

29*th*. I returned to London.

November. This term I paid my Lady Coventry one hundred pound she freely lent me.

1650. *January* 7*th*. From London to Bagshot.

8*th*. From Bagshot to Sutton.

January 9th. To St. Giles.

10*th.* To Dorchester.

11*th.* Dine at Woolton at Sir Thomas Trenchard's, and came home to St. Giles.

17*th.* To Salisbury, to the sessions and oyer and terminer ; present, Mr. Bond, High-sheriff, myself, Colonel William Eyres, Mr. Tooker, Mr. Hussey, Mr. Swanton, Mr. Free of Wishford, Mr. Ayres of White parish, Colonel Thomas Eyre, Colonel Read, Mr. Gabriel Martin, Mr. Coles, Mr. Shute, Mr. Littleton : we all this day subscribed the Engagement.

18*th.* The commission lasted.

19*th.* The sessions ended, and I came home to St. Giles.

22*nd.* I went to my commission at Wimborne betwixt Mr. Banks and I.

23*rd.* Returned.

29*th.* Myself, Captain Dewe, and Mr. Baker sat on a commission from the Council of State to give the Engagement at Blandford. I returned at night.

31*st.* To Winchester, on my way to London.

February 1st. To Bagshot.

2*nd.* To London, my cousin Day's.

7*th.* I received a commission to me and others from the Commissioners of the Great Seal for the giving the Engagement in Dorsetshire. I sent it by the next post to Captain Dewe.

8*th.* I received a second commission as above with the time enlarged, and sent it as above.

February 2nd. I paid Mr. William Hinton 500*l.* I owed him on bond, and cancelled.

This month I borrowed 150*l.* of my cousin Day, on mine and my brother John's bond.

March 5th. I came to Bagshot on my way to my house in Dorset.

6*th.* To Twyford in Hamshyre, to Mr. Wool's, where my aunt ———— ¹ lived.

7*th.* Home to St. Giles's.

11*th.* To Salisbury assize. Judge Nicholas² Chief Justice.

¹ A blank in the manuscript.
² Robert Nicholas was made serjeant October 30, 1648, and a Judge of the Upper Bench (the Commonwealth name for King's Bench), June 1, 1649. He was afterwards moved by Cromwell to the Court of Exchequer. (Foss's Judges, vi. 463.)

March 13*th*. Home to St. Giles's.

14*th*. To Dorchester assize. I was of the oyer and terminer for the circuit.

16*th*. We sat on the commission for militia. In the afternoon I returned home to St. Giles's.

19*th*. I laid the first stone of my house at St. Giles's.[1]

20*th*. I came to Winchester.

21*st*. To Egham.

22*nd*. To London, to my cousin Day's.

29*th*. I removed my lodging from Ax Yard to Bedford Street.

April 15*th*. I was married to Lady Frances Cecil,[2] and removed my lodging to Mr. Blake's, by Exeter House.

July 2*nd*. My wife and I and my sister came from London to Bagshot, on our way westward.

3*rd*. We came to Basingstoke.

4*th*. We came to St. Giles Wimborne.

10*th*. I went to the assizes at Shaston, where were present justices[3]

---

[1] The right wing of the present house was built in 1651. (Hutchins's Hist. of Dorset, iii. 186.)

[2] Daughter of David, third Earl of Exeter, who had died in 1643, and sister of John, fourth Earl. Cooper's connexion with the King's enemies and adherence to the Commonwealth did not prevent his marrying a noble lady of a Royalist house. This second marriage was also of short duration; the lady died some time in 1654. But it was not without issue; two sons were born of this marriage.

[3] Here ends the Diary, as abruptly as the Fragment of the Autobiography written by Shaftesbury late in life ends. Nothing more is known of Shaftesbury till he is named by the Parliament nearly two years after a member of a Commission for the reform of the laws, January 17, 1652; and we learn this only by the Journals of Parliament.

APPENDIX III.

*Suppressed Passages of Edmund Ludlow's Memoirs, referring
to Sir Anthony Ashley Cooper, collected by John Locke,
1653—1660.*[1]

(1) WHEN by the Instrument of Government whereby
Cromwell was set up Protector he had issued out writs for
choosing a parliament, General Ludlow in his manuscript
history has these words[2] (p. 344, 1. 33):—

"And though I was in Ireland and under a cloud, and that
there was the like packing of the cards for the election in
the county of Wilts as in other places, the Cavaliers and the
imposing clergy, the lawyers and court interest, all joining

---

[1] These suppressed passages of Ludlow's Memoirs, all relating to Sir
A. A. Cooper, are in Locke's handwriting among his papers in the
possession of the Earl of Lovelace. There is no explanation in the
manuscript as to how Locke obtained these suppressed passages. I
have made many endeavours to trace the manuscript of Ludlow's
Memoirs, but have entirely failed to obtain any clue. If it is in
existence, it would probably be found that more has been suppressed.
Ludlow's Memoirs were first printed at Vevey in Switzerland, and
published in 1698 and 1699 : Ludlow had died there in 1693. Locke
died in 1704. There is no trace, that I am aware of, of intercourse
between Locke and Ludlow. It is clear that every passage containing
depreciatory mention of Shaftesbury was purposely suppressed, when
Ludlow's Memoirs were published. At that time the memory of
Shaftesbury was dear to Whigs; and Ludlow had possibly himself
lived to wish that these passages should not see the light. It is stated
in Tyers's "Political Conferences" (p. 88) that Ludlow's Memoirs were
prepared for the press by Littlebury, translator of Herodotus, a very
strong Whig.

[2] This short introduction and other similar explanations are by
Locke. The pages and lines referred to are, it is to be presumed, of
the manuscript of Ludlow's Memoirs. This passage is to be inserted
at p. 498 of vol. ii. of the three-volume Vevey edition, 1698-9, and at
p. 211 of the quarto edition of 1771.

against that of the Commonwealth, and having preferred a
list of ten men (the number which was to be chosen by that
county) as those whom they would have to be chosen, they
cite the parishes and every particular person therein to
appear, who when they came upon the hill were headed by
Sir Anthony Ashley Cooper, a man of a healing and reconciling spirit of all interests that agree in the greatening of
himself, being now one 'of Cromwell's Council. The well-
wishers to the public interest, according to the practice of
their antagonists, prepared a list of such as they judged
faithful to the public cause, but the other party not contented with their policy make use of force, threatening those
who oppose them as such who designed disturbance in the
State by promoting the election of such as were dissatisfied
with the present Government; but notwithstanding all they
could say or do, and though the under-sheriff was made
for their turn, the high-sheriff being absent, the Commonwealth party appeared so equal, that it could not be decided
without a poll, and both parties were so numerous that the
usual place for election was too strait, so that they consented
to adjourn the meeting unto Stonnage,[1] where there was
room enough. The great work is to keep me from being
elected who knew not of one person's intention to appear for
me, being at that time in Ireland, neither had I been free to
have sat had I been elected as a member to serve in that
assembly (a parliament I could not own it to be, the Long
Parliament being only interrupted by the sword), knowing
well that they were called together for no good end, and that
if they should beyond expectation do anything for the good
of the people, they should receive an interruption by the
power of the sword, under which they then were. Yet did
Sir Anthony Cooper and Mr. Adoniram Byfield, a busy
clergyman, not contented with their share in that tyrannical
Government, or hoping that it would conduce to that which
was more so, make harangues to the people, labouring to
convince them that it was desirable to choose such as were of
healing spirits, and not such as were for the putting of all
things into confusion and disorder; but the people well
knowing their persons, designs, and interests, and that yet
nothing could prevent tyranny and confusion but the settling
of such a Government as would provide for common good,

---

[1] So in the manuscript; Stonchenge.

and needed not the military sword to uphold it, but would be
supported by the affection of the people, stick close to the
former resolution, and pleased in the first place to cry up me
as one they would entrust in that assembly. The other
party, finding mine greater than any of theirs when divided,
unite in their first vote for Sir Anthony Cooper, whom the
under-sheriff on the view adjudgeth to be first chosen,
though the party that appeared for me conceived themselves much injured therein ; but the other party had all
the power in their hands, and knew they should be pro-
tected by him, who called himself the Protector, do they
what they would."

(2) P. 377, l. 22 is thus :[1]

" Sir Anthony Ashley Cooper, who was first for the King,
then for the Parliament, then in Cromwell's first assembly
for the reformation, and afterwards for Cromwell against that
reformation, now being denied Cromwell's daughter Mary in
marriage, he appears against Cromwell's design in the last
assembly, and is therefore dismissed the Council, Cromwell
being resolved to act there as the chief juggler himself, and
one Colonel Mackworth, a lawyer about Shrewsbury, a
person fit for his purpose, is chosen in his room, &c."[2]

[1] This is to be inserted after the words "departed from that kingdom," vol. ii. p. 53 of the Vevey edition, and p. 224 of quarto edition,
1771.

[2] The "last assembly" spoken of in this passage is Cromwell's first
parliament under the Instrument of Government, which met September 4, 1654, and was dissolved on the 22d of January, 1655.
There are several mistakes in this passage of Ludlow. Cooper had not
been "in Cromwell's first assembly for the reformation and afterwards
for Cromwell against that reformation." In Cromwell's first assembly,
the Barebone's Parliament, he had acted in accord with Cromwell, and
was a leading member of the party of moderate reformers, and, as
Burnet says, "was of great use to Cromwell in withstanding the
enthusiasts." It is not true that Cooper was dismissed from the
Council, or that Mackworth took his place. Cooper continued to
attend the Council until December 28, 1654. Mackworth had been
appointed a member on the previous 7th of February. A dismissal
from the Council could only have taken place, according to the provisions of the Instrument of Government, on a specific charge of misconduct after inquiry by a Committee jointly appointed by the Council
and the Parliament. It does not appear even that Cooper resigned
his seat in the Council, when he ceased to attend in the end of
December 1654. His name is included in a list of members of the
Council, prepared at the end of 1655, printed in Thurloe's State
Papers. (iii. 581.)

Note that this is in the book eleven leaves after that he gives account of the dissolving of this called here the last assembly, in which eleven leaves he writes of Cromwell's proceedings against the Cavaliers, and many other particulars, and immediately after the imprisonment of my Lord Grey and his baseness to Colonel Sexby. This concerning Sir Anthony is written p. 377.

(3) When the Long Parliament was restored by the army in Richard Cromwell's time, and the Parliament had appointed a Council of State which was to consist of thirty-one persons, p. 513, l. 6, it is thus:[1]

"Mr. Love (in consideration that Sir Anthony Ashley Cooper had voted with the Commonwealth party in the last Convention) moved that he might be one, though his affections were well known to be to another interest, and Mr. Nevill having hopes that Sir Horatio Townsend was a friend to the Commonwealth, for the same reason, moved for his addition, which two motions being upon the rising of the House made on a sudden before any could recollect themselves to speak against them, there being also an unwillingness to disoblige those of whom there was any hope, were consented to."[2]

(4) In the following page, line 21 is thus:[3]

"And when the Wallingford House party (which was the Council of officers, Lieutenant-General Fleetwood, &c.), had taken the oath that was directed by the Parliament to be taken by every member of the Council of State before he took his place, the effect whereof was to be true and faithful to the interest of the Commonwealth, and to oppose Charles Stewart or any other single person whatsoever, they came

[1] Vol. ii. p. 656, line 11 from bottom of Vevey edition, and p. 277 of quarto edition of 1771.
[2] There is an interval of more than four years between the periods referred to in this passage of Ludlow and in the last. Richard Cromwell's parliament was dissolved April 22, 1659. The Rump of the Long Parliament was then resuscitated; and this body proceeded to elect a Council of State on May 13. It was resolved that the Council should consist of thirty-one members, twenty-one members of the parliament, and ten who were not members. Seven of the latter were elected on that day, and two of these seven were Sir A. A. Cooper and Sir Horatio Townshend.
[3] At the bottom of page 657 of vol. ii. of Vevey edition, and at page 278 of quarto edition of 1771.

but seldom to discharge their duty, pretending that, by reason of Sir Anthony Ashley Cooper's being of the Council and Sir H. Townsend, they could not with freedom speak their minds there nor carry on the public work, they supposing these persons to be assured to Charles Stewart's interest, and that they would give intelligence to him of all that passed. That we might remove this rub, endeavours were used with them both to manifest their affections to the public, for removing of jealousies between the Parliament and the army, by desiring the House to excuse them from that employment, or at least to forbear coming to the Council. Sir H. Townsend very ingenuously chose to do the latter, pretending occasions of his own which drew him into the country. But Sir Anthony having it in design to be a *boutefeu* between the Parliament and the army, as his after carriage will make appear, makes use of this occasion and comes into the Council with much confidence, and moves with much importunity to have the oath administered to him, professing himself ready to take the same, yet having a secret resolve to break it at the same time (as there was ground to suspect), but the Council not having any power to refuse it him permitted him to take it. And being thus ensnared, as the best remedy to prevent inconveniences, they appoint a Committee of examination and secrecy, whom they entrusted with great powers, to wit, Lieutenant-General Fleetwood, Sir Henry Vane, Major-General Lambert, Major Salloway, Mr. Scott, Serjeant Bradshaw, and myself: yet so hot and confident was Sir Anthony grown, that to pursue his mischievous design, he solicits the Parliament that they would admit him to sit upon an election of seventeen or eighteen years' standing, which never was adjudged, and we could find no better way to put him off (so far had he insinuated into the members) than to refer the consideration thereof to the committee of five formerly appointed by the Parliament for the receiving of satisfaction touching those members who had not sat from 1648, who alleging their powers were at an end, it was referred to them to search their books, and state matter of fact in relation thereto."[1]

---

[1] The case of Sir A. A. Cooper's election for Downton was referred to the Committee named by Ludlow on May 10, the day after the restoration of the Parliament, and three days before Cooper's election to be a member of the Council of State. Cooper was not yet admitted to sit in the House.

(5) P. 571, l. 9 : 1

"The Parliament sent a committee to the Tower to examine Sir George Booth touching the plot wherein he had been engaged, both as to the authority which he pretended to act by, and as to those who were engaged to join with him therein ; he confessed he had received a commission from the King, and that many of the nobility and gentry were engaged with him for the carrying on of the design ; some he discovered, but took time to discover the rest ; and upon examination of a boy which brought, as was supposed, a letter from Sir George Booth before his rising to Sir A. A. Cooper, it was found that he dismissed the boy with much civility, in token of consenting to what was done."

(6) When the Wallingford House party had put a stop to the sitting of the Parliament, and Monk marching from Scotland had declared against, pretending to be for the Parliament and Commonwealth, but underhand carrying on his design of setting up King Charles, p. 621, l. 19, it is thus : 2

"Sir Anthony Ashley Cooper, also a great instrument in this horrid treachery, as he was most active amongst those of the Parliament who were consulting for their restitution, so notwithstanding the affronts he had formerly put upon me, the Lord Arundel being pressed by the trustees and contractors at Drury House for the paying in of thousands of pounds which he was in arrears for some lands which they had sold of his to some of his friends, and which Cromwell had discharged him of, they not allowing that to be a sufficient discharge threaten him to sell the land again according to a command they had received from the Parliament to that purpose, if he forthwith paid not the said arrears. It being apprehended that my letter to them might be of service to him therein, he the same Sir Anthony, coming to me with him to desire me to write on his behalf, professed to be very affectionate to the interest of the Commonwealth, which he did so to the life that I was much pleased therewith, having always believed him to be otherwise inclined. But notwith-

1 Vol. ii. p. 696 of Vevey edition, and p. 294 of quarto edition of 1771. The whole of this passage, except the last sentence referring to Shaftesbury, is printed in Ludlow's Memoirs in somewhat different words.

2 This passage should be inserted probably at p. 765 of vol. ii. of the Vevey edition, and at p. 323 of the quarto edition of 1771.

standing his fair words, I was not so confident of him as to repose any great trust in him, he having played fast and loose so often, declaring sometimes for the King, then for the Parliament, then for Cromwell, afterwards against him, and now for the Commonwealth."

(7) When Monk drew nigh to London, and was always declaring highly for the Parliament and Commonwealth, whereas he modelled his army for another design, p. 690, l. 11, it is thus :[1]

" It was wonderful to consider how with fair words those who used to be watchful to discover what was for their interest were lulled to sleep : Chief Justice St. John himself, who even in this session prepared and procured the Parliament to pass a declaration against Monarchy and for a Commonwealth, and Reynolds who had bought public lands as well as the other, in crushing the friends of the Commonwealth and preferring those of a contrary principle (if of any), acting as if they had designed nothing less than what they pretended to and what their interest led them to ; scarce one of ten of the old officers of the army are continued ; Sir Anthony Ashley Cooper, a known bitter enemy to the public and to all good men, on a disputable election of eighteen years' standing, against all reason and common justice, is admitted to sit as a Member of Parliament because he had joined with some of them in opposing the army at this time, which Charles Stewart himself would have done, might he have been admitted into the confederacy. They bestow also a regiment of horse upon him, which by his policy he modelleth with officers for his turn, and by his smooth tongue and insinuating carriage bears a great sway in Parliament."

(8) When Monk was come to London, p. 705, l. 35,[2] it is thus :

" In the meantime the secluded members held their cabals with the city of London for the carrying on of these designs, and some of those members who sat, especially Sir Anthony Ashley Cooper and Colonel Feilder, had correspondency with them."

[1] Vol. ii. p. 809 of the Vevey edition, and p. 342 of the quarto edition of 1771.

[2] At p. 822 of vol. ii. of the Vevey edition, and p. 347 of the quarto edition of 1771.

APPENDIX IV.

Speech in Richard Cromwell's Parliament, March 28, 1659.[1]

MR. SPEAKER,

This day's debate is but too clear a proof that we Englishmen are right islanders; variable and mutable, like the air
we live in : for, Sir, if that were not our temper, we should
not be now disputing whether, after all those hazards we
have run, that blood we have spilt, that treasure we have
exhausted, we should not now sit down just where we did
begin, and of our own accords submit ourselves to that slavery
which we have not only ventured our estates and lives, but I
wish I could not say, our souls and consciences, to throw off.
What others, Sir, think of this levity, I cannot tell. I mean
those who steer their consciences by occasions, and cannot
lose the honour they never had : but truly, Sir, for my own

---

[1] I have no doubt that this long elaborate speech, which was published by Sir A. A. Cooper at the time, is the one thus referred to in
Burton's Diary on March 28: "Sir Anthony Ashley Cooper made a
long speech till the House was fuller of those of his party, and would
to second the motion that they be but for this parliament, and would
have them bounded in time." (iv. 286.) It was made in support of a
motion for limiting the existence of the "Other House"—Cromwell's
House of Peers—to the time of the Parliament then sitting. The
speech here printed has been published in various works; it is to be
found in the Somers Tracts and Harleian Miscellany, in Morgan's
"Phœnix Britannicus," George Villiers, Duke of Buckingham's Works,
2 vols. 1715, the old Parliamentary History, and Martyn's Life. In
the Somers Tracts it is reprinted from a republication in 1680 with
the following title: "A time-serving Speech spoken once in a season
by a worthy member of Parliament, and now thought fit to be
reprinted, to prevent the occasion of having it respoken." (Vol. vi.
p. 466.)

part, I dare freely declare it to be my opinion, that we are this day making good all the reproaches of our enemies, owning ourselves oppressors, murderers, regicides, subverters of that which we do not only acknowledge to have been a lawful government, but, by recalling it, confess it now to be the best: which, Sir, if it be true, and that we now begin to see aright, I heartily wish our eyes had been sooner open ; and, for three nations' sake, that we had purchased our conviction at a cheaper rate. We might, Sir, in '42 have been what we thus contend to be in '59 ; and our consciences would have had much less to answer for to God, and our reputations to the world.

But, Mr. Speaker, I wish with all my soul I did state the case to you amiss ; and that it were the question, whether we would voluntarily relapse into the disease we were formerly possessed of, and of our own accords take up our old yoke, that we with wearing and custom had made habitual and easy, and which, it may be, was more our wantonness than our pressure that made us throw it off. But this, Sir, is not now the question : that which we deliberate is not whether we will say, we do not care to be free, we like our old masters, and will be content to have our ears bored at the door-post of their House, and to serve them for ever ; but, Sir, as if we were contending for shame as well as servitude, we are carrying our ears to be bored at the doors of another House ; an House, Sir, without a name, and therefore it is but congruous it should consist of members without family ; an House that inverts the order of slavery, and subjects us to our servants ; and yet, in contradiction to Scripture, we do not only not think that subjection intolerable, but we are now pleading for it. In a word, Sir, it is a House of so incongruous and odious a composition and mixture, that certainly the grand architect would never have so framed it, had it not been his design, as well as to show the world the contempt he had of us, as to demonstrate the power he had over us.

Sir, that it may appear I intend not to be so prudent, as far as my part is concerned, as to make a voluntary resignation of my liberty and honour to this excellent part of his Highness's last will and testament, I shall crave leave to declare iu a few particulars my opinion of this other House; wherein I cannot but promise myself to be favourably heard by some, and patiently heard by all : for those Englishmen who are against that House will certainly with content hear the reasons why others are so too ; those courtiers who are for it give me evidence enough to think that in nature there is nothing which they cannot willingly endure.

First, Sir, as to the author and framer of the House of Peers ; let me put you in mind it was he who with reiterated oaths had often sworn to be true and faithful to the government without it ; and not only sworn so himself, but had been the chief instrument both to draw and compel others to swear so too. So, Sir, the foundation of that noble structure was laid in perjury, and was begun with the violation and contempt as well of the laws of God as of the nation. He who called monarchy anti-christian in another, and indeed made it so himself ; he who voted a House of Lords dangerous and unnecessary, and too truly made it so in his partisans ; he who with fraud and force deprived you of your liberty when living, and entailed slavery on you at his death : it is he, Sir, who has left you these worthy overseers of that his last will and testament ; who, however they have behaved themselves in other trusts, we may be confident will faithfully endeavour to discharge themselves in this. In a word, had that other House no other fault but its constitution and author, I should think that original sin enough for its condemnation : for I am of their opinion who think that, for the good of example, all acts and monuments of tyrants are to be expunged and erased ; that, if possible, their memory may be no longer-lived than their carcases ; and the truth is, their good laws are but snares for our liberty. But to impute to that other House no faults but its own, you may please in the first place to consider of the power which his Highness hath left it, according to that "Humble Petition and Advice," which he was pleased to give order the Parliament should present to him. For as the Romans had kings, his Highness had "parliaments amongst his instruments of slavery ;" and I hope it will be no offence for me to pray that his son may not have so too. But, Sir, they have a negative voice, and all other circumstances of that arbitrary power which made the former House intolerable ; only the dignity and quality of the persons are wanting, that our slavery may be accompanied with ignominy and affront. And now, Mr. Speaker, have we not gloriously vindicated the nation's liberty,—have we not worthily employed our blood and treasure to abolish that power which was set over us by law, to have the same imposed upon us without law ? And after all that sound and noise we have made in the world, of

the people's legislative power, and of the supremacy and
omnipotency of their representatives, we now see there is no
more power left them but what is put into the balance, and
equalled by the power of a few retainers of tyranny, who are
so far from being the people's choice, that the most part of
them are only known to the nation by the mischiefs they
have committed in it.

In the next place, Sir, you may please to consider that the
persons invested with that power are all of them nominated
by the Lord Protector (for to say by him and his Council, has
in effect no more distinction than if one should say by Oliver
and Cromwell). By that means, the Protector himself, by
his own and by his peers' negative, may become in effect two
of the three estates ; and by consequence, is possessed of two
parts of the legislative power.   I think this can be a doubt to
no one who will but take the pains to read over the catalogue
of those noble lords ; for certainly no man who reads their
names can possibly fancy for what virtues or good qualities
such a composition should be made choice of, but only the
certainty of their compliance with whatsoever shall be
enjoined them by their creator.   Pardon, Sir, that name, for
it is properly applicable where things are made out of nothing.
If, in the former government, increase of nobility was a
grievance, because the new nobility, having fresh obligations
to the crown, were more easily led into compliance with it ;
and if one of the main reasons for exclusion of bishops out of
the House of Lords was because they were of the King's
making, and were in effect so many certain votes for whatever he had a mind to carry in the House ; how much more
assured will that inconvenience now be, when the Protector,
who wants nothing of the King but (in every sense) the title,
shall only make and nominate a part, but of himself constitute
the whole ?   In a word, Sir, if our liberty was endangered by
the former House, we may give it up for lost in the other
House : and it is in all respects as secure and advantageous
for the liberty of the nation, which we come hither to redeem,
to allow this power to his Highness's officers and chaplains,
as to his other creatures and partisans in this other House.

Now, having considered, Sir, their author, power, and constitution, give me leave to make some few observations,
though but in general, on the persons themselves who are
designed to be our lords and masters ; and let us see what
either the extraordinary quality or qualifications are of these

egregious legislators, which may justify their choice, and prevail with the people to admit them at least into equal
authority with the whole representative body of themselves.
But what I shall speak of their quality, or anything else concerning them, I would be thought to speak with distinction,
and to intend only of the major part; for I acknowledge, Mr.
Speaker, the mixture of the other House to be like the composition of apothecaries, who mix something grateful to the
taste to qualify their bitter drugs, which else, perhaps, would
be immediately spit out and never swallowed.   So, Sir, his
Highness, of deplorable memory to this nation, to countenance
as well the want of quality as honesty in the rest, has nominated some against whom there lies no other reproach but
only that nomination ; but not out of any respect to their
quality or regard to their virtues, but out of regard to the no-
quality, the no-virtues of the rest ; which truly, Mr. Speaker,
if he had not done, we could easily have given a more express
name to this other House than he hath been pleased to do ;
for we know a house designed for beggars and malefactors is
a house of correction, and so termed by our law : but, Mr.
Speaker, setting those few persons aside, who, I hope, think
the nomination a disgrace, and their ever coming to sit there
a much greater, can we without indignation think of the rest ?
He who is first in their roll, a condemned coward ; one that
out of fear and baseness did once what he could to betray our
liberties, and now does the same for gain.[1]   The second, a
person of as little sense as honesty ; preferred for no other
reason but his no-worth, his no-conscience ; except cheating
his father of all he had was thought a virtue by him, who, by
sad experience we find, hath done as much for his mother
—his country.[2]   The third, a Cavalier, a Presbyterian, an
Independent ; for the Republic, for a Protector, for everything, for nothing, but only that one thing—money.[3]   It

[1] Nathaniel Fiennes, second son of Viscount Saye and Sele, who in
the beginning of the Civil War had surrendered Bristol to the King's
army without making any defence, and had been condemned to death
by a court-martial, but pardoned by the Earl of Essex, the general-in-
chief.   He was now one of the Commissioners of the Great Seal, and
one of Richard Cromwell's chief advisers.   His father and a younger
brother John were also named by Cromwell members of his House of
Lords : the father did not sit.

[2] I do not know which of Cromwell's Lords is here referred to.

[3] This is generally supposed to refer to Lord Broghill, after the
Restoration created Earl of Orrery.

were endless, Sir, to run through them all; to tell you of the lordships of seventeen pounds a year land of inheritance; of the farmer lordships, draymen lordships,[1] cobbler lordships,[2] without one foot of land but what the blood of Englishmen has been the price of. These, Sir, are to be our rulers, these the judges of our lives and fortunes; to these we are to stand bare whilst their pageant lordships deign to give us a conference on their breeches. Mr. Speaker, we have already had too much experience how insupportable servants are when they become our masters. All kinds of slavery are miserable in the account of generous minds; but that which comes accompanied with scorn and contempt stirs up every man's indignation, and is endured by none whom nature does not intend for slaves, as well as fortune.

I say not this, Mr. Speaker, to revile any man with his meanness; for I never thought either the malignity or indulgence of fortune to be, with wise or just men, the grounds either of their good or ill opinion. Mr. Speaker, I blame not in these men the faults of their fortune any otherwise than as they make them their own: I object to you their poverty, because it is accompanied with ambition; I remind you of their quality, because they themselves forget it: it is not the men I am angry with, but their Lordships. Sir, though we easily grant poverty and necessity to be no faults, yet we must allow them to be great impediments in the way of honour, and such as nothing but extraordinary merit and virtue can remove. The Scripture reckons it amongst Jeroboam's great faults, "that he made priests of the meanest of the people:" and sure it was none of the virtues of our Jeroboam, who hath set up his calves too, and would have our tribes come up and worship them, that he observed the same method in making lords.

One of the few requests the Portuguese made to Philip the Second, King of Spain, when he got that kingdom, as his late Highness did this, by an army, was, that he would not make nobility contemptible by advancing such to that degree whose quality or virtue could be noways thought to deserve it. Nor have we formerly been less apprehensive of such inconveniences ourselves. It was, in Richard the First's

---

[1] This refers to Colonel Pride, who had been a brewer, and, it is said, had begun as a drayman.
[2] Colonel Hewson had been a shoemaker.

time, one of the Bishop of Ely's accusations, that castles and forts of great trust he did "obscuris et ignotis hominibus tradere"—put in the hands of obscure and unknown men. But we, Mr. Speaker, to such a kind of men are delivering up the power of our laws, and, in that, the power of all.

In the 17th of Edward the Fourth, there passed an Act of Parliament for degrading John Nevil, Marquis Montague and Duke of Bedford : the reason expressed in the Act, because he had not a revenue sufficient for the maintaining of that dignity ; to which was added, when men of mean birth are called to high estate, and no livelihood to support it, it induceth briberies and extortions, and all kinds of injustice that are followed by gain. And in the parliament of 2d of Charles, the peers, in a petition against Scottish and Irish titles, told the King, that it was a novelty without precedent that men should possess honours where they possessed nothing else, and that they should have a vote in parliament where they have not a foot of land. But if it had been added, or have no land but what is the purchase of their villanies, against how many of our new peers would this have been an important objection ! To conclude : it has been a very just and reasonable care among all nations, not to render that despised and contemptible to the people which is designed for their reverence and awe; and, Sir, an empty title, without quality or virtue, never procured any man this, any more than the image in the fable made the ass adored that carried it.

After their quality, give me leave to speak a word or two of their qualifications; which certainly ought, in reason, to carry some proportion with the employment they design themselves. The House of Lords are the King's great hereditary Council ; they are the highest court of judicature; they have their part in judging and determining of the reasons for making new laws and abrogating old : from amongst them we take our great officers of State: they are commonly our generals at land, and our admirals at sea. In conclusion, they are both of the essence and constitution of our old government ; and have, besides, the greatest and noblest share in the administration. Now, certainly, Sir, to judge according to the dictates of reason, one would imagine some small faculties and endowments to be necessary for discharging such a calling ; and those such as are not usually acquired in shops and warehouses, nor found by following the plough : and what other academies most of their lordships have been

bred in but their shops, what other arts they have been
versed in but those which more required good arms and good
shoulders than good heads, I think we are yet to be informed.
Sir, we commit not the education of our children to ignorant
and illiterate masters; nay, we trust not our horses to unskil-
ful grooms. I beseech you, let us think it belongs to us to
have some care into whose hands we commit the management
of the commonwealth; and if we cannot have persons of
birth and fortune to be our rulers, to whose quality we would
willingly submit, I beseech you, Sir, for our credit and
safety's sake, let us seek men at least of parts and education,
to whose abilities we may have some reason to give way. If
a patient dies under a physician's hand, the law esteems that
not a felony, but a misfortune, in the physician: but it has
been held by some, if one who is no physician undertakes the
management of a cure, and the party miscarries, the law
makes the empiric a felon; and sure, in all men's opinion,
the patient a fool. To conclude, Sir, for great men to govern
is ordinary; for able men it is natural: knaves many times
come to it by force and necessity, and fools sometimes by
chance; but universal choice and election of fools and knaves
for government was never yet made by any who were not
themselves like those they chose.

But methinks, Mr. Speaker, I see ready to rise after me
some gentlemen that shall tell you the good services their
new lordships have done the commonwealth; that shall extol
their valour, their godliness, their fidelity to the cause. The
Scripture, too, no doubt, as it is to all purposes, shall be
brought in to argue for them; and we shall hear of "the
wisdom of the poor man that saved the city;" of the "not
many wise, not many mighty;" attributes that I can no way
deny to be due to their lordships. Mr. Speaker, I shall be as
forward as any man to declare their services, and acknowledge
them; though I might tell you that the same honour is not
purchased by the blood of an enemy and of a citizen; that
for victories in civil wars, till our armies marched through
the city, I have not read that the conquerors have been so
void of shame as to triumph. Cæsar, not much more indul-
gent to his country than our late Protector, did not so much
as write public letters of his victory at Pharsalia; much less
had he days of thanksgiving to his gods, and anniversary
feasts, for having been a prosperous rebel.

But, Sir, I leave this argument; and, to be as good as my

word, come to put you in mind of some of their services, and the obligations you owe them for the same. To speak nothing of one of my Lords Commissioners' valour at Bristol, nor of another noble lord's brave adventure at the Bear-garden,[1] I must tell you, Sir, that most of them have had the courage to do things which, I may boldly say, few other Christians durst so have adventured their souls to have attempted : they have not only subdued their enemies, but their masters that raised and maintained them; they have not only conquered Scotland and Ireland, but rebellious England too, and there suppressed a malignant party of magistrates and laws ; and, that nothing should be wanting to make them indeed complete conquerors, without the help of philosophy they have even conquered themselves. All shame they have subdued as perfectly as all justice ; the oaths they have taken they have as easily digested as their old General could himself; public covenants and engagements they have trampled under foot. In conclusion, so entire a victory they have over themselves, that their consciences are as much their servants, Mr. Speaker, as we are. But give me leave to conclude with that which is more admirable than all this, and shows the confidence they have of themselves and us : after having many times trampled on the authority of the House of Commons, and no less than five times dissolved them, they hope, for those good services to the House of Commons, to be made a House of Lords.

I have been over long, Sir, for which I crave your pardon ; therefore, in a word, I beseech you let us think it our duty to have a care of two things : first, that villanies be not encouraged with the rewards of virtue; secondly, that the authority and majesty of the government of this nation be not defiled, and exposed to contempt, by committing so considerable a part of it to persons of as mean quality as parts. The Thebans did not admit merchants into government till they had left their traffic ten years : sure it would have been long before cobblers and draymen would have been allowed.

---

[1] The person here referred to is Colonel Pride, who is accused of having cruelly killed a number of bears, in suppressing bear-baiting, as Sheriff of Surrey. See a lampoon printed in the Harleian Miscellany vol. iii. p. 136: "The Last Speech and Dying Words of Thomas (Lord, alias Colonel) Pride, being touched in conscience for his inhuman murder of the Bears in the Bear-garden when he was High Sheriff of Surrey, taken in shorthand by T. S., late clerk in his Lordship's Brewhouse."

Sir, if the wisdom of this House shall think we have been
hitherto like the prodigal; and that now, when our necessities
persuade us, *i.e.* that we are almost brought to herd it with
swine, it is time to think of a return; let us without more
ado, without this motley mixture, even take our rulers as at
the first, so that we can but be reasonably secured to avoid
our counsellors as at the beginning

Give me leave, Sir, to release your patience with a short
story. Livy tells us there was a state in Italy, an aristocracy,
where the nobility stretched the prerogative too high, and
presumed too much on the people's liberty and patience;
whereupon the discontents were so general and so great,
that they apparently tended to a dissolution of government,
and the turning of all things into anarchy and confusion.
At the same time, besides these distempers at home, there
was a potent enemy ready to fall on them from abroad, that
had been an over-match for them when united; but now, in
these disorders, was like to find them a very ready and easy
prey. A wise man, Sir, in the city, who did not all approve
of the insolence of the nobility, and as little liked popular
tumults, thought of this stratagem, to cozen his country into
safety. Upon a pretence of counsel, he procured the nobility
to meet all together; which when they had done, he found
means to lock the doors upon them, went away himself, and
took the keys; then immediately summoned the people; told
them, by a contrivance of his he had taken all the nobility in
a trap; that now was the time to be revenged on them for
their insolences; that, therefore, they should immediately go
along with him and despatch them. Sir, the officers of our
army, after a fast, could not be more ready for the villany
than these people were; and accordingly they made as much
haste to the slaughter as their Lord Protector could desire.
But, Sir, this wise man I told you of was their Lord Protector
indeed. As soon as he had brought the people where the
parliament was sitting, and when they expected but the word
to fall to the butchery; "Gentlemen," says he, "though I
would not care how soon this work of reformation were over,
yet, in this ship of the commonwealth, we must not throw
the steersmen overboard till we have provided others for the
helm. Let us consider, before we take these men away, in
what other hands we may securely trust our liberty and the
management of the commonwealth." And so he advised
them, before the putting down of the former, to bethink

themselves of constituting another House. He began and nominated one, a man highly cried up in the popular faction, a confiding man, one of much zeal, little sense, and no quality; you may suppose him, Sir, a zealous cobbler. The people, in conclusion, murmured at this, and were loth their fellow mutineer, for no other virtue but mutinying, should come to be advanced to be their master; and by their looks and murmurs sufficiently expressed the discontent they took at such a motion. Then he nominated another, as mean a mechanic as the former; you may imagine him, Sir, a bustling rude drayman, or the like : he was no sooner named but some burst out a laughing, others grew angry and railed at him, and all detested and scorned him. Upon this a third was named for a lordship, one of the same batch, and every way qualified to sit with the other two. The people then fell into a confused laugh and noise, and inquired, if such were lords, who, by all the gods! would be content to be commoners? Sir, let me be bold, by the good leave of the other House and yours, to ask the same question. But to conclude this story, and with it the other House, when this wise man I told you of perceived they were now sensible of the inconvenience and mischief they were running into, and saw that the pulling down their rulers would prove in the end but the setting up their servants, he thought them then prepared to hear reason, and told them, "You see," says he, "that bad as this government is, we cannot, for anything I see, agree upon a better: what then if, after this fright we have put our nobility in, and the demonstration we have given them of our power, we try them once more whether they will mend, and for the future behave themselves with more moderation?" The people were so wise as to comply with that proposition, and to think it easier to mend their rulers than to make new. And I wish, Mr. Speaker, we may be so wise as to think so too.

APPENDIX V.

A Letter from Sir Anthony Ashley Cooper, Thomas Scot, Josias Berners, and John Weaver, Esquires, delivered to the Lord Fleetwood, owning their late actions, in endeavouring to secure the Tower of London for the better service of the City and Commonwealth, December 16, 1659.[1]

SIR,

Understanding you have received some disturbance of late, in examining divers persons about a design to surprise the Tower; to save you further trouble, we do hereby freely own our utmost and hearty endeavours to have put that place into more faithful and confiding hands, and that by authority from the Council of State, who at the passing of that resolve had the sole legal power from the Parliament of ordering, directing, and disposing of all the garrisons and forces of this Commonwealth, both by sea and land ; an action so honest and honourable as would not only have given check to the exorbitances at Wallingford House and Whitehall, but was

---

[1] This letter is printed in the Thurloe collection of State Papers, vol. vii. p. 797, and in the Somers Tracts, vol. vi. p. 542. Ten days after the date of this letter, on December 26, the Committee of Safety was overthrown, Fleetwood and Lambert discomfited, and the Rump Parliament restored ; Sir A. A. Cooper, Scot, Berners, and Weaver were then entrusted with the temporary command of the Tower, which they had secured. Whitelocke, under date of December 24, records : "The Speaker with Cooper, Reynolds, Weaver, and Berners went to the Lord Mayor and discoursed with him and the Sheriffs, touching the Parliament's meeting again speedily, and found them to like well of it; from him they went to the Tower and secured that." (Memorials, p. 691.) The letter in the text describes an unsuccessful attempt made before December 16.

almost necessary to the preserving the peace and safety of this
great city, by giving advantage to them to put themselves into
a regular posture of defence, and such an encouragement to
the sober party among them as would through God's mercy
have utterly defeated the designs of the common enemy. Sir,
let us tell you this design was not so vain but that we had by
the blessing of God possessed that place some weeks since,
had we not been frustrated by our mistake in the courage and
fidelity of a person, whose opportunity, interest, and duty, if
not principles, gave us better hopes.[1] But in this age we are
to complain and wonder at nothing ; yet we cannot but highly
resent the confidence of sending for one of our number by
a party of soldiers, as if red coats and muskets were a *non
obstante* to all laws and public privilege. Not as if that
person or any of us are afraid or ashamed to own the enterprise before any that have a lawful authority to demand an
account of it ; which we are sure no single person, junto, or
pack of men at Whitehall or Wallingford House have a pretence to. Sir, we have the witness with our own spirits, that
we have and do cordially wish the preservation and good of
you and your family : but if the Lord hath said, " You shall
not hearken, but be hardened in your way," we must acquiesce
in His providence, and with sorrow look upon that ruin which
is flowing in upon you, as upon one in whom we thought we
had seen some good.

Sir, consider that in the day of trouble, which is certainly
coming upon you, what support you will have to your spirit,
when you shall be assaulted with the shame you have brought
upon God's people ; with the breach of faith to the Parliament

---

[1] Compare Ludlow's Memoirs, ii. 763 : "The Parliament party was
not wanting to promote their interest, and to that end formed a design
to get the Tower into their hands. Colonel Fitz, who was then Lieutenant of the place, had consented that Colonel Okey with three
hundred men should lie dispersed about the town, prepared for the
enterprise, promising that on a certain day he would cause the gates to
be opened early in the morning, to let him pass in his coach ; which
opportunity Colonel Okey with his men taking, might easily seize the
guards and possess himself of the place ; and their attempt might have
succeeded, had it not, by I know not what accident, been discovered
to the Lord Mayor, who informed the army of it the night before it
was to be put in execution. Whereupon Colonel Desborow with some
forces was sent thither, who changed the guards, seized the Lieutenant
of the Tower, and left Colonel Miller to command there till further
order."

from whom you received your commission ; with the ruin you
have brought upon your native country (unless the Lord by
His own Almighty arm prevent it); and with the misery you
have led the poor soldiers into, who, instead of being the
instruments of renewing and settling the peace and liberty of
these nations, enjoying the honour and quiet thereof, their
arrears fully paid, future pay and advancement settled and
established in order and with the blessing of their countrymen,
are now become the instruments of nine men's ambition,[1]
have made the whole nation their enemies, and are exposed
again to the hardship and hazard of a new unnatural war,
without prospect of our hoping that the issue of these affairs
can leave their new masters so rich as to satisfy their arrears,
or so secure as to trust preferments in any hands, but such
whose fanatic principles or personal relations make them
irreconcilable to the public interest. But God, we trust, has
raised up a deliverer, having by admirable providence put an
opportunity and power into the hands of General Monck, the
ablest and most experienced commander of these nations ;
whom he hath also spirited to stand firm for the interest of
this Commonwealth, as well against a rebellious party of our
own forces, as the designs of the common enemy, notwithstanding all causeless and false aspersions maliciously cast
upon him ; being warranted in his present actings by especial
commission and authority from the Council of State, whereas
yours is that only of the sword. Our prayers and earnest
request for you and all honest men amongst you are that you
may timely join with him, and partake of the honour and
blessing of his actions, and your true repentance shall be a
greater rejoicing than your desertion was trouble ; when
Providence shall have separated the precious from the vile,
and not have suffered our scum to boil in, but shall have
placed the sword and civil authority in the hands of men of
the best and soberest principles. Sir, be not so far deceived
as to think sober men see not through the mask of this
strange new parliament, whose liberty and safety either of
meeting or debating must be at your pleasure, who, having
taken upon you to be conservator of the cause, will only make

---

[1] The nine men here referred to are probably the niue officers who
subscribed the circular letter which, produced by Colonel Okey in the
Parliament, caused the commotion which brought on Lambert and
Fleetwood's revolution of October. See p. 189 of the " Life."

use of them as your assessors and tax-gatherers ; the present interrupted parliament being the sole lawful authority, and which can only be hoped to make the sword subservient to the civil interest, and settle the government in the hands of the people by successive and free parliaments unlawfully denied to them. Sir, we have in sincerity given you our sense, and shall leave you to Him that disposes of all men's hearts, and remain,

Your servants,

So far as you shall be found to serve the public,

AN. ASHLEY COOPER.
THO. SCOT.
JOS. BERNERS.
JOHN WEAVER.

APPENDIX VI.

A Proviso for the Bill of Uniformity, presented to the House of Peers from the King by the Lord Chancellor, March 17, 1662.[1]

PROVIDED always that, notwithstanding anything in this Act in regard of the generous offers and promises made by His Majesty before his happy restoration of liberty to tender consciences, the intention whereof must be best known to His Majesty, as likewise the several services of those who contributed thereunto, for all whom His Majesty hath in his princely heart as gracious a desire of indulgence as may consist with the good and peace of the kingdom, and would not have a greater severity exercised towards them than what is necessary for the public benefit and welfare thereof, it be enacted. And be it therefore enacted, that it shall and may be lawful for the King's Majesty by any writing and in such manner as to his wisdom shall seem fit, so far to dispense with any such Minister as upon the nine-and-twentieth day of May, 1660, was and at present is seised of any benefice or ecclesiastical promotion, and of whose merit towards His Majesty, and of whose peaceable and pious disposition, His Majesty shall be sufficiently informed and satisfied, that no such Minister shall be deprived or lose his benefice or other ecclesiastical promotion for not wearing the surplice, or for

---

[1] This Proviso is here printed for the first time from the Rolls of the House of Lords. Though presented by Clarendon, the Lord Chancellor, from the King, it was rejected by the House of Lords. See Chapter IX. of "Life;" and Lords' Journals, March 17, 18, and 19; Rawdon Papers, pp. 141—143, and Pepys's Diary, March 21, 1662.

not signing with the sign of the cross in baptism : so as he
permit and bear the charge of some other licensed minister
to perform that office towards such children whose parents
desire the same, and so as such Ministers shall not deprave
the Liturgy, rites, or ceremonies established in the Church
of England, or any person for using them, by preaching,
writing, speaking, or otherwise, upon pain of forfeiting the
benefit of the dispensation.

And be it further enacted, that such dispensations as aforesaid being granted by His Majesty shall be a sufficient
exemption from such deprivation in the cases aforesaid.
Always understood, that this indulgence be not thought or
interpreted to be an argument of His Majesty's indifferency
in the use of those ceremonies when enjoined, though indifferent in their own nature, but of his compassion towards
the weakness of the Dissenters, which he hopes will in
time prevail with them for a full submission to the Church
and to the example of the rest of their brethren.

*A Bill, entitled " An Act concerning His Majesty's power in
Ecclesiastical Affairs," presented to the House of Peers,
February 23, 1663, by Lord Roberts, Lord Privy Seal.*[1]

WHEREAS divers of His Majesty's subjects through error of
judgment and misguided consciences (whereunto the licentiousness of these late unhappy times have much contributed)
do not conform themselves to the order of divine worship
and service established by law ; and although His Majesty
and both Houses of Parliament are fully satisfied that those
scruples of conscience from whence this non-conformity
ariseth are ill-grounded, and that the government of the
Church with the service thereof, as now established, is the
best that is anywhere extant, and most effectual to the preservation of the Protestant religion : yet, hoping that
clemency and indulgence may in time wear out those preju-
dices and reduce the Dissenters to the unity of the Church ;
and considering that this indulgence, how necessary soever,

---

[1] This Bill, which caused considerable public excitement in 1663, is
now printed for the first time from the Rolls of the House of Lords.
See Chapter IX. of " Life ; " also Lords' Journals, February 23, 25, 27,
28, March 5, 6, 12, 13.   The bill was dropped in committee.

cannot be dispensed by any certain rule, but must vary
according to the circumstances of time, and the temper and
principles of those to whom it is to be granted; and His
Majesty being the best judge when and to whom this indulgence is to be dispensed, or as may be most consistent with
the public peace and without just cause of offence to others;
and to the end His Majesty may be enabled to exercise it
with universal satisfaction : Be it enacted by the King's most
excellent Majesty by advice and with the consent of the
Lords Spiritual and Temporal and Commons in this present
Parliament assembled and by the authority thereof, that the
King's Majesty may by letters patent under the Great Seal, or
by such other ways as to His Majesty shall seem meet,
dispense with one act or law made the last session of this
parliament, entitled " An Act for the Uniformity of Public
Prayer, and Administration of Sacraments and other Rites and
Ceremonies, and for establishing the Form of Making, Ordain-
ing, and Consecrating Bishops, Priests, and Deacons in the
Church of England," *and with any other laws or statutes concerning the same or requiring oaths or subscriptions, or which
do enjoin conformity to the order, discipline, and worship
established in this Church, and the penalties in the said laws
imposed or any of them,*[1] and may grant licences to such of
His Majesty's subjects of the Protestant religion, of whose
inoffensive and peaceable disposition His Majesty shall be
persuaded, to enjoy the use and exercise of their religion
and worship, though differing from the public rule, the said
laws and statutes, or any disabilities, incapacities, or penalties in them or any of them contained, or any matter or thing
to the contrary thereof notwithstanding. Provided always,
and be it enacted, that no such indulgence, licence, or dispensation hereby to be granted shall extend or be construed to
extend to the tolerating or permitting the use or exercise of the
Popish or Roman Catholic religion in this kingdom, nor to enable any person or persons to hold or exercise any place or office
of public trust within this kingdom, who, at the beginning of
this present Parliament, were by the laws and statutes of

---

[1] On March 5, the House of Lords adopted a recommendation of
the Committee to omit the words which are printed in italics, applying to other acts besides the Act of Uniformity. A list of such acts
was brought in to the House on that day by the Attorney-General in
pursuance of a previous order: the list, which is curious, and is not
professed to be complete, is printed in the Lords' Journals of March 5.

this realm disenabled thereunto ; nor to exempt any person or persons from such penalties as are by law to be inflicted upon such as shall publish or preach anything to the deprava- tion or derogation of the Book of Common Prayer or the government, order, and ceremonies of the Church established by law.   Provided also, and be it enacted, that no such licence or dispensation shall extend to make any priest or minister capable of any ecclesiastical living or benefice with care, who shall not before the Archbishop of the Province or Bishop of the Diocese where he lives, make such subscription to the Articles of Religion as is enjoined by the statute of 13 Eliz., made for reformation of disorders in the Church ; nor shall extend or be construed to extend to dispense with the Book of Common Prayer, but that the said book shall be con- stantly read in all the cathedral and collegiate churches, and in all the parish churches and public chapels.

END OF VOL. I.

www.ingramcontent.com/pod-product-compliance
Lightning Source LLC
Chambersburg PA
CBHW022026110726
47901CB00006B/1662